Among the Lesser Gods

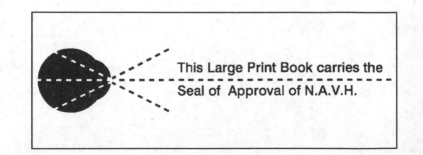

This Large Print Book carries the
Seal of Approval of N.A.V.H.

AMONG THE
LESSER GODS

MARGO CATTS

WHEELER PUBLISHING
A part of Gale, Cengage Learning

GALE
CENGAGE Learning·

Farmington Hills, Mich • San Francisco • New York • Waterville, Maine
Meriden, Conn • Mason, Ohio • Chicago

GALE
CENGAGE Learning®

LIBRARY OF CONGRESS CATALOGING-IN-PUBLICATION DATA

Names: Catts, Margo, author.
Title: Among the lesser gods / by Margo Catts.
Description: Large print edition. | Waterville, Maine : Wheeler Publishing, a part
  of Gale, a Cengage Company, 2017. | Series: Wheeler Publishing large print
  hardcover
Identifiers: LCCN 2017015531| ISBN 9781432840976 (hardcover) | ISBN 1432840975
  (hardcover)
Subjects: LCSH: Women—Colorado—Fiction. | Large type books. | BISAC: FICTION /
  Literary. | FICTION / Contemporary Women. | FICTION / Family Life. | GSAFD:
  Suspense fiction.
Classification: LCC PS3603.A89865 A46 2017b | DDC 813/.6—dc23
LC record available at https://lccn.loc.gov/2017015531

Published in 2017 by arrangement with Skyhorse Publishing, Inc.

Printed in the United States of America
1 2 3 4 5 6 7 21 20 19 18 17

For Stephen,
for everything.

Thus have the gods spun the thread for wretched mortals: that they live in grief while they themselves are without cares; for two jars stand on the floor of Zeus of the gifts which he gives, one of evils and another of blessings.

— Homer, *The Iliad*

1

I wasn't thinking about rescue when my grandmother's letter came. Nothing in my life had given me reason to expect divine giveaways, and I certainly didn't deserve any. No, to be honest, I was thinking about a nap.

I'd started out well. Made an effort to tackle the day or shape my destiny or whatever useless crap the placement office motivational posters said would fix everything. I really had — went to campus, checked in at the job board again, added my name to the Physics Rules! advisement list to show my availability to tutor. Again. For another week.

But that's where my effort ended. The idea of listening to one more lecture while I grew more sure, every day, that the diploma about to be stuffed in my hand was going to be completely useless here in greater Los Angeles or anywhere else in the goddamn country, for that matter, was just too much. My advisor was right. I should've applied to grad school. But she'd moved away last semester, which meant there was no one left to tell me what to do or say she'd told me so. What was the point of hanging around campus? So I left.

I caught the next bus to West LA and sat facing a sign that told me a career in auto mechanics would've been a better choice, then got off to walk the rest of the way home, head down, fists shoved in my sweatshirt pockets against the morning chill. I thought first about whether I'd hate waiting tables or selling shoes worse. Then I thought about the throbbing spot on my jaw and what lies would most plausibly explain the bruise beginning to ripen there. I thought about the worthless bastard who'd given it to me. I thought about the nauseated knot in my belly, not sure whether it was just anxiety that my period was well over a week late or already the consequences of it. And that's when I started to think that sleep was the only way to *stop* thinking about how thoroughly I deserved my spot at the bottom of this pit I'd dug for myself.

I stopped in the breezeway to check the mail before going upstairs to my apartment, a trip that always unnerved me a little. The balcony that led past my door appeared slightly off plumb as it wrapped around the courtyard, no matter where you stood, bad enough that I had to look away from a woman leaning too far over the metal railing to yell something in Spanish to a lower apartment. A brown palm frond drifting on the surface of the pool was the finishing flourish to an overall air of dilapidation. Carlo was a terrible super. And, as I should have been able to tell, a terrible person. A girl with reasonable faculties would have known there were better ways to avoid thinking about the future than allowing him to only make things worse.

I put my key in the mailbox lock. The door was dented and the lock tarnished, my roommate's and my names caught behind a yellowed plate. Actually, mine had slipped so that *Alvarez* appeared just below the edge of the frame. I tugged it the rest of the way out and threw the scrap on the ground. For better or worse, I'd be out of this apartment soon enough.

I grabbed the stack of envelopes and mailers and shut the door. Footsteps coming down the stairs behind me rattled the banister.

"Hey."

I looked up. My roommate, wearing a

bathrobe over jeans, carrying car keys.

"Hey."

"I'm going for coffee," she said as she passed me.

"Okay."

I watched her walk toward a sagging Impala parked too close to the curb. Her steps were slow and heavy but straight. Probably just hungover. Of all my questionable roommates, I had to admit that this one had worked out pretty well. She was a sleepy drunk rather than a delusional one, self-absorbed and undemanding, prone to go limp rather than drive a car at her worst, so it didn't trouble me to watch her sink into the driver's seat and start it up. Better still, she had a father who paid her share of the rent on time. Little favors.

The car coughed to a start and pulled away, puffing clouds of blue smoke. I went back to the mail. *UCLA Class of 1978: DO YOU HAVE YOUR CAP AND GOWN YET?* demanded the postcard on top. I flipped past. Electricity bill, sale flyer from Tower Records, something from a law office addressed to my roommate. A letter from Lockheed I didn't need to open because that pimply shit Terrence from second quarter General Relativity had already told me he'd gotten the job that had been my last hope.

Then I saw my grandmother's handwriting and stopped.

It's not as if getting something from her was uncommon — far from it. Her letters were usually short and, of themselves, insignificant: *We had a late storm, and Merle lost two calves — real nice ones. School closed around here for two days. The snow is already pulling back up the slopes, tho, so this'll be gone real soon. I'll probably be able to get back to the cabin in two or three weeks.* They said that as far as she was concerned, it didn't matter that I lived in California. That I had always been as much a part of her life in Colorado as the snow and the calves. And that I always would be. The easy, impersonal notes invited easy, impersonal responses, so it never took me long to answer; we probably exchanged letters every two or three weeks and had since I was old enough to write.

I tucked the rest of the stack under my arm and worked my thumb under the flap. Folded inside the envelope was a single sheet torn from a legal pad, yellow and lined, with my grandmother's angular writing nearly filling the page.

My dear Elena,
    Do you remember Paul and Carrie,

out on the east edge of town? Paul fixes my truck. He has that mark on his neck. They have two children, and now Carrie's gone. Paul drives a truck some and is gone a few days at a time. Are you still looking for a job? If you can put it off a few months and come help out this summer, that'd be real good. Folks are all doing what they can but they can't take those kids full-time much more. It's hard on the kids, too. Nobody can pay you anything, but you won't spend anything, either. It'd give Paul more time to save money and figure out what to do. This is just all so sudden. Let me know quick as you can.

Tuah

I looked out over my roommate's empty parking spot with the oil spots on the pavement toward the stucco face of the Whispering Palms Apartments across the street, rust stains weeping from the corners of the windows. A few shreds of morning fog were still caught in the lower leaves of the jacarandas. An old woman labored along the sidewalk beneath them, pulling grocery bags in a child's wagon.

What did she mean by "gone"? Dead? Run away? Imprisoned? And why? What had happened? How old were the children? Girls or boys? What exactly would I be doing? I hadn't been around children much. What about their father? I had a vague memory from one of the monthlong visits my own father and I made each summer, sitting three across on the front seat of my grandmother's truck, fanning dust from my face as she stopped to talk to someone at the dirt crossroads: a man in another truck with a dark birthmark that wrapped across his throat and reached for his ear. But other than that, I knew nothing. Would I be staying in the house of a stranger? How long would he be gone? How often?

I realized all at once that it didn't matter. The questions swooped through my mind and away again like passing birds. The only one that pressed on me very seriously was *How did she know?*

My mind was already made up. I could smell the thin, clear air, see the aspen leaves twisting in the sun, feel the heat on my skin. Go home to the only place where my guilt grew faint around the edges. A turn of events like this was more than I could've hoped for. More than I deserved. If I could take this life I'd wrecked and trade it in for another, I would accept almost anything in return.

■ ■ ■ ■

The class of 1978 graduated without me. I'd dreaded parading across that stage. Besides — my father was the only one who would've come, and he, ever anxious to please his mother, agreed that it was good for me to leave for Colorado as soon as I finished my last final. I put my key on my roommate's windowsill and loaded my car early in the morning, long before there was any chance Carlo would see me carrying bags and make me question what I was doing. It was better this way.

I followed the route my father and I had always taken together, every summer since my mother had left us — and probably with her, as well, if I'd been paying attention when I was that young. Leaving the coastal fog behind me, I crossed the Mojave on the first day. Hour after hour of desolation, a landscape of gray: rocks and grit and miserly, grasping, starving plants. Of radiant heat. My father always made sure we had plenty of water — in stoppered Pyrex bottles that sloshed and clacked against each other in the backseat and made me want to go to the bathroom more often than I probably needed — and his farewell gesture this morning had been to make sure I was well supplied now that I was traveling alone.

I drove with one wrist hung over the top of the steering wheel, the opposite elbow out the open window. The air blowing in felt as if it came out of a furnace and smelled of dust and tar and fumes, but the Pinto had no air conditioning, so it was better than the alternative. I wore shorts and a tank top, and sat on a towel to keep the sweat from gluing my skin to the vinyl. From time to time I would turn on the radio, occasionally picking up some nattering Spanish or a few country songs, then shut it off again a few minutes later, preferring the sound of the wind and the feeling it gave me of being carried, floating across the landscape like smoke, touching nothing.

My father had never talked much as he drove, so I didn't particularly miss his company. Once every hour or so he used to clear his throat and call out over the wind and the engine, "How're you doing?"

"Fine," I would yell back.

He'd follow up with, "You hungry? Need anything?"

It was a ludicrous question. Unless I needed rocks or cactus thorns, the offer was hollow. We'd lapse back into silence, and I would entertain myself by lining up the edge of the window with the edge of the road or seeing how long it would take for a near Joshua tree to seem to pass a farther one.

Dreary as the drive was, there was only one year I hadn't wanted to go. I was fourteen, and complained I was missing out on beach trips and slumber parties that I'd never really cared about before or since. But I hadn't put up a serious fight. My resistance was just a convenient weapon, readily available to prove my lack of freedom whenever I felt nagged about picking up clothes or cereal bowls or books left wherever I last touched them. But I never brought it up independently. I think, deep down, I knew we were only posturing, my father and I, taking care to maintain a delicate balance of opposing weight and force. I feared that if I pushed with any real effort our lives would tip, he'd give way, and I'd find myself holding power I didn't want. While around my grandmother, though, we both ceded control to her, and for just that month, I relaxed.

Our dining routine saved the drive, and I followed it now as if collecting stamps in a pilgrimage passport. The staff of Santo Burrito. The mustard smear of the Cross. At home, my father cooked at a survival level, overwhelmed by the grocery store and accused by the presence of a kitchen in every home. But we almost never ate out, sitting instead at our silent table, cutting, chewing, looking at our plates or at the wall. On the road, though, we ate at coffee shops, diners, and truck stops. We went to the same ones every trip, each the campiest, most lurid landmark in sight, and together they represented the only hint of playfulness I ever saw in my father.

The Cactus Blossom in Nevada, where we had pancakes with nopales syrup, was an adobe cube of weathered green, with hand-painted brown spines a foot long hashed all over it and electric pink tin flowers anchored to the roof. They'd been folded and twisted by the wind so often that fragments of broken petals peppered the sand outside. Dino's Drive-In in western Colorado had a life-size plaster brontosaurus wrapped around the building and the tyrannosaurus-head speaker that took your order. A western cheeseburger for my father; a plain single for me with onion rings and a Dino's Dessert Pie.

The highlight, though, was Harvey's, in southern Utah, which boasted only a giant frosted cup tilted at the top of a twenty-foot pole. Against the competition, it should not have captured my father's attention, but it seemed the frosted cup was enough to capture anyone's attention, standing as it did above the sandstone grit, not a hint of green anywhere in sight, the sun glinting off the Lucite droplets on the cup's surface. Ranchers, with their hats and their snap-front shirts, their dark jeans hollow over flat bottoms and bowed legs, would bring their families into the air conditioning from thirty or more miles away. Their wives had lines around their mouths, their sons were laconic and polite, and their daughters were wiry and as sharp-eyed as birds. Harvey's served fresh fruit shakes made with watermelon and cantaloupe and peaches, ice cream, and cold milk, and we would sit inside at a white table, our hands wrapped around the sweating cups, icing our throats and shivering while we looked out the window at the heat waves rising off the car.

I found I liked traveling alone. I stopped and started at my own choosing. I ate unselfconsciously alone at restaurants. I could have sat for hours at the window at Harvey's with my blackberry shake, elbows on the counter, heels hooked on the rail of my stool, watching the shadow of the giant spinning cup lengthen and shrink again across the sand.

I arrived at the Travelodge a couple of hours farther on, and paid for my room with a credit card I was using for the first time. I savored the hard edges of the key in my pocket, and spread my things out in the room as if I planned on staying a week. As I turned on the TV and lay back on the bed, crossing my arms behind my head and arching my feet, I felt the cords connecting me to Los Angeles stretch to their limit, vibrate for a moment, then break.

I was free. And at the end of the summer I would just drive on. Waitress at a beach bar in the Keys. Cook lobsters in Maine. Save money. Get this baby into more responsible hands and take a stab at grad school in another year or two. I had left behind nothing I cared about, no responsibilities or obligations, no family. My mother existed only in memory, and my father's vague, disapproving presence served little practical purpose and could be invoked from anywhere. Whether he was in the room or across the country made little difference. Was this all there was to it? Could I actually just drive away from my old life and my colossal debt would be canceled? If so, well, I'd be the last person to insist that I owed more.

I woke early the next morning, feeling

more rested than I had in weeks, and left when the rocks were still deep red and cast long shadows. For this part of the journey, the desert was framed by cliffs and mesas in the distance in one direction and rusty canyons and mountains in the other. Sometime after midday I began to see occasional trees, then a snaking line of green along a river, and finally fields and orchards and sagebrush rangeland. I watched for the first pine. And then I began to climb.

I left the interstate near Vail, its lift chairs idle over boulevards of grass curving through the trees, and started to wend my way south, higher and higher, through Leadville, casting a glance toward the neighborhood where my grandmother kept her winter home. Somewhere, that same direction, was the home of the family I had supposedly come here for, but all I cared about now was getting up to the cabin. I stopped at Safeway and bought fresh fruit and meat and a gallon of milk, then drove on. After Leadville, the way became narrower and more precipitous, and I saw few other cars. Spruces and firs crowded against the road, then would break open to reveal a glacial valley, newly green in early summer. In the darker hollows I could see patches of snow lingering under the trees. It was hard to remember I'd started the day in the desert.

Eventually I left the pavement. I had some miles to go over washboard dirt road before the turnoff to Hat Creek. From time to time barbed wire would emerge from the trees to meet the road at a cattle guard, or an archway of timbers would announce the entrance to the Bar Lazy something-or-other. My elementary school classmates had been fascinated by my summer trips, which must have seemed to them like journeys into a Wild West story. They probably doubted my honesty.

"She lives in a real ghost town?"

"You cook on a fire?"

"There's no sink inside?"

"No toilet?"

"Where do you go to the bathroom?"

"You go *outside*? At *night*? What if it's cold?"

"Are there bears?"

There were, but my grandmother had plenty of experience in keeping them at bay. She had already made her way into the local history books as the last resident of Hat Creek, a gold mining outpost that grew and died within the span of thirty years. She had even been featured in a human interest story in the *Rocky Mountain News* a few years ago.

The photo showed her in profile, leaning one shoulder against a porch post at her cabin and cradling a coffee mug in her hands. "Miriam Alvarez marks her seventieth birthday at her solitary mountain home," read the caption. The article mentioned her husband, Eduardo, who died nearly twenty years earlier, and two children born and raised there: a daughter, Benencia, who had died as a teenager, and a son, my father, now living in California "with his family." The last year-round residents had left decades earlier as gold mining ceased and wartime molybdenum mining drew them to Leadville.

My grandparents had gone as well, but every spring since my grandfather died, my grandmother would follow the retreating snow up to the valley just below timberline, her car loaded with flour and beans and canned ham and dried apples and bottled peaches. She would unlock the door to the old cabin, take down the sign advising hunters that the home was still occupied and to please look to any of the other structures for shelter, hook back the shutters, sweep out the mouse nests, air the blankets, and start a fire in the stove. Its wavering trail of smoke against the late-afternoon sky would be the signal that I was almost there.

Though my grandmother made the cabin her summer home, she made enough trips back and forth to Leadville that the road to Hat Creek stayed reasonably navigable. I drove with my chest close to the steering wheel, peering over the hood, easing the Pinto into each dip and around muddy spots, careful to avoid any rocks that threatened to scrape the oil pan. On the necessity of this my father had been quite fixed, standing on the curb yesterday morning, giving instructions with one arm folded across his chest and the other chopping the air to *make . . . things . . . very . . . clear.* I'd wondered briefly whether there might be a story or two to explain his stress on this point but didn't really want the information badly enough to work or wait for it.

At last I eased through the center of Hat Creek, driving slowly to keep the dust down, passing between the abandoned shells of lives long gone. My grandmother had spun stories for me, though, bringing the silent town to life. To the left, Hamilton Brothers General Merchandise, the name still red, outlined in blue, on the false front where the boards had cupped and split. It had been run by a pair of Scottish brothers who slept on cots behind the counter for a

25

decade before one got married to a large, loud woman, and the other left within a month with nothing but a suitcase.

To the right the saloon entrance gaped empty and dark between broken hinges, where identical twin brothers who had been secretly sharing a job at the mine surprised themselves and their coworkers by stumbling through it — one going in, one going out — at the same time.

Ahead lay the scattered logs of a cabin knocked over by a mule skinner who yanked the reins in the middle of an argument with the foreman about how much longer he could wait for a full load. My grandmother had told me the story more than once, each time demonstrating with her forearms the way the cabin had leaned over and lain down in the dirt: upright, lying down.

Beyond that, the road bent to the left at a rocky saddle and dropped out of sight on its way to the jumble of abandoned machinery and the locked gate of the old mine entrance. But my path lay in the other direction, up a track that bent to the right behind the schoolhouse, where my grandmother had shown me the marks children made against the doorsill to measure how tall they were. The tires crunched as I turned uphill and into the trees.

She'd heard me coming, of course. Plus the dust must've been visible for miles. She stood on the edge of her porch, one hand braced against the small of her back, the other shielding her eyes. She wore a chambray shirt and twill work pants and work boots, with her steely hair pulled into a bun. She held her arms open and unbent as I got out of the car.

"You look tired." She gave me a stiff embrace, then pulled back, holding me by the shoulders and studying my face. Mac, the latest in a line of wise and shaggy dogs, stepped off the porch and shambled toward me, pressed his nose into my hand.

"Thanks, Tuah. Aren't you supposed to wait till people are fifty or sixty or something to say that?"

"No. Not when you really do look tired." She narrowed her eyes. "What's that on your chin?"

I put my hand over it. "A bruise. I slipped getting out of the pool."

"Huh." She continued to study my face. "You feel all right?"

I wasn't inordinately tired; nothing felt sore or strained or different. I hadn't gained any weight. I felt a little unsettled first thing in the morning and needed to eat something right away, but as long as I didn't let myself get hungry, I didn't notice anything else. Surely she couldn't have.

"Well, I've been in the car for two days. I'm sweaty and dirty and the last time I ate was about two hundred miles ago. Is that it?"

She tilted her head as if really thinking the answer through. "No," she finally announced, releasing my shoulders. Then she turned and went inside. "Did you bring any fruit?" she asked over her shoulder. "I've been thinking about a banana all day."

2

I slept for the better part of three days.

I sat outside in a porch chair my grand-father had made, moving it from time to time to follow the sun. When awake, I only bobbed on the surface of sleep. Then sea-weed fingers would twine around me and drag me back under without warning, sometimes for only a few minutes, other times for an hour or more. The clearing around the cabin became an island where I washed up from time to time. While there, I would start to think about my choices, my future, the clock ticking in my belly, but then the breezes stirring the upper limbs of the pines would sound like the surf, hushed and rhythmic, and I would doze again, wrapped in a quilt, my head cradled against the worn boards.

Tuah eased the threads of truth free care-fully, one at a time, without me noticing what she was doing. She waved off my help with chores she excused as being "a one-man job" or something that would take "just a moment," then asked questions as she worked that came across as mere efforts to pass the time.

She started on the first day as she squatted in her small garden patch, pinching weeds and overcrowded plants between her fingers. Greens thrived under the intense sun and the cool nights at this altitude, and she grew varieties that I knew only by her pet names. Corn Salad. Ragged Jack. Foreign Shoes. She dismissed my offer of help in this case by claiming she'd staggered the planting and I wouldn't be able to tell the difference between weeds and immature lettuces. I should rest after that long drive.

"Graduating must feel like a real accomplishment," she said as she parted two bunches of spinach to peer beneath them for intruders. Or maybe they were chard.

I shrugged. "It's what happens when you run out of classes."

"That's not true."

"Close enough. I took some classes, then I took the ones that followed, and then there weren't any more."

She peered up at me from under the brim of her straw hat. "You do know I didn't go to college."

"Of course."

"Going to college is a remarkable opportunity."

I twisted my finger into the edge of the quilt. "Yes, ma'am."

She gave a *pheh* through her lips and crab-stepped a few inches to the side, parting another pair of plants. "Now don't go acting like a child, like I'm correcting you. You're a grown woman. But I grew up different and I just want to understand your way of thinking." She probed between the plants as if that was the primary focus of her interest. A mountain jay made a blue slice across the upper corner of my field of vision.

"It's just — going to school. It's what people do. And now . . ."

"Time to pick your own path. That's a privilege, too," she said when I failed to complete my own thought.

"I know."

Tuah gave a single nod, the brim of her hat dipping down, then up, but she didn't look at me. She prodded at the ground with a sticklike tool, working something back and forth with her other hand.

"Hah!" She yanked upward, holding a weed aloft for me to see, its dirty taproot dangling below her thumb and forefinger.

31

"Even up here. Dandelions. If you don't get the whole thing, it'll just come back." She continued to look at me for just a fraction longer, whether to emphasize the magnitude of her victory or to allow some metaphoric meaning to sink in, I didn't know.

She tossed the weed into a growing pile a few feet away from her. "I think I would've studied biology. Understanding how things live, how they keep living . . . now that would be interesting." She moved again, plucking the little grasses that poked up between the plants.

I looked down at the quilt, the binding now wound around my finger. I could remember having picnics on it as a child. I used to aggravate my parents to no end by taking an apple or a piece of bread, bunching this quilt under my arm, and disappearing for hours with Rex, Tuah's dog at the time. I took perverse pleasure in defying the order that I tell someone at least what I was doing or the direction I was headed before I left. I cared nothing for my mother's anger, which was constant and meaningless and only shifted from one object to another. During our Colorado visits she tried to keep it from showing, which made it all the quicker to flash through any little fissure of irritation. My father's frustration at things

32

that wouldn't stay in their places was endless, so his anger here seemed more born of helplessness at his inability to keep her happy or me leashed. It produced pleading rather than volatility, oil rather than heat.

But I didn't care. I wanted only my freedom, and my parents' anger was too slight a consequence to matter. Announcing a plan and getting permission would defy the point of going in the first place. At the time I couldn't yet imagine any consequence to my actions that should inhibit them in the slightest.

I worked my finger free, then slid it along the edge to a new spot and started over. I envied Tuah. She lived as she pleased, moving between town and the cabin, answering to no one. As far as I could tell, she enjoyed what I had been dreaming of for a decade: perfect solitude, with no one to be responsible for, no one to harm.

I pulled my finger free again, then balled my hand under my temple. "I'm not sure what I'll do next, just yet," I said. "There's time."

I wasn't sure whether she heard me, but then she looked up at me, considering.

"I see," was all she said. She waved a hand as Mac sauntered toward her. "Shoo," she said, then turned her attention back to the ground. I was asleep before she got to the end of the row.

I woke the next morning to the murmur of voices, overlaid by the crack and clatter of wood chopping. Dammit. Cowboys. I dragged my hand out from under the pillow and squinted at my watch. Not even seven o'clock yet.

The remains of Hat Creek were in what was now open rangeland, the countryside peppered with cow pies in various stages of desiccation. Wandering Herefords, with their white, expressionless faces, would meander single-file down the main street from time to time as the empty windows watched them pass, or bed down in the shade uphill from the cabin to chew their cud.

Stopping at Tuah's house was something the ranch hands liked to do whenever they could reasonably claim to be in the neighborhood — rounding up calves for branding, looking for strays, following up on reports of bears or mountain lions. She'd offer them a meal, they'd do a chore, and everyone would feel pleased with the exchange. But I'm pretty sure the cowboys were really just checking on her, though they never said so. By virtue of longevity, she'd become a communal grandmother, both in town and up here, and pretty much everyone who knew her called her Tuah as I did. I'd been told the name came from my grandfather repeatedly introducing her to me as *tu abuela* when I was little. When he died not long after, the name became an echo of his voice, and she never wanted to be called anything else.

As great as it was that folks cared about her like family, they weren't *my* family, so I would have to march to the privy in front of strangers unless I wanted to stay in the house indefinitely. I sat up, rubbed my face, and raked my fingers through my hair a few times. Now that I was awake, waiting them out was no longer an option. To hell with it. I pushed my feet into my flip-flops. The sweats I'd slept in would have to be good enough for the occasion. I grabbed my toothbrush and toothpaste, then stepped out onto the porch to meet three horse faces lined up along its edge, one black, one brown, one spotted black and white.

"Well, hi, kids," I said. The brown one shook, setting off a jangling of harness.

"There she is," Tuah said, straightening, a piece of wood in each hand. Two cowboys that looked to be not quite out of their teens wielded hatchets at the splitting stump. The third, rolling a log toward them with his

35

foot, was much older, leathered and weatherbeaten. He could have been forty or eighty.

"You make it sound like I'm stumbling out at noon."

"Just glad to introduce you. Gentlemen, this is my granddaughter. Elena, this is Tom, Leo, and Rich."

"Pleasure."

"Pleased to meet you."

"Yes, ma'am."

"Pleased to meet all of you. But I need to" — I gestured over my shoulder with my thumb — "you know."

"Of course."

"Well, sure."

"Yes, ma'am."

I scuffed off the side of the porch and along the path toward the privy. After they finished chopping, they'd expect breakfast. They'd be here half the day. I yanked the outhouse door open and let it slam behind me. I just wanted to eat a bowl of oatmeal in privacy and sit in the sun. And probably go back to sleep.

I took as long as I could possibly justify, brushing my teeth to a level my dentist would admire, washing my face, neck, arms, feet, counting the cold water as a small price to pay for the extra moments of privacy. By the time I came back down the path, I could see the first trails of smoke rising from the chimney.

"I wanted you to start the fire but I couldn't wait any longer," Tuah said as I stepped onto the porch.

Twelve years, now. When would she let it go? I was never going to start another fire. Period. "Sorry. It took a while to wake myself up, you know, after sleeping so late."

"Sure," said one of the younger cowboys. "The night life around here can be pretty crazy."

"Thank you for understanding." I wiped my still-damp hands on the seat of my sweatpants. "Tuah, you want me to start some pancakes or something?"

"That would be nice."

Thank God. I managed to fill enough time getting dressed, mixing the batter, wiping plates, and getting the table set that I didn't have to go outside again before calling everyone in to eat.

The cowboys ate with their heads bent over their plates, hair pressed to their scalps but for the ridge that marked the place where their hats usually rested. A smattering of conversation about the weather helped me know it had been an unusually dry spring so far. Finally the older one pushed back from the table.

"Rich, Leo, we best get going."

"Thank you, ma'am."

"Thanks a lot."

Tuah stood as well. "No, thank you. That wood will last me half the summer, and breakfast won't last you more than a couple of hours."

"And the work only took a couple of hours. We're more than square."

"And thank you," the older one said to me, extending his hand. "Those were some real fine pancakes."

I hoped my smile looked warm, rather than as if I was about to laugh. Only the use of "flapjacks" would have made him sound more like a character from an old Western. "You're very welcome."

"Yes, thank you," the next one said, shaking my hand as well.

"Of course."

"Thanks a lot," the final one said, taking my hand in turn. But then he held onto it a little longer. "I hope to see you again real soon."

Good God. What was he, sixteen? He had rosy cheeks and skin that looked as if it had never been shaved.

"I'm sure you will." I pulled my hand away and sidestepped to follow the others out the door. They got on their horses, and the older one touched the brim of his hat.

"Bye, now," he said.

They turned and fell into line, but as the black, the brown, and the spotted tails swished away, the cowboy at the rear turned around with one hand against the back of his saddle to give me a long final look. He grinned, nodded once more, and then the three of them faded away into the trees.

"My," Tuah said as the last tail disappeared. "Looks like you caught somebody's eye."

"Spare me," I said, turning to go back inside.

"What? There's no rule against you enjoying yourself while you're here."

I twisted around in the doorway. "Tuah! Aren't grandparents supposed to be overprotective? He's a *cowboy* — bar the door and all that."

"Leo is a scholarship student at Mines."

"What?"

"School of Mines, down in Golden. One of the best engineering schools in the country. This is his summer job, at the dude ranch. Don't be so quick to judge. There's always more to things than you think."

Had my father, master of the snap judgment, really been raised by this woman?

39

"People are the same the day you meet them as the day they die, so you might as well figure out what you're dealing with up front."

I first remembered hearing that when I told him about a sixth-grade classmate who'd called me a babykiller. I had not yet found any reason to doubt him.

"I'm going to wash up," I said, and went inside.

3

In the time it took me to wash the dishes, get the blanket, and go outside, Tuah had started sorting and stacking the split pieces of stove wood. She dismissed my offer of help this time by saying I'd helped a lot already and besides, she was particular about how the stack was built. It was easier to do it herself than to correct me as I worked. I was fairly sure I remembered doing that very chore without supervision when I was no more than thirteen years old, but I didn't argue. It was certainly possible I'd done it in a way that bothered her for weeks after I left. So I pulled up the quilt as she nested the firewood and inquired about people she remembered me mentioning in letters or in summers past, her work-gloved hands serving as the front stop to keep the face of the stack even. She remembered most of these people better than I did, so I let her remind me of any necessary context and lead the conversation as she wished.

She started with "that girl who lied" and moved through "the marijuana boy" and "the dropout," and then to "the advisor," the one who had pushed me to go to grad school. I could tell Tuah was annoyed that the advisor's move to Florida made it easier for me to ignore her advice. But she didn't belabor it, moving easily enough to "the lazy girl," a neighbor who never went to class or, as far as I could tell, got out of her bathrobe. As we talked, "lazy" started to sound a little harsh. Maybe she was just tired. For a really long time.

"You don't tend to pick the best friends," Tuah said as she whacked two sticks against each other so that the dirt showered around her feet.

At this point we'd drifted so far into the swaying rhythm of unimportant questions and rambling answers that it didn't bother me in the slightest to agree with her. I gave a half-effort, one-sided shrug.

"Them's my people."

She stood there for a moment, the two sticks against the sides of her legs. "They don't have to be," she finally said.

"Why force myself in where I don't fit?"

"Well, what about the piano player? He sounded like a nice young man."

He actually had been, which proved my point. That was precisely what made it all the worse the night he found me in Carlo's apartment rather than my own. Carlo was a disaster, as I knew long before I noticed him watching me at the pool, but he had a dark smile and as little regard for the future as I did, which made things more comfortable. Time I spent with Carlo was time I didn't have to spend thinking about it.

"He broke up with me."

"I see," she said, then turned toward the sticks scattered like dropped matches around the splitting stump and started kicking them into a group, herding them toward the stack. A breeze tugged at my hair and ruffled the edge of the quilt, carrying the scent of cut pine. She added the two sticks in her hands to the pile, then put her fists to her lower back and arched against them. "That Carlo you mentioned yesterday, I don't suppose he might've had something to with that bruise on your face."

I looked down. Didn't answer.

"But you're gone now." It wasn't a question. "You won't see him anymore."

This was easier to confirm. "No. No, I won't. Ever."

"That's good." She bent for another piece of wood and returned to stacking. Bend, clack, smack. Bend, clack, smack.

"You've been picking bad friends ever since the fire," she said without looking at me. "But it's getting worse."

Against the pull of gravity, I lifted my head. "What?"

She went on as if I hadn't spoken. "Other than that piano player, I haven't heard you talk about a decent friend in years. All these people that don't care about you, and you don't care about them. And then you don't want anything to do with the good ones, like Leo. I can't make sense of it to save myself. And this Carlo . . ." She shook her head, patting the top of the woodpile as if she had spoken to it rather than me. "He's the worst one yet."

I felt my spine stiffen against the slats of the chair. "Are you — trying to *fix* me?" I was too stunned to frame out an entire sentence before I started speaking. "You think I go around looking for people to hurt me? Because of the *fire*? And *Leo*? That kid? What are you *thinking*?"

She stopped and looked straight at me. "I think you're in trouble." She tapped the stick in her hand against her leg three or four times, then turned away, laid it on top of the pile, fitted it, moved it, then reached for another.

She was being manipulative, I was sure. She would leave that loaded statement lying between us forever, stack wood until the bottom of the pile dissolved into the earth rather than say anything else before I asked. Asked for clarification I didn't want to hear. I knew it. But I still couldn't stop myself.

"I'm *normal,* okay? Lots of girls make stupid mistakes with guys and it doesn't *mean* anything. It's over, and I got away, didn't I? I left *everything* behind."

"Everything?" she said. She stepped back and eyed the front line of the stack. "You sure have been sleepy."

"I'm *tired.*"

"You're twenty-two." She tapped a couple of straying sticks back into place and spoke to the pile. "When Eduardo and I came up here I was expecting your aunt Benencia. Six years before your father, that would've been. Anyway, I couldn't keep my eyes open, either. When you're pregnant, the altitude really gets to you."

Denial, with its props and buttresses and scaffolding, collapsed as unceremoniously as the abandoned structures in the valley below me. How delusional had I been? Escape? I would never detach myself from my sins. They weren't car parts I could remove and replace, but pieces of my identity, and now I'd dragged them here with me: the walnut-sized life buried in my gut, the ghosts of the dead that clung to me like burrs. My body sagged into place where it was, quilt drawn up to my chin, forearms against my chest, feet pulled away from the cabin's encroaching shadow. I squeezed my lip against a quivering I couldn't stop, then uncovered one hand to brush a strand of hair away from my face. Waited for an answer to come out of a space inside me that suddenly yawned wide and empty and dark. My resources of denial were gone. I had no argument against the truth.

"I don't know what to do," I whispered. The muscles of my throat and chest and eyes contracted. Like a tired child, I started to cry.

In physics, I learned equations that define a universe in balance. What happens on one side of the equation matches and predicts what happens on the other. But these equations prove true only in systems of infinite scale. I learned at the age of ten that in the observable world, where interference is the norm and time and space create artificial boundaries, almost nothing happens in proportion. Tiny actions set off reactions that multiply exponentially, so that the final

46

effects are far out of scale to the original trigger.

No explanation of the persistence of mass and energy could make sense of the harm a seventy-pound girl with a magnifying glass could do on a dry, blustery day in the Los Angeles foothills. No amount of replaying it in my mind would arrest that dot of light quivering on a pile of weeds before it grew to a flame, still the winds that carried it away, divert the fire from the homes I destroyed or the family I killed, or silence my mother's words.

"How are we supposed to live with what she's done?"

They couldn't, it turned out. My parents blamed each other. The community blamed my parents. But I knew the truth. Only I knew what had taken place in my own mind as I gathered those weeds and pointed the light at them, the fascination, the triumph, the absolute knowledge that what I was doing was wrong. And the fully conscious way I did it anyway.

No, there was no way to atone. No forgiveness to be granted. No way to put things back in balance, and no way, now that I carried a child, to escape this world without ever doing more harm to another soul.

There is always a moment, though, where

the laws of physics do work. Where everything can be stopped. The reaction — just in that moment — is equal to the action, and smothers the first puff in a cloud of billowing magnitude so that the outsized trouble never takes form. A sliver of time, barely there at all, where if a person's reach is just long enough, the feet quick enough, the eyes sharp enough, disaster can be averted. The ripping grocery bag. The knife at the top of a toddler's reach. The hot spot widening to a flame. If the moment is missed, everything changes. Forever.

For once, the reaction came at the right moment. As I sat curled in the chair seeing my past flare up and consume the future, Tuah squatted in front of me. She pried the ends of the quilt from my fingers and pulled it away from my shoulders the way someone might open a pair of cupboard doors.

"Now, that Carlo, does he know anything about the baby?"

I shook my head, which made me feel loose and slightly dizzy.

"That makes things simpler. Now, there are doctors. We can find one, if you want to, right away, and talk about some options —"

The dizziness bloomed into a flush of hysteria. "No! No! After what I did — I can't — I can't ever —"

48

"Hush. Then you're gonna have a baby. People do it all the time, and they live after. Don't be saying you don't know what to do. You did the right thing coming here. You're not alone." She gave my forearms a pat, then straightened and returned to the woodpile. "Get a rake," she said over her shoulder. "I need some help clearing this away. It's time for you to get up."

I did as she asked. The ground leveled itself under my feet, and I left the open quilt behind me.

4

My shadow fell in a sharp-edged circle on the concrete around my feet as I stood in front of the Kofford family home, a flat-fronted, one-story gray house on the frayed edge of Leadville. Whoever had originally chosen the color showed foresight: the fading that happened so quickly at this altitude was slightly less noticeable. The peeling, however, couldn't be disguised. Grass stood in clumps around the house, kept back from the foundation by a line of bricks set into the soil. Behind the battle line, tulip leaves, curled and brown, surrounded a concrete rabbit at watch beside the porch. Other frame structures — neighboring houses, sheds, neglected barns — were scattered along this stretch of black-top, and the wind eddied around them, whipping strands of hair across my face that I tried to brush away with one hand. Though I was here in response to a recent crisis, what I was seeing suggested these people had been a mess for a long time.

"Don't look so angry," Tuah said over her shoulder, pausing as she raised her knuckles to the door.

"I'm not angry."

"Then don't look that way."

She rapped on the door. The house shuddered in response, quieted, then gave another rumble. A curtain twitched at a window, and then a moment later, the door swung open.

"Tuah!" A girl with tangled blonde hair catapulted through the opening and threw her arms around Tuah's waist. I felt a twinge of something too sudden to identify. This stranger acted as if she were more involved with my grandmother than I was. Tuah put one arm around the little girl's shoulders and bent to speak to her.

"Sarah, I'd like you to meet my granddaughter. This is Elena."

The girl half-unwrapped herself but kept her cheek pressed to Tuah's hip. She wore a pair of pink shorts and a gray T-shirt that looked as if it belonged to her brother. I watched a frown start to form between her eyebrows as she appraised me.

"Hi, Sarah," I said.

She didn't answer but turned to look up

at Tuah instead. "She's your *granddaugh-ter*?" she asked. She looked back at me, still frowning. "She's a grown-up."

"That's right." Nothing in Tuah's tone would suggest that she wasn't speaking to an adult. "One day you'll be a grown-up, too, but you'll still be your father's daughter, and your granny's granddaughter. That's what happened with Elena, too. She used to be a little girl, just your size, and then she grew up."

"Huh." It was a sound from her chest, more than a word, and she let it linger only a moment before she grabbed Tuah's hand in both of hers and started to pull her inside. "I wanna show you my somersaults."

I followed the two of them inside. I don't know what I'd expected, but it wasn't this restless bird hopping from one thing to the next. Tuah had told me only that neighbors said Sarah caused trouble when she didn't get her way. Her brother, Kevin, on the other hand, had the opposite problem, withdrawing to the point where other children were uncomfortable and would ask their parents when he was going home.

She'd told me all this yesterday, when she must have concluded I was never going to ask on my own. While we shelled peas, she said that Carrie, their mother, had been on her way to visit her own mother in Minturn on an icy February night when her car missed a curve, went through a guardrail, and landed on its top on the rocks far below. It wasn't found until the next day.

Paul, her husband, was a truck driver and part-time mechanic. Tuah had first gotten to know him over the engine of her own truck. His road trips often kept him away for four or five days at a time, which was impossible work for a single father of young children — Kevin was eleven, and Sarah, five. Carrie's mother had come to stay for a while after the funeral, but she drank too much to be trusted with the children. No other family lived nearby. Paul had stayed home as long as he could, trying to take care of the children and the home while finding full-time work as a mechanic, but nothing was available and the ends wouldn't meet no matter how hard he stretched. Carrie had worked as a hairstylist and the family had always needed both incomes, so they certainly couldn't last long on less than one, and he began to worry he'd stop getting calls if he didn't start taking trucking jobs again soon.

Neighbors and families from school rallied and took turns having the children as long-term guests. It soon became clear, though, that neither the children nor the caregivers could go on this way indefinitely. As word got out that Tuah had found help, a breath of relief passed through family kitchens and school corridors. My summer help would buy Paul more time to find a way to start earning a decent living from home.

I closed the door behind me, then had to blink and wait for my eyes to adjust to the dark. To the brown, to be more accurate. Beige pinch-pleated drapes covered the windows, screening out most of the sunlight; earthy shag carpet covered the floor. I could see a sliver of the kitchen from where I stood inside the door, with a chocolate stove, a tan-and-gold vinyl floor, walnut-stained cupboards, and at the window, a linen panel embroidered with chickens. A tweed sofa the color of toast had its back to me, its cushions lined up, runway-style, across the floor.

"Watch this!" Sarah perched on the sofa back, her bare feet where the cushions used to be, her hair splaying out from a snarl at the back of her head. Without waiting for a response she tipped forward, caught the edge of the sofa with her hands, then executed a loose, beetle-like somersault across the cushions. At its end, she twisted on her bottom to face us, eyes sparkling. The tangle's source was evident.

"That was amazing," Tuah said. "Did you work that out by yourself?"

Sarah nodded.

"That was really good," I added. She gave no sign she'd heard.

"Where's your brother?" Tuah asked.

Sarah shrugged. "Watch me again," she ordered, pushing herself off the cushion.

Tuah ignored her. "Kevin?" she called, turning toward the hallway that ran away from us, presumably toward bedrooms.

"Watch me!"

"I'm watching," I said.

"Kevin?" Tuah disappeared into the hallway.

"Watch me!"

"Go ahead," I said. "I'll watch you."

Sarah glowered at me from her seat atop the sofa back, and I imagined an internal wrestle with whether to raise her demand level upon Tuah. After a moment, options and consequences considered, wisdom prevailed. She folded her arms.

"Why are you at my house?"

"I'm going to stay with you sometimes when your dad goes on trips." God, what was I saying? Trips? Really? For days on end? I glanced at the window, covered, and the door, closed, and in that moment wanted nothing more than to fling them both open and flee.

"Is he going on a trip today?"

"No, not today. We thought it would be nice for me to meet you first. He's going on a trip tomorrow."

"Who are your kids?"

"I don't have any kids."

She rubbed the corner of her eye with one knuckle, pushing some hair away from her forehead. "What dinners do you make?"

I groped through my mind to find something I could remember fixing for myself. "What do you like?" I said when my search produced nothing but toast and canned soup.

"Samwiches."

"Do you like peanut butter sandwiches?"

She pushed up her bottom lip and shook her head.

"Bologna?"

Another shake.

"What kind do you like?"

"My mom's samwiches."

She twisted back around to face the somersault lane.

"Watch me," she ordered.

"Okay." I came around the sofa and sat on the arm. Now, at least, I had something to say. It would be what I wished someone had said to me when I was twice her age but felt just as bereft, my mother gone without explanation, staring at a plate of eggs my father had made, dark yellow and folded and nothing like the creamy mounds I was used to.

"Will you teach me how to make your mom's sandwiches?"

Sarah tumbled across the cushions and turned around to look at me, head tilted as she pushed her hair away again with the backs of her hands.

"I'm not hungry right now," she said after a moment. She got up and pushed the end cushion back against the one before it. I heard a door close, then Tuah's voice, thank God.

"Elena, come meet Kevin," she said.

A boy who reminded me of the ranch sons at Harvey's Milkshakes entered the room from the hallway, Tuah behind him with one hand on his shoulder as if propelling him forward.

"Hi, Kevin," I said, rising from the sofa.

He stuck one hand out, elbow straight. "Pleased to meet you," he said. He wore a smudged white T-shirt, dark jeans, cowboy boots, and held a hat in his other hand. Wavy, light brown hair was crushed to his forehead in the front and on top, but stuck out defiantly at the back. He gave off a sharp, grassy smell. I took the offered hand.

"Pleased to meet you, too," I said. "Looks like you were busy. I'm sorry we interrupted you."

He nodded, chin high. "I was helping my dad in the shop," he said, leaning on the word *dad.* He withdrew his hand and pushed it into his pocket. "School's out, now."

"Paul will be right in," Tuah explained. "Have you two eaten lunch?"

Kevin and Sarah glanced at each other, then both nodded.

"Yes, ma'am," Kevin added.

I heard a door slam shut. Clearly the hallway led to more than bedrooms. A man entered, wiping his hands on a blue rag. He wore a chambray shirt, untucked in the back, with the edge of that identifying birthmark showing below his ear. I saw the connection to the children right away — a certain pulling at the corners of the eyes, a point to the chin. Mimicking his son, he held out his hand.

"Paul Kofford," he said. "Pleased to meet you. I can't tell you how much I appreciate you coming."

"Of course." I avoided Tuah's eyes. "It was

58

a good time for me to be here."

He looked away. "I'll show you around," he said. He turned and started toward the kitchen, stepping over a cushion Sarah hadn't needed and must have tossed aside. Apparently she hadn't broken any rules in making her tumbling mat. She sprang off the corner of the sofa to attach herself to her father's hip. Kevin trailed behind us. Tuah started putting the sofa cushions back.

"So tell me —" I started.

"You have to watch out when you open the oven," he said, bending to demonstrate, thumb over the handle, fingers splayed across the panel to support it. "I need to get a new screw to hold the front panel on, but you know how it goes . . ." He shrugged without looking at me and didn't wait for a response. He closed the oven and stuffed the blue rag into his back pocket. "You get used to it, don't think about it anymore. It's just a plain metal screw . . . I probably have something the right size in the shop . . ." He flipped on the faucet, inexplicably. "Just don't think about it when I'm out there." Shut off the faucet. "If I'd think about it for once while I'm in here, then just go out there and look around, pick up some things, bring a few different ones back in, I'm sure I could find something . . ."

He moved on to the refrigerator, opened it as he was talking, waved vaguely at the contents, and closed it again. A pantry door next to it swung open under his hand as well, the boxed and canned goods inside acknowledged with another wave before he closed it.

". . . nothing much right now, but you should feel free to get whatever you want. The kids will tell you what they like. I'm still figuring it all out myself. I'll just leave some money in the jar" — he lifted the head off a fat porcelain cat near the sink to reveal a dark cavity — "for the groceries or anything else you need. Cleaning stuff . . ." He glanced down at his daughter, then away again. "Hair stuff. Soap. All that."

Tuah had described him as quiet, a responsible man who'd be grateful for whatever I did but never directly ask me for anything. I'd pictured an already taciturn cowboy, now silenced by grief — far from the rambling reality I now followed through the kitchen and into a utility room. The flow of words felt like water filling a closed chamber, steadily rising around me.

". . . and the laundry soap is in here" — he opened a cupboard, waved in front of it, and closed it again — "and you have to watch out for the washer getting unbalanced. It'll start banging. You just need to open the lid and move things around."

I wondered how long it took him to figure that out. I doubted he had known a great deal about doing the laundry while his wife was alive. Maybe one of the neighbors had shown him. Maybe Tuah had. I glanced back through a slice of the kitchen. Tuah nodded at me from the living room, waved me on with a little sweeping gesture, then sank onto the sofa.

From the utility room, we passed through a bathroom that served as an odd connection to the bedroom hallway. A door at the end of the hallway led outside and would explain the comings and goings from what I'd thought were only bedrooms. But the door had three narrow windows, hashed like bars at eye level, which did little to illuminate the hallway and only intensified the prison-like atmosphere.

"This is Sarah's room. You'll have to get on her pretty hard to keep it clean."

I stood at the door and stared. The floor was covered with the ordinary detritus of a girl child — scattered paper, crayons, dolls, socks, stuffed animals — but it was the walls that arrested me. From the baseboard to as high as I imagined Sarah could reach while standing on the bed or a chair, the wall was papered with drawings. I turned to look down at her, just behind her father's hip.

"Are these all yours? You did them all yourself?"

She nodded, looking up at me.

"Is drawing your favorite thing to do?"

She squinched her faced together and looked sideways, thinking. After a moment, she shook her head.

"What do you like better?"

"Parties," she said.

"Parties are stupid," I heard from the hallway. I'd almost forgotten Kevin was there, but even if I'd been aware of him I wouldn't have known that was a wrong thing to say.

"That's enough," Paul said. "This way."

I followed him down the hallway, stealing a glance at Kevin as I did, but he was looking down and fiddling with something in his pocket.

"This is Kevin's room," Paul said, opening the next door. "He needs to work on keeping it clean, too."

I looked inside. Clothes were on the floor, but in piles that at least suggested some sort of order. The bed was unmade, and gum wrappers, scraps of paper, buttons, and baseball cards covered the top of a dresser against one wall. The room smelled like cat litter.

"What's your favorite thing to do, Kevin?" I asked, leaning back from the doorway.

He took no time to think about it. "Working in the workshop," he said, tapping his hat against his knee.

"And this is my room," Paul said, crossing the hall.

I took in the unmade bed, the clothes heaped on a chair, the cluttered dresser top, a folded hide-a-bed against the wall, and a stiff family portrait from Sears or JCPenney looming over all of it.

It was too much. Too much. The weight of suffering in this place squeezed against my lungs. The children of all this deserved better than me.

"I spent a lot of time thinking about where you could sleep," Paul said, swallowing so that I saw the birthmark swell outward and lie down again, "since I don't have an extra bedroom. You could've had Sarah's room, but when they share Sarah won't settle down, and then Kevin gets mad at her, and that can go on for hours, so I thought I'd better leave them where they are. But the sofa isn't comfortable in the living room, and people don't like to sleep in other people's beds, no matter what, but then I remembered that Carrie's mom has this hide-a-bed for when her sister came to stay, so I asked and she said it would be a good idea for me to have it for a while, so I've got it in here just so it's out of the way, not because you'd have to sleep in here — you could put it wherever you want. You can sleep in here if you want to have a door you can close, but don't feel like you have to, because we can just roll it down the hallway and set it up in the living room, and then you could have the TV, too, and get to the kitchen better, and the bathroom is kinda in the middle anyway . . ."

I couldn't stop him. I nodded and made occasional hums of agreement while his eyes flitted to the hide-a-bed, the hallway, the floor, the children. I felt acutely aware of being a strange female intended to sleep in the house his wife had abandoned, and felt the pull of the open door behind me.

He eventually paused and looked toward the toe of his boot.

"I'll use the living room," I blurted into his hesitation. "What time do you want me here?"

He finally met my eyes. "About seven," he said.

5

Much as Tuah loved the cabin, my grandfather's pride had always been the house in town. It was to serve as my home base when I wasn't staying with the Koffords, and it was where Tuah dropped me off after we left their house, telling me to settle in while she went to the market.

Narrow and Victorian as the cabin was squat and plain, the house had a place for every twentieth-century luxury. Those white folks who thought he wasn't good enough to marry one of their own? *Mi abuelo* had shown them, all right. The bathroom, once a butler's pantry, included both the original oak cabinetry as well as a tub and shower, a porcelain sink with chrome legs, and a toilet with an overhead tank and a pull chain. The kitchen wall had a pass-through with a tin door on each side where the milkman could leave his deliveries, so Tuah didn't have to walk outside or do so much as bend over to get fresh milk. A coal-fired furnace had been converted to gas, with scrolled iron grates in each room so the entire house was comfortable, without extraordinary effort, on even the coldest nights of the year. Refrigerator, electric stove, washer, dryer. Wallpaper. Carpet. Neighbors on every side. It was hard to believe this belonged to the same woman who happily hauled water at the cabin.

My room, the spare bedroom beside the kitchen, must have been meant as a sick-room when the house was built. Now, with its wallpaper of tiny violets, the carved cherubs at the corners of the headboard, the mounded quilts and extra pillows, the room felt grandmotherly in a completely different way than Tuah did in person. Old family photos in scrolled frames, under domed glass, fanned above a bureau. A stiff wedding portrait of Tuah and my grandfather. Tuah as a girl with her older sisters, all of them wearing petticoated dresses and gigantic bows in their hair. My father, in short pants and curls and ankle boots, sitting on a mule with its ears turned sideways, looking grim. And the only two pictures I'd ever seen of Benencia, my father's older sister, who died while he was still a child.

For some reason I had grown up thinking

benencia was the Spanish word for blessing. I had thought it the most beautiful name in the world to give to a child. *Blessing.* It wasn't until I was in high school that I learned the Spanish word for blessing is *bendición.* Or *gracia.* Or *beneficio.* Not *benencia.*

"So what does *benencia* mean?" I had asked my Spanish teacher, feeling stunned and cheated and somehow wronged. I was far from his first student with a Hispanic surname that didn't know the language.

He'd brushed chalk from his hands. "*Nada.* Just a name somebody made up, I guess."

I set my duffel on the floor and bent to peer at the pictures. In the first Benencia and Tuah stood in front of the Hat Creek cabin, before the porch was added, before the deforested hillsides grew up to be as I now knew them. Benencia looked like a little girl from a pioneer story in button-up boots and a full skirt and a sunbonnet, maybe five or six years old, holding her mother's hand, head turned to look over her shoulder. The rim of her bonnet hid her face completely. The other picture must have been taken not long before she died. She was a teenager, long-limbed and athletic, caught midstride, walking uphill but looking back. She wore a midcalf skirt, ankle boots, and a short-sleeved blouse. One hand atop her head held her hat in place, while the other trailed behind her. The sun was before her, and the long shadows suggested it was morning or late afternoon. As in the first picture, her face was turned away. Her profile was strikingly similar to Tuah's. In neither picture was she looking at the camera; there was no way to see the emptiness in her eyes, the mental handicap I always assumed to be just one symptom of the problems that must have made her life so short.

What *were* those problems, anyway? I had never asked. Growing up, grains of family history dissolved into my pool of knowledge without me noticing, the same way salt dissolves in water, the same way you can't remember anyone ever telling you that school starts in the fall. Benencia was disabled, somehow, and she had died, somehow. Was her condition genetic? Did I carry the gene? Would I pass it on?

God. A child. Some unformed creature receiving all nutrients, light, sound, and experience through me. What a terrible situation for a kid to be in. And now Kevin and Sarah, entrusted to my care. Actual people, rather than the abstractions they'd been in my grandmother's letter. What was their father thinking? Me, them, this fetus. How could so many desperate creatures wind up in the same place together?

I sat on the bed facing the window, then leaned to my side, then pulled my knees to my chest and stared out. Aspen leaves rustled against each other and a pair of girls with legs like colts revolved back and forth across my framed view, practicing cartwheels on a neighbor's lawn. I closed my eyes. My head hurt, and the relentless motion made it worse.

I'd made a colossal mistake. All I'd wanted from life was to be left alone, sitting in a laboratory every day working through calculations that had defined, knowable answers. So now, to put off facing the reality of a baby, I'd taken on responsibility for two children? Damaged children needing unknown amounts of unspecified care? At what point had this idea ever made sense to me? Why did it make sense to anyone else?

When I heard the back door squeal, the girls were gone. I blinked once or twice before realizing I must've dozed off. I sat up and scratched at the roots of my hair, heard the door again, then went into the kitchen. The truck door slammed. With yet another squeal from the back door Tuah came in, looking down and wiping her feet on the rag rug. Mac stepped around her and shook, then went to his dish and started drinking.

"I found some cherries," she said. "Early this year. We can have them with dinner."

"Okay."

A lawn mower hummed from somewhere out of sight.

She set down the bags she'd been carrying and looked at me. "Sleeping again?"

"I guess."

"Those kids won't take care of you, you know."

"I know." I cleared my throat. "Is there more outside?"

"Just one. On the seat."

By the time I got back, she had fruits and greens and vegetables queued up by the sink like cars at a car wash. It seemed like a lot. She had no refrigeration at the cabin and couldn't keep things cold for more than a couple of days in the ice chest she took with her.

"How are you going to keep all that fresh?" I asked.

"What?"

"At the cabin. Isn't that a lot for you? You're not just going to leave it all here, are you?"

"No, I'm not going up tomorrow. I'll stay here for your first week, in case you need anything. Oh —" She put a hand in the pocket of her pants and got out a folded piece of paper. "I ran into a friend at the market. She lives over by the Koffords and wanted you to have her number. Said to call anytime you need help. She knows the kids real well."

She pushed the paper toward me and turned back to the sink. I felt a stray pang of hope. Tuah would be nearby. Other neighbors wanted to help. This would've been a good moment to believe in God, to believe that some force in the universe had a compelling interest in protecting those children, to think I could stay and this could really work. But then that would mean it had also let their mother die. And that it had let me kill three other people before deciding I could use a little help. Too late. "Thanks," I said, stuffing the paper into my pocket.

Tuah twisted the knob and started filling the sink, then tore the stems off a bunch of spinach and dropped the leaves into the water.

"Would you get a towel out of the bottom drawer so I can lay out this spinach?" She twisted the faucet off.

I spread the towel across the counter while she swirled her hand through the water so that the leaves seemed to move like a school of fish. I smoothed the towel more than it needed and spoke without looking up.

"I don't know if I can do this."

"Do what?"

"Take care of those kids. I don't know anything about kids."

"You didn't get through college thinking you can't do things you haven't done before."

"But I *did* do science before. I like it. Everything works in science."

"Don't be so afraid of everything, Elena. You're braver than you think. You weren't doing science when you found your first apartment by yourself."

"Yeah — *by myself.* That's the point — I'm *fine* by myself. This has nothing to do with being afraid. I just know what I can and can't do."

"Oh, good heavens. That's what fear *is.*"

"God, Tuah. It's *reality.* I'm great by myself but I know I get in trouble with people. I should be living like you. Off alone somewhere. You could drop me in the middle of Africa and I'd be fine. I'm not *afraid* of anything, but I'll be a disaster with those kids."

Tuah stared at me for a long moment without speaking, then her eyes narrowed. She turned back to the sink, took the spinach out by handfuls, and laid the leaves on the towel. She pulled the plug from the drain and set it on the counter. As the water swirled and gurgled, she turned the faucet back on and caught water in her cupped hand to rinse away the lines of sand left behind. Only then did she shut off the water and turn to face me.

"Elena, I don't go to the cabin to be by myself. I'm not getting *away* from people. I'm going *because* of people."

"Right. Because they drive you crazy."

"No." She took a deep breath. "What do you know about Benencia?"

I must have looked as startled as I felt.

"You know who she is, don't you?" Tuah asked.

"Yes — it's just — I was wondering about her, just now, from the —" I gestured toward the bedroom with my thumb. "Pictures, you know."

"All right, then. What exactly do you know?"

I wasn't quite sure how to put it. "She was . . . handicapped, somehow. She died when she was a teenager."

"Do you know how she died?"

73

"I just thought — it had something to do with the handicap, right?"

"Do you know where she's buried?"

When I was little, I had liked to go to the cemetery in Hat Creek. In its weathered abandonment, it was spooky enough for a child, even during the daylight. I would kick the sagebrush and rub the wooden crosses with my fingers to read them better, sorting out where the bodies themselves must be lying, figuring out how old people had been. I clearly remembered my grandfather's marker. I couldn't do the same for Benencia's.

"Somewhere by Abuelo, I guess. I don't remember seeing a marker, though."

She took the dishtowel from her shoulder and wiped her hands. "No, you haven't. She's not there."

"But — why would you bury her somewhere else?"

"We didn't," she said. She tilted her chin toward the window, which looked out toward the mountains that framed Leadville. "She was lost."

"What do you mean?"

"I mean — *lost*. She got lost. She wandered away, and we never found her."

How had I not known this? It should have been important. My father had been eight when she died. Or — became lost. Old enough to remember, and something like that certainly would have hung over the family as he grew up. I could still remember a mother I'd seen at Disneyland who thought her daughter had fallen into the water at the jungle ride. She'd clutched the boat rail and screamed. Like an animal. I couldn't imagine he was unaware. Why had he never told me?

"I — I didn't know."

"No, I'm sure you didn't. I know your father doesn't talk about her. He was very young. They were six years apart."

"But, what happened?"

"Benencia stayed like a little child her whole life. She wandered off and disappeared as easily as a five-year-old. More easily — she was bolder and faster. On the day it happened, we thought she was playing with other children. We didn't figure out she was missing until it was almost dark. The whole town went out searching with lanterns, calling her name —" Tuah shook her head. "Nothing. But she had always been afraid of men and especially of anyone yelling. I tried to tell them. I've always wondered if she was somewhere nearby and hiding, afraid to answer."

"I'm so sorry." It was the only response I

could find.

She looked back at me with a faint smile. "Thank you," she said.

"I should have known —"

She shook her head. "No. No. It would have been a terrible, hard thing for you. It's nothing to hide from you, but I never found the right time to tell the story. And it would've made staying at the cabin kind of strange, don't you think? This is better."

I looked down at my finger, now outlining a tile at the edge of the counter. My aunt. My father's sister. I cleared my throat.

"How long did you search?"

"Weeks. But it was already autumn, and the nights were cold. No one expected to find her alive after the first few days. We had snow only a week later. But I was her mother. I couldn't just give up like that."

Unfound forever. "Of course not."

"No." Tuah put a hand on her hip, the bunched towel hanging like a tassel. "Now, I want to explain something," she said. "When I go to the cabin, I'm not waiting for her. She hid, and went to sleep, and froze, I'm sure, and animals found the body. Benencia is gone. And Eduardo is gone. And your father —" She looked down, then out the window. "In his own way, he's been gone a long time, too." She was still a moment, then looked at me. "But in the cabin, we were together. *That's* why I go back. To me, a house holds memories, keeps them safe for anyone who wants to come back. A place keeps things you might forget yourself, and then when you're there it gives them back to you. Does that make any sense?"

When I got my driver's license as a teenager, one of the first places I drove by myself was to the house where we lived when I was ten, when I'd started the fire. We had moved four times since then. Ironically, unfairly, the wind had swept the infant blaze up the hillside and away from us so quickly that even with the thousands of acres ruined, the homes burned, the lives lost, no firefighter had stood on the ground of our canyon or had to fight to save our house.

Even at the time, the scorched path it had left was narrow and only lightly gray. Six years later, it had healed completely. I had cut school, and was there midday on a Thursday, when no one was home. With my car idling in the driveway, I forced myself to stand behind the garage and stare at the weeds. I squatted down as I'd squatted over the fire, put my elbows on my knees and my face in my hands and wept. When the school called later that afternoon to check on my absence, I shrugged my shoulders and let my father assume whatever he wanted about where I'd been. The Plaza. Cliff jumping. Taking heroin. I didn't care.

Yes. I understood. I nodded.

"That's why I go. That's where we were a family, where all four of us were together. I'm lucky. I can go back to the place that held our family. I've never had to leave it without knowing I'll be back. I've never had to leave behind the part of myself that stays there."

What had become of the pieces of myself left behind over the years? I could see them clearly — gossamer shreds, snagged like tissue and fluttering faintly behind me. One caught on the corner of the kitchen table at the neighbor boy's house where I'd been having dinner the afternoon of the fire, just before we evacuated; another on the carpet threshold in the apartment where my mother last lived with us; another on the oleander bush sprawling over the grave I dug for the rabbit my father bought me after she left. If I returned to gather them all, what would I have? Did I even want them back?

"I don't go to the cabin to be alone," Tuah said. "I go there to connect myself *with* people. Do you understand?" She paused, one eyebrow lifted, then bent to get a plastic basket from the cupboard at her knee and started stacking squash in it. "You need those children as much as they need you. You need to start thinking about other people besides yourself. It's the only way you'll ever stop being afraid."

"I'm *not* af—"

"Stop it. Now blot that spinach and don't give me another word about what you can't do."

6

Paul Kofford made small ceremony of saying good-bye to his children the next morning, ruffling Sarah's hair and giving a nod to Kevin before he pulled his Dodgers cap down low over his eyes. The handling made little difference in Sarah's hair, which formed a mazy halo as she sat with her head bowed over her cereal, elbow out, spoon clutched in her fist. She swung her bare feet below her nightgown but didn't look up. Kevin managed a solemn nod of his own before his father opened the front door. Nearly horizontal rays of sunlight cast a blinding rectangle across the floor, which narrowed and then disappeared as the door closed again.

"Can I please have some sugar?" Kevin asked.

"Sure. Where is it?"

He turned and pointed toward an upper cabinet in the kitchen. "In there."

I found a mason jar topped with a salt-box top that had been trimmed and secured under the jar's ring. I put it on the table, where Kevin picked the spout open with his fingernail and started to pour sugar over his Cheerios like sand over paving stones.

"Easy, there," I said, reaching to take the jar out of his hand. He stopped pouring and looked up at me.

"This is how I have it," he said.

"It is?"

"Uh-huh."

I decided today wasn't the day to remake anybody's eating habits. "Are you done with it, then?" I asked.

"Uh-huh." He put the jar down and gave his attention to the bowl. I put the sugar back in the cupboard, then stood in the kitchen for a moment, arms folded, absorbing the scene before me: the shade-darkened family room, the dinette table with a few days' mail scattered around the sleepy children, the muffled sounds of chewing.

I had no idea how the day would unfold or the three that would follow until Paul returned. Tuah had helped me come up with some ideas the night before. The library had a summer reading program. We could go to the municipal swimming pool. We could play Monopoly or the children could build forts. The children could certainly invite friends over, which would help. She did warn me that most children were unlike me, and wouldn't want to roam aimlessly in the wilderness for hours on end, especially children who lived here and saw no novelty in the landscape. She encouraged me to put them to work — cleaning their rooms, doing household chores, helping to get groceries and cook meals, doing yard work. They needed normalcy and routine. A schedule they could depend on. Discipline. A steady hand.

"What would you like to do today?" I asked.

"Shoot cans," Kevin answered.

What were the household rules about firearms? I knew nothing about them myself. And I most definitely wasn't going to have the children handle lethal weapons on my first day, especially when they knew more about them than I did.

"You'll have to save that for when your dad's home. Anything else?"

Sarah stared at me, chewing, a drop of milk clinging to her lower lip. She looked as confused as if someone had lifted her out of a dead sleep and slung her into the chair only seconds before.

"Sarah?"

"Uh-huh?"

"What would you like to do today?"

A blink. Swallow. "Color," she finally said.

"I hate coloring," Kevin announced.

"That's okay. You don't have to do the same things."

My response seemed to catch him by surprise. He looked at me guardedly for a moment, as if waiting for me to say something else, then turned his attention back to his cereal. I glanced at the clock. Five minutes after seven.

I cleared my throat. "After breakfast, I think we should do some chores, and then later we can go to the library, and you can pick out some books."

"What kind of chores?"

"Cleaning your rooms." They said nothing, but in the way they both stopped chewing and straightened their backs against their chairs I could feel the resistance. *Be firm,* I heard Tuah say. *Do what you say. But be reasonable.* I plowed on.

"I think doing everything at once is really hard. This morning I'd like you to show me your clothes. We can decide what to wash and what to put away. Then I'll do the laundry later and you can show me where everything goes."

The chewing resumed, though they continued to study me.

"Okay," Kevin finally said.

"Good."

I told myself I had successfully navigated the first passage.

Kevin's room was fairly easy. He had a drawer of underwear that I confirmed was fresh. Everything else was on the floor, and though he showed me which were dirty and clean, I opted to wash everything. I hoped it would do something about the pet-like smell. I stripped the bed, as well, and left him absorbed in a box of what appeared to be trash that I'd inadvertently kicked out from underneath it.

Sarah, and Sarah's room, were more complicated. She seemed to come more fully into herself after breakfast, brightening as I washed the dishes, and by the time we got to her room she had started to chatter. *This* shirt had kittens on it, see? This one was Lisa and this one was Jenny and this one was Fluffy and this one was Anna-mara-something or other. *This* skirt could spin, and she pulled it on and demonstrated, whirling on her toes, skirt standing out like a plate, nightgown hiked around her ribs. *This* was her watermelon top, and this one had daisies. Her jeans were comfy. Her green pants were soft. A glacier might grow more quickly than this laundry pile.

Finally I couldn't take it anymore. Sitting cross-legged on the floor, I pointed to the picture directly in front of me on the wall, hoping to distract her enough to move a few pieces across to the laundry pile without commentary. The picture included four stick figures with large heads. One had no face, and the others had eyes and noses but no mouths.

"Who are those people?" I asked.

She jumped to her feet to point to each one, going first through the figures with faces. "That's my daddy. That's Kevin. That's me." Then she pointed at the featureless face. "And that's my mommy. She died."

Oh, God. I scanned other pictures, searching in vain across the wall in front of me for one that included four complete faces. I realized as I did that the pictures all appeared to be of about the same skill level — all included arms, legs, faces, hair, dresses on the girls, some with mountains or houses of fairly consistent geometry.

I rotated so I could look along other walls. Faces. Finally. "Sarah, did you draw all these pictures just recently, while you've been in kindergarten?"

She shook her head. "I drew some of them at home," she said.

"I mean — just, while you've been a big kindergarten girl?"

She nodded. "Since I was a *second half* kindergartener."

Since her mother had died. I would confidently place that bet on all my scant possessions.

"But kindergarten's over," she added. "I'm a first-grader now."

My longest day before this had moved at least twice as fast as this one. The level of room-cleaning I'd agreed to was finished by 8:00. The library wouldn't open until 10:00, though I got no sense that the outing meant very much to them. I had the children sit on the floor with me and help sort the laundry — do you think this is dark or light? — a game Sarah enjoyed, but in Kevin produced mounting frustration.

"This is *stupid*!" he finally snapped after wadding a pair of jeans and chucking them into the pile of whites.

Don't make excuses for them. They need a firm, calm hand, not pity. I took a deep breath. "That's a rude word, Kevin," I said. "You don't like it, but it's not stupid. It's what we have to do to get clean clothes."

"I don't *do* this!" he shouted, far too loud for the narrow hallway where we sat. Before I could say anything, he pushed himself to his feet and fled outside, slamming the door behind himself so that the glass panes rattled.

"Kevin's mad," Sarah offered.

"Yes." I looked down at the heap of jeans and shirts by my knee. "Does he get mad a lot?"

She shrugged. "I dunno." She picked up a flowered shirt. "What's this?" she asked.

"Light." So she'd seen Kevin have an outburst of temper more than a few times before. I uncrossed my legs. "I think I'll go talk to him."

"Is he in trouble?" she asked.

I had no idea what I'd say to him. I could ask questions and listen. That was something I'd wished for, at least.

"No," I said. "You wait inside."

I pushed through the hallway door, which opened to a concrete stoop only as wide as the door, just deep enough to stand on. Packed dirt marked the spot where the first step afterward would land. The landscape was too bare to hide a sulking boy, so I headed toward the former barn, now serving as Paul's mechanic's shop. I found Kevin squatting in the shadows on the far side, out of sight from the house, stabbing a hole in the dirt with a pointed stick.

"Hey," I said, seating myself beside him.

"I don't want to do laundry no more."

"I figured."

He twisted the stick to drill into the dirt. Chipped some to the side. Drilled again.

"I'm sorry I said *stupid,*" he said, his tone draped with theatric remorse. I doubted he was sorry in the slightest.

"Where'd you find your stick?"

He glanced at me, pale blue eyes on either end of a bridge of freckles, then pointed toward a runoff ditch a dozen yards away, choked with branches and debris. I got up, brushed the dirt off my seat, and took my time picking a better digging stick than his. Eventually I returned and started digging beside him. A meadowlark lilted a scrap of song from the top of the barn. I felt chilly in the shade.

"Are you a mom?" he said after I'd dug out a four-inch circle.

"Not yet."

I deepened the center of the circle.

"Are you a teacher?"

"Nope."

He seemed to need some time to absorb this. Then, "Where do you work?"

"I just finished college. I'm going to stay

here with you and your sister for a while."

"Taking care of us is your job?"

"Sort of."

"Is my dad paying you?"

I was baffled by his line of questioning but couldn't see a reason to do anything other than answer.

"No. I'm just helping. My grandma is helping me, and I'm helping you. But I'll stay here as long as you two need me." Where had that come from? Ignore it. Plow on. "Your dad is trying to figure out a way to stay home more so he won't need other people to help."

Kevin didn't respond, but concentrated on working around the edges of a buried rock he'd encountered.

"What *do* you do?" I asked. I kept my eyes on the tip of my stick and the bowl of grit forming in front of me.

"What?"

"When you left the house, you said you didn't do laundry. So what *do* you do?"

"I dunno."

"Did your mom always do the laundry?"

I kept my eyes down, resisting the temptation to make eye contact as I waited for an answer.

"I guess," he said eventually.

"You know, everybody needs to do the

things your mom used to do now."

Still I kept my eyes down. So I didn't see the expression on his face when his stick skipped across the dirt and a kick of sand sprayed my leg before his shoes crunched away from me.

7

Anxiety consumed me for the rest of the day. I could think of nothing but anticipating sensitivities. The library, at least at Sarah's level, turned out to be a minefield of stories about children and animals and their mothers. Terrified of stumbling unawares into something that would upset her, clueless about how to distract her or respond to her flood of *What about this one? Or this one?* I shifted my attention to Kevin and dragged her with me. He'd found a stack of books about machinery and stood unsmiling beside a table, flipping pages. Despite my insistence that he could take as many books as he wanted, he took a particularly dull-looking title about the world's biggest engines to a chair and said he didn't want anything else.

Without any further ideas on how to handle Sarah, I let her go back to the picture books without me while I started looking for something to read aloud to them, something simple but entertaining enough to bridge the age gap. Reading and study were the only places where I used to be able to lose myself as a child, to close a door against the ghosts of the burned who otherwise trailed behind me night and day. So, thinking through the books I re-read most as a child, I looked first for *James and the Giant Peach,* but when I opened it I realized I'd forgotten about the parents that were killed on the first page. *Charlotte's Web* promised emotional reactions to Charlotte's death. *The Black Stallion* came to mind next and was as quickly discarded for the shipwreck that kills everyone but the boy and the horse. Children, it seemed, were meant to be exposed to grief early.

"Lookit *this!*" Sarah held a book out to me. *My Mommy's Pocket,* with a picture of a cartoon kangaroo and its smiling baby waving from the safety of her pouch.

Oh, hell no.

In the distance behind her I could see Kevin slumped in a chair flipping through a car magazine. He wouldn't last much longer.

"That looks great, sweetie. I'll hang on to it and you look for some more."

Sarah bounced away, waving to a librarian

with great swooping wings of hair sprayed into place, pushing a cart toward me as she passed. The librarian smiled back at Sarah, then looked at me.

"Excuse me," I whispered. "Can you recommend something I can read to a first-grader and a sixth-grader where nobody dies?"

"Oh, honey," she said, stopping the cart. "Bless your heart." She turned away from me to scan the featured books displayed across the top shelf. "Let me . . . Oh. There." She reached over a book with a dog on the cover to get another and held it out to me. *Tales of a Fourth Grade Nothing.* "Take this," she said. "They'll love it." Then she returned to the cart, but instead of taking hold of the handle, she scooped up a stack of picture books and pushed them into my arms. "And I got these for Sarah," she added, lowering her voice. "I'm Mrs. McKee — Alice." She tilted her head back toward Kevin in his chair and the tea-party table where Sarah had started flipping through something new. "I work at the school library, too. Look — can I just give you a quick piece of advice? Don't make yourself crazy trying to protect them. There's nothing but kids with mothers all around them. You can do a lot for them this summer by getting them used to talking about it, before they go back to school."

Then she winked at me and rumbled away before I could breathe out anything other than an automatic, "Thanks."

What she hadn't accounted for was my discovery that morning that I was afraid of their feelings. My goal now was to sidestep through the summer and hope they'd deal with their grief after I was gone. The weak and ugly truth.

From the library it was home to the laundry and the traps awaiting in the harmless-looking pile of clothes. Should socks be doubled over or balled? Underwear rolled or stacked? Shirts folded or hung? Eventually it was time for lunch. What did they expect? Did they like peanut butter or bologna? Grilled cheese? Would they eat fruit or vegetables? Should sandwiches be cut into rectangles or triangles?

Over the course of just these few hours, a vision for the summer started to take shape. If I was going to stay, my objective was to pad everything they touched with the familiar and comfortable. They'd been subjected to nothing but other mothers' food and other families' routines for three months, and chances were their days at home hadn't been much better. Everything about the house — from the chaos in the children's rooms to the useless assortment of canned goods in the pantry to the sticky dust on the washing machine — suggested that their father was barely functioning.

On a notepad in the kitchen, beside the phone, I started a list of questions to cover with their father when he called. How much TV were they allowed to watch? Did they have an afternoon snack? What kinds of chores were they supposed to do? Were they expected to finish their dinner, whether or not they liked what was on the plate? Were desserts allowed? Did they take baths or showers? For now, I had only them to ask, and every expectation that the answers would be based on whim rather than truth.

Still, we moved smoothly enough through afternoon TV, macaroni and cheese, and toward bedtime until Sarah went into her room to get a stuffed animal after her bath and I heard, in a tone that accelerated upward like a fighter jet swinging into the sky, "Where's my *BUFFERS*?"

My hands dripping dishwater, I ran down the hallway.

"What is it?"

"Where's my *BUFFERS*?" She stood facing her bed, hands on her nightgowned hips, bath towel in a heap at her feet. Her hair, wet and uncombed, straggled across half her face. She smelled of baby shampoo.

"What's your buffers?"

"He's my *RABBIT*!" She pointed at the stuffed animals on her bed, arranged against the corner of her room as if the wall had erupted and poured out a lava flow of multicolored fur.

"Oh." I felt my shoulders relax. I shook the water from my fingers. "I'm sure he's in there. I washed your sheets, remember?"

She thrust her upper body toward me with a look of hatred that shocked me. "He goes in the *FRONT*!"

It was impossible. There was no way in heaven or earth that I could reassemble their broken world as it used to be. I could never be wise enough or quick enough to steer them around every heartbreak and disappointment and frustration. And I knew in my belly that if I let her treat me this way — even once, no matter the reason — the summer would be unendurable. I straightened myself as I could envision Tuah doing.

"Stop this."

"He goes in the *FRONT*!"

"Sit down. Right there. This instant."

"NOOO!" she shrieked, elbows bent, white-knuckled fists pulled close to her chest like a boxer about to lash out. Her cheeks had

flushed, and a webwork of mottled pink spread down her neck. Forget flight or invisibility — refusal is the ultimate superpower. What was I supposed to do in the face of it?

"I think I see his ear," said Kevin, from the doorway. I had forgotten him and wondered how long he'd been there. I waved him quiet without looking. I had to find a way to get this girl in possession of her faculties again. Scrambling to give her the actual rabbit at this point would leave me worse off than before.

"Sarah, no one will help you until you calm down. Sit on the floor. Right now."

"NOOO!" She threw herself on her bed and burrowed into the pile of animals. "Stop *LOOKING* at me!"

I had no idea what to do. This was a full-scale tantrum. She screamed and wailed and sobbed, kicking her feet as she lay facedown on the bed, head lost in the pile of animals.

"I think he's right there," said Kevin again. I could see his arm extended, pointing, from the corner of my eye.

"Shhh."

Instinct. Nothing else remained. I squeezed my eyes shut, which did nothing to shut out the shrieking. I grasped through my mind like a secretary flinging files everywhere until I found something. A memory: babysitting. Me standing in a burnt-orange living room, ankle deep in shag carpet, reporting to a neighbor woman with a set curl that her little boy had thrown a tantrum about some candy she'd specifically told me not to give him. The woman had laughed, much to my irritation.

"Oh, I'm sorry," she'd said. "The thing that causes the tantrum is never what the tantrum's about. If it happens again, start talking about something else. He was just tired."

I avoided babysitting whenever possible after that.

I opened my eyes and looked around the room. The pictures in which all four family members had faces were clustered by the door. On a bookshelf nearby, a snapshot leaning against a jar of rocks showed the family in front of a Ferris wheel. The tumult on the bed made the jar rattle. I picked the picture up and studied it.

"Where was this picture taken?" I asked Kevin.

"At the fair. It was fall. We got to miss school."

"DON'T LOOK AT ME!"

"For the whole day?"

"Uh-huh."

"That must've been great."

Sarah's crying rose to a high, thin wail, sharp as a spear.

"Did you ride the Ferris wheel?"

He nodded.

She'd lost control of her breathing, her chest pulsing to the sobs.

"Were you scared, being up so high?"

"Nope." He shook his head, clearly pleased to be able to tell the tale. "Not even Sarah. Not even when it stopped at the top."

"Wow."

She squirmed backward on her elbows to pull her head out of the pile, turned her face toward us, and pressed her cheek against the pillow. She sobbed now in shuddering moans with her fist against her mouth. She'd stopped kicking.

"And that's your mom?" I asked, pointing. In the picture she had her arm across his shoulders and had Sarah pulled tight against her hip. A beautiful woman with a generous mouth and a wide smile. She and the children wove together into a triangle. Paul stood just behind Kevin, and though one arm wasn't fully visible, he didn't appear to be touching any of the others.

"Yeah."

How many times had I vacillated today between imagining myself a hero and seeing myself a coward? The bed shook beside my knee as I continued to gaze at the picture. There was something off, something ominous about the way the Ferris wheel loomed over them, the size and angle of their combined shadow resting on the pavement like a creature about to rise up and strike them. It looked a little like a book I'd read as a child, a boy with a staff, fighting a shadow on the cover. The boy was a wizard, and the shadow was a demon he'd accidentally conjured, made of his own darkness and fear. It grew in power as he grew, and in the final battle, with nowhere to turn, he turned and embraced it. In that instant, it dissolved. Maybe I should have tried to find that one at the library.

I took a deep breath. Looked up. Yes, I was afraid of their pain. But avoidance had clearly already failed. "Sarah, do you remember when this picture was taken?"

She nodded, unable to control her breathing enough to speak. She hitched her knee and twisted onto her side. I sat on the bed beside her, holding the picture. Kevin stood still as time in the doorway.

"Do you think about your mommy a lot?"
Huh-huh-huh-huh.

I looked at Kevin. "You too?"

He nodded. His eyes filled half his face. No, I wasn't without resources when it came to lost mothers. The wanting to remember. The fear of it.

"What kinds of things do you think about?"

"Driving in the car, sometimes. I always sat in front. And bedtime." He looked down.

"Sarah, what do you think about?"

She reached out for the picture and brought it close to her eyes.

"Sarah, it would be okay with me if you wanted to tell me about your mommy sometimes."

"I-I-I'm forgetting my *memories* about her."

I looked up at the walls around me, blinking and swallowing. The crayon families looked back at me, Sarah and her mother in their triangle dresses, their wide-open hands with the stick fingers, their long hair colored yellow or brown, and all those empty, empty faces. I looked back at Kevin. No amount of blinking would clear the pool of liquid gathering at my lower lids, so I didn't try to hide anything from him. I squeezed a smile and willed my throat to relax so I could speak evenly. He met my gaze and gave me the tiniest nod in return. Shared sorrow connected us.

"You too, Kevin?"

"Yeah."

The question nobody had ever asked me. I looked back at Sarah.

"How does that feel, forgetting?"

"Terrible." As if she was spelling it out mentally, she formed her mouth around every letter.

"Do you remember what she looked like?"

"No, not at *all.*" She brought the photo closer to her face.

"Sarah, if you could remember more things, and if you could talk more or see more pictures, do you think you'd feel better?"

"Uh-huh." She put the picture down on the blanket and rubbed her eyes with her fist.

"Would you like that too, Kevin?" I asked.

Standing motionless in the doorway, his hands hanging empty at his sides, he nodded twice.

"Then that's what we'll do," I said.

We started reading our book gathered on the floor of Sarah's room, leaning our backs against the side of the bed. Sarah sat with her arms wrapped around Buffers the Rabbit, at peace now that the rest of the pile had been properly rearranged. She'd given Kevin a bear that he accepted as if doing her a favor but that remained in exactly the place she'd put it on his lap.

I wished I had one of those other books now. I wished I had James and his miraculous peach, with his new friends who cared about him and gave him hope again after an undeserved awful fate had stripped everyone he loved out of his life. I wished I had Alec Ramsay and his stallion, needing each other and surviving together when everyone else on the ship had been lost. I wished I had wise Charlotte saving Wilbur's life and teaching him how love itself equips you to carry on after the one you love is gone. Things I had never learned successfully on my own.

"Chapter one," I began. " 'The Big Winner.' "

8

The next two days passed in utter calm, as if nothing had ever happened. The children whined as morning chores were announced, but they did them without argument or tears. I knew what was going on: I was well versed in resistance meant only for show and the nominal dramatics didn't trouble me. By the third day, in fact, as he herded Cheerios into his final spoonful, Kevin even asked what they had to do after breakfast.

What proved far more difficult than managing the children was figuring out how to interpret and deal with the glimpses I got into the family's private life. Things I was certain I needed to ask about seemed unimportant, but things I never would have thought to question had gravity I couldn't understand. At the grocery store, the children fretted about having a list their father had not first approved. They lagged behind me and kept to the center of the aisle, as if afraid a hand would snatch at them from between the cereal boxes.

When I selected individual items and asked whether they usually got *this* kind or *that* kind, they cast worried looks at each other and Kevin would say something like, "I *think* that one's okay. But just one." Trying to buy a jar of grape jam got me an alarmed look and then a firm, "No. We're not buying any jam." I pointed out that the jar I'd seen in the refrigerator was almost empty, but Kevin just said, "No. That's enough." Mystified but unwilling to probe, I elected not to argue.

An elderly man at the foot of the road, who introduced himself as Mr. Fousek, made a point to wave me down and ask our destination every time we left the house. The first time he had been washing paintbrushes in his driveway, and I figured he was just the neighborhood busybody. But the next time he lurched out of his garage, waving with both arms as if afraid we'd pass without stopping. As we returned, he let another car go by with only the barest nod. Why was he so anxious to keep track of our movements and ours alone?

My direct interactions with the kids were simpler. I learned Sarah drank from the plastic cups, and Kevin insisted on glass.

Guns remained off limits, but Kevin had a surprisingly powerful slingshot, and teaching me how to aim and shoot it provided plenty of entertainment. Sarah loved to dress, arrange, and care for her stuffed animals, and she showed genuine awe when I showed her how to apply her new shoe-tying skills to making bows for their ears, arms, tails, and manes.

Evening, though, was when they pulled the coverings off their wounds, washed them, let them weep under the little canopy of light from Sarah's bedside lamp, and dressed them again before sleep. In just one dose, they discovered storytime as the balm that soothed them.

Bless Mrs. McKee and the book she'd chosen for us.

During dinner, the children would talk about what we might read that night, using their spoons or the backs of their hands to keep food in their mouths while they laughed. What would Fudge do next? What did they think Fudge would do if he was at their house? What would happen if Fudge met an elk or saw a beaver pond? As the mountain's shadow spread across the valley and stretched its covers over the house, they'd abandon the TV without me saying anything and start to get ready for bed —

Sarah's bath first so I could comb her hair while Kevin showered. Then we would gather in Sarah's room, where Kevin would sprawl on the bed and supposedly read his book while I read picture books on the floor to Sarah. But Kevin's book lay open and ignored while he leaned over my shoulder to follow along with the children's stories. At one point he even said "Read that one" as Sarah struggled to choose.

After I finished reading a few of Sarah's, the last pretense would drop and they'd take equal places at my sides, hair slicked and smelling of soap, Sarah pressed against my hip and Kevin leaning on my shoulder, while I read from *Tales of a Fourth Grade Nothing.* We read probably longer than we should've each night. But what did it matter? They didn't have school in the mornings, and the gash of need was so raw I couldn't deny them. Besides, we had a lot of pages to get through. I didn't want them to finish it without me over the weekend.

On Thursday night, they started to talk about their mother. While we read *Jack and the Beanstalk,* Kevin said she'd packed magic beans in his lunch one day last year. I wasn't clear on whether he was embarrassed or pleased. Perhaps both. Sarah said they'd talked about a princess party for her

107

birthday at the end of the summer, where they'd have a real pony and build their own castles. They started interrupting each other in an effort to tell their stories, and before long I wondered how much was real and how much an effort to outdo one another in how wonderful, magical, and loving of a mother they each remembered.

Their father did not fare as well in these stories. I tried to keep in mind the context, but I couldn't help noticing that if he entered the narrative at all it was only as the rule-maker, the permission-denier, the authority. I felt some code-of-adults obligation to support him, to suggest good reasons why he might have said they couldn't have a dog, couldn't throw a party, mustn't go to friends' houses after school unless he was home and gave permission, but they didn't seem to need them. They mentioned their father's policies offhandedly, as a way of painting the background in a story meant to be about their mother, without complaint or judgment or any apparent wish for things to be any different.

Then Kevin, rubbing his eyes with one hand, stuck the book in my hand and said he wanted us to start reading. So I read. And they hugged me before they went to bed.

By the next morning I had to admit that, on balance, the week had gone well, but I was still glad for Friday. Paul was due back that afternoon, and I'd have four days to spend at the cabin with Tuah before the Koffords needed me again. I anticipated the ease of waking and sleeping on my own schedule, of being free of needs and questions, and felt a general sense of well-being as I squatted on my heels with the morning sun on my back, idly pulling weeds from the bed around the front door.

Kevin threw and fielded a tennis ball against the side of the shed as I half listened to Sarah, sitting on the step, telling me stories from the lives of her stuffed animals. The elephant's best friend was the blue cat. The blue cat loved pretzels because they were her favorite because she liked them. But the elephant liked peanuts, so sometimes they had fights. But the doll could stop them because they were afraid of her because she was the ghost.

"She's a ghost?" I said without looking, wiggling at a long-rooted finger of grass between the stones.

"You know, the miner's daughter. The one who got killed."

I dropped back onto my heels. A miner's

daughter? "No, I don't know about that ghost."

"She has blue ribbons," Sarah said, holding the doll out for me to see. It was a child doll, upright and stiff, with cloth Mary Jane shoes and a pink dress, and blue bows in her hair. "The ghost is looking for her dog, and if you're alone in the woods at night she might *get* you."

"Who told you this story?"

"Cindy's brother. It's true."

I hated this kid, who must have thought it was fun to frighten little girls. And at the same time, I needed to hear the rest of the story. A miner's daughter, killed in the mountains? Was it crazy to wonder whether there was a connection? Would a more complete telling make it any clearer? But I had the wrong storyteller to extract anything close to a clear version.

"Are you scared about the ghost?"

Sarah tilted her head back, face to the sun, closing her eyes with a wide smile. She shook her head. "Nope. I'm not scared at *all*."

"Really?"

"Miss Poppy told me when people die, and you love them, they're angels that wrap love all around you, like my mom. Not ghosts. Ghosts come from bad thoughts, so she said I won't ever see one."

My own ghosts, made of smoke and regret, shimmered silently from their usual place at the edge of my field of vision. A mother, a baby, and a little girl. I refocused on Sarah.

"Who's Miss Poppy?"

Sarah pointed her arm straight ahead, over my shoulder. "She has Bella."

Good God. Every answer this child gave was wrapped in another question. I tried to pull her back.

"Does she know about the miner's daughter, too?"

But Sarah was looking past me now. I heard a car and turned to look over my shoulder.

"Katy!" shrieked Sarah, dropping the doll into the dirt.

A little girl launched herself, feet first, out the back door of a gold sedan as a wire-thin teenager emerged from the driver's door. Another woman, with round cheeks and curly hair, got out of the passenger door and set a dungareed toddler on the ground. Sarah threw her arms around the little girl, and they both started shrieking with laughter, at what I didn't know. I eased my knees and back straight as I stood.

"You're Elena, right?" the round-cheeked

one asked, giving a tug to the toddler's overall straps. The child lifted his arms to right himself, then took a tentative step toward the little girls.

"Yeah. Hi."

"I'm Joan. That's Mindy." She tipped her head back to the far side of the car, where the teenager slammed the back door, a baby on her hip. "We were just on our way back from the park. Thought we'd come see how you were doing."

I had a sudden picture of Mr. Fousek, at the end of the street, flagging down passersby and sending one to check on me because I hadn't been past his house since yesterday. Sarah grabbed the other girl's wrist and started pulling her toward the front door.

"Good to meet you," I said.

The screen door swung open beside me. "— and we got pizza, and Fritos, and some cheese. I'll show you," Sarah said. The two girls disappeared and the door slammed behind them.

"Can I use the bathroom?" the teenager asked as she approached.

"Ah, sure."

"Here." She held the baby out to me.

My hands closed automatically on the baby, and the teenager disappeared into the house. The other woman took the hands of the toddler over his head and directed his walking toward me, falling into step with his rolling gait. "Boy, we sure came in here like a freight train, huh?" She squinted up at me, smiling.

"I — it's fine. I wasn't really doing anything."

I lowered myself onto the step and perched the baby on my knee. He stared back at me. He was heavier than I expected, solid and dense. I had scarcely ever handled a baby. Should I be supporting his head? I saw no sign of wobbling. His neck seemed thick, though the head above it was so large the ears were almost as far apart as the shoulders. Could he sit alone or crawl? What did he eat? How much did he sleep? The round, steely eyes offered no answers.

The walking baby continued to teeter toward me. Should I hold out a hand to encourage him? Or would that constitute neglect of the one on my knee? His mother spun him around and dropped onto the step beside me, sparing me the decision.

"How are you?" she said. "How's it been?"

"Uh, good, I guess."

The toddler twisted sideways and plunged his head into Joan's lap, laughing. Mindy came out of the house wiping her hands on the seat of her jeans.

"I'm gonna air dry," she said. "The towels looked a little —" She tipped one hand from side to side.

"Oh," I said. "Those are the kids' bath towels. I haven't found more."

Joan craned her neck toward me. "Really?"

"Yeah, really. Looked everywhere I can think."

"No, the week. It's been good?"

"It's fine," Mindy said before I could answer. She sat on my other side and held her hands open to the baby, twiddling her fingers. A wide smile broke across his face and he dove toward her.

"What?" Joan and I said together.

"The towels. It's fine. I'm just trying to be polite and not use somebody else's towel."

Too many people all at once, too many conversations. Me, pressed on both sides by them. "How old is he?" I asked, gesturing toward the baby I'd just been holding.

"Seven months, but he's huge. I can't wait for him to walk 'cause right now the idea of carrying him much longer makes my back hurt."

I blinked at Mindy. "He's *yours*?"

She laughed. "I know. I look like the babysitter, right? Yes, he's mine — Alex. And Katy, too, inside. She's friends with Sarah, and we've been pretty close to the family through, you know, everything." She nodded toward Joan. "I'm married to Joan's brother."

"Ah." I looked back and forth between them.

"I've got an older one, too," Joan said. "A boy, eight. He's with a friend. He's a little young for Kevin but they get along okay."

This avalanche of children and relationships was more than I could capture at once.

"I'm the one who gave your Gran my phone number," Mindy said. "At the market. Do you still have it?"

"Oh! Right. I, ah, think so."

"You should've called. I can help anytime. Just a sanity break. It's rough, I bet. Being new here, nobody to talk to but the children." She wrinkled her nose. "It'd make *me* crazy."

"We get it," Joan said. The toddler gave a sudden squeal and yanked free of her hands, then dropped onto his hands and knees in the stubbly grass.

Mindy nodded. "Completely. Carrie always wanted more kids, but I guess it's probably just as well now she never had them."

"She lost one, you know, between the other two," Joan said.

"No. Wow. I didn't."

"Just a couple of months old. Perfect baby. She woke up one morning, surprised he'd slept through the night, and found him just gone in his bed."

"Oh, God," I said. "I had no idea. Was Kevin old enough to remember?"

"Not really. Less than three."

"Oh." I picked some soil from under my thumbnail.

In my experience, tragedy was never evenly distributed. Its concentration in this family didn't seem unnatural to me. And maybe it explained some of their odd behaviors. But Joan and Mindy gave me no time to think. They chattered on together, back and forth, painting Kofford family backstory for me the same way Sarah had been doing for her animals. Kevin broke his arm at school in the fourth grade sliding on the ice at recess and was laughed at for crying. Sarah had been slow to take to potty training. Contrary to what the children had told me about their father forbidding a puppy, I learned that Paul once *had* gotten the family a dog — a big one, which he declared a necessity with him being gone so much — but Carrie said the dog was judgmental and got rid of it.

I didn't ask for an explanation of that puzzling little detail, having already discovered that I wasn't really needed for the conversation to go on. I closed my eyes and turned my face to the sun. Joan would get up and knock a dirt clod out of her son's hand from time to time, still talking, while Mindy elaborated now and then and bounced the baby up and down, up and down on her knee. My back eased into the cradle of conversation that spanned the space behind me, and I let my mind wander.

I heard a shriek of girlish laugher. The *thwak, thwak* of Kevin throwing a ball against the shed wall. I had survived my first week and wasn't afraid of the next. *Thwak.* What had life been like for Carrie? Had she been blamed for the baby's death, then distrusted and policed in every small thing to ensure no other accidents? *Thwak.* The dog had been judgmental? *Thwak.* Had Benencia lived on in folklore, a face for the universal fear of what lurks in the dark around us? How long would it be before Carrie joined her — a ghost car, perhaps, on icy nights, or a frozen woman at the side of the road waving for help?

"— but Carrie wouldn't hear anything bad about that old crank, no matter what."

My wandering thoughts snagged at the mention of the woman whose place I was so scantily filling. I opened my eyes and looked at Joan.

"Who?" I said.

"I'm sorry — Paul's dad. He was just plain mean."

"But Carrie wouldn't say a word against him," Mindy said. "Never. She was always up to something but she'd never hurt a soul."

Ghosts come from bad thoughts.

Carrie would never be a ghost to Sarah or to these women gilding her memory. Only to those who never knew her, who were afraid of the icy dark, who wanted to shape and focus on their fear.

Thwak.

My ghosts were different. No matter what Tuah said, no matter what this Poppy said, they weren't made from fear. They were real and they deserved to be. I owed it to them, in fact, to think about them every day, to let them follow me and watch me and take some meager satisfaction in my failures.

"Here," Mindy said, pushing a piece of paper into my hand. "In case you can't find it. I mean it — call me. You do not have to do this by yourself."

"Now *I'm* the princess!" Sarah's voice from inside.

A squeal from Mindy's baby, frustrated

that she wasn't giving the paper to him. My hand, closing around it. The ghosts wavered.

Thwak.

9

"You got the paint?" Tuah called as she rummaged in the bed of her pickup. Mac sat on the passenger seat, waiting.

The sun hadn't topped the mountains, and birds fretted from their perches without yet leaving them, so I thought she ought to keep her voice down and be a little more careful about the clanging as she threw metal and wood and plastic into the truck this early on a Saturday morning. This was town, after all. She had neighbors. But the truck was years past anyone caring about additional scratches or dents, and Tuah felt no need to inconvenience herself for the benefit of people staying in bed longer than they should. I jounced on the balls of my feet beside the tailgate, wearing a sweatshirt and the boxer shorts I'd been sleeping in, my legs as pale and bumpy as chicken skin, my arms folded tight against my chest.

"Right here in the back," I said.

"Thinner?"

"You said you had it."

"Oh." More screeching and clattering. "There it is. And I've got the brushes. You got the cooler?"

"It's on the front seat. With the grocery bags."

She straightened and looked at me with her hands on her hips. "So that's it, then?"

"I hope so. Can I go back inside?"

"Haven't you learned by now to leave your shorts in California?"

"Nope. I haven't."

She leaned against the truck panel on one forearm. "You're not going to wear those riding, are you? Or are your jeans getting tight?"

"*No.*" God, did she not notice how loud she was being, or how many open windows were around us? "I'll see you up there." I waved and ducked back into the house.

The original plan had been for me to drive up behind her in my own car, but Leo the cowboy had called me Tuesday with some confusing tale about needing to bring new horses up to the ranch, asking if I would want to come on a daylong horseback ride Saturday. My exits were all closed: he'd called Tuah first to learn how to reach me, and she'd not only told him but said yes, it would be fine for me to arrive later on Saturday, and yes, she could drive me back down to Leadville on Tuesday before I was needed again at the Koffords'. Plus he'd caught me at the right moment. The kids had been arguing, the house was dark, the sun was shining outside, and I loved riding as a kid. So I said yes.

Now with Tuah's early start, I had plenty of time to shower, cook myself some oatmeal and eggs and the last of the sausage, clean up, and still get to the meeting spot a few minutes early.

Nevertheless, Leo was already waiting for me. Or I presumed it was him. At a picnic table beside the Mother Lode Motel on Highway 91 sat someone in a cowboy hat hunched over a newspaper. Two horses were tethered to a parking barricade, one brown and the other a black-and-white pinto, saddled and ready, heads down, swishing tails at their flanks. I parked nearby and heard boots crunching across the gravel as I reached to get my backpack from the passenger side floor.

"A backpack?" he said as I got out. "You know we're only going for the day, right?"

Wow. Condescension was a pretty bad place to start for anyone interested in being liked. I took a slow blink. "Well, it's where my driver's license goes. You know, for the driving I had to do to get here. And my keys, because I have to put them somewhere. Toilet paper. Some snacks. Not my first day in the mountains."

He didn't seem to pick up on my tone. "Good for you. Just wanted to make sure you didn't set your expectations too high."

"Nope. Pretty much figured I'd just be watching a horse's ass the whole way up."

He laughed. Genuinely laughed. Completely unoffended. Delighted, even. "Then maybe you'd better ride in front."

"Deal." I hitched the backpack onto my shoulder, and we walked toward the horses. "Which one's mine?"

"Whichever you want. Although" — he glanced back over his shoulder toward my car — "the pinto seems logical."

"Works for me." I tied my backpack to the back of the saddle, then we mounted up. I scratched the horse's neck, black under a coarse white mane, warm against my fingers. I felt a little foolish now about my snippy start. It really had been a pretty innocent comment. "Honestly, you go first. I have no clue where to go. And no offense meant to your horse's ass."

"None taken, I'm sure," he said with a grin, shifting in his saddle. "He's pretty confident." He bent the horse's head away from me, starting forward toward a path that dipped from the parking lot into a wide meadow separating the motel from the river. "We'll cross the river over there," he said, pointing to his right. "It's just a little upstream of where Hat Creek comes in."

"You're the tour guide." I hoisted my leg and lifted a flap on the saddle to shorten one stirrup. "So how is it we can make this trip in one day when the drive takes so long?"

"We're following the creek. The road goes the long way around over Trapper Pass."

My horse shook his head, flopping the scraggly mane back and forth.

"What are their names, anyway?"

"The horses? Brownie." He glanced back at me. "And Spot."

"You just made that up."

"Maybe. But when I hand them off to the wrangler they'll be whoever I say they are. You don't know it yet, but I'm a very important person."

I allowed myself a smile. The day would be fine, and just what I needed after all. I'd gone to sleep last night pressed under the weight of all I still didn't know about the children. I had asked my accumulated questions when Paul got home yesterday afternoon, but the conversation had been frustrating and disjointed, with him going off on tangents rather than answering my questions, so that it ended with me wondering not just whether this or that was allowed but whether a family made of such disconnected people could ever be all right. Now, though, I felt my hips relax into place and the weight slide off my shoulders. I'd lost track of how enjoyable it was to be on a horse. It had been years since I'd ridden — certainly not during college and probably not in high school, either.

We splashed across the river, gravel crunching under the horses' hooves, then wound our way through the trees on the far side and started working our way uphill, on a path made spongy by fallen needles and bark. I leaned forward, breathed in the warmth of the horse's neck and the bright scent of pine. I let my mind rest on the slow beat of hooves, the crunch of a twig, the color of the sky, the twist of a leaf. I began to be profoundly glad I'd come.

We chatted easily as we rode — college trials, bad roommates, cooking disasters, getting by on a student budget. These horses were of a different caliber than the plodding trail horses I'd ridden as a child, and we moved up the trail quickly. I heard water again about fifteen minutes after the main river crossing, and soon the path widened and flattened to meet a small river spread less than a foot deep over a broad bed of stones.

"This is Hat Creek?" I asked.

"Yup."

"I expected it to be bigger downstream. Not much for a whole town to be named after it."

"Not much of a town."

"True."

The horses splashed across, then continued along the grassy shore. I inhaled deeply, smelled the warming grass and pine. The morning sun spread across the valley, sharpening the edges of trees and rocks and the ridgeline above. I was glad no one had ever felt it worthwhile to build a road here. I ducked my head as the trail led us into an aspen glade, then involuntarily pulled up.

"Whoa," I said.

"You don't need to say —" Leo started, then saw that I'd stopped moving and did the same. "Oh. You weren't talking to the horse."

The trees overhung the creek, which ran between ferns along the banks. They cast dappled shade on long grass, and a few

126

sprays of blue columbine poked through the ferns.

"No. I just — wow. What a beautiful spot. I've never seen anything so lush around here before."

"Pretty, isn't it? People hike along here a lot, too."

"They do? Isn't it too far?"

"There's an access road that starts you closer. There's just no good place to leave a car for four days, so I had us start at the motel. Nice, though, huh?"

"Definitely."

The creek chugged over the rocks. The contrast between shade and sun made the shaded grass look richer, the sunlit grass look brighter and greener. My horse thought well of it, too, and had taken advantage of my distraction to start grazing.

"Glad you came?"

I found Leo looking at me with eyebrows tilted and a knowing grin. So my earlier snark had not, in fact, gone unnoticed.

"Yeah." I gave the reins a tug to pull my horse's head out of the grass. "But only for this. Nothing else. Just this. The rest of the day has been terrible so far."

"Nowhere to go but up," he said, nudging his horse forward.

■ ■ ■ ■

I lost track of how many times we crossed and recrossed the creek. As promised, the vistas, small and large, only multiplied as we climbed. We passed through pocket valleys and aspen woods, places where the creek ran wide and shining, others where it tucked under its banks and only the shush and rustle gave it away. Sometimes the path would open and reveal the bare slopes ahead, high above timberline. Other times I'd twist around in the saddle to look at the view behind: pine and rock etched against a china blue sky, white still icing the tops of the distant peaks. As the sun climbed, the warmth eased into my back.

Around noon, Leo reined in at the edge of a meadow in the center of an aspen grove. The creek murmured at its edge.

"You hungry?"

"Always."

"Let's stop here. I brought lunch."

We dismounted, and he fastened strap cuffs around the horses' forelegs as they plunged their heads into the grass.

"I probably don't need to hobble them," he said as he squatted by the pinto's fore-legs. "I don't imagine they'd go far no matter what. But I'd rather not take chances. One day spent walking is enough to make you cautious."

"Which you've done?"

"Which I've done. Nothing makes you feel more stupid than walking down the trail into a dude ranch. In front of all the guests, all the other hands, even your horse."

He did the same for the brown horse, then got a pair of paper lunch sacks and a rolled-up sheet out of a saddlebag.

"Nothing fancy," he said as he handed a bag to me.

I opened it to see a tuna fish sandwich on white bread, a bundle of crackers in plastic wrap, a greenish banana, and a pair of store-bought cookies. It looked like a lunch a third-grader would spread out on his desk.

I looked up at him.

"This is enough for you?" I asked.

"Well sure. You?"

His look of genuine concern made me laugh. "Oh, *I'm* fine. I just think of guys eating three sandwiches and a box of cookies and looking around for more."

He grinned. "Ah — you should've seen breakfast." He pointed to a flat spot in the shade a few yards away. "I'll just spread this sheet out over there and we can sit and eat. If you want to go to the bathroom first" —

he tilted his head toward a jumble of boulders some distance in the other direction — "that's a good spot over there. You said you have toilet paper?"

Caught completely off guard, I had to laugh. He was as matter-of-fact as a child. I patted my back pocket. "Already got it ready."

By the time I got back, he'd not only spread out the sheet but had unwrapped and arranged our lunches in two identical place settings. He lay on his back, boots crossed, looking up into the leaves with his arms folded under his head.

"Need a pillow?" I asked as I lowered myself to the ground.

"Just trying to prove I didn't care how long you took."

I laughed again. "You must have sisters," I said as I reached for a sandwich.

"What makes you think so?"

"The whole bathroom business. Most guys would be uncomfortable."

He nodded as he sat up and swung around on his hip to a face me. "Good guess. One sister."

"Older?"

"Right again. With friends. Lots of inside intel on why girls think boys are stupid. She's married now, to an idiot, which she deserved."

"Brothers?"

"One." He looked down and reached for another cracker. "Plus Dad, stepmom, Mom, and some flaky dude that lives with her when he runs out of money. The all-American family."

"So you grew up here, right?"

"Whole life."

"Your dad's a miner?"

"Of course."

I took a cracker between my fingers. I'd been putting off this question all day. But now I was a person who embraced what I feared, right? I put the cracker in my mouth and leaned back against my hands.

"So, growing up, did you ever hear ghost stories about a girl who disappeared up here?"

He looked surprised. "Yeah, sure — you know about that?"

"A little. Sarah said something about a ghost that would get you if you went in the woods. But she also said it could stop her stuffed animals from fighting over what to eat, so I might not have the details quite right."

"Yeah, the stuffed animals part is new. It's way scarier than that, or it was the first time I heard it. Scout campout. If it was meant to keep a bunch of stupid kids from wandering around after the adults went to sleep, it worked." He picked up his banana and dug at the stem with his thumbnail, then pulled back a section of peel. "Okay, here goes. There was this girl who lived at one of the old mining camps with her dad. She had a dog that stayed with her no matter what, so he felt okay about leaving her alone all day while he worked in the mine. The dog was as big as a bear, and mean, and nobody ever caused trouble with that dog around. Bears, mountain lions, drunks — nobody."

My father used to talk about the dogs they'd had when he was growing up. One had died when he was fairly young, and another had grown up with him after that. Both were big, like Mac was now. It often came up as he was scoffing at some tiny creature he saw at the end of a rhinestone leash in Los Angeles. He disdained small dogs.

"Nice touch," I said.

"Thank you." He took a bite of banana. "Anyway, the girl loved the dog. It slept with her, and every night when she cooked dinner, the dog had the first plate. The girl was a real camp princess — always in a pretty dress, wearing a hair ribbon, smiling at everybody and dancing around with that dog."

Sarah's doll, in her dress and hair ribbons. Benencia in the pictures — simple as a child. Beautiful.

"What about the rest of the family?" I asked. "Mom? Any brothers or sisters?"

"It's supposed to be a mining camp, you know. Not a lot of families up there."

"So how come there's a daughter?"

"Hey," he said, putting his hands up. "I'm just telling it like I heard it. Isn't that what you wanted? Or should I add seven dwarves?"

"Sorry. Go on."

"Okay, one day the dog went missing. Just gone. And the girl went out to find it."

"Where was her dad?" I asked.

"Work. When he came home she was gone."

"So how does he know she's gone after the dog?"

"Geez — do you want the story or not?"

"Sorry. Really."

"So the dad calls together all the other men at the camp, and all the crazy old coots in the hills, and they all go out searching. Nobody goes to work for days — they're all calling and looking. But nobody ever found anything. Not so much as a hair ribbon."

He broke off another chunk of banana and put it in his mouth.

"That's it?" I asked.

"That's just the setup. Especially the hair ribbon — remember that. Now's the part that keeps little boys in their tents.

"The search was finally abandoned, but the dad wouldn't give up. Winter came, and he got caught out in a storm, still looking. Folks found him frozen to death with his lantern still in his hand. Years went by. People started to talk about other strange disappearances, but it's the wilderness, so folks figure it's just what happens sometimes. A couple of hunters that never came back. A geologist. Finally some old miner crawls out of the hills into town for supplies, gets drunk, and brags to some guys in a bar that he hated that girl's dog and killed it." Leo sliced a finger across his throat. "Like that. Then while he was burying it, the girl found them, and he killed her, too. Folks thought he was just talking, but he was never seen alive again. Somebody found him in his cabin a few weeks later, strangled with a *blue ribbon*. And all around the cabin were these *giant paw prints* in the dirt."

He'd finished on a melodramatic flourish, voice lowered, slowing with each of the final words. But I was finding it harder to play along. The name had just come to me. *Gus.* The dog my father remembered them having when he was small. Big enough for him to ride, he would say, but too dignified to let him.

"Wow," I managed, looking off somewhere over his shoulder.

Leo didn't seem to notice anything but lowered his voice still further and leaned forward. "The girl and the dog still wander through the trees — right here." He made a wide gesture with one hand to take in the circle of aspens around us. "Looking for each other, looking for revenge. The miner wasn't enough, and nothing ever will be. Pity the soul that crosses their paths."

The pinto snorted into the grass and shook its head, then stomped one foot and continued grazing. Leo leaned back again and returned to his normal voice. "You like that? Then the scout leader added some stuff about hearing the dog snuffing around in the leaves. Sealed the deal. Nobody left camp after that, but I think a few kids wet the bed 'cause they were afraid to go out to pee."

It had been a mistake to ask. Maybe it was better to stay away from what you feared, after all. My family's tragedy was now a grotesque ghost story used to frighten children and test teen bravado. Something for them to laugh at when they got older. I unfolded one leg, then wadded my wrappers and banana peel into my fist and shoved them into the brown bag.

"My leg's going to sleep. Can we get going or walk around or something?"

A shadow of a smile, there and gone in the moment Leo looked at me. Then he stood and brushed his seat. He'd thought something, I could tell. Made some judgment. Oddly, it mattered to me that it not be wrong.

"What?"

"Nothing." He extended one hand to help me up but pointed to the corner of his mouth with the other. "You got a little left over, there."

10

After lunch, we ducked into a stand of lodgepole pine and climbed away from the creek, Leo still riding in front. The branches and needles knit themselves together high overhead to such an extent that the ground was free of undergrowth and I could detect no trail at all. Browning needles underfoot muffled the hoofbeats, and the silence rested on us like a blanket. We wove around the tree trunks and I fished for a new subject.

"So your family," I said. "You don't like your brother-in-law?"

"Nice guy," he said. "Dumb as a box of rocks. I'm not sure how he comes out of the mine every day under his own power."

"And your brother. You didn't say what he's doing."

"Ah, my brother." Leo shifted in his saddle. "He's kinda messed up. Honestly, he's crazy. Not weird crazy. Lunatic crazy."

"Oh. I'm sorry."

"That's how most folks around here know me — the crazy guy's brother."

I looked at his back for a moment, relaxed under a drape of faded chambray, curving and straightening in response to the horse's gait.

"And I thought you were just Leo the Cowboy."

"God, really? That? All the education, the great conversation, the cooking skills, the good looks, and *that's* how you think of me?"

"First impressions stick."

"Shoot."

I smiled. "Where is he now? Your brother."

A tilt of the head. "We don't know. Colorado Springs, last we heard. It's been a few weeks, so no telling for sure."

"Was he always that way?"

"Nah, it started while he was in high school. Till then, he was a great guy. Super-smart. Great sense of humor. Then he started shutting down. Holing up in his room, staying up all night, talking to himself. He started having these outbursts at school, yelling at people out of the blue. After every weird thing he did he'd just say 'I had to.' He was hearing voices."

"Is that why your parents split?"

138

He twisted in the saddle to look back at me, then turned back to the front. "Didn't help. But that's not how it works, you know. Trouble comes to everybody and a marriage that can't handle it isn't much to begin with." He raised his wrist to his face, brushing his nose or the corner of his mouth. "I've seen folks weather worse."

I elected not to answer. Anyone who'd grown up in a town like this one had certainly spent a lifetime in close proximity to the spectrum of human experience and reaction, choice and consequence. Let him think what he pleased. No point in arguing just because my own life had taught me something different about the power of a child in trouble to drive a wedge between parents.

Within a couple of hours we reached landscape I thought I started to recognize. Then — yes — through the trees a glint of old mine equipment. Steps later, the trees thinned, then ended. A dirt road cut across the stripped mountainside, around a brassy lake of poisoned water, toward the mine entrance. Uphill was a rusted crane, buckling as thinner supporting pieces oxidized and gave way. Narrow-gauge railroad tracks passed below it to the mine opening, now gated and padlocked. Like heaving sea waves and just as devoid of life, piles upon piles of rubble and tailings rolled away toward the line of trees just visible on the far side of the slope.

At some point when I did not yet fully grasp money and what constituted a lot or a little, I thought Tuah must be unimaginably rich. My grandfather had mined gold, after all. Gold, wealth; they went together. I pictured vast quantities of gleaming metal spilling out of the ground. Nuggets the size of eggs. I no longer recall what I'd said or why I'd gotten this response, but I remember her laughing and saying no, my grandfather had worked for a paycheck just like anybody else. And what came out of the ground was measured in ounces, not tons or even pounds. I must have looked puzzled, because she showed me what she meant by ounces. She squatted in the dirt by the cabin porch, scooped some grit in her hands.

"That much," she said. "That much gold would make a good day."

Whenever I saw the colossal wreckage around the mine, I thought of those cupped hands. By itself, the scale of the destruction was tragic. But compared to the physical size of the reward, it was offensive. The imbalance insufferable.

We didn't speak as the horses picked their steps over the railway ties, then followed the road up the slope, past the cabin knocked over by the mule skinner, and onto the level ground of Main Street. Given my feelings about the mine, I'd always been grateful for the topography that hid it from town. We rode side by side between empty windows that stared at each other across the street. General store. School. The paymaster's office, where a blue flax blossom had worked its way up between the porch slats. Past the turnoff to Tuah's cabin, I figured he had a reason and just rode alongside, little puffs of dust rising around the horses' hooves.

"I love this place," Leo said, looking from side to side. "I wish it could stay like this but I know it can't. Things will fall down. People will find it and mess around. They're talking about bringing trail ride groups over here from the ranch next summer." He made a face. "Ghost town tour."

I didn't like to think about it. These places were mine.

I pointed to a house one street away from the main road, visible because of a vacant lot in front of it, where the roof had caved in under the combined weight of neglect and decades of snow. "My grandmother said the guy who lived there drew birds. Pencil drawings all over the walls so it felt like an aviary when you went inside."

"Really?" Leo looked as if someone had just told him he'd won a prize. "You know the stories about these places?"

"Well, I know a lot of stories. I might not have them attached to the right houses."

"Really," he said again. "That's so cool. What about that one?" He pointed to one with a collapsed chimney a couple of lots away from the first.

"That's easy. The Diazes'. They had twin boys my dad's age, Jaime and Jorge. He played at their house all the time. The mom's name was Juanita, and I think she was probably Tuah's best friend."

"Wow. That one. The one that's leaning to the left."

"I'm not sure. Maybe the whore. Or the bootlegger."

"Wait — bootleg? Wasn't that a saloon back there?"

I shrugged. "Yeah. Or music hall and coffeehouse, depending on who the customers were. I think they kind of did their own thing up here. Not a lot of G-men around."

"I guess not."

We'd turned uphill, then turned again so that we were heading back toward the track that cut through the trees to Tuah's house.

We passed an empty foundation and a patch of bare ground, then Leo tipped his head toward the next house. The siding boards had started to cup, but the roof was intact, the walls perpendicular, so that it gave off an air of prim shabbiness, a proper lady fallen on hard times. Other than the window glass, only the front step was missing, the board split in half lengthwise and fallen into the opening.

"What about this one?"

"My favorite. It has the most stuff in it — furniture and clothes. Well, had. The clothes are gone now. But I used to put them on and play house, then put them back exactly the way they were. Sort of my secret place."

"It has stuff inside?" He reined his horse, and mine stopped beside it. "Can I see?"

"Sure."

Leo dismounted and dropped the reins. "We'll only be a minute," he said. "They won't drift too far. Lead on."

I swung down, stiff now as I hadn't been at lunch. I lifted the door against its hinges, enough to open it but not enough to keep it from scraping against the plank floor. Inside, debris showed animals reclaiming the space for themselves — tangled twigs, bird droppings, feathers, shredded cotton and newspaper. The empty fur of a dead

143

chipmunk tufted one corner. A stovepipe hole now jammed with a bird's nest. The room smelled of dust and decay and time demanding its due. I stepped inside and Leo followed.

"Man," he said. "What a relic."

Like Tuah's cabin, it had three rooms: the front room in which we now stood, then two rooms dividing the back of the house. Neither of the small rooms was big enough to hold a modern double bed. In front of us stood a table. A single chair with a broken leg lay on its back nearby.

The floorboards creaked under Leo's boots as he crossed to the table. He traced its surface with his fingers, then squinted at a piece of paper tacked to the wall above it.

"How long ago do you 'spose this was written?"

"Most people left here in the thirties and forties. So not the Wild West exactly, but what, maybe . . . forty years?"

He took off his hat to get closer, then leaned back. "Yeah, too faded."

He peered in the doorway of the first bedroom. It had an iron bedstead with the springs unattached at the bottom and one side scraping the floor. After looking around for a moment, he took a couple of steps to the side and went into the other bedroom.

"That was still a mattress when I was little," I said, following him. I leaned against the doorjamb and pointed to a pile of shredded cotton and droppings now drifted against the wall.

"And this is where the clothes were?" he said. He stepped over broken wardrobe doors lying on the floor to peer into the cabinet. Bent and darkened hinges marked where the doors would have attached.

"Yeah, women's clothes," I said.

"Just women's? In a mining town? There's usually only one reason for that."

"Ha. You wouldn't think so if you saw the clothes. Lots of gingham and buttons. Tuah never gave me much of a story about this place, but I remember when I did ask, she just said, 'John and Olive ended bad.' "

He turned to look at me, then back into the empty wardrobe as if ghostly clothes might appear. "That's it? You never found out anything else? Who they were? Where they went?"

"Never asked."

"How come?"

"I dunno." And I didn't. I really, truly didn't. There'd been a sense of finality about Tuah's answer, I remembered — or thought I did now — but fresh from my week with the children that hardly seemed reason enough. The children I had left yesterday were not only far too self-absorbed to care about an adult's tone, but aimlessly, irrationally, unstoppably curious, puzzling over their books, following bug trails, trying to understand where I'd come from and why. Could I really have been nothing like them? How was it that I had stories for all the other houses but not the one I'd always felt was especially mine? The year I returned and found the clothes gone, I felt personally violated. But I hadn't said or asked anything about that, either. What was *wrong* with me? I kicked at a sliver of broken lath. This place was mine to know about, not his. And what were we doing, stringing the day on like this? It wasn't a date. I straightened and turned away.

"I think I heard thunder," I said. "Let's go."

I already had my foot in the stirrup by the time he pulled the door closed. I swung up onto my horse and turned away, along the road toward the turnoff to the cabin. Within a few moments he'd caught up.

"Hey," he said as his horse fell into step beside mine. "You want to go for another ride next week?"

"I have to watch the kids."

"No, I mean, just, sometime when you're

back up here."

"I think Tuah needs a lot of help with the painting."

"And if she doesn't?"

I glanced sideways at him. Was he incapable of taking a hint? Fine, then. "I just don't think it'd be a good idea."

"Why not?" He looked at me with eyes wide, as frank as a child, as if he had not yet learned that all possible answers to that question are bad.

"Look — thank you. I've had a great day. But this just isn't a good time for me."

"Time for what? We're having a nice day. I'd like to have another nice day. Seems pretty simple. What's the problem?"

"Nothing. Can we drop it? It's just me."

"What is it?"

Oh, good God. "Maybe it's none of your business."

"Why?"

Would nothing make him stop? I'd only agreed to come today in the first place because I'd been backed into a corner. There was no point in dating, in creating some drawn-out romantic charade, in taking up with some other decent guy I'd only treat badly. Better to cut it off now. Firmly.

"Since you're so curious, I'm *pregnant,* all right? I'm going to have a baby."

But the embarrassed retreat I'd expected didn't happen. Instead he stood slightly in his stirrups, centering the saddle. "Oh," was all he said. "When?"

"What?"

"When? Like, when are you supposed to stop riding?"

"What?" I was completely disoriented. "I — I don't know! That isn't it! What are you talking about?"

"What are *you* talking about? I'm still talking about the same thing. Do you want to go for another ride sometime?"

"But I'm *pregnant*!"

"I went to prom with a girl that turned out to be pregnant, and we had a great time. It's summer, it looks like whoever the guy was is history, and I'd rather spend my time with an attractive girl than a bunch of ranch hands any day. It's okay for you to ride, right?"

"Why won't you just let this go?"

"I thought I just explained that."

The circle of logic had closed around me, leaving me nowhere to go. "Fine!" I snapped. My horse's ear twitched and he bobbed his head. "*Fine!* I'll go!"

"Well, I don't want you to go if you're mad."

At that, the wave of absurdity that had

been carrying me through the whole exchange curled over my head and tumbled me under. I collapsed over the saddle horn, laughing, rocking with the horse's gait.

"What?" he said.

I sat up after a moment and ran a hand over my face. "Does nothing shock you?"

"I have a crazy brother, remember? He said he was pregnant once, too."

11

I pulled the stirrer through the paint bucket between my feet, watching the pigment from the bottom lift and working the streaks through the lighter base. The shade Tuah had chosen was the color of daffodils, buttered and creamy. I could picture the bright yellow house alone in its clearing in the pine woods, dainty white curtains in the windows, a pot of geraniums on the front porch. Cheery and strange and wonderful. And so alone.

I sat on the edge of the porch with little curls of gray littering the ground at my feet, shadows long and blue in the afternoon light. Tuah had scraped the cabin while I'd been on the ride with Leo and was now at the truck, gathering pails and brushes.

"I've never painted, you know," I called to her as I stirred.

"Just slop it on there." Tuah folded her waist over the truck's side wall and reached down into the bed. "You can't go wrong. Do you see anybody looking?"

"Well, you."

"Go with the grain, then. That's my quality tip. All that matters is protecting the wood. The wind and the sun and the ice around here will bring a house down in no time if you don't take care. You've seen plenty evidence of that."

I kept twisting the stirrer through the paint. The color was even now, but I liked the weight of the paint against the stick, the way the tracks of movement melted away behind it. Was that all we were doing? Only forestalling the closure of time over our heads? At some point, unmaintained, the boards of Tuah's cabin would warp and separate, the roof would cave in, and the cabin would collapse in exactly the same way as the houses already ahead of it on the road to decay. Who would tell the story of it, as Tuah had told me theirs? For how long? In time, all these lives would fade away along with the houses that had sheltered them, the joy and sorrow, good and evil. Did those things, as well, blend together and dissolve over time?

"Tuah, can you tell me about John and Olive?"

Metal pails clashed against the truck wall.

151

"Janoliff?"

"John. And. Olive." I looked up. "The house in town where I found the clothes when I was little. I know other stories from around town, but all I can remember about them is that you said they ended bad. Who were they? What happened?"

She pushed herself upright, a pair of small aluminum pails in one hand. Her reading glasses, perched on top of her head, glinted in the fingers of light that came through the aspen leaves.

"Well, all right then," she said. She tipped her head toward the bucket between my feet. "I think you're done stirring. Come pour us some paint and let's get started."

"John was no good, I'll tell you, though Olive never said anything ill about him."

Tuah and I stood on chairs, stroking yellow paint along the underside of the eaves where our work would be safe if it started to rain.

"Sure," I said. My dad had never uttered a bad word about my mother, either, come to think of it.

"They'd been dryland farmers, blown out by the Dust Bowl. They got a fresh start here, but it didn't take long for John to get restless. Then one day, he was gone. Just like that. Olive said he'd gone to look at a business opportunity or some such thing. Said he'd told the foreman he'd be back in a few weeks, but the foreman didn't know anything. As far as he was concerned, John was fired. But they let Olive stay — no reason to throw her out of a house nobody needed in the dead of winter."

Tuah got down from the chair, refilled her small pail, and stepped back up again. One hand on the back of the chair, no hoisting, no grunting, no wobbling. Seventy-three, just stepping up the same way I would.

"Olive was pregnant," Tuah said, dabbing the bristles into a knot over her head.

I stopped painting. "You mean — John left with her expecting?"

"Well, to be fair he didn't know that part. She didn't even know until later." Tuah dipped the brush in the pail, worked at the knot some more, then rolled her shoulders and looked at me. "Olive was my dearest friend, but she was a fool. A dear, gentle, hopeful fool. The way she kept faith in that man . . ." She shook her head, then turned back to painting. "She kept saying he'd send money soon, or send for her, that he'd written from this or that place and was about to get things fixed for her to come, but she never even had an address for him."

"So what happened?"

"Everybody adopted her. There was a lot more love around her than she'd had before, I promise you. She'd find a loaf of cornbread on the porch, or a sack of beans, or flour. Ladies would drop off a dress here or there, saying it didn't fit or they used it when they had their own babies. She was so grateful, dear thing. In tears. Then when time came for the baby, it was a terrible labor. She was just a tiny thing."

"I remember the clothes," I said. "In the house. They were my size."

Tuah threw me a crooked smile. "You tried them on?"

"Yeah. I was eight or nine."

"Huh." She returned to painting. "Well, you were tall but still a child. Try to imagine having a baby when you were that size. We didn't have a doctor, you know, just a lady helping her, and she was about ready to give up. I told her to just reach in there and get that baby out, no matter what it took. She did, and Olive was torn up something awful, but she made it. And the baby was healthy. A boy. She named him Charles Thomas. After her father and grandfather. Not a word about John from her or any of us, you can be sure of that. And rightly so. I don't think she'd heard from him in weeks.

Maybe months." Tuah switched the brush to the hand holding the pail and stood on her toes to tug at a shingle that held firm. She resumed painting.

"She stayed in bed for two days. Third day she got a fever. Sixth she died."

"Oh." The tiny sound escaped me by surprise. I'd lost track of the tragic end I expected, and must have taken misplaced hope when I heard she survived the childbirth. Tuah dipped her brush and turned her back to me to work in the opposite direction.

"So the house was just left there after she died? Everything in it?" I asked.

"Yes."

There had been an eyelet blouse, I recalled specifically. A skirt with buttons along the side. Two calico dresses with a print too faint to discern. The tiny shoes.

A drip of paint started to run down the back of my hand, so I wiped it against the edge of the pail. "No one else needed the house after that?"

"The place was too sad. Besides, folks started to leave during the war. The mine was about tapped out, and there was lots of work in Leadville."

I could see why she hadn't told me all this when I was a child.

"So that's the story, then," I said.

She nodded.

"What ever happened with the baby?"

"Adopted," she said. She stepped off the chair and tipped her chin toward the horizon behind me. "Storm's getting closer. We best get things cleaned up before it hits."

We washed our brushes at the pump, icy water pulsing through the bristles, then gathered all the supplies onto the porch and sat there to watch the storm. The mountains sent grumbles of thunder back and forth to each other as the clouds thickened and darkened. The temperature dropped.

"I'm going in for a blanket," I said, standing. "You want anything?"

Tuah shook her head without looking at me. "No. I'm fine. Thank you, though."

I came back out with the quilt and an orange. I dropped into my chair, quilt across my lap, and dug into the orange with my thumb. A clash of thunder sounded overhead and a few raindrops plopped into the dust.

"So John never came back?" I asked as I kicked the quilt open around my feet.

"What?"

"John and Olive. John just disappeared? I mean, since the baby was adopted."

"Not exactly."

"Oh. So he didn't want the baby?" I laid a cupped piece of orange peel in my lap and started filling it with shreds of pith.

"I didn't say that."

I looked up. "What?"

"It's none of your affair," Tuah said after a long pause.

"Good God, what happened? It's fifty years ago."

She looked up at me at last, eyes narrowed, and seemed to consider her options for a few moments. She got up and went to the edge of the porch, then squinted up at the clouds. She whistled and clapped the side of her leg, and Mac, who must have been lying in the dirt off the end of the porch, jumped up, tail waving.

"This storm isn't going to do anything," Tuah said. "We're taking a walk."

12

I pulled on a sweatshirt and followed as Tuah walked downhill from the cabin, strides firm over sage and weeds and rocks. A test pattern of raindrops struck us, but she paid no attention, and the cloud thought better and withdrew. She didn't speak as we walked along Hat Creek's upper road and cut through an empty lot, side by side, Mac ranging in front of us with his nose to the ground. The scent of dust and sage swelled up with the evaporating moisture.

Tuah took us to the charred remains of a house on the edge of town, which as I recall had burned down when a toddler tipped over a kerosene lantern. She picked her steps over the rocks and half-burnt stubs, then turned so that we were looking back at the town, the main street with Hamilton Brothers looming over the far end, the sagging rooflines, the weeded foundations, the utter and complete stillness. She sat on a log that was blackened on the underside and patted the spot beside her. I sat.

"You see a ghost town when you look at this, don't you?" she said.

I wasn't sure how she wanted me to answer. "Well, yeah, I guess."

"We like the idea of ghosts because they say a story is over. Unresolved, maybe, but nothing can be done about it. Lets us say things are done. But no story is ever over. Everyone who lived here was just passing through. These houses don't have ghosts. They're just skins that folks outgrew and left behind. The stories go on."

She tipped her head toward the ground. "This place, for example. Ed died a year or so after the fire. Alcohol. Florence moved down to Leadville and turned into a real good plumber. Their oldest boy runs the trucking company now where Paul gets most of his work. And the girl that knocked over the lantern? She's a kindergarten teacher at Sarah's school. This place is the beginning of their story, not the end." She reached forward and plucked a coral-colored sprig of Indian paintbrush, twirled it between her fingers for a moment, then held it up to me. "Beauty from ashes, right here. Tragedy and blessing. Leave them alone long enough and it gets real hard to tell them apart."

She flicked the blossom away, and I watched it fall like a feather a few feet in front of me. I looked at the still-visible foundation lines of the house, then up at an aspen sapling that had sprouted near the far corner, its leaves sparkling in the late sun that stretched its rays under the clouds.

"So what happened to John and Olive's baby?" I asked.

"That house." She pointed. I wasn't sure which she meant, but it probably didn't matter. "The Rodels. Quiet folks. Emma baked such good pies." She looked down and brushed something away in her lap. "We weren't going to just give Olive's baby to the county. Nobody outside Hat Creek knew she'd died or that she'd even had a baby. I kept him for a while. But with Roberto, and Benencia . . ." The silence carried her sentence further than the words did. This, then, was the first child she lost.

I tried to understand. *Bambi. Dumbo. The Secret Garden.* From infancy I had been surrounded by stories meant to reinforce the idea that nothing is more tragic than a mother losing a child — or a child its mother. But those situations were different. My own mother disappeared one morning about six months after I started the fire, after a fight I'd heard between my parents in which she said her life was ruined, *ruined* by what I had done. I didn't know the specific gravities of sin or love. In a laboratory setting, with all external variables removed, which should outweigh the other? My observations in the natural world showed only that a parent's love was overcome relatively quickly. What — if anything — I would feel for the being in my belly was something I had no way to know.

"You just gave them the baby? Didn't they have to adopt him somehow?"

Tuah shook her head. "They moved down to Leadville as a family. Come spring we told the sheriff Olive and the baby died in childbirth. Nobody ever knew but us in Hat Creek."

I'd read *The Grapes of Wrath.* I visualized a Depression-era world of migrants and vagrants and dispossessed that surely couldn't be troubled with getting a government agency to give an official stamp to a birth. Perhaps this situation was far from unique.

I rubbed a stripe in the dirt with my foot. The ashes had long since dissolved, now indistinguishable from the soil.

"John came back, didn't he?" I said.

Tuah glanced sideways at me. "That next

summer."

"And?"

She squinted into the distance. "Folks stuck to the plan. We told him the same thing we told the sheriff. And that nobody felt sorry for him."

Cause and effect, action and consequence. "You *kidnapped* his baby?"

She shrugged. Nonchalant. A technicality.

"Tuah — you're saying you took a man's child and never told him." I paused for another response. There was none. "*I'm* not disagreeing, but — you're saying *everybody* was okay with that? A whole town of people?"

"Absolutely." She turned to face me. "You do realize you're doing the same thing, right?"

"It's not the same thing — you even agreed with me." I looked down at the ground between my feet. Then up to the clouds. "And it's not like I made some detailed plan. I just — left," I finally said.

"Not making a decision is a decision, too. And I'm not saying you made the wrong one. But you did make one."

I doubled over my knees and wrapped my arms around my shins, pressing myself and my tiny, tiny baby into my lap. I didn't know what to feel. I just wanted to think about someone else's story instead of my own.

"What did he do?" I finally asked.

"John? He left. If he wanted comfort, he wasn't going to find it here."

How could someone identify all the consequences of what they'd done? Olive's story was like a ball of yarn scraps, loose ends protruding in every direction, nothing to make it clear which strand led to which other, which ended, which carried on.

"What about the son?"

"He never knew any of it. Still doesn't."

"He's alive? He lives around here?"

"Well sure. He's a little younger than your father. He lives in Leadville and works at the mine, like everybody else. Grew up, got married, had two children. And now grandchildren."

"Who all think they're Rodels."

"Yes, that's right."

"Tuah, this is *huge*. How did you know you were doing the right thing?"

"He's had a good life, Elena. His folks loved him and taught him to work and do the right thing, and he did the same for his own children."

"But don't you still wonder?" Suddenly, I needed the answer to this question more than any others. "How did you know that was the best thing to do? I mean really *know.*"

"The best? We didn't. Nobody can know that. But we knew it was good. And it was what we could do at the time. That's all anybody ever gets to work with."

"But — what about Olive? When you're gone, she'll be totally forgotten."

"That happens to everybody, eventually. Her son was safe, and he got to have children of his own, who grew up to be good people raising more good people, who will do the same after that. That's the important part."

I could understand the logic, but did the important part also have to be the only part? The idea that I was now one of only a handful of people on earth who knew Olive had ever walked upon it felt like a weight.

"Is she buried here?"

Tuah tipped her head in the direction of town. "Yup."

"Is the grave marked?"

"Sort of."

I knew what that meant. A wooden cross in a graveyard no one ever saw, with a name and dates carved into it, which by now was becoming too weathered to read and would soon fall over, would split as the wood dried and endured relentless freeze-thaw cycles, and would finally disintegrate into splinters on the ground. When that happened, she'd be gone. What she'd done, how she lived, even her name — all vanished.

Tuah rubbed her shins, then put her hands against the log and pushed herself to her feet.

"Time to get back to work," she said, brushing the seat of her pants.

I squinted up at her. "Who are they?"

"Who?"

"Olive's descendants. You want me to know. You want somebody to always know who they are. That's why you told me the name."

Tuah smiled. She looked down at her boots, then swiveled one at the heel like a windshield wiper to make an arc in the dirt.

"Look up Rodel in the phone book," she said. "Charles T. Rodel. Jack Rodel is his son. The daughter's married so she doesn't show up as a Rodel, but you already know her anyway." She looked back down at me. "Those girls you said stopped by? Mindy? She's Olive's granddaughter."

13

I arrived at the Koffords' home Wednesday morning before the children were awake. I balanced on the edge of the living room sofa, hands folded around one knee, while Paul stood in the kitchen drinking a mug of coffee. He wore dark, stiff jeans, a plaid shirt, and a denim jacket and leaned back against the counter with one boot crossed over the other, blowing and sipping, gaze fixed on the oven door. I looked at the top of one curtain, where a pleat sagged away from the rod, or at the kids' framed school pictures on the mantel, with their slicked hair and fixed stares against marled blue backgrounds. After the strained conversation we'd had before I left Friday — him seeming puzzled by my questions, giving answers off-target from what I was asking, me feeling as ignorant after as I had before — I didn't really want to start a fresh one. And so I sat, acting alert and interested, listening to nothing but the hum of the refrigerator.

Finally a creak of leather — whether belt or boots I couldn't tell — as he straightened and turned to rinse the mug and upend it over the other dishes in the sink.

"Well, guess I'd better get along. Cash's in the jar. Might wanna get to the market first thing. Not much here to eat. Not enough milk for cereal." He opened the fridge and took out the jug, sloshing it to demonstrate.

"Oh, sure. That'll be fine."

"They can have some toast or something for breakfast." He opened a cupboard. "Cinnamon and sugar here, some honey. Bread's on top of the fridge. You probably want something yourself. There's some eggs. Not enough to just eat, but maybe you could make some French toast. There's enough milk for that. And sugar. Or pancakes. There's pancake mix. The kids like pancakes. Syrup's here, too. Butter —" He opened the refrigerator door and stooped to peer inside. "Yeah, there's enough. You probably want butter. I got no powdered sugar, though. You probably want powdered sugar, so that won't work . . ."

Powdered sugar, a deal-breaker? I didn't know how to respond. He faded back into

167

silence as he started opening cupboards and checking for mystery ingredients.

"I'm sure we'll be fine," I said after I guessed the monologue wouldn't resume. What would it be like to be married to someone like this? Only the knowledge that he'd be gone in a few minutes kept me from shoving back against this takeover of my needs and wishes. I contented myself with changing the subject. "They knew you'd be gone this morning?"

He closed a cupboard and stood for a moment with his hand on the handle. "I think so," he said.

I wasn't convinced and foresaw potential disaster when the children woke up and found him gone. But as soon as the idea formed to suggest he go in and wake them to say good-bye, I pictured a bad reaction intensified by grogginess. Which would be worse? Telling them he'd left without saying good-bye or starting their day off confused and unhinged?

"Maybe you could write them a note," I said. "Just something quick. Tell them you'll miss them. Stuff like that."

"That's a good idea."

He opened a drawer near the door to the back porch, took out a pad and a pencil, wrote for a few moments, then folded the piece of paper and left it on the counter.

"There you go. I thought Sarah might want to try to read it, so I tried to write real clear. Kevin can read it to her, but that might make her mad if she wants to try by herself, so you'll probably want to let her have it first. You could maybe give it to her while she eats her breakfast, when Kevin's on the other side of the table and can't see it too clear right off. Then you could help her if she needs it. Kevin'll be just fine that way, just fine, I think . . ."

He was already turning away, pulling on his ball cap. I caught myself thinking I'd do almost anything rather than whatever he said I'd probably want to.

"Well that's it, then," he said, turning back at the door. "I'll be back on Friday, y'know. Probably late. Then out again Sunday night. So you'll probably want to just stay in town for the weekend. You can stay at your grandma's, I guess. I mean, we'll leave your bed up here, but y'know . . ."

He trailed off, gave a little cough, and shifted his weight, clearly having been dragged by the current of his own stream of consciousness into uncomfortable water. To my discredit, I left him there, waiting with a smile for him to extricate himself however he saw fit. He tugged at the bill of his cap.

"Well, anyway, I guess I'll be going."

"Have a good trip," I said. "We'll be fine."

The back door squealed on its hinges, then latched closed again. And I was glad of it.

"Are kittens stronger than puppies?" Sarah sat on a kitchen chair, legs swinging, chin close to the edge of her plate, scooping sodden toast into her mouth.

There had indeed been just four eggs, but that was enough for me to make each of us a piece of toast and a single egg, with an extra to spare for Kevin if he was hungry. By the time I'd ruled out everything Paul had suggested, it was my only idea.

I'd involved the kids in buttering bread, cutting a circle out of the center of each piece with a jar lid, then breaking an egg into the center as soon as the bread started grilling in the pan. Kevin, I'd already seen, was willing to eat almost anything put in front of him, and though Sarah said she didn't want her eggs and toast to touch, as soon as she cut her circle she couldn't wait to see the egg break into it. She was now eating the result with gusto. Neither one seemed upset that their father was gone.

Her question caught me by surprise. "Uh, I don't know. I guess it depends."

"On what?"

"Whether they're big dogs or small ones, how old they are, what you mean by stronger. Lots of stuff."

"What if they're big dogs and little kittens?"

"Dogs," said Kevin. He herded a bite of toast through the yolk slurry on his plate, then pushed it onto his spoon with his thumb.

"Hands out of your food," I said.

"Yes, ma'am."

"What if they're mean kittens and little puppies?"

"Kittens," I said.

"What if they're both little and they can't see?"

She knew a lot about kittens and puppies. "Then they just trip over each other."

Sarah giggled.

"They could bite," Kevin offered.

"No teeth," I said. From my seat at the head of the small table I reached out to pluck a fold of each of their arms between the edges of my fingers. "They'd just suck on each other."

They both giggled, scrunching their necks down between their shoulders, and Sarah had to catch some food that burbled out the corner of her mouth, which made them both laugh harder. I started laughing, too.

"You want more?" I said to Kevin as he chased down his last bite.

He nodded. "Yes, ma'am."

"Then go fix it yourself. I'll watch."

"I want more, too!" Sarah wailed. I looked at the bites mashed and scattered on her plate.

"No, you don't. If you finish yours before Kevin's ready you can have some of his. That's all we've got. If that's not enough, we'll just have to be hungry bears when we go to the store."

"Are bear cubs stronger than puppies?"

"Yes. Always. Why do you want to talk about animal babies so much?"

"Miss Poppy —" Kevin started as he stood with his plate.

"Her dog had puppies!" Sarah yelled before he finished. "I drew a picture!" She started to push herself away from the table.

"Finish your breakfast," I said. "When did —"

"She said we could come see them *every day*!" Sarah shouted. She held on to the back of her chair and bent at the waist from the effort.

"Wow," I said again.

"Can we go after breakfast?"

"No," I said reflexively. This must be the

same woman who'd told Sarah about the ghosts. I did remember Paul mentioning a neighbor with a flower name — Rose or Daisy, I would've said — who knew the children well and could help if I needed anything, but even assuming this was the same one I had no idea whether she'd ever really invited the children to come over. And she certainly wouldn't want them at eight o'clock in the morning. "We need to go to the store. Plus I think we need more library books. Maybe this afternoon."

"She likes the mornings," Sarah grumbled, getting back into her chair and turning her attention back to her plate.

"She does," Kevin added. "Where's the circle cutter?"

"Right by the sink."

"Where's the bread?"

I eyed him from my seat at the table. I had a sudden memory of my father calling questions like these out to my mother. Was kitchen-blindness a genetically male trait?

"Maybe you could find it yourself," I said. "It looks like a bag with bread in it."

"One puppy died," Sarah offered, without preamble, during lunch.

After shopping and restocking the kitchen, we had decided to eat our ham sandwiches

173

outside. The morning had gone smoothly, except for the moment when I suggested that we pack our lunches in sacks. Sarah told me her dad would have to check them. I looked to Kevin for explanation or confirmation, but he looked down and shoved his hands in his pockets.

"Okay," I finally said, electing to sidestep rather than challenge. "We'll just carry everything outside on a cookie sheet."

So now I sat on the tufted, uncut grass with my legs crossed, feeling moisture wicking onto my seat and considering putting the cookie sheet underneath me. Sarah, oblivious to the damp, sat with her knees turned out, her legs forming a *W*. Kevin ate potato chips out of a wad in his hand.

I waved a fly away from my face. "My," I said. I wished I knew what Sarah was thinking. "That happens with puppies," I added.

She nodded, sure of herself and emphatic. "Uh-huh. The mom squashed it."

Oh, good grief. "That's too bad," I said.

"Do you think the mama is sad?"

I looked at the potato chip bag. They were the last of an old bag and slightly stale. I took one anyway to avoid her eyes. "I do. Moms love their babies."

"Miss Poppy doesn't think so. She says the mama never even knew she did it."

"Well, that's true. It was an accident, but she loved her puppy."

"Miss Poppy says some mamas don't care."

Who *was* this woman? What she said was certainly true, though it was nothing I wanted to think about right now. And I wouldn't say it to a child who had just lost hers. So where Miss Poppy said what was true and difficult, I dug deeper in the potato chip bag and opted for something I didn't believe but thought sounded soothing.

"Dogs aren't the same as people, you know."

The children prevailed. Within a few moments after throwing away the potato chips, I found myself on Miss Poppy's front porch, wind chimes swaying and jangling around my head. This house had been a curiosity to me from across the road. Whether it was a small Victorian that had suffered from homespun repairs or a miner's shack embellished with Victorian flourishes, it was hard to tell. A plastic stag and doe reigned over a mound of frowzy peonies beside the porch. Mr. Fousek, mowing his lawn at the bottom of the road, waved to me. Kevin let Sarah ring the bell.

I had to stop myself from taking half a

step back at the sight of the woman who opened the door: certainly six feet tall, broad-shouldered, wearing a vast muumuu that floated a few inches above ankle socks and men's sandals. A puff of silver hair ended in a walnut-sized knot on top of her head.

"Angels!" she cried, holding her arms open.

Sarah dove into the folds of fabric while Kevin succumbed to a shoulder squeeze.

"And you're Elena," she said. She released Sarah and extended her hand. "Poppy Cosby."

"Pleased to meet you," I said.

"Come inside!" She released my hand and stood back, holding the screen with one arm to allow the children to pass.

"If it's okay. I don't want to intrude. The children said —" But it was too late. They were already inside.

"Of course! Anytime!" But she lowered her voice as I passed her. "Just not *all* the time," she added close to my ear. "Hah!" she barked.

It took a moment for my eyes to adjust. I turned my head from one side to the other.

"Quite a collection, eh?"

Miss Poppy stood, hands on her hips, evidently pleased at my reaction. But if it was a collection, I couldn't tell of what. The walls were so covered the paint color was a mystery. An inspirational poster. An Indian rug. A boot. A roll of tape. A dream catcher, feathers dangling over a child's drawing, probably Sarah's. A postcard. A license plate. A sombrero. A book jacket. A 1968 calendar, open to January. A file folder with something written in pencil on the tab. A flattened red playground ball. A yellow window shutter.

"Uh, yeah."

"Can you guess what it is?"

I felt trapped. Would a failure here cause offense? Brand me as ignorant?

"I — I'm sorry — no."

She smiled with what looked like satisfaction and lifted her chin a little. "Keep your eyes open. You'll get it sooner or later. Everyone does. You want something to drink?"

From a faint sour smell, I guessed the puppies were being housed inside.

"No, thank you."

"A beer. You need a beer."

"Oh, really, no. Thank you. I'm fine."

She leaned toward me and winked. "I tend bar, you know. Professional service, but no I.D. required."

"Thank you, but no, really. You know, the kids."

She tilted back again, hands far apart on her hips, and squinted slightly. "Huh," she said after a moment. "Fair enough. Well, I want one and I don't wanna drink alone. Water?"

"Thank you," I said. "That'd be fine."

Without warning, she turned toward the back of the house and yelled, "You kids aren't touching those puppies, are you?"

"No, Miss Poppy!" they called back in unison.

"C'mon back," she said, waving me to follow her as she turned toward an open door. "Let's sit down and have that drink."

I followed her through a doorway into the kitchen. A short ledge capping a half wall was covered with porcelain animal figurines. The windowsill held a collection of colored bottles and empty flowerpots. Plates and platters crowded every square foot of wall space not already hung with cupboards, and flowered wallpaper kept the spaces between their edges busy. She opened a crowded cupboard, took out a glass, and started filling it at the sink.

The children knelt beside a hard-sided blue wading pool in the corner.

"You're not making Bella nervous, now,

are you?"

"No, ma'am."

"We're just watching."

She shut off the water. "That's right. Now Miss Elena and I are gonna sit down for a visit. If you get tired of watching, you can go outside."

I glanced out the window. I could see the top of an on-end sofa, a barrel, some boards leaned against the fence, and some unidentified lengths of metal tubing or pipe.

I started at a tug on the hem of my jeans. I looked down to see a small, snub-nose dog with the denim between his teeth.

"Sugar! Stop it!" Poppy bent to wave a hand at the dog, who skittered aside, then darted out of the kitchen. "Sorry about that. Can't stand that damn dog. I don't know why he's so fixated with fabric." She handed me the glass. "He's always nipping at the hem of my dress in the morning when I'm dancing."

Poppy was backlit, hands on her hips, flyaway hairs shining around her head. Behind her, crystals sparkled in the window and fairy decals flitted across the cupboards. Puppies mewed and rustled against the newspaper lining the bottom of the pool, and Kevin and Sarah leaned over the edge like eager gargoyle statues around the roof-

line of a cathedral. I smelled dogs and coffee and soap, and from nowhere felt a stab
of pure, childlike delight. I didn't laugh, but
must have looked like I was going to.

"What?" she asked, tilting her head a little.

"Nothing. I'm just thinking I really ought
to dance in the mornings."

She pursed her lips and shook her head.
"So many don't," she said. She turned to
the refrigerator and got a bottle, then
popped the cap against the edge of the
counter.

"Stop bothering my dog!"

The voice was querulous and high-
pitched, and came from another room. I
twisted toward it.

"Nobody's doing anything, Mama," Poppy
called back. "Miss Elena's just here for a
visit, and Sugar was biting." I heard no
response.

"Who's that?" I asked, turning back.

"Mama Ruth. She mostly stays in her
room and watches TV. Sugar is her dog."
She peered over the children into the wading pool, weight on one foot, the other in its
man-sandal hovering over the floor so that
she assumed, for a moment, the position of
a very large and ill-dressed statue of Mer-
cury. She looked back at me over her shoulder. "You wanna see the pups?"

"Sure."

"C'mere. They're just starting to wake up."

I found a brown dog of no particular breed lying on her side like a brood sow, crumpled newspaper around and underneath her, a mash of hairless guinea pigs attached to her teats. Their backs undulated as they shouldered each other and pressed against her belly.

"How many are there?" I asked.

"Six." Poppy took a swig from the bottle. "She had seven, but we lost one."

"That's the one that died!" Sarah blurted without turning her head. Kevin knelt motionless beside her. The magnetic power of those barely moving puppies was extraordinary.

The mother raised her head and thumped her tail, then started to push herself up on one shoulder.

"Hey, now," Poppy said. She bent over, muumuu billowing away from her waist, to push the dog's head back down with one hand. "Not now, girl." She looked up over her shoulder at me as she waited for the dog to relax back into her lying position. "She's a terrible mother."

Something in my reaction must've made her feel a need to reassure me. "Oh, there's

181

nothing wrong with that," she went on. "Some of 'em are just like that. She probably had a bad mother herself. She just needs a little help, somebody to show her what to do. They can learn, you know."

Mama Ruth's voice came from closer this time. "Where the hell's my chips?"

I turned to see a stoop-shouldered old woman in a nightgown and slippers, a roll of Life Savers caught between the fingers of one hand. She was as notably small as Poppy was large, with short white hair mashed to the back of her head.

"Mama, this is Elena. She's looking after Kevin and Sarah."

"These are my chips," she said, grasping a bag on the kitchen counter. She shuffled away again, crinkling the cellophane in her fist as she went.

"But still," Poppy said to me with a wink, "some mamas will always be better than others." A door slammed. "Hah!" she barked.

14

Joan was formidable. She hid it pretty well with the rosy cheeks and the round face and the springy little curls, but that was the only explanation I could come up with for how Saturday night found me in the doorway of the Powder Keg, where Poppy worked, craning my neck in an effort to find Joan and her friends. When Joan had come to pick up Kevin Friday morning for a birthday party, saw the bartender she already knew gardening across the road, and found out I'd be alone in Leadville over the weekend, the plan clicked together and locked into place before I fully understood what it was. Girls' night at the Powder Keg, seven thirty. Sharp. These women didn't have kid-free time to waste with people being late.

The tavern was a century-old saloon with plank floors and a tin ceiling that had expanded into a former bank lobby next door. I'd pictured something darker and more secluded, but it was loud — with voices and laughter and jukebox music clanging off the ceiling and the hard floor, ceiling-hung televisions competing for attention with their separate offerings of a Dodgers game and an episode of *Hawaii Five-O* — and it was full of men. Alternating as I had been between the worlds of an old woman and children, I'd lost track of the way that even a century after the prospectors, Leadville was still a town of men. Uncomfortably so, at the moment. With no sign of Joan or a likely-looking group of women, I locked my eyes on an empty seat at the bar as I threaded my way through the room.

"Hey, doll!" Poppy hailed as I sat down. She wore another loose caftan, now cinched around the middle with an apron so that she looked like a pair of sacks stacked on top of each other, rather than just one. "What can I get you?"

"A Coke, I think."

I'd had alcohol only once in my life, getting drunk at a party during my freshman year of high school. The feeling of lost control, the sense that I might lack the capacity to stop myself from doing something with everlasting consequences, frightened me as nothing had since the fire.

Not drinking now had nothing to do with the pregnancy. I had not yet been to a doctor, I ate without a thought to nutrition, and I took no vitamins. Still, Poppy eyed me, then leaned toward me and lowered her voice.

"No kids here now, you know," she said.

"Thanks, but no."

She leaned back, still studying me, then gave a single nod. "All right, then," she said. She pulled a glass off a shelf that barely cleared her head, scooped ice, and started filling it.

"Hey, Poppy! How 'bout another?"

She turned her chin to speak over her shoulder without looking away from the tap. "I'm cutting you off, Bill."

I glanced at my watch. It was just after seven thirty.

"He's a vet," she said as she slapped a napkin in front of me and set the glass on top of it, as if that was all the explanation anyone would need.

"I heard you!"

"Oh yeah? What'd I say?" Poppy snapped back without looking.

"That I ain't done yet."

"Sorry, Bill. That wasn't it. I'm gonna pour you some coffee. You can stay here or go home. Don't matter to me."

The man lifted his empty beer glass and gestured toward me. He wore a plaid shirt, open at the collar, where an impressive mat of dark hair pushed out.

"Who's 'at?" he asked.

"That's my friend. You leave her the hell alone. She's new in town and doesn't need your crazy talk."

"Huh." He pulled his glass back toward himself and looked down into it, either satisfied or distracted. But I sensed a shift of nearby heads and shoulders toward me as soon as she said "new in town."

"Joan will be here soon," I said, a little louder than I probably needed for just Poppy to hear me.

"Oh, sure. They'll be here any minute. Once a month, regular as old Aunt Flo. Bah!" She leaned toward me confidentially. "That's probably half the reason they do it." She straightened, then cleared a couple of empty glasses into a plastic tub below the bar.

"See that man over there?" She tipped her head toward the threshold between the original tavern and the bank lobby. "In the toupee."

He was easy to spot. The ginger nest distinguished a short man in a denim jacket from the group of five or six around him.

"Wow. Yes."

"That's Roger Hoopengarner. You need to talk to him. Assistant principal at the high school. I hear they're looking for a science teacher."

"Oh, no. I'm not looking for a job."

"Really? With your grandma here and everything? You said you studied science. Seems like it'd be a great fit."

"No, I don't think so."

"Shame." She leaned forward on her elbows and lowered her voice. "The last one had a little . . . trouble. Little situation with the law. And the Department of Wildlife. Some poaching, maybe. And trafficking. And maybe a little farming what he shouldn't have been, where he shouldn't have been doing it, if you know what I mean. And resisting arrest. That's just what I heard. Anyway, he won't be back, and Hoop tells me they're having a hell of a time coming up with a replacement."

"I really don't want to teach."

Poppy shrugged. "Suit yourself. But it's summer, and they're desperate. He might hunt you down if you don't talk to him tonight. And it's a job. Yours for the asking."

I looked at the man in the toupee again. He didn't look predatory. He was short, a

187

little thick around the middle, and stood with a glass mug in one hand and a plump woman hooked on his other arm, talking to another couple. The woman on his arm was watching him with an expression of pure delight. He looked — jolly. He would be the least threatening adult in any high school.

"Well, still," I said.

"Hey Poppy! How 'bout another?"

"I got that coffee coming right up for you, Bill." She patted the counter in front of me, then nodded toward the door. "Your friends are here," she said. She took a coffee cup down from overhead and walked away, the ties of her apron bouncing against her backside.

"Elena!" Joan called, waving overhead. With her were three women I didn't know and, mercifully, Mindy, who stopped at the door to talk to someone else. Joan worked her way between the tables toward me. She had on a lot of blue eyeshadow, and her hair was fixed and shiny. She gestured in order to the three women just behind her. "This is Lizzie, Kim, Leslie."

One had a narrow, severe face and long neck; the second had striking silver-blue eyes; the third had black hair, parted in the center, that hung glossy and straight on both sides of an oval face. I already couldn't remember which was which.

"Good to meet you," I said, as much to myself as to them.

Polite agreement, pleasantries, and I trailed along behind them as they ordered a round of margaritas from Poppy and picked their way to a table near the back of the room.

A girl probably only nine or ten lined up a shot at the pool tables nearby. She wore white sandals, a sundress, and a red cardigan, and stood on her toes as she wiggled the cue back and forth in front of the white ball. With a sharp rap she struck it, sending a green one spiraling toward the side cup.

"Good job, baby." A man with a gray mustache at a nearby table raised his glass toward her.

A waitress set a basket of tortilla chips and a cup of watery salsa in the center of the table, pulling my attention back to my own group. In just that long, I'd already become unhitched from the conversation. Someone was sick, I inferred. Or maybe not. The tone suggested that whatever it might be was commonplace, more annoying than worrisome, and whoever this woman was she couldn't expect a lot of sympathy from this group. Loose pieces of the conversations going on at the tables around me fluttered past like scraps of paper on a breeze.

". . . the first one after that was . . ."

". . . went with him, too . . ."

". . . is no way in hell . . ."

". . . before she ate it . . ."

". . . one that got stuck on his ass for . . ."

I was particularly intrigued at the last, but like the others, the edges were torn off, this time by Mindy.

"Hey," she said, sliding into the empty chair beside me.

"Oh, hi."

She reached for a chip, coated it in salsa, then popped the whole thing in her mouth.

"They sure didn't waste any time, did they?" she said, voice low, tipping her head a fraction toward the rest of the table.

"What?"

"The gossip." She caught a dribble of salsa on her lip with one finger. "Sheesh. How bored are you?"

"Completely." Why did I say that? No, I wasn't bored, even though I had no specific interest in the health of some person I'd never met or heard of. But agreeing was easy, and the path of least resistence usually led to the closest outlet. Sometimes I had to do a little digging to create the path, but I most certainly found my way onto it. Always.

"Sorry it took so long for me to rescue you," she said with a grin, then popped another whole chip into her mouth. I wouldn't have thought she had a large enough mouth. Perhaps her bony jaw hid it. Was that Olive's mouth? Olive's chin? I thought of the splotched mirror hanging near the wardrobe in John and Olive's house in Hat Creek. If only it could've retained one image of Olive before she was gone forever.

I could already tell I didn't like knowing Mindy's secret when she didn't even know it herself. It turned things upside down. We were scarcely better than strangers. I glanced at the little girl at the pool table, now on her toes again, digging balls out of a corner pocket. Cleared my throat.

"No problem," I said.

"Here you go." The waitress put a margarita in front of Mindy and another Coke in front of me.

"Oh — I don't need another —"

"Fella over there sent it."

I twisted against the back of my chair. Leo, sitting on the far side of the bar at a table of cowboys, raised a glass. With his hat off and his peachy complexion, he didn't look old enough to be in a bar. Though admittedly, it *was* a bar that had a little girl playing pool. I put on a smile and waved.

"Who's that?" Mindy asked.

"Don't go anywhere," I said, turning around just as I saw him pushing his chair back.

"Why? You know him? Is something wrong?"

I shook my head. "No, nothing like that. My grandmother knows him. She had me ride horses with him last weekend."

"*Had* you?"

"He asked, she pushed it — it's weird. So don't leave us alone. Please. He wants a summer girlfriend. I just — don't."

Mindy grinned and reached for her drink. "You don't want a girlfriend?"

"No, I just . . . don't want to make any more people mad at me than I have to this summer. I'm already waiting for Paul to start asking what made him think it was a good idea to have me watch his kids."

Mindy laughed. She thought I was joking. People usually did, which was fine. Sugar coating on a bitter pill. Prepping the patient, so to speak, for the inevitable bad turn.

"And Coke? Seriously? Is he Mormon or something? Or did he get you pregnant?"

I felt a snatch at the top of my gut, something like the feeling when a school-teacher caught you passing a note or trying to hide something in your desk. Approaching from behind me, the boy I'd already foolishly told I was pregnant. In front of me, a table of women I really, really didn't want to talk about it with. In a bar. I couldn't figure out how to arrange my face, and felt it freeze.

"Is everything okay?" Mindy said.

"Hey there."

I found the smile I needed and turned around. "Well, hi! Thanks for the drink. I'm surprised to see you back in town."

Leo shrugged. "Yeah, my friend's brother is home this week so they don't need me at the ranch. I'm picking up some shifts in the mine instead. I'm surprised you're not up with Tuah."

"Short weekend for me. I'm back at the Koffords' tomorrow."

"Ah. Great. Hope to see you around town this week, then. I'll let you get back to your friends."

"Great! Thanks again!" I turned back to Mindy, hardened cheer in place. She put a hand on my wrist.

Are you okay? she mouthed.

Applause went up from a table in front of the TV. I glanced at it to see Steve McGarrett standing beside a car on a promontory, pushing his suit coat open to rest his hands

193

on his hips, Danno just rising out of the passenger seat, both of them watching another car settle into the ocean. At the bar, drunk Bill hunched over his coffee.

"Elena?"

The other four women had closed into their own circle, leaning toward each other, talking intently. Balls clacked against each other at the pool table. *No. No, I'm not okay. I'm pregnant. And I'm a little more pregnant every day. And I can't move or stand still without fucking something else up.*

I pushed hard against something tight in my throat. "Yeah," I said. Another squeeze. "Yeah."

"Is it him? Is there a problem?"

"No — no, he's fine. I'm fine."

"No you're not. You can say you don't want to talk about it, but I'm not going to pretend I can't tell."

I scarcely knew Mindy, but I'd known people like her before. Intrusive. Blunt to the point of insensitivity. Tactless. I wanted to like her for the sake of what I knew, but right now I just wanted to make it all stop.

"Okay, fine," I said. "I don't want to talk about it. Can we talk about something else? You can't fix this."

"So?" She looked sideways and tilted her head ever so slightly to indicate one of the other women at the table, probably the one with the long dark hair. "Just because I can't fix Leslie's MS doesn't mean I don't talk to her about how she's doing, maybe help with her kids once in a while."

She let go of my wrist. "I was kind of a bratty teenager." A shrug. "I know, hard to believe. But when I was sulky my mom used to say that not talking about stuff is like growing mold." She took a sip of her drink. "Talking airs it out. You still have the stuff, but it keeps it from getting furry and gross."

Involuntarily, I started to laugh. And then my eyes started to burn. "Smart mom," I managed to say.

"Yeah, my dad and my brother are idiots, and don't tell Joan I said so. The men in my family are hopeless. But my mom's pretty great."

The burning in my eyes tightened and spread. I couldn't process everything as quickly as it was coming at me. *The men in my family.* I knew so much more than she did about how true her assessment was. The threads of generations and intersecting lives crossed each other, knotted, and wound around others. The threads ran through me, pulling forward and backward, twisting through the tiny fingers in my belly. Olive's tragedy, leading to Mindy, who now connected to me and to Sarah and to Tuah, who connected back to Olive, whose story shared so much with me and my own unwanted child. When Olive was alone, had Tuah ever just asked, like this, whether she was okay? How would she have answered?

"I'm pregnant," I whispered.

Mindy's hand on my knee. A squeeze. The dark-haired woman laughed, flipping a lock over her shoulder. I glanced sideways, but none of the other women showed any sign that they noticed our absence from their conversation.

"Does your grandma know?" Mindy said.

I nodded.

"That's good. And she's okay?"

I nodded again.

"Where's the dad?"

I shook my head, which seemed to be enough. Mindy looked hard into my eyes. "This is *not* a big deal around here. You understand? We talk" — she tipped her head toward the rest of the table — "but it's harmless. We're all misfits. This place is small, we're isolated, and the winters are awful. The only reason to stay is because folks take you as you are. Well, and there's work. But nobody cares about your prison history or who your daddy was or where that baby came from." She gave my knee a pat and took another sip from her drink. "So what are you going to do next?"

A weak, involuntary giggle started in my nose and then spread into my shoulders so that I finally hung my head, trying not to cry, as they shook with laughter I couldn't control. When I could finally speak, I looked up. "Are you serious?"

She furrowed her brows. "Of course. Isn't that about the only thing you think about?"

"I try not to. I have no *idea* what I'll do next."

"Huh. Well, don't you kinda have to think of something, eventually?"

"No kidding."

The waitress's arm appeared, setting a second margarita glass on the table in front of Joan, salt snowy on the rim against the pale green liquid inside. The silver-eyed woman gestured to show that something was much, much taller than the top of her head, and Joan waved her hands in front of herself in denial.

"When are you due?" Mindy said.

"Sometime around the middle of January would be nine months, I think."

"It's forty weeks, hon. Since your last period. When was that?"

"Oh. The end of April was when I started to think I'd missed it."

"No dates?"

"I didn't exactly keep track."

Mindy rolled her eyes, then bent over the sacklike bag on the floor beside her chair, digging in its depths for a few moments before emerging with a checkbook. She flipped it open in her lap and started counting weeks on the calendar, her lips moving slightly as she ran her finger down the columns. Finally she looked up.

"That puts you more like Christmas or New Year's."

"Oh."

"You're like" — she looked back down at the calendar, tracing the numbers again — "thirteen or fourteen weeks now. You're out of your first trimester." She tucked the calendar back into her bag and picked up her drink, tilting it toward me. "Cheers."

"Hey — what are we toasting?" the silver-eyed woman said.

Mindy, bless her, didn't miss a beat. "New beginnings." The glasses came together over a bowl of salsa and I touched rims with them.

There were assurances that summer was great here, that I would make lots of friends, that I would never want to leave. It was a few minutes before Mindy could speak to me privately again.

"Do you have a doctor?" she said.

"Not yet. But I feel good. I haven't been sick or anything."

"It's not about *you,* silly. It's for —" She tipped her head slightly and looked pointedly toward my belly. "You know."

"I know." But I didn't. Not really. I hadn't thought about it much.

Mindy studied me for a moment. "Are you giving it up?" she asked quietly.

I looked at the basket of chips. It was red plastic and had a waxed-paper liner. Oil from the chips had soaked through the liner, making darkened shapes that you could probably imagine as bears or trees or someone's face. If you stared for long enough.

"Yeah," I finally whispered. "I think so. Yeah. I mean, it makes sense, right?"

I felt the hand on my knee again. Another squeeze.

"You'll figure it out." She released my knee and pushed the tortilla chips toward to me. "Now eat some chips before I finish this thing off by myself." She leaned closer. " 'Cause I'm not eating for two."

15

When I arrived at the Koffords' house Sunday afternoon I found Paul far from ready to leave. He seemed as surprised to see me at the door as I was to see him barefoot and shirtless, hair mashed flat on one side of his head.

"I'm — ah — I'm sorry. Am I early?"

He just stared at me, then gave a slow blink. "What time is it?"

"Five."

"Yeah."

What did that mean? Yes I was early? Yes he agreed about the time? His gaze wandered off to the distance over my shoulder.

"I thought — you're leaving tonight, right? Because of the heat? The desert?"

"Yeah." He stepped back, opening the door wider. He rubbed his fingers in his hair. "Yeah. Just trying to get some sleep first. Come on in."

I hesitated. "Should I just come back a

little later?"

"Hi Lena!" Sarah burst around the corner, her greeting sounding like one word. She wrapped my hips in a wiry embrace and pressed her cheek against my belly. I was too startled to say anything. My free arm shaped itself around her shoulders and then my hand moved to her hair. My fingers caught in the knots.

"Will you braid my hair?" she said, looking up.

"Sure. Will you let me brush it first?"

She made a sound in her throat, annoyed, martyred. "*Okay.* I'll get the twisties."

"Get the *brush,*" I called as she started toward her room.

She ran past Paul as if he wasn't there. He stood with his back to the wall, hands hanging empty at his sides. He didn't shift away as I looked at him, but only stared back, eyes stark, face as naked as his chest. I knew his expression, could feel the way it had rested on my own cheekbones and lips and eyes in years past.

"How are you?" I whispered, pushing the front door closed behind me.

"Rough day." He swallowed. "We went to see Carrie's mom yesterday. Pretty hard on all of us." He looked down. "I'd better go get my stuff."

Sarah passed him as he started away from me down the hallway.

"I got the twisties."

"What about the brush?"

"Oh." She pivoted and ran away again. I could hear the tiny thunder of her feet, the slam of a drawer, then she reappeared with the brush and a photo album tucked under her arm.

"You sit here." She pointed the brush at an upholstered chair the color of dry lumber. I set my bag beside it and obeyed her. As soon as I did, she wedged herself between my knees, back to me, and handed the brush and elastics over her shoulder. It was as if we'd gone through this routine a thousand times, but I'd never braided her hair before. I stared at the back of her head, afraid to feel her mother's fingers in her hair, the same way I felt her mother's shape in the chair beneath me.

"How about we sit over on the sofa?"

She shook her head. "Huh-uh." Her shoulders shifted between my knees as she pushed herself more firmly into place.

This had nothing to do with me. It was something I could do for her. I squeezed my fingers around the brush amd smoothed it over the top of Sarah's hair.

"Ow."

This, now, I knew.

"I hardly touched anything."

"It hurts."

"Do you want braids or not? And if you don't, we'll still have to comb it out tonight after your bath."

A deep sigh widened her back against my knees.

"Okay." She opened the photo album and started flipping pages. Then stopped. Then flipped back a few. Then ahead again.

"Do it like this," she said. She held the book up over her head so I could see. The pages were plastic sleeves that each held three pictures. In the center picture on the left page, Sarah was squeezing Buffers against her chest and leaning forward, eyes squinted shut against the sun, nose wrinkled, grinning to the camera. Tight pigtails curved behind and under her ears like rams' horns. She looked younger, but only slightly, and the leafy background behind her suggested the picture must've been taken last summer. It was leafy in a way that wasn't typical around here, though — ferny and shady and cloistered. Like the enclave I'd seen the day I rode up to Hat Creek with Leo. The picture above and below it must have been taken in the same place: in one Sarah had her back to the camera, squatting at the edge of a little brook; in the other Kevin held her over the water by her arms. They were both laughing.

"Where were you in that picture?" I said as I returned to brushing.

She lowered the album to her lap. "In the fairy woods. It's my mom's secret place. We didn't tell it to anybody."

"Oh." She sounded so casual and matter of fact. "That looks like a great book," I said.

She nodded. "I found it under Kevin's bed."

"Does he know you have it?"

Her head moved from side to side this time. "Huh-uh."

Oh, dear God. Kevin would be furious to find Sarah had gotten into his private treasures, and then add the sentimental worth of the photo album in both their eyes . . . "Where is Kevin, anyway?" I said.

She shrugged her shoulders. "I dunno."

We sat in silence as I brushed and braided her hair and she turned pages in the photo album. I was just getting to the bottom of the second braid when the phone rang. A few moments later, Paul reentered the room. He stopped short at the mouth of the hallway, now wearing his Dodgers cap and a plaid shirt, an overnight bag in one hand, staring at his daughter and me. His shoulders curved as if shaping themselves around something pressed into the center of his chest. I wanted to apologize, to somehow silently let him know that I understood and I was sorry, but I hadn't known what else to do.

Sarah looked up, so that the soft little braid slipped out of my fingers and started to unravel. "Daddy, can you take us to the fairy woods?"

He swallowed hard. "What, honey?"

"The fairy woods. Mommy's secret place."

He drew a deep breath, then started turning his head from side to side, denying her request absolutely and firmly and finally. "I don't know where that is, honey," he whispered. He cleared his throat. And again. "I, ah, need to pick up Kevin."

"Right."

I looked down, pretending that repairing and finishing the braid required my undivided attention. A moment later the door closed with a soft clack, letting the blanket of silence settle back over us. I fastened the end of the braid, rubbed my hands on my thighs, then pushed against Sarah's shoulders.

"Come on," I said. "Let's see what's in the kitchen for dinner."

The freezer yielded ground beef and English muffins and the pantry a packet of sloppy joe mix. The potential for these ingredients brought Sarah up onto her toes, hands clenched and vibrating with excitement, making it all the worse when I had to report that there was no tomato sauce.

"But we *have* sloppy joes," she insisted, holding the picture on the front of the packet to my face as proof.

"Look." I took a deep breath. I wasn't sure that reasoning with a five-year-old would work. "Does that feel like a sloppy joe to you?" She drew the packet back to study it herself. "Is it big enough? Do you think there are sloppy joes inside?"

A moment for consideration. "No," she finally said, reluctant and sulky. "You make it with the stuff."

"Exactly. And we don't have all the stuff."

"We *always* have the stuff!"

"We can get some at the store tomorrow and have it tomorrow night. I promise."

"No! You have to get the stuff!" Sarah grabbed my wrist and pulled. "You have to *look* for it!"

I followed, bewildered and obedient, as she led me to her parents' room, then heaved open a door I'd always presumed led to a closet. Women's clothes on hangers filled the space along one side, but darkness on the other suggested a larger room.

She looked over her shoulder at me. "You have to *look*!"

I cast my eyes around at the stiff family portrait on the wall, the dresser topped by coins and a button and wadded Kleenex, a *Trucker* magazine and a half-empty packet of Juicy Fruit. A stack of shirts, plaid on plaid, hung over the back of a chair. Paul would be back any moment.

"Oh, I don't think so. This is your daddy's room. He doesn't want me looking through his things."

"These aren't his things. They're Mommy's."

She wrapped her arm around the door casing and disappeared, then emerged with something in her hand. She held up a can of asparagus.

"Do you need this?" she said.

I took a hesitant step forward. "No. Is this another pantry?"

She disappeared and reemerged a moment later with a can of sauerkraut. "Is this the right thing?"

"No." Another step.

She reappeared again, this time with tomato sauce. "Is this right?"

I blinked, baffled. "Well, yes it is." Sarah

gave a yelp of joy. I took another step. "What else is in there?"

"*All* the stuff." She disappeared again, and this time I followed her into the darkness. A string hung from above, and I tugged it. Light.

To one side hung blouses, shirts, dresses, and skirts, pants and sweaters folded over hangers, crisp and exact, shades of emerald and garnet and topaz and amethyst, sorted by color, all looking far nicer than anything I'd ever dug out of a drawer for myself.

It was hard to imagine that the other side of the closet belonged to the same woman. Shelves held a baffling assortment of objects. Magazines. Teacups. Photo envelopes. A lightbulb. A china dog. A ball of string. Things behind things too deep for me to guess the depth of the shelves.

And food. Cans, jars, bottles, and boxes, piled and packed. Vegetables, cereal, sauces, beans, juices, and soups in no discernable order. A bottle of clam juice crowded between a can of baby formula and a flowerpot. Two jars of pickles supporting a box of melba toast. But soon I started to see repetition: somewhere on every shelf was grape jam. Jars, and jars, and jars of Welch's grape jam.

Eventually, my eyes finally found the floor.

In the corner, against the wall and a case of macaroni, was a blanket, a pillow, and Buffers. And jam. So much grape jam.

Paul brought Kevin home, bare-chested and shivering, a towel wrapped around his waist, rolled-up jeans and a shirt under his arm. I glanced up from the stove where I stood over a hissing pan, scraping shreds off the block of frozen ground beef as they thawed. The two of them stood just inside the door, looking at me. I prodded the meat, flipping the block over, setting off a fresh round of spitting. I looked back up to find them still there. What were they waiting for? I was not the mistress of this house here to give them direction and wouldn't let my position at the stove tell them I was.

Kevin's chest was pale and sinewy, his shoulders drawn forward, hands clasped over the towel at his waist, lips clenched together. Paul looked off slightly to the side. I flipped the meat again. Forfeited the battle.

"Kevin, why don't you get in the shower right now and warm up. Dinner won't be ready for a while."

"Yes, ma'am."

The still life dissolved as Kevin shuffled toward the bedrooms, laces trailing on his untied shoes. Paul tugged at his cap.

"Guess I'd better be going," he said.

"Okay, then." In the worst way, I did not want to end up sitting around the table as a family, but anything else felt like I was shoving Paul out the door and supplanting him in his own home. I ran the wooden spoon around the edge of the pan. "Or if you want to wait a little longer, I can fix you a sloppy joe before you leave."

He nodded. "That'd be real nice. Thank you."

He left the room and went outside. I could hear the shower water running through the pipes, a door slam as I guessed Sarah followed her father outside, and then a while later another bang as she came into the laundry room beside the kitchen. She brought with her a smell of leaves and the puppy-like scent of childhood sweat. The meat had finally relaxed into the pan and was almost finished browning, and she bounced to my side to see.

"When's it ready?" she asked.

"Soon. Would you set the table?"

She jumped onto the counter and swung her head to one side as she opened the plate cupboard. She set the stack of plates on the counter and jumped back down, and it was only as she laid the last plate on the table that I realized she'd laid out four rather than three. I hesitated, unable to think of a tactful way to correct the situation quickly enough. She returned to the kitchen for silverware and glasses.

"Sarah, I think your Daddy has to go. I don't think he's going to eat with us."

She nodded her head. "He's gonna have a sloppy joe, too."

That could mean anything. I put my hand on my hip and looked back down at the pan. This was not a fatal situation. It was entirely possible that Sarah's assumption was not Paul's. And even if it were, sitting at the table with the family would not, in fact, kill me. Surely I could manage to perform that simple task with enough grace to not embarrass or offend any of them and keep my own discomfort to myself.

A door opened, creaked, and closed again, and Paul came into the kitchen holding his hat in one hand, scratching his hair. Grace. I would comport myself with grace.

"Are you going to eat here, or do you want to take yours with you?" I asked.

"I put your plate *here,* Daddy," Sarah said, patting the plate at the end of the table with her open hand. "Like always. Lena sits there." She pointed to the other end. Perfect. So I'd been sitting in her mother's spot all this time.

His eyes flitted to the table, then settled somewhere along the edge of the counter. "That's great, honey, but I really gotta get going." He glanced at me. "I'll just take it with me, thanks." He turned and left again the way he'd come, with "I'll just take my stuff out . . ." trailing behind him as he pulled his hat back over his brow.

What had he been doing all this time, going in and out, if not taking his bag at some point? I scooped the meat onto a paper towel and poured the grease into a cup, then went mining in the refrigerator for something fresh to serve on the side. Nothing. Mercifully, I found peaches in the pantry and didn't have to wrestle with whether to send Sarah for whatever pleased her in the closet.

"Do we put the stuff in now?" she asked from my elbow as I dumped the hamburger back in the pan.

A squeal in the plumbing let me know Kevin had shut off the shower.

"Yes. Here you go." I handed her the opened can of tomato sauce.

"I can do it *myself*?"

"Well sure." I couldn't imagine a problem. The sharp-edged lid was already in the trash and the burner was off.

She looked up at me and gave a single

slow blink. *"Really?"*

Was there history here I was unaware of? Was I being unsafe, doing something her father wouldn't have let her? It seemed like a harmless enough thing for a child to do. But if something bad happened, it would be my fault. My fingers hardened around the spoon.

She seemed to sense my hesitation and stared at me, eyes round. I forced my hand to relax.

"Really. Just pour it in."

She stood on her toes and arched her arm over the pan, keeping her skin as far as possible from its edge, and started to tip the can. I put my hand over her wrist to lower it.

"Careful. It'll splash if you hold it too high."

"Uh-huh."

I doubted she heard me. Her concentration was absolute.

"Good job. You want to do the packet?"

She nodded, too awestruck for words, and although she did sprinkle a little outside the pan, in this she was largely successful as well.

"Now stir."

My shoulders released as abruptly as if a belt had come unbuckled, surprising me with how tense I must've been. I watched her swirl the spoon in the pan for a few moments before I turned the heat back on.

"You did a really good job," I said. "I'll put the sandwiches together. Now go tell Kevin dinner's almost ready."

I toasted the English muffins in the oven while the filling heated through, filled them, and wrapped one in foil for Paul. As I stood over the table dishing peaches, the back door squealed, then banged shut.

"Your sandwich is on the counter," I said. When he didn't answer, I looked up to find him standing over the wastebasket, staring into the trash.

"Is something wrong?" I said.

He shook his head, then looked at me and scratched the back of his head.

"Where'd you find that tomato sauce?" he said.

"Sarah found it," I said, heat spreading across my face.

"Mmm." He pulled his upper lip between his teeth, nodded, then took the sandwich in his hand. "Thanks. I appreciate it."

"Sure. You'll be back Friday?"

"Yup." He cleared his throat. "Money's there in the jar for groceries. You just buy whatever you need. I know there wasn't much for you to work with tonight, so I really appreciate you taking care of things."

Sarah swung around the corner of the room with one hand on the wall.

"I gotta go now, honey," he said.

"You got a sloppy joe?"

He held up the foil disk as Kevin came into sight, hair slicked back, wearing a sweatshirt and a pair of jeans, heading straight for the table.

"I'll see you on Friday, okay, buddy?"

Kevin nodded, pulling his chair out. "Bye."

"Okay." He touched the brim of his hat to me. "Thanks again."

And with no ceremony, no wails of protest from children who'd already had a mother drive away and never come back, he was gone.

"Can I have milk?" Sarah asked.

I stood in the center of the kitchen, more bewildered by this family than ever.

16

"Can we start reading early tonight?"

We'd left off last week in the middle of *James and the Giant Peach,* which I could tell the children enjoyed, but Kevin's request surprised me. The sloppy joes were done and cleaned up and they were watching a Sunday movie about a bear cub while I flipped through a magazine. He sat at the far end of the sofa from me, and I would have thought he was completely absorbed. I closed the magazine over my finger.

"What do you think, Sarah? Do you want to finish the movie?"

She lay on her belly in front of the TV, Buffers wedged under her arm, and didn't turn her face from the screen.

"Uh-huh."

"Is that okay, Kevin? Can you wait a little longer?"

He glanced at me and shrugged one shoulder. "I guess."

But something caught my eye. He looked different. One of his eyes looked — smaller somehow.

"Kevin — look here a sec."

He turned to face me. Yes, one eye was certainly puffy. I moved over and bent closer.

"Does your eye feel okay? Is something itchy or sore?"

"Nah." He looked away.

"No, really. Let me take a better look." Not that I knew what to look for or what I'd do if I saw something. Call Joan or Mindy, probably.

"It's nothing."

I pulled back a fraction. *It's nothing.* This wasn't an allergy or infection. Something had happened. I laid the magazine beside me.

"What happened? Did you hit it on something?"

The corner of his mouth wrinkled. "Kinda."

I lowered my voice, but Sarah seemed oblivious to everything but the television. "Did you get in a fight?"

No response.

"What was it about?"

A faint shrug. "Nothing."

At last one of the many loose strands of

the afternoon caught on to something solid. "Did you call your dad to come pick you up today? Is that why?"

He looked down at his lap, where he scratched at something on the surface of his jeans. "Yeah."

"What was it about?" I repeated.

"My mom," he said. His voice was barely above a whisper.

"Oh."

"A kid said she was crazy."

"Ah."

A roar and a yowl. I glanced at the screen. A bear — the cub's mother, I guessed — fought a pair of coyotes.

"Did he say it to you?"

He shook his head. "He was telling other kids. They were laughing."

"Oh." Children as a dog pack. I understood the behavior well. We moved so frequently as I grew up, I had to face it over and over. Someone would find out about my connection to the Arroyo fire, an event that didn't fade from public memory, and the one who learned first would pull others into the name-calling. Before long, I'd be glad to hear we were moving again. Never far enough, though. My father, a teacher, wouldn't look for a position outside the district where his employment was secure.

So the cycle would repeat itself.

But now, after these few weeks here, I'd started to see familiarity as a robe you pull over the odd or the shocking. As with any other clothing, everyone knows what's under there, but folks ignore it and focus on other things. Because everyone has something to cover. If the crowd at the Powder Keg was any indication, most people understood that, and in time made a loose, careless peace with each other. Maybe I could've learned that sooner if we'd stayed in one place longer. Given the chance to stick trouble out, Kevin might fare better than I did.

"You were at the pool?" I asked. "Just on your own?"

He shook his head. "I was with some kids."

What had Kevin been like when his mother was alive? I doubted very much different. Serious and stern, dark-browed and sober, his jeans hard and his shirt tucked in tight; he would never be one of the gang. Anytime he thought he was, they'd surely turn on him. No, if they didn't have this, they'd be teasing him about something else. The trick was to get him through this time.

"Well." I stood up. "We need to get some ice on that."

■ ■ ■ ■

The phone jangled me out of a sleep so heavy I'd forgotten where I was. I was in the Koffords' living room. It was night. Vague, formless panic preceded rational thought.

The rollaway creaked as I sat up. I rocked backward slightly, then swung my feet to the floor and staggered across the living room to the kitchen.

"Hello?"

"Hi. It's Paul. You up?"

My response was instinctive, spoken before my mind could process the irony of the question. "Yeah, sure." I blinked. With the phone cord stretching behind me, I took the additional steps to switch on the light inside the stove hood, then bent and squinted to read the clock below. The white plastic hands cringed against each other. Three twenty. "Where are you?"

"Green River."

Consciousness stretched and stirred. Utah. The desert. Driving at night. "Oh. What is it? What's wrong?"

"It's Kevin. I wanted to talk about Kevin."

That's when I heard it. The slight stumbling, the hesitation over the hard consonants in "wanted to talk about." He was drunk.

"It's three in the morning."

"I know — I know." Pleading. "It's just — I wanted to talk to you while I knew he wouldn't hear anything."

Snappy retorts would only occur to me later. "Okay." I leaned against the wall beside the phone, then slid to the floor and put my elbows on my knees. Closed my eyes.

"He got in a fight today," Paul said. "He's not a fighter. He doesn't fight."

"Uh-huh."

"It was about his *mom.*"

Oh, God, please don't let him start crying. "Yeah. He told me."

"He did? That's good. That's really good. I'm really glad."

Who would serve alcohol to a man who pulls up in a heavy rig along an interstate highway in the middle of the night? Or did he just carry a bottle with him?

"Sure," I said.

"What'd he say?"

"That some kid said she was crazy." Weariness made me blunt.

"Is that all?"

"Yeah."

"There's more. They said Kevin was crazy,

too. They said that's why she died — she couldn't stand the sight of him. Him being as crazy as her."

"Oh." The word faded into a sigh. "Oh, no."

"He wanted to know, in the car — we were driving home. He said, 'Am I crazy?' But he's not. You understand? He's not. He's not. He's a good kid. He's kinda quiet, that's all. He looks angry sometimes when he's not, that's all. That's all. He's not crazy."

"No — I know. You're right."

"Carrie was — it was hard, all right? People talk, but they loved her. She never acted crazy around anybody. She never did anything wild. She never *hurt* anybody. She just wasn't the same as everybody. That's all. That's all." He'd begun to cry.

I listened to him in the dark, the receiver pressed to the side of my face, my head bowed over my knees. I saw the closet full of objects and food. The pressed clothes. The jam. Things were so much more complicated than I'd first thought.

"Everybody loved her," he went on. "She just — did that to people. They couldn't help it. But then she'd get ideas that didn't make any sense, and it's like she *knew* they didn't make sense, a little bit, because she'd do things but then she'd hide them. And she'd forget things and I'd worry about the kids. Whether they were safe. And I worried, you know, how it was for them. I tried to keep everything — okay. Everything together, you know?"

I didn't. And I didn't want to. He'd come out of this a few hours from now and remember bits of it and wonder how much he'd told me.

"Oh, God, it was the *secrets.* I couldn't handle all the *secrets.* Secrets she had with the kids, secrets she kept from me —"

I couldn't let him go on any longer. "I *know,* I know. It's okay. We're okay here. Is there anything you want me to do for Kevin? Anything you want *him* to do? Are they going to let him go back to the pool?"

There was no answer. I could hear crying.

"Anything at all? Just tell me what you want me to do."

Finally, a deep breath and he spoke again, very low. "Just — take care of him. Watch out for him. Don't ever joke with him about being crazy. He's gotta toughen up but he needs more time. Just more time."

"Okay, now tell me where you are right now."

"Green River."

"That's right." It was like talking to Sarah,

coaching and managing. "But are you at a truck stop or a bar or something?"

"A truck stop. There's a room with phones."

"That's good. Is there a place to sleep there?"

"I don't know."

"I think you need to find a place to sleep. I don't think you should drive for a while."

"I'll be fine. I'll be fine."

"No, you should ask somebody where to go. Just for a few hours."

"I'll be fine. You just — you watch out for Kevin, okay?"

"Of course, but —" I could hear the emptiness, the way my own voice sounded flat and dead against a connection that had been closed.

Eventually, when the phone started beeping in my hand, I stood and hung it up, then went back to bed. But against my eyelids, I saw headlights sweeping the darkness and deep inside my skull I heard the moan of trucks. I didn't sleep anymore that night.

Sarah was up first, as usual. When she saw the empty rollaway bed, she hesitated at the end of the hallway, nightgown floating over her feet, Buffers dangling below her elbow. My first few nights, she would come into

224

my corner of the living room and start patting my arm to wake me. From there she'd graduated to sitting beside me while patting, and lately she'd started lying down, nesting against my back or belly, the springs squeaking as she worked her feet into the folds of the blanket.

"Are you awake now?" she'd say after she was satisfied that she'd done enough pushing and jostling to make herself comfortable.

"Yes," I'd say.

"When can we have breakfast?" was the follow-up. A full night was a long time for her to go without food.

But this morning she found me sitting at the table, flipping through an illustrated children's book on mythology I'd found in a basket. It had been that, hairstyle magazines, or a book of Bible stories with Jesus and the children on the front and no creases in the binding. Why was it so hard to find a book in this house? I'd been breaking bites off a piece of toast, most of which still lay, cold and dry, on a plate at my elbow. She padded across the carpet and stood beside me. She watched me turn a few more pages before she said anything.

"What are you doing?"

"Looking at this book."

"What is it?"

"A bunch of stories people made up a long time ago about the way the world works. You never saw it before?"

She shook her head.

I gestured toward the basket in the living room. "I found it over there."

"Oh," she said, unimpressed. She pointed at the picture. "What's that?"

"That's called a chariot. It's a kind of a wagon for horses to pull."

"What's that?"

"The sun. It's a story about how a god would hitch a flying chariot to the sun and pull it across the sky every day."

She wrinkled her nose and pulled her head back. "That's crazy."

"I know. People had some crazy ideas back then. They used to think that gods did everything, but now we know science, and that people do most things themselves. Kind of like we're little gods."

"We're God?" Her wide-eyed amazement gave me a glimpse of just how this conversation might sound in the retelling.

"Oh, gosh, no." I had enough trouble without kicking up a religious scandal. "I just mean, uh, there's just a lot of crazy ideas in that book. They're really funny. We're just people, you know? Making our own things happen."

Mercifully, I'd lost her, and I hoped the boring end to the religious conversation would drain the whole thing out of her mind. She put her palm over the picture and pushed a clump of pages aside, then pointed at the picture on the new page.

"What's that?"

"That's a girl being born out of her father's head."

Sarah remade her last face and exaggerated it, then turned to show it to me so I could see what she thought of the idea before she said anything.

"Daddies don't have babies. And they don't come out of people's heads."

"That's right. I told you it was crazy."

"My mom was going to have a baby. But then she died."

Stunned, I didn't answer. She turned another clump of pages.

"What's that?"

Apparently I didn't answer quickly enough.

"What *is* it?"

"Ah, that's a man looking at himself in the water. He got stuck there because he thought he was so beautiful he couldn't look away."

She laughed. "He just looked at himself

all day?"

"That's what the story says."

"That's funny."

I looked at her and the inevitable bird's nest that sleep made of her hair. From time to time I checked on her at night to see whether I could figure out how it happened, but I only ever found her motionless, splayed across the mattress, sheets snarled around her knees, head buried in her pillow.

"I don't know," I said. "You look pretty great right now, yourself. I bet if you went in the bathroom and checked the mirror you'd get stuck there, too."

She darted away and thundered down the hall. I heard a thud I knew to be her feet kicking the cabinet as she jumped onto the bathroom counter, then another thud as she jumped down. A few seconds later she was back at my side, giving me less time to gather myself than I wanted.

"Huh-*uh.*"

"Wow. You're amazing. Most people would've had a hard time."

"My hair looks messy."

"Well, maybe. Do you want toast or cereal this morning?"

"I want frosty flakes."

"Okay."

I pushed myself back from the table and she sat down at her place, pulling the book in front of herself and starting over as I went into the kitchen.

"What's that?" she asked, pointing to another picture.

"Hold it up so I can see." She raised it as high as she could, looking up toward the ceiling, arms straight overhead. "That's Athena. She's Zeus's daughter, the one that came out of his head. She was supposed to be very wise."

She turned the page. "And that."

"That's Poseidon. He's the god of the sea."

She lowered the book and studied the picture of Poseidon rearing out of the water with his trident, arms outstretched over a roiling sea full of bizarre creatures. "He looks mad."

"Uh-huh. Now if you want breakfast, you're going to have to stop showing me pictures for a minute."

She turned pages slowly while I poured cereal into a bowl and got milk. Kevin shuffled into the room and pulled out the chair across from her. He sat heavily, looking down at the place mat.

"What were you doing in the bathroom?" he said. "You woke me up."

"Looking in the mirror."

"Why?"

"To see if I'd get stuck." Sarah turned another page. "I didn't."

"You should've."

"I know. Lena thinks so, too."

I glanced at him sharply, but since Sarah had missed the insult I didn't want to make more out of it.

"Good morning," I said. No response. "Do you want cereal or toast?"

He shrugged one shoulder. "Crunch," he said after a moment.

"Excuse me?" Kevin might not be chatty but he was always polite.

"Cap'n Crunch, please."

"That sounds better." I filled the bowl and poured milk around the edges. We had less than I'd thought, and left to his own devices he had a tendency to overdose himself, then pour the remainder down the drain.

I placed the bowls and spoons in front of the children and took my seat at the end of the table. Kevin picked up his spoon without response, while Sarah was too absorbed in the book to even notice the food.

"What do we say?" I prompted.

"Thank you," they replied automatically.

"Who's that?" Sarah asked, pointing at another picture as she picked up her spoon.

"Oh. That's Pandora. That's a box full of all the troubles in the world and she wasn't supposed to open it, but she was curious and let all the trouble out."

Sarah stopped her spoon above the bowl and glared at me. "*All* the bad things in the *world* were in that box?"

"It's just a story."

She shoved the book aside. "I hate her."

I'd probably had less than four hours of sleep. I'd spent the next four replaying the conversation with Paul, imagining myself saying something that would have stopped him. Now I'd just learned that her dead mother might also have been pregnant. I was powerless to think of a helpful way to respond. I pulled my plate closer and broke off another piece of toast.

"I do, too," I said.

I glanced over at Kevin, whose eyes stayed on his cereal. He pushed the floating squares down into the milk with the back of his spoon, an endless game of Whac-A-Mole that resulted in very little cereal consumed.

"Let me see your eye," I said.

He turned to face me for just a moment, then went back to tapping the surface of his cereal. The skin was puffy, the eye reduced, with a purple streak extending from the bridge of his nose along the curve of the socket.

"Bad night?" I asked.

He shrugged.

"You and me both," I muttered, standing with my plate. I hadn't meant to say it, but my resistance was down. The children didn't react, though. Sarah sucked milk from her spoon with her chin stretched over her bowl, feet waving back and forth above the floor, while Kevin continued tapping. I let my remaining toast slide into the trash on my way to the sink.

"Quit kicking," Kevin snapped. I glanced up to see him glaring at Sarah.

"You quit kicking."

"I'm not doing the kicking."

"I'm not doing the kicking."

"Quit it."

"Quit it."

"Quit copying me!"

"Quit copying me!"

"Shut up! I hate you!"

"Kevin!" I was too late. He lashed out with one foot, missing her, then swung again, catching her heel. Sarah shrieked, far out of proportion for the glancing barefoot blow, then started to wail.

"You apologize to your sister!"

"I'm *sorry* you're *stupid.*"

"Kevin!" His behavior was so far out of character that I had no framework for how to handle it.

He slammed his spoon down on the table, knocking the edge of the bowl so that it sloshed milk across his hand and the place mat, then shoved his chair back and ran out of the room. A door slammed.

"Hush, Sarah. You're not hurt."

"Am too!"

"Enough. He's gone."

It was going to be a very long day, indeed.

By mid-morning I felt myself fraying. Though he eventually emerged from his room with a muttered apology, Kevin continued morose and brittle, and tension shimmered from him like fluorescent light. My own anxiety multiplied the effect, and Sarah, caught between us, alternated between whining and withdrawal.

I skipped chores. We needed groceries, and a trip out would've done us all good, but I was desperate for Paul to call and report he was all right and afraid to do anything that might result in a missed call, including one that might tell me he *wasn't* all right. Sarah wanted to have her friend Jenny come over, but tying up the phone would've been just as bad, so I endured her pleading and nagging while I struggled to come up with reasons why it wouldn't work. Finally Kevin announced that he wanted to watch TV, and I gave them both over to *The Price Is Right.*

I braced myself against the sink and stared out at the service shed and the mountainside and fought to keep the bile out of my throat. This was the first time I'd felt nauseated since I'd gotten pregnant but I didn't think the baby was to blame.

A flutter of movement caught my eye in the sliver I could see of Poppy's front yard. I darted across the living room and grabbed the front doorknob.

"I'm just gonna say hi to Miss Poppy," I said. The children, immobilized, didn't respond. I left the front door open so I could still hear the phone.

"Hey there!" I called, too loud, waving everything above the elbow.

Poppy, doubled over a spray of blue flowers so that she presented nothing but a dome of calico to the road, straightened and put a hand over her eyes.

"Well, hey there yourself," she called back.

"How are the puppies?"

"Fine, just fine. They change every day. You all wanna come see?"

Stupid question. I'd been too absorbed by my own fear to anticipate that obvious response. "I — I can't right now. I . . ." The only thing I knew was that I couldn't let her go. She was an adult. A lifeline. In a way I'd never felt before, I needed to not be alone. I dropped my hand, still up in a half wave, to my side. "Can you come over and help me with something for a minute?"

"Well, sure, honey." She hoisted herself out of the flower bed, pushing a wind chime away from her face, laid a handful of dead flowers on the step, then ambled across the road. "What do you need?" she asked as she came into the front yard.

I glanced inside at the children, still safely staring at the TV, and pulled the door ajar.

"Do you mind sitting down here for a sec?"

"Not at all." She turned sideways and braced herself against the concrete with one hand before lowering herself onto the stoop with a grunt. I sat beside her, hands tucked under my thighs.

She eyed me, squinting though we sat in the shade, her face ruddy and creased. Her hair was in a braid that looked as if she'd probably slept in it, gray and fuzzy and caught on her shoulder, and an enormous turquoise squash blossom pendant lay on her breastbone like a fist. She smelled of cold cream and grass. "You okay?" she said.

235

"I think I need some help."

"Yes, that's why I came."

I clearly lacked experience at asking for help. I wasn't sure where to start.

"Do you know Paul pretty well?" I asked.

"Not really. I knew Carrie better."

Just like Paul had said — everyone loved Carrie.

"He called me last night," I said. Poppy waited. "I mean, early this morning. Really early, like three o'clock. He was drunk."

"Ahh." Poppy's face eased, comprehending. "That happens, you know. Folks say some crazy things. What was it?"

"No, that's not it — he's on the road. I tried to tell him to get a room and stay wherever he was, but he didn't really answer me. He just kept saying he'd be fine and that I needed to watch out for Kevin." Through the sliver of open door behind me came faint dinging from the television, then a shimmer of applause.

Poppy looked at me, waiting. "That's it?" she said.

"Yes!"

Another pause, then, "What do you want me to do, honey?"

"I — I don't *know*! But I'm afraid to leave the house or tie up the phone. I don't want to miss a call."

"What kind of call? You mean, that he'll call again and be mad if you don't answer? Was he acting mean or something?"

"No! I *hope* he calls again. That would mean everything was all *right!*" I rolled my lips together. What I wanted to say next might become more real if I said it aloud. I put my elbows on my knees and rested my forehead on my fists.

"It sounded like good-bye," I whispered.

Poppy put a hand on my back and leaned over to peer at my face.

"Honey, what are you afraid of?"

I put my knuckles to my cheekbones and looked toward the wind chimes sparkling in Poppy's front yard. Took a deep breath. "I'm afraid he got drunk and started thinking about how he can't take it anymore and the kids would be better off without him and that I didn't say anything about how much they need him and he decided to drive his truck off a bridge and the highway patrol is going to call and those kids are going to be *orphans.* With *me.*" I glanced over my shoulder at the door. I sounded insane. And awful. Only the sound of a slide whistle, a fortune lost, came from the TV in return.

"God damn." Poppy straightened and rocked back a little, then looked back at me. "And all he said was 'I'll be fine'?"

"But you didn't hear it! He was weird when I got here last night, and then there was this call . . ." I trailed off, looking for support, then did my best imitation of what I recalled of Paul's tone. Heavy. Labored. *"I'll be fine. Take care of Kevin."* I waited. "Don't you get it?"

"No, I don't. Do you always expect terrible things to happen?"

"But that's how people talk when they're about to leave! Making arrangements and leaving messages and everything."

Poppy tilted her head slightly. "Where the hell do you get an idea like that?"

I considered, then looked away. "It's a long story."

"And maybe you don't want to tell it now while you're worried about something else."

"Probably not."

"Another time."

Slowly, I nodded.

She threw her heavy arm around my shoulders. "You know, having those kids wouldn't be the worst thing in the world." A squeeze and a smile. "I mean, I've got Mama." She added a slap on my back as punctuation. "Hah!"

I must have looked horrified. I already knew what awaited me. Forget the kids — I could see my father in another ten years, shuffling around my house, disapproving of the TV shows I watched or the way I kept the shades open to let in the sun, petulant if I was gone for too long. A strangling necklace of need. Now if you added the baby and these children . . . All my efforts to break away and flee were only making things worse.

"Wrong time for a joke, huh?" she said.

"Kinda."

She folded her hands back in her lap. She spoke very softly. "So how can I help you?"

I had no idea. She couldn't answer my questions about what Paul meant or what might have happened in the desert overnight. She didn't know him well enough to explain him to me. She couldn't tell the future and say that yes, it would be fine to take the children shopping for an hour or two right now, but that I should be home at, say, one fifteen.

"I don't know. I just don't know what to tell the children and I'm afraid to leave the phone. If I do the wrong thing right now —" I swallowed. "I guess I wanted you to tell me this was something normal for him and I don't need to worry."

"Oh, honey, you never *need* to worry."

"You mean, about Paul? It's okay?"

"No. The worrying — what does it do? It

doesn't make a single thing happen. Look at yourself. You're saying you'd keep the children cooped up in the house all week just because you're afraid something awful has happened — something you can't do anything about — and you'll miss hearing about it. Is that right?"

"Not all week."

"Till when, then?"

"Until I heard something."

"So, maybe all week."

I shrugged.

"And that doesn't sound crazy to you?"

Lacking a better answer, I gave another shrug.

"Well, that's pure bat shit crazy, is what it is. Staying here, waiting by the phone, that doesn't do anything. If something has happened, sitting here isn't going to change one thing. You're just going to make those children miserable and nervous and fretful, and more misery is the last thing they need. Go on, now. Give them a good day. And have one yourself while you're at it."

In one motion she put her arm across my shoulders again, squeezed, and planted a kiss on my temple.

"You're all right now," she said as she moved her hand to the center of my back and pushed herself up. "Sometimes folks just need a little help to flush out the crazy. That's what friends are for." She looked down at me, then waggled her first two fingers toward the door behind me. "I'll expect you and the kids to come see the puppies as soon as that show's over," she said.

From inside, a bell rang and the audience cheered.

17

Like a child, I did as Poppy told me. I pulled a brush through Sarah's hair, ignoring the yelps and flinches, ordered Kevin to dress, then eased them into cooperation by asking for their input on a grocery list. They had come to accept our un-reviewed shopping, and when I suggested we put Ding Dongs on the list, the mood brightened instantly.

With the paper tucked into my back pocket, I led them across the road to Poppy's. We laughed as the puppies stumbled over each other, but before long, one balled itself into Sarah's lap and two into Kevin's and fell asleep. I'd found one that seemed sleepy when we arrived, and had already withdrawn to a chair in the corner, under a mobile of tropical fish and beside a collection of turtle figurines. Sugar snuffled around my shoes for a moment, then clicked away across the kitchen floor and disappeared toward the bedrooms. The warm body against my legs felt as soothing as a heating pad on sore muscles. Poppy, who'd left the room to take Mama Ruth a sandwich, eased herself into a chair beside me when she returned.

"You ever wonder why people give stuffed animals to sick kids?" she said quietly.

"Uh — for presents?"

"Yes, but why *that*? Why not cars or Barbie dolls or games?"

I thought. Why would *I* give a stuffed animal to a child? "I don't know. Just because children like them."

She shook her head. "It's instinct. We just know that taking care of another creature makes us feel better."

I looked at the children, their backs to me, stroking the sleeping dogs in their laps. I supposed people gave stuffed animals to victims, not perpetrators, or else I might have had more experience with the phenomenon myself. Kevin pointed toward the remaining puppies, kneading their mother's belly in their sleep, and said something to Sarah.

"What happened there?" Poppy whispered to me, tilting her head toward Kevin and pointing at her own eye.

"Fight."

She nodded. "Ah. I see."

She probably did. Better than I did.

She eyed me for a moment. "You're worried about him, aren't you?"

I looked at Kevin now petting the two sleeping puppies in his lap in methodical, simultaneous strokes. I nodded. She nodded in response.

"You need some coffee?"

"That'd be nice. Not much sleep."

"I figured." She pushed herself out of her chair but stopped and looked down at me before going any further. "You figured out the collection yet?"

I'd gotten so accustomed to the chaos of items covering the walls and surfaces that it took me a moment to understand what she was talking about.

"No."

She nodded. "You're getting there."

As we stepped out into Poppy's overgrown front garden a half hour later, I discovered that under the full sun, my fears turned pale and shrank away. Other than this morning, Paul had yet to call during one of his trips, and I now couldn't explain why I ever imagined he would today. If everything was fine, he had no reason to make a special effort to tell me so. And if anything had gone seriously wrong, someone else would've called right away. So I told Kevin and Sarah to get in the car, then after we passed Mr. Fousek and let him know we were going to the store, I turned and asked if they'd like to go boat racing instead. They stared at me. I couldn't tell whether they were unsure what I was talking about or surprised I'd suggest we do anything fun. Perhaps they suspected I was trapping them into a chore.

"No, really," I said. "We'll go to the river and build boats and race them."

"How do we build them?" Kevin said.

"However you want. Use leaves, sticks, anything. They're just going to float away, so you don't want anything great. What do you think?"

"Who do we race?" Kevin again.

"Each other. Or nobody. It doesn't matter. There's no prize or anything. Come on — it's just for fun."

"I wanna go!" Sarah said, kicking the back of my seat and bouncing.

"Well?"

"Okay," Kevin said.

I drove them past the edge of town, to a place where the Arkansas River was shallow and wide, tumbling across the rocky stream-bed. Clumps of willows crowded the shore, and a sandy island split the river into twin

245

cords that twisted together again past its tip. I parked the car along the side of the road, and we walked together to the bank.

"Here," I said, bending over to pick some of the long, thin grasses at my feet. "You find some sticks and leaves. Use the grass to lash them together, any way you want. Then we'll let them go."

They were unsure of themselves at first, asking whether it was all right to use this leaf or that, to use a stick this big or that small, to try to make a sail or a mast. I agreed to everything. After she understood how to lash, Sarah adjusted quickly and started tying things together in any way that pleased her — four sticks bundled together with a leaf for decoration, a cluster of leaves joined at their stems and arrayed like a fan, a cracked Styrofoam coffee cup she'd found behind a rock, with a twig for a sail.

But Kevin struggled.

"Will this work?" he would ask at every design decision point.

"I don't know," I would say. "Try it and find out."

The answer frustrated him. For some reason, he needed to know exactly what result would come from his actions before he took them. He would turn away from me, wrestle a while longer, look at Sarah squatting at the river's edge with her strawberry-print shirt riding up her back, launching yet another craft, and then — though he surely knew he'd get another unsatisfactory answer — turn to me and ask my opinion again.

"Kevin," I said at one point as he frowned over a raft platform that had, for the third or fourth time, collapsed in on itself. "Lots of stuff won't work. That's okay. You have to see what *doesn't* work to find what *does.*"

"This is *shit.*" He froze momentarily, as if the word had escaped him by surprise, then flung the wad of sticks into the weeds.

My heart squeezed tight around the base of my throat. The sensation startled me. I was only a tick away from tears welling up over this bottled-up, earnest, anxious, angry boy at the intersection between adulthood and childhood, suffering in his grief the pains of both and therefore suffering more intensely than either. I wanted to pull him into my arms, tell him not to worry, to never mind about these dumb boats, that I was sorry I'd brought them here and would think of better things for him to do from now on.

"Lookit *that* one!" Sarah squealed, jumping up and pointing at the river. I could just make out something sticking upright from the water, bobbing along at a steady ninety-degree angle to the surface. She turned back to look at me, eyes round with delight and surprise. "It's my *best ever!*"

"That's great," I called back. She ran to a nearby clump of grass and doubled over to forage for raw material for another. I looked back at Kevin. No, avoidance wasn't the best strategy.

"Forget about the boats for a minute," I said. "I need to tell you a story."

He gave me a dark look, then started plucking grass from between his thighs. Perhaps he was relieved to not be in trouble over the profanity and therefore willing to listen.

"I had a friend a while ago." I cleared my throat. "A musician. A piano player." Kevin didn't need to know that the friendship, or whatever it was, had ended when I'd slept with Carlo. "He was a really, really good piano player. I used to watch him play, the way his fingers just seemed to feel the music. He could play the piano like other people sing. The music just came straight out of his fingers. Have you ever tried to play a piano?"

He snatched a fistful of grass. Nodded.

" 'Chopsticks'?"

He nodded again.

"Anything else?"

A pause. " 'Jingle Bells.' "

"Did you play it perfectly the first time?"

He shook his head.

"Me neither. My friend tried to teach me to play. But I was scared. I wouldn't let him."

Kevin looked up at me. Finally. "What were you scared of?"

"Mistakes. I was so afraid of making mistakes I wouldn't even try. My friend didn't understand that at all. He got kinda mad at me, actually. 'What's the problem?' he used to say. 'A mistake won't kill you.' He said he made mistakes all the time but he'd just keep playing straight on through. He said perfect wasn't real — painters made flubs, and actors forgot lines, and writers couldn't find words. The mistakes make things worth looking at." I squinted up toward the sun. Good God, I was an idiot. I looked back down. "But I still wouldn't do it."

Kevin had returned to plucking grass. Rip, toss. Rip, toss.

I picked up a stick and flicked it at him so that it grazed his neck. Startled, he looked up at me. "Listen," I said. "I was *wrong*. I missed out on a chance to learn how to play piano. How stupid was that?"

It's possible the corner of his mouth twitched. "Really stupid."

"Thank you. Now don't you be stupid. I don't care whether they're shit, but we're not leaving here until you've launched at least ten boats."

He took a deep breath and let it out slowly, then pushed himself off the ground and walked, gangly and stiff at the same time, toward a willow bush that leaned over the water like Narcissus himself.

I wrapped my arms around my knees and rested my chin on them, smelled the marshy tang of the water's edge mixed with the clear scent of sun-warmed grass. Kevin's first effort was a four-stick bundle, similar to one of Sarah's first but without the ornamental leaf. But she shrieked and cheered for him as if he'd just launched the *Queen Mary*. It bobbed briefly, then got sucked under in an eddy and emerged as four separate sticks. Sarah only clapped harder. Kevin glanced back at me, then set to work on his next one. His humility astonished me.

Mistakes are what make things interesting.

Sunlight glinted on the water as it tumbled over the rocks, icy and clear. After a few more efforts, Sarah and Kevin made a pair of boats they launched together, chasing them downstream and cheering them on until one came apart. I couldn't tell from their reactions whose it had been.

A mistake won't kill you.

Sure it might. Or worse, others. But I had to admit that being governed by that possibility hadn't served me especially well, either — expecting the worst from everything I touched, believing my actions would do only harm, then not accounting for my deliberate acts of sabotage in measuring the carnage around me. I hadn't been making mistakes all these years; I'd been trying to prevent unintentional disaster by taking paths I knew would end badly, in predictable ways, rather than those that only might. Calculated, manufactured, anticipated disaster would always be preferable to an accidental fire raging away from some misbegotten effort to enjoy myself.

I should have left Carlo alone.

I should have tried to play the piano.

I should have been willing to try something, anything, and allowed myself to make honest mistakes. Small ones. Maybe seeing small mistakes resolved would have made me less paralyzed by the fear of making another big one.

I lifted my hand to brush tears off my cheeks. Kevin stretched a hair beyond his reach to retrieve something from the current, slipped, and landed spread-eagled in the water. Sarah squealed with laughter, then Kevin pulled himself to his hands and knees, scooped a handful of water, and threw it at her.

At the far end of the valley, white mountaintops capped the steely blue of the lower slopes. The river's colors flowed from them — white ripples, blue water — like paint from an overloaded brush. It tumbled toward us, interrupted by rocks and plants and children at play, then carried on past no matter what they did in the midst of it.

I shouldn't have taken up with Carlo, whom I knew to be toxic and chose because I thought I could predict exactly how it would turn out. That was sabotage.

Now I was going to have a baby. That was a mistake.

But in time, it might not turn out to be the worst thing in the world.

After we got home and the children changed into dry clothes, I sent them outside to picnic on butter-and-sugar sandwiches and potato chips. They asked for Ding Dongs, and I gave them those, too. I even had one myself, and if it wasn't as good as I remembered, it was good enough. I took it outside and sat in a circle of sun on the back steps, watching the children peel the foil wrappers back from the cake to make little hats just as I used to. In fact, I got so absorbed making a foil airplane out of mine that it wasn't until the doorbell rang twice that I remembered how anxious I was to hear from Paul. Or news of him. I jumped to my feet, dropping the airplane onto the concrete. By the time I got through the house I had already placed the sheriff on the front step — the sweaty uniform, the hat in hand, the pursed lips. I yanked the front door open.

"Well?" Mindy said. Katy held a fold of her pants and the car idled in the road behind her.

"What?"

"Didn't you get my message?"

A chill touched my chest. "What message?"

"I called this morning. Hours ago. Have you been gone all this time?"

"Mostly, I guess."

"Look — could Katie stay while I take Alex to the doctor? I'll be back in an hour."

My shoulders relaxed. "Oh — sure. No problem."

"Are you positive it's okay? I tried Joan first, but she's at the dentist with Ben. I just thought for sure you'd be here."

"Of course." I looked down at the little girl. "Sarah will be really excited to see you. They're having a picnic in back. You go ahead, and I'll bring out some more food."

Without an answer, Katy darted past me and disappeared into the house. I figured she knew her way to the back door.

Mindy took a deep breath. "I'm sorry. You're saving me. I would've taken her if you weren't here, but she's horrible when Alex is getting all the attention. This is huge."

I heard the back door bang and a shriek of joy from Sarah. "It's nothing. Go."

"Thank you!" she called again as she turned back to the car.

I waved, and she blew me a kiss from over the hood. Was I missing something? The gratitude seemed out of scale. Perhaps there was some protocol for help-giving and help-receiving that I didn't understand. Or was this just honest adult friendship?

When everyone had finished eating, the girls shut themselves in Sarah's room, and I shooed Kevin away on his bike to go find some action somewhere. After yesterday's disaster at the pool, I thought it was important to get him back on the social horse. And maybe this morning's small success would make him a little more willing to just try something.

Mindy was back before the hour was out.

"Well, that was quick," I said as I let her in. "Is everything okay?"

"Yeah, I thought he was sick, but it's just teeth." She dropped her bag at the foot of my rollaway bed and switched the silent, staring, snot-nosed baby to her other hip. "Look, I'm really sorry about the way I just dumped Katy on you like that. It never occurred to me you wouldn't get the message. I'd been gone, too, so I thought I must've just missed you calling back."

"Not a problem. They've been playing the whole time. What message, anyway?"

"There's an answering machine. You need to check it."

"Are you kidding? That's none of my business."

Mindy rolled her eyes. "Oh, come on. You're the one who's here all the time. Nobody's leaving private messages for Paul. What if somebody wanted one of the kids to come play? Or if Paul wanted to tell you something, like he's been delayed for a day?"

Oh, God. Had I been missing it all along? "But I don't know where it is," I said.

"Can't be that hard. It's by one of the phones. Where are they?"

"I dunno. The one in the kitchen is the

only one I use."

She looked at the phone hanging on the kitchen wall. "Well, it sure isn't there. Bedroom. Come on."

As reluctant as I felt about prying any further into personal Kofford spaces, I was even more uncomfortable having Mindy lead me around the house. And more uncomfortable yet about how to say so, so I followed silently.

I could hear high-pitched chatter as we passed Sarah's closed door. Kevin's door hung half open, revealing an unmade bed and a pair of jeans on the floor, and the back door, half open as well, showed a sliver of uncut grass through the screen. Mindy opened the only other closed door, paused for a moment to look around, then said, "Ah! There we go."

A three-drawer dresser served as a bedside table, topped by a lamp, a half-empty glass of water, a dish containing some change and a paperclip and a couple of screws, then the phone and the flat black recording machine with its blinking light. Dust was thick in the dish and along the back of the dresser, though it looked like someone had tried to swipe the front part clean.

"I've never used one," I said. As close as we might have been to the same age, I felt a generation gap yawn between us. What need did anyone in my sphere have for an answering machine that would capture invitations to a Bad Company concert, date-stamped in proper order? Meanwhile, Mindy lived in a world of people arranging pediatrician appointments and needing to know whether a child had gotten hurt at school.

"Easy." Mindy pressed a button as I sat on the edge of the bed.

A whir, a click, and then a voice I didn't recognize: "Hey. I had to go to Mom's. The kids are sleeping over at Cathy's, so you can get them in the morning if you get back late. It's just . . ." There was a long pause, a noise that might have been a sigh, then, "I really need to get away. I need it. But we're gonna be fine, okay?" Another pause, then a click.

Mindy looked at the machine for a moment, then pressed another button. Mindy's voice: "Hi. Elena — it's Mindy. I just wonder if I could bring Katy by for a little while this afternoon. I have to take Alex to the doctor and she's driving me crazy. Let me know. It's at two. Thanks — bye." A click. Mindy pressed another button.

"I erased it," she whispered.

"The *whole thing*?"

"No — no. Just mine. It should be back to the way it was. I don't think he'll know you heard it."

I looked at the machine, then back up at Mindy. "That was Carrie, wasn't it?"

She nodded. Then dropped onto the bed beside me, Alex facing forward on her lap. She wrapped her arms around his belly. "The date was on the screen. It was the night she died."

Sarah's door banged open hard against a doorstop that was only marginally successful in keeping her from putting dents in the wall, and the two girls flashed by the open bedroom door, a swirl of sundresses and loose blonde hair, wiry arms and legs. The screen door squealed, then clapped shut, leaving only emptiness behind them.

"They were wearing shorts when they started," I said.

Mindy gave a half-laugh and rested her lips against Alex's head. "Girls can't do anything alone," she finally said.

We sat in silence while the sun played through the leaves outside the window and into our laps. Alex tugged at his shirt and watched his hands twist in the fabric.

"Look, I don't want be nosy," I said, "but can I ask you some questions? About the Koffords, I mean."

"Sure."

"Okay, so, why am I here, really? I mean,

why doesn't Paul just get a job at the mine like everybody else?"

Mindy took a deep breath. "It's — kinda complicated. His dad died in a mine accident when Paul was — I dunno. A kid. Anyway, his mom always felt like the dad was made into a scapegoat for the accident, that she didn't get enough of a settlement. She wound up being kind of a nut around here, always going on about Climax being evil and trying to get more money. She only died a couple of years ago. I don't know how Paul felt about it, but, this is Paul, you know? He'll be loyal to his mother forever. I think it's a principle thing to make it on his own, not walk in there with his hat in his hand asking for work."

"I get it," I said. I sat for a moment, then took a deep breath. "Okay, next. Was Carrie pregnant when she died?"

Mindy didn't answer right away, then turned to face me, her cheek now resting on the baby's head. "Why do you ask?"

"Sarah said her mom was going to have a baby. And then she started talking about something else, so that's all I know."

"Hmm." She looked down and stretched the hem of Alex's shirt to wipe a puddle of facial fluids that had started to form on her arm. "That makes sense, actually. The last

259

time she did my hair I noticed this sleeve of crackers on her counter, and then one of the other girls walked by with a hamburger and she made some comment about the smell. So I remember I wondered for a sec. But she didn't look sick — she looked really happy." She put her lips back on the baby's head. "Hmm," she repeated. "I bet you're right." Another pause. "Wow." And another. "I wonder if Paul knew."

"What?"

She took a deep breath. "Carrie kept a lot of secrets. But she never kept them to herself. She'd tell one person something and say not to tell anybody else. Then she'd tell somebody else something different. And they usually weren't any big deal — things like 'I have a rip in this shirt — don't tell anybody.' Or 'I took Sarah for ice cream. Don't tell Paul.' There was a lot of 'don't tell Paul.' "

"You think she'd really tell her five-year-old and not her husband?"

"Honestly?" Mindy nodded. "I do. I loved her, but it's so easy to see her saying 'It's our little secret' that I hardly have to try."

I pondered for a moment, then pushed my hands against my knees and stood. I went around the foot of the bed and swung the closet door all the way open. I tugged the string.

"And what about this?" I asked.

Mindy hitched one leg underneath herself and twisted toward the closet. It took a moment for her eyes to focus on the overflowing shelves.

"Oh, that poor, poor man."

Sensing opportunity, Alex dove out of her arms, face-planting himself on the bed. Mindy let him go.

I took a deep breath. "Mindy, I'm about to ask you one more thing you'll probably just laugh at but I really, really need you to give me a serious answer."

She nodded.

"Is there a chance, *any* chance at all, that Paul is going to give up and run away and leave me with these children?"

Her eyes met mine and held. Mindy knew nothing about my history or her own, which made her answer all the more miraculous to me. "No. People can be incredibly selfish and stupid, but they aren't all that way. That's not what Carrie was doing when she died, and it's not something Paul would ever do. He stood by Carrie no matter what. He will never leave his children. Never."

18

Mindy had insisted on paying me back for my minimal babysitting by taking both children the next afternoon. She said she had some yard work to do and Kevin could help with the baby while the girls played. She told the kids to bring swimsuits to play in the sprinkler.

It was a hot day, by local standards, though far from what southern California had taught me to label that way. But I felt perfectly comfortable on a lawn chair in the Koffords' backyard, shaded by the house, a glass of iced tea nested in the long grass beside me, the mythology book open on my lap.

The illustrations were strangely compelling — Prometheus chained to a rock, head thrown back in a cry for relief as an eagle tore at his liver; Demeter bowing into herself in grief, with all the plants of the earth wilting around her as her daughter returned to Hades. The stories were at once simple and profound — the jealousy, the grief, the anger, the longings and disappointments, the little victories and unintended consequences. I could see that mythology was not so different from physics: both trying to explain that all the disproportion and imbalance in the world only appeared that way and were the products of forces we could not see.

When I heard Paul's pickup pull up in front of the house, I was looking at a picture of Zeus in a columned hall, surveying tiny fields and towns below Olympus. He held a white urn against his hip, tilted, and reached into it with one hand to cast blessings, the story told me, on those he chose to favor below. A black urn of sorrows stood at his feet. Actual people were minuscule from that perspective, so insignificant in their joys or troubles that the gods could rub them between their fingers like sand. I'd been looking at the picture for some time.

I heard the pickup come to a stop but couldn't stir myself. Paul was early, by a few hours. He went into the house through the front door, and I heard him calling for someone to answer but I waited until he came closer.

"Out here," I said when I believed he'd

hear me.

He pushed open the screen door and stood in the opening, four fingers in his jeans pocket, birthmark wrapped around his neck.

"Hey," he said. "Where are the kids?"

"At Mindy's. She invited them to play in the sprinkler. She said she'd bring them back before dinner."

"What's for dinner?"

The question shouldn't have bothered me. He hadn't been expected until early evening, so of course I would've planned dinner, and of course he had a right to show up early and eat his own food with his own family. But I felt as if he was checking on me in my momentary idleness. Suddenly he was Paul the dictator again. A fissure opened, releasing the fear and anger I'd sealed away since his call at the beginning of the week.

"I don't know. Did you have a good trip?" I made no move to get up.

"Fine. Just fine."

Confronting a problem acknowledged its reality and was something I would ordinarily avoid at all costs. But I wasn't going to do that today. The knowledge surprised me.

"Your call on Monday night really scared me," I said.

He frowned, whether unable to remember or unhappy that I had I couldn't tell.

"I guess it was Tuesday morning," I added when he didn't answer. "From Green River. At the truck stop. I couldn't get back to sleep. I waited by the phone for hours."

"You thought I'd call again."

"I thought it'd be the highway patrol. To tell me you'd driven the truck off a cliff somewhere."

He looked down, dug with the toe of his boot against the threshold.

"You were drunk," I said.

He took a deep breath. "Yup." Twisted his toe again. Then he looked up and met my gaze. "I didn't drive," he said. "I went to sleep in the cab. I wouldn't take chances. You need to know that."

His eyes were level and hollow, unflinching. Honest.

"You wanted me to call and say I was all right," he said.

"Sure did."

He bent his head and nodded to his boot, then shook his head. A deep breath and a pause. "So I guess you checked for messages."

I was an only child and therefore a terrible liar. "Yes."

"Did you listen to the tape?"

I looked down at the book folded over my finger. Zeus, with the jar of troubles at his feet, perhaps growing bored with bestowing blessings and about to return to what he did best. By the time I looked back up I probably didn't need to answer.

"Yes."

He looked at the hand in his pocket, then pulled out a piece of lint or dirt that he rolled between his fingers and flicked away. He stepped outside and let the screen door close. He sat heavily on the top step and faced me, forearms on his knees, hands dangling. The ends of his fingers were stained.

"It's probably time I explained some things. You live with my children. In my house. They say things. *I* said things the other night. You probably have some ideas about us."

I didn't know how to answer. I waited.

"And you've seen things. The closet. You've seen what she collected in the closet."

I nodded. I wished I didn't have to.

He took a deep breath. "Carrie was the most popular girl in school. You've seen pictures. Probably can't figure out why she picked me. So beautiful — that huge smile, so much life. Everybody wanted to be around her. I couldn't believe how lucky I was. I didn't ask why. God, why would I?"

He turned his hands over and curled the fingers toward himself as if checking the cuticles, then dropped them again. "Carrie was — reckless, which was part of why she was so much fun. She'd get an idea and act. Didn't matter if it made sense. When she was younger, it was just Carrie being crazy — fun crazy, coming up with stuff that other people wouldn't think of or would be afraid to do. Let's skinny-dip at Twin Lakes. Throw firecrackers down an old mine shaft. That kind of stuff. Everybody loved her. Everybody — they told me so, all the time. And sure, it's fun, but when you live with her, it'll wear you out. You know anybody like that? Of course you do." His own answer seemed sufficient and he went ahead without waiting for one from me. "It's hard," he said, shaking his head. "Real hard. And then the ideas got to be just plain crazy."

He took a deep breath that lifted his shoulders. "You know," he said, looking off to the side, "I can say that now. Crazy. I didn't when she was alive. She was just lively. Or moody. Or sensitive. Never crazy. But that's not right. Sometimes, the ideas took over — let's throw Sarah a princess party in the snow when it's ten below and the wind's blowing. Kevin should learn how to knit. Foods shouldn't touch each other. Let's get in the car right now and go to the beach." He gestured upward with his hands, offering the ideas to heaven. "And when I said no, she'd get angry. Whatever she wanted to do was the most important thing in the world."

I'd had it all wrong. All, all, all wrong. The controlling husband, the abused wife. Instead Paul, so ordered and predictable, must have been an anchor to the storm-tossed Carrie. She might have flailed against the restraint, but the anchor was what kept her from being swept out to sea.

"That's why I got the answering machine, you know? If I couldn't stop her from launching off on some half-baked scheme, I wanted to give her a way to at least let me know where she was and what she was doing. It worked, some. Better than nothing."

He looked at me. "Like you wanted me to call you. I'm sorry."

"It's okay."

"You've had Mr. Fousek stop you, at the bottom of the road, to ask where you're going?"

I nodded. I could feel my face warm.

Paul shook his head and looked away.

"God, you must've thought I was some kind of tyrant." He brushed his knee with the back of his hand. "He's a good man. I just asked him to keep an eye out. Can you imagine how embarrassing that was? But he never asked me a thing, just nodded and did it. Couple times I knew Carrie was in a bad spell, came home, and everybody was gone. Middle of winter, cold, ice on the roads — I was scared to death. But he told me what he knew and let it be. Good man."

"Of course."

"I made sure they had the right food in their lunches. Even food at all, sometimes. Made sure Sarah was dressed okay. That they went to school."

His voice had gotten tighter as he spoke, and now I could see the rims of his eyes start to thicken. I looked away and watched a squirrel spiral its way up an aspen tree and disappear into the leaves. After a few moments he cleared his throat and went on.

"I was afraid of losing her," he said. "From the beginning. It never went away. That's why I keep that message."

I looked at him, not comprehending. All I remembered was, "I really need to get away," which seemed like the last thing a husband would want to hear over and over.

"You remember what she says at the end?"

269

I shook my head.

"She says, 'We're gonna be fine.' " He paused. *"We."* He shifted his weight on the step. "When I think about it, by myself, run through it a few times in my mind, I start to hear *I*. She says *I'm* gonna be fine." He shook his head. "No. She didn't leave us. The ice took her away. That's what I have to remember."

He put his hands to his knees and stood, then brushed the seat of his jeans. "I'm sorry I worried you. You're doing a real fine job with those kids. They're doing better than I've seen since their mama died. I appreciate it more than I can say."

He gave me a nod, turned, and went back inside, the screen clapping shut behind him. I looked down at the book in my lap. There was no reason to be surprised. Whether it was the tiny Greek man and his plow, or Paul and his truck, or me and a spark in the weeds, the giant god remained overhead. It didn't matter who you were. If you got in the way of the divine debris, you were screwed.

Though I was invited, I didn't stay at the Koffords' to eat the spaghetti dinner I'd thrown together. I could tell Paul's invitation was only polite and I couldn't imagine sitting at that table and making casual eye contact with any of them. I wasn't family. I shouldn't know the things I now did. I folded my bed and pushed it against the wall while Paul unpacked in the bedroom, then called to him that I was leaving to pick up the kids from Mindy's. I found them all behind the house, where the girls, in swimsuits, ran and shrieked while Kevin kinked the hose to make the fountain sprinkler stop and start. Mindy sat on the shaded steps, elbows on her knees, with a magazine folded over itself.

"Hey, there," she said, looking up as I rounded the corner of the house. She set the magazine behind herself and scooted a few inches to the side, leaving room for me to sit. "What are you doing here? I was going to bring them home."

"Paul got home early." I turned toward the sprinkler. "Kevin! Sarah! You need to dry off. Your dad's home."

They continued without so much as a glance my way, as if separated from me by a wall of glass.

"Is everything okay?" Mindy said.

"It's fine. Sarah! Come get your towel!"

"Do I have to go through the whole thing again about not pretending things are fine when they aren't?"

271

Kevin released the water just as Katy was at mid-jump over the sprinkler, and both girls squealed and ran away. I sat. "He figured out I heard the tape."

"Oh, no." Mindy squinted and wrinkled her nose at me. "Is it bad?"

"No, it's fine. I'm fine. He's fine. I just — wish I didn't know any of it."

"Of what?"

"Stuff about their marriage. Their life. He told me a lot. And none of it is any of my business, and here I am living with them — it's just weird. And so sad. Now I just want to take the kids back to their house, leave them there, and disappear."

"I'm sorry."

Kevin had started shutting off and releasing the water in a steady rhythm, and the girls began to sidle back toward the sprinkler.

"How much did you know?" I asked.

"Not much. Just guesses. She was so kind, but — I dunno. On edge. There was always — something. Tense, maybe. Like a deer ready to bolt."

I sighed. "I had everything wrong. Paul's a really good man. I thought he was some kind of tyrant — all these weird rules, the way he needed to tell me every little thing to do. He was just doing the best he could.

It was an awful situation. I was an idiot."

"Hey, don't misjudge yourself the same way. You're doing great things with those kids." She lifted her thin chin toward the children. Kevin had let the girls start to trust the rhythm and they were now leaping across the sprinkler during the shut-offs. "Look at them. Even when their mom was alive, I don't think I ever saw them play together like that. I think Kevin's learning how to be a kid. You're making things better, you know."

I didn't, but she was kind to say so. And it was a nice idea to return to late that night, after I took the children back to their father, waved good-bye, and then couldn't stop thinking about them the rest of the evening. Working on my list of what to take to the cabin in the morning didn't distract me. Leo calling and asking for a ride up to the ranch didn't distract me. Instead I just kept replaying the conversation with Paul, circling around again and again to examine it and pick at it like a caged bird given a ball of yarn. The ramifications of what I now knew — on what the children's real needs were, on what I could or should or should not say or do — were larger and more complex than I could sort out, and worrying at the yarn was only making me feel more tangled in it. But finally, alone in the dark, as I curled under the quilts that night, the picture came back: I saw Kevin, spraying the girls in mid-leap one last time. I saw the girls shrieking and laughing and wiping water out of their eyes, then grabbing the sprinkler and turning it on him so that he jumped up and started to run as well. I saw three children, laughing in the sun, and the shining drops falling around them.

19

"How was your trip?" Tuah asked when I got out of the car beside the cabin Saturday morning.

"Fine. Did you set that up, too?"

"Set what up?"

I squinted at her, then lifted the back hatch of the Pinto. It was possible, I supposed, that she hadn't been involved. I handed her a stack of mail, folded in the current week's newspaper.

"Leo. I gave him a ride to the ranch."

"So that's what took you so long. Why didn't he drive himself?"

That was the right answer. "He lent a guy his car. It worked out fine. I just thought you might have been meddling."

"I didn't meddle last time."

I rolled my eyes.

"And I trust he didn't try to steal your virtue?" She played the straight man perfectly, reading a postcard with some sort of

275

beach picture on the back, not looking at me, giving no hint of a smile.

"Ha, ha." I hoisted a bag of groceries onto my hip. "Maybe tomorrow. He asked me to go to some Fourth of July cookout at the ranch before I go back to town."

"That sounds nice." She shoved the mail into one of the grocery bags and picked it up, then got another. She started inside, then turned her head back to say over her shoulder, "You talked to your dad?"

"What? No. Why?"

"That card was from him. You didn't look through the mail?"

"No. What's it say?"

"He's coming."

She disappeared into the darkness through the door. It took me a moment to fully register what she was saying but less to realize what unwelcome news it was. I crumpled the top of another bag in my fist and followed her.

"What? When?"

"A couple of weeks." She set her bags on the table.

"Well, what's he going to do?" I said. "I'm busy with the kids. He knows we can't just hang out, right?"

"Of course."

"So he'll just sit around up here with you?"

"I can come up with some chores for him. But I've got things he can do in town, too, where he can see you some."

What was I doing? Trying to argue with the universe about why he shouldn't come? I set down my own bags, then glanced at Mac, who thumped his tail once in acknowledgment of my slight attention without looking away from the food. He probably already knew which bag held the bacon.

Tuah reached inside the first bag, set the mail on the table, then followed it with two cartons of strawberries, a block of cheese, and a bunch of bananas.

"Have you told him about the baby?" she asked.

"No." I hadn't called since confirming my safe arrival weeks ago.

"Have you called the doctor?"

Tuah had left a name and number on a pad of paper beside the phone in the Leadville kitchen. I'd seen it but had observed a perimeter around it as if it were nettles or poison oak.

"No."

"Have you told anybody?"

"Mindy." I rolled my shoulders. "It was kind of an accident." I looked out the open door at my car, the hatch still gaping open. "And Leo. That was an accident, too."

She folded the bag flat. "And it looks like you survived."

"I guess."

"I think a few more accidents like that won't kill you, either."

"So you want me to march up to strangers and tell them I'm pregnant?"

"Nope. But it doesn't have to be a secret, either. And you need to get to the doctor and make your plans. Besides — pretty soon folks'll start wondering anyway, and then they'll just gossip about it." She pulled the next bag closer to herself, then reached inside. "I'll give you a tip. When you live in a small town, tell your own secrets. People have to think they can talk *to* you about anything. Then they won't talk *about* you."

I felt cords tighten around me. Plans and a future. *When you live in a small town.* Well, I didn't live in a small town. I was here only temporarily. Given my typical wardrobe, I'd be gone before anything really showed. In the two weeks since I'd seen her last, what had put the idea into her head that I would live here? And even if I did, I doubted her advice about preventing gossip was right. I'd sat at the Powder Keg last weekend with a table full of gossips. And those stories about Benencia could only have been started by people talking to each other behind her back.

"I've been in the car for a long time," I said. "I'm gonna go for a walk."

"Take Mac with you," Tuah said. "And some water." She held up a package of Oreos. "Good thinking on these, by the way."

I walked wherever Mac led. He ranged back and forth into the trees, snuffing at elk droppings or cow pies or dead things I didn't want to imagine, stopping to investigate some new scent, then loping ahead, tail waving, checking over his shoulder from time to time to see whether I was having as much fun as he was.

I needed to take lessons from the dog. Yes, my father was coming, but why did that matter? I would tell him about the baby when I was good and ready, without regard for when he scheduled his visit. Or never tell him at all. When had he ever noticed me cutting my hair or getting new clothes? Surely unbuttoned jeans and loose T-shirts would get me through his visit without him suspecting anything. And as for my inference that Tuah had some hidden agenda to keep me here — that's all it was. Inference.

Even if she *had* stood there in her canvas pants and ordered me to get a job at JCPenney and marry a miner and stay in Leadville forever, she had no power over me. I wasn't being forced into anything by anybody. I'd overreacted. Maybe it was hormones. Calm down.

We climbed toward timberline along a cow path, sat side by side at a rock outcrop where I could look back down over Hat Creek and watch cloud shadows drift over it, and then Mac led the way back to the house. Like him, I smelled the cabin before I saw it, but only barely, just as I rounded a landmark boulder that diverted the trail and blocked the house's rear from view. He'd probably been able to smell it the whole time.

Take Mac with you. The refrain had been the same my whole life. *Take Rex with you,* Tuah had said when I was small. She never joined in my parents' lectures and scoldings about needing to tell them where I was going, but it was probably her doing that the dog would inevitably appear somewhere nearby after I'd slipped away.

She had a dog that stayed with her no matter what.

I missed a step, scuffing my foot against a

rock. My memory, Leo's story, Benencia's loss.

Well ahead of me now, Mac jumped onto the porch and disappeared. He still had his head in the water bowl when I rounded the side of the house and stepped onto the porch.

"Nice walk?" Tuah said as I came through the open door. She sat at the table, a cup of coffee at her elbow, reading the newspaper, glasses perched halfway down her nose. Two dishpans of water — one soapy, one just murky — sat at the other end of the table. The groceries had all been put away.

"Yeah. Sorry — I should've stayed and helped with the groceries. And you should've waited on the dishes. I would've done them."

"There weren't many. Groceries or dishes. You can dump the water."

I poured the contents of the soapy water into the rinse water, nested the full pan into the empty one, then went outside and tossed the water into the bushes set back from the trail. After rinsing the pans at the pump, I came back inside and got a towel to dry them.

"You know, I wonder," I said as I wiped. "With Benencia, did you have a dog that went with her, too?"

Tuah looked up over the rim of her glasses. A faint smile.

"Yes." She set the newspaper down and took her glasses off. "Why do you ask?"

"It's just — for as long as I can remember, if I was going farther than the privy, you've always said, 'Take Mac' or 'Take Rex.' "

"You remember Rex?"

"Of course. I cried for days when I heard he'd died."

"He was a good dog. He had a big job, keeping you out of trouble."

I tucked the dishpans into their spot below the shelves.

"I wondered about Benencia getting lost," I said. I pulled a chair out and sat facing her. "Whether there was a dog. If there was, and he was anything like Mac or Rex, I don't know how she could've stayed lost."

She'd started nodding before I finished. "You're right," she said. "We did have a dog. Gus. Just a good ranch dog. Common sense dog. He seemed to know Bennie needed extra help, and he never let her out of his sight. But your father —" She shook her head. "Your father was a handful. Gus felt like he needed to watch out for him, too. If he had to choose, he'd follow Benencia, but you could see he didn't like it. He'd hang back and try to watch both of them as long

282

as he could, but the minute Bennie disappeared, he'd go straight after her."

"She did that a lot?"

Tuah smiled and nodded. "Like you."

"So how did she get lost?"

She gave a long, deep sigh. "Gus died."

"He did? When?"

"A few days before. I don't think Benencia understood. I've always wondered if she went looking for him."

"He just — died? You mean, old age or something?"

"No. He was old, all right, but no. He was shot."

"What?"

"Shot. By a hunter. It was fall — things like that happened every year. Ranchers would have cows getting shot — they still do, in fact. Folks had to be extra careful walking around up here."

"But a *dog*?"

She shrugged her shoulders. "People don't think. They're looking for deer, thinking about deer, something moves just out of sight, and they shoot. Besides — he was a big dog."

"Dad remembers a dog big enough to ride."

"That'd be Gus, all right. Such a good dog. I'm surprised he remembers. He was pretty young."

"Oh, he remembers a lot."

She glanced at the newspaper, then looked back at me. "But he never said anything about Gus being shot?"

It seemed like I wouldn't have just lost track of him mentioning something like that. "No, I don't think so."

"Huh. Maybe he didn't know." She looked down at the glasses she still held by one earpiece, which she rolled between her thumb and forefinger so that they tapped a couple of times against the table. She looked back up at me. "You've heard the stories, then."

I didn't know how to answer. I felt as if I'd been caught spying.

"Who told you?" she went on. "One of the children?"

"Ah —"

"Because that's how I first heard. I was at the school, telling about Hat Creek, and when they found out I lived up here I could see their eyes get big as dishes. A little girl said, 'Aren't you *scared*?' I thought they were talking about bears or the dark or being alone, but then they started to tell me about the ghost."

"How awful."

She set down the glasses and reached for

284

the coffee, took a sip, then set the cup back down. "It's all right. I grew up in Arizona hearing about a railroad ghost. After that," she gestured vaguely down the mountain with her thumb, "with the children and the story, I wondered whether that railroad ghost had a widow walking around town with us."

I could hear the faint drone of a plane passing by, high overhead. The question that had been nagging me since I first learned Benencia's story wouldn't let go.

"Have you ever thought," I started. "I mean, about what happened to Benencia, have you ever thought about it being — something else? I just — it's the stories. Could a part of them be true? Could somebody have done something to her?"

"No." The firmness and finality of her answer surprised me. I waited for elaboration that didn't come.

"You sound sure."

"I am. The stories don't mean anything. I know how they work. There has to be something evil, something tragic to make it a story. People make up whatever they want."

"But still — nobody really knows what happened. And stories get started somewhere. You said yourself you're only guessing."

Tuah leaned forward on her elbows. "How far did you walk today?"

"I dunno. A couple of miles."

"And all your years here, all your walks, how many miles?"

"I — have no idea."

"Have you ever just run into somebody? Said howdy?"

"No."

"Listen to me," she said. "This town is all there ever was up here. There's these houses, then nothing. A handful of ranches. All we had was each other. I *knew* these people. Can you understand that? Living up here — it makes you family. Bennie was their child as much as she was ours. No one had secrets here, or secrets that lasted very long. We knew the truth about each other and hung on together anyway. Every soul in this town helped look for her. Some got sick trying. Women fed us and did our wash and took care of Roberto when I couldn't do any of it."

She made a sweeping gesture toward the open door. "And that's all there ever was. It was one of us — someone that was part of this whole big family — or she got lost."

She took the coffee mug in one hand and

stood, looking down at me.

"She got lost," Tuah said.

20

"Any idea what this is?"

I held up a small bolt I'd just found near the paint bucket. It was afternoon now, warm and still, and we were painting the porch. We'd said nothing further about Benencia, and I was glad to be busy.

The wide plank siding was finished, deep yellow, as rich as butter. The porch posts and trim, streaked with whatever gray remained after scraping, would be white. But first we had to paint the underside of the porch roof, for which she'd chosen a robin's-egg blue. She'd finished the worst part of the job — scraping and caulking — before I came, so together now we stood on chairs and craned our necks backward, pulling the color of the sky through the roof and spreading it across the boards. Mac lay dreaming and twitching below us.

Tuah squinted. "Is it part of the bucket?"

"No, it's too big."

"Huh. Just toss it in the jar."

In Leadville it was on the utility room windowsill; here it was on the shelves by the stove. The magpie jar, she called it: a mason jar of collected odds and ends — buttons, screws, clips, rings, lids, springs. "If you don't know what it is, where it goes, or what it's for, it goes in the jar," Tuah would say.

"Okay."

"Oh!" she said as I started inside. "There was a letter for you. It's on the table. Probably under the paper."

"For me? Who from?" Instinctive fear pushed a picture of Carlo into my head, but that was impossible. And a *letter*? No way. I don't think I ever saw him write anything longer than a phone number. No one knew where I was, and beyond him — allowing, of course, for the supernatural power that would advise him about the baby in the first place — I couldn't imagine anyone who would go to extraordinary efforts to find me.

"I don't know. It's your letter."

I went inside, dropped the bolt in the jar, and after a moment's rummaging with the newspaper, found the envelope. It was from the Florida Institute of Technology, with a logo showing a Florida map with tiny star along the Atlantic coast. My name and the

Leadville address were typewritten on the front. Why and how would someone there find me here, when I'd never so much as heard of them? I tore it open. The letter inside was on university letterhead, typewritten, and nearly filled the page. I glanced down to the signature — *Cora,* with the flourish at the end of the *a* resolved into a heart, and below it, *Cora de la Cruz, Student Advisement.* Good God. Cora had been my advisor at UCLA, the one who had taken me on as some sort of special case and hounded me to go to grad school until she moved away. What had it been — six months ago? Quite the display of dedication.

She started with small talk — congratulating herself on the detective skills she'd exercised to get my grandmother's address, asking whether I'd made it through graduation all right. And finally, the reason for writing: She wanted to let me know about a teaching-exchange program specifically for female graduate students in the sciences. I'd be perfect for it, she thought. It would let me get a master's degree for almost nothing. I could take admission tests in the fall. Be accepted by January. Go back to school next fall.

I could start over.

I sank into the wooden chair and looked

out the window. The glass pane had been swung open to the inside and pushed the white curtain aside. I could see a section of the porch roof, still brown, and Tuah's paintbrush spreading blue into the edge of the visible square, then dragging back out. In and out.

I reread the letter a half dozen times. *Go back to school.* By the time I had the baby, the door to Florida would just be opening. I could erase this year altogether and return to the world I knew. Bodies at rest. Bodies in motion. Energy expended or conserved. Action and reaction: weighed, measured, and accurately predicted.

Once the baby was delivered and taken away, I could do anything I wanted. I just hadn't thought about it lately. What better option could I have than this? Staying here, taking a job as a store clerk or a secretary at the mine office? Looking at every woman with a baby and wondering if it was mine? I'd be winding myself into Tuah's apron like a scared four-year-old. And the longer I did it, the harder it would be to ever get away.

I'd already started, I could now see. Grabbing hold of one apron string when I unpacked my clothes, winding it around my finger when I bought toothpaste and a toothbrush to leave at the Koffords', wrapping my wrist when I told Leo I'd see him again. I just hadn't been paying attention to what those things implied, hadn't thought to resist each inference and expectation as it appeared. Nothing in Tuah's comments that morning should have surprised me. No, my need to get out of the house in that moment had come from feeling the strings pull, not because they were touching me for the first time. And certainly not because of hormones. Reading this letter, though, made me feel as if tightening restraints had just dropped off. I flipped over the envelope. Melbourne, Florida. There would be classrooms and laboratories. Columns of figures. Formulas. Outside, the roll of waves, on and on into eternity. Me, standing on the sand. Alone. Free.

A thump and a scrape. Tuah getting off the chair and moving it a foot or two.

"Are you all right?" she called.

"Fine. I'll be out in a minute."

Free.

"You know who I feel sorry for right now?" Tuah said.

We sat on opposite ends of the porch, backs to each other, doubled over, reaching under our backsides to slop a base coat under its edge.

"What?" I twisted upright. She'd caught me completely off guard.

"Not what. Who. And it's your mama. She's missed out on a lot."

This turn of conversation disoriented me. Just a minute before we'd been talking about how much ice I should bring up next time I came, which was about all the complexity I was capable of processing at the moment. I'd woken up with a headache, having spent most of the night with my thoughts chasing each other in the dark. Now, a full day after reading Cora's letter, I was, if anything, even farther away from resolving what to do with myself. Or any other self. What seemed so simple when I first read the letter had grown complicated when I started to consider the realities. Where would I find a job? Or live? And how, with a pregancy that would be fully visible if I went to Florida at the end of the summer? Or would I stay here to give birth, then flee, leaving Tuah with the knowledge that there was a great-grandchild somewhere nearby? Available decisions and consequences circled and twisted until my head throbbed with knots. And here, on the edge of the porch, I'd suddenly found it impossible to sit and bend with the top button closed on my jeans. Of course. Today.

These boards, this house, these mountains were my family's history. They were baked into my bones and were being transferred, cell by cell, into the bones of the creature pressing against my pants. If I went to Florida, what, really, would happen to that child there? What would life be like in the family that took it in? Would they stay there? Stay together? Break apart as my family had done? How could I ever satisfy myself that I had done the right thing?

I rubbed my nose with the back of my wrist. "I don't think she cares," I said.

"Only because she doesn't know what she's missed. I'm sorry for her."

A jumble of scenes crowded into my head like shoppers shoving through the door for a clearance sale. My mother bending over me at night, a kiss on my forehead, my father telling me in the morning that she was gone. Sitting alone in the lunch shelter at my first new elementary school, in fourth grade, plucking grapes from their stems as if they needed my full attention. Packing moving boxes. Watching *Marcus Welby* with my father, the room dark, both of us silent.

"Why are you saying this?"

"Well, it's true."

"It's true that it's summer, but you're not talking about that."

She scooted sideways along the edge of the porch, her back a rectangle of chambray, her head invisible between her shoulders. "Well, now, that's right. I guess just because I'm thinking about the baby."

Gear teeth of logic dropped into place against each other. Now I could see where she was going: My mother had left me, and I would probably leave my own baby. My mother had missed my childhood, for better or worse, and I might miss my own child's life. My mother's absence had scarred me, and my absence would — do what, exactly? I pressed my lips together, dipped the brush in the can, and spread more paint. Yes, leaving my baby — whether here or in Florida — would entail pain I had glossed over in my rush to embrace an escape. But focusing on that would only cost me more sleep.

"You know, having a child hurts," Tuah said. "Don't let anybody fool you on that score. But then the pain is over, and you've got a baby."

You've got a baby? *Got?* I straightened again and twisted toward her. "But I don't *want* a baby."

"Well of course you weren't setting out to have one," she said. "But something seems to happen, no matter what. When those eyes look at you, well, the whole world changes."

What was she talking about? Eyes? Looking at me? It was hard enough to figure out
what to do with something I only imagined
as a swaddled bundle or a faceless person
leading a separate life somewhere. Not an
actual soul I would have to engage with.
Not a sentient child anchored to a life I
couldn't even manage for myself. No, no,
no.

"I can't keep a *baby*!"

She laid her brush across the top of her
paint can, got up, and walked across the
porch to sit down beside me. She put a
hand on my knee.

"I didn't say you *should* keep the baby. Or
give it up. I've got no place to say one way
or another. I just want you to be prepared
that whatever you decide, it'll be hard. Real
hard."

"I *know.*"

"No, I don't think you do. Nobody does.
Nothing can prepare you for what you'll feel
for that child in your arms. Nothing about
it will be easy."

"But my mom —" I'd gotten ahead of
myself and bit off the rest.

"Your mama was a frightened woman, her
whole life. When she left you and your dad,
she didn't make that decision because it was
easy. She did it because she was afraid, and

I can promise you she regrets it every day of her life." Her hand tightened on my knee. "The decisions you make when you're scared . . ." She shook her head. "You'll always wish you could go back and do something different."

I looked down. Her hand on my knee was sinewy and corded with veins. The nails were rough. I had the same oval nail beds that went to the tips of my fingers.

"I can't keep a baby," I whispered. Were the baby's fingers forming like that, too? What other traits from me, from my father, from Tuah and Abuelo, or traits from my mother I didn't even know about, were reaching through me like rhizomes through earth, now pushing up a new shoot?

"That's not a decision. That's an objection. If you've made your decision, then what are you afraid of? Be brave. See the doctor. Make your plans. Figure out what you're going to do between now and the delivery, then start thinking about what's next."

"But, who do I talk to? How am I supposed to handle everything? What if I make the wrong decision?"

"There may not be a right one. But there's going to be one. You need to give yourself a fighting chance to have some confidence about it."

"What if . . . it . . . winds up someplace bad? Has a terrible life?" My voice was creeping higher. This was an awful time for me to be talking about this. The center of my chest, on the inside, already felt as raw as an open blister. My head throbbed. "I can't live with . . ."

Tuah didn't wait too long for the words that wouldn't come. She rubbed my knee. "People live with a lot of things. You do what you have to. And then you go on living."

I looked back up. "How? *How?* How do you know? What decision have you *ever* made that you regretted?"

She released my knee and leaned back. "Oh, good heavens. Lots of things."

"Name one."

"Oh, I don't remember. Not just off the top of my head like that."

"Of course not."

"Lena, that's because it happens all the time. That's the nature of life. You can only go down one path and you don't get to know ahead of time what's down the other. Pick and go. Sometimes it turns out better than you expected. Sometimes worse. No point dwelling on the path you didn't take. And no matter what happens, some good will pop out of it somewhere. Just because it came from something awful doesn't mean it's poisoned, somehow. You gotta hang on to it anyway, be grateful for it."

She bent forward, picked up a rock, and tossed it, backhanded, it toward a tree. A mountain jay lifted out of it and winged slowly away, black over blue.

She brushed her hands against each other. "Look," she said. "Your life, it's a gift. It's a good gift. And the child you're carrying, that's a gift, too. But no gift comes for free."

Sunlight on water as Kevin and Sarah cheered for their haphazard sailboats. The circle of lamplight as we read stories together and talked about their mother. Mindy's hand on mine; Olive's living, loving granddaughter bearing me up in a cowboy bar as I said that yet another soul was on its way into the world.

Gifts, all, it was true, no matter how small they were or from how much filth they might have been recovered.

Tuah put her hand on my knee again and patted it, then pushed herself to her feet. "Start making some decisions, Lena. Good and bad will come, no matter what you do. Accept it, and look for the good."

I squinted up at her. Fuzzy strands stood out from her head, silvered by the sunlight behind her.

"You haven't answered my question," I said.

"What question?"

"About a decision you regretted."

"Why do you want to know?"

"I want to figure out how you make decisions after you know how much harm one person can cause."

She looked down at me. "Ah, my Lena," she said. She pressed her lips together, then turned to look downhill, toward town. The jay swung back into view, settling into a different tree, willing to wait for whatever scraps our dinner might offer. Just when I began to wonder whether I'd gotten all the answer I was going to, she spoke.

"I let Benencia go," she said. She cleared her throat. "In her blue calico dress with the pink flowers, with no coat or shawl, and without Gus. I didn't want to let her go, but she knew she wasn't a child, and she'd get angry with me when I tried to keep her safe. So against my better judgment, I let her go." She looked back down at me. "I let her go. I shouldn't ever have let her go. I live with that every day, but I live. It's the best anybody can do."

21

Dust rose and sparkled as I turned onto the lane for the Flying J Guest Ranch, the setting sun straight in my eyes. I squinted, my head still throbbing. I would be spending the night in Leadville anyway, before going to the Koffords' early in the morning, so I would far rather have skipped the cookout and headed straight there. Pulled the blind and put my head into the pillow. But Tuah didn't have a phone for me to let him know, so here I was.

I passed the opening in the split rail fence where I'd turned off when I dropped Leo here yesterday morning. As he'd instructed me, I followed the sign for guest parking to a gravel lot with flower boxes lining the fence, each with a little American flag stuck into it at a jaunty angle. Yes, it was a parking lot, but the sight of my mud-crusted Pinto between a Mercedes and a Lincoln Continental made me wonder whether I'd really gotten the directions right.

I got out and shoved my keys into my pocket. A cabin of polished logs had a sign nailed to the corner, pointing along a boardwalk to "guest registration" and "lodge" and "mess hall." I followed it around the corner of the cabin, then stopped. Before me spread a wide lawn that ended half a football field away in front of a log lodge, three stories high, with green shutters and red geraniums at the windows, a deep porch, and an American flag swaying beside the steps. Red, white, and blue bunting ran along the porch railing. A life-size chainsaw-art bear held a welcome sign and a flag. Smaller cabins encircled the green, with paths around them disappearing into the pines. A couple of girls in white shorts swatted a shuttlecock across a net stretched near the corner of the lodge.

"Hey! Elena!"

I turned to see Leo stepping down from a seat atop the split rail fence.

"Right on time," he said. He wore dark jeans, boots, a hat, and a snap-front plaid shirt. A pressed stars-and-stripes bandana was knotted around his neck.

"You didn't tell me this was evening dress," I said. I had on jeans, a pair of Chuck Taylors frayed along the tongue, a

Who '76 concert T-shirt, and a sweatshirt knotted around my waist.

"You look great." He pointed to a golf cart, the nose of which protruded beyond the corner of a cabin near where he'd been sitting. "You want a tour? We've got about an hour before dinner."

"First I want you to tell me how I never knew this was here."

"The ranch?"

"No, *all* this. That place I dropped you off, where it looked like a regular summer camp? I expected more of that. This is . . ." I looked back toward the lodge, now noticing little croquet wickets set into the grass near a pair of Adirondack chairs. "I had no idea. And —" I waved from the boots to his dove-gray hat. "Is that a costume?"

God, I sounded like a snotty teenager. But he just grinned.

"Something like that," he said. "But as long as I'm in it, I can let you drive."

We followed a sand-and-gravel cart path that curved into the trees and led us past the pool. Tennis courts. Mini golf. A recreation building with Ping-Pong, billiards, board games, a library, and a toddler playroom. In addition to the twenty guest rooms in the lodge were family cabins, nestled into little aspen groves around the property.

Lanes and paths wound through the trees. Finally he had me stop at the corrals, downhill and downwind from all the guest quarters so no one would be troubled by the smells of an actual ranch. A dozen or more horses stood in a clump at the far side, a head shake here, a foot stamp there, tails swishing without regard to whose faces or flanks benefited. I parked the golf cart beside the barn, and we got out.

"There's Spot," I said as we leaned against the fence rails, pointing at a black and white pinto. "Right? The one I rode?"

Leo nodded, squinting under the rim of his hat. "He's pretty busy this week."

"Busy?"

"Every guest gets assigned a horse. The lucky ones get the ten-year-old girls, and the new guy hit the jackpot. Little girl from Florida. He's getting a lot of goodies."

Florida. The setting sun, behind me, warmed my shoulders and lit the ridge in the distance. *These mountains.* I squeezed my eyes shut. *Stop.* I crossed my arms on the top fence rail and dug my chin into the back of my wrist. "The ponies are for little kids?"

"Yup. But they're all kinda stubborn and mean, so one of us has to be right there with them if a kid wants to ride."

"And guests can just go on rides anytime they want?"

"There's a schedule of planned rides, and most folks just do that." He pointed past the horses to a large, empty corral with wooden bleachers outside the far fence. "They can ride anytime in the rodeo ring. We get the beginners started in there, and we use it for roping, barrel racing, all that stuff."

"Roping? With actual calves?"

"Sure. You can do as much real work around here as you want. Go on roundup rides during the summer, do some branding, the works."

"Cowboy play land."

"That sounds about right."

Suddenly one of the ponies, tucked in between larger horses, pulled its head up, ears back, so that its bared teeth were just visible over another horse's rump. It snapped, and there was a muffled percussion of hooves stamping the dust, a shifting in the crowd, but within a few seconds everything settled back down.

Leo shook his head. "Ponies. Always with the Napoleon complex."

Or maybe it was just a completely reasonable reaction to bodies that were too big, too immovable, and too oppressive getting

305

way too close. That pony understood me. I shoved myself away from the fence.

"Dinner soon?" I said.

"Sure."

We got in the golf cart and wound our way back uphill, humming past the mini golf, the pool, the tennis courts, some larger guest cabins, to a spot behind the mess hall where three other golf carts were parked. I heard a clank of horseshoes and smelled charcoal smoke as we got out.

In the time we'd been gone, an honest-to-God Conestoga wagon had been pulled onto the green in front of the mess hall, a shelf laden with serving dishes running the length of the sideboard, bunting swagged just above it, a flag at each end. Vacationers in shorts and jeans, some with cowboy hats, some with boots, had started to gather in clumps, and the first to eat were already lined up. A pair of ranch grills gave off smoke at the back of the wagon, and a man in an apron stood behind them with a spatula. He too wore boots, a hat, and a slash of stars and stripes around his neck.

I looked at Leo. "Does everybody who works here have to wear that bandana?"

"Usually it's just red, but yeah. That's how people spot us."

"As if the rest of the getup weren't

enough."

"Oh, you'd be surprised. We have guests showing up in some pretty serious duds."

I closed my eyes and took a deep breath. Here I was, rude again, and him letting it roll off his back. He was just so benignly *likeable.* Where was the behavior that would mark him as one of my own tribe? The temper, the alcoholism, the abuse, the selfishness that could exist on a parallel track with my own wrecked train? I didn't make a habit of hanging out with nice people who'd never done awful things. Nice people had their own soft little world where I would only feel my own jagged edges more acutely. As I did now.

"Sorry," I said. "That came out wrong. Can we get food or something?"

"Sure."

We joined the line leading to the grills behind a balding man with a red-striped shirt hanging like a circus tent over a pot belly.

He turned slightly toward us. "Howdy," he said to Leo, giving a little nod to me.

"Hey," Leo said. "You had a good day?"

"Yup." The man turned another step toward the grill. "Hamburger," he said to the cook.

Howdy? I mouthed to Leo.

He pinched a little smile and shook his head. *Later.*

We got barbecued chicken, a scoop of baked beans out of a blackened kettle at the back of the wagon, then waited as a round woman wearing a denim skirt and little red sneakers stood on her toes to peer into each dish and serve herself dainty spoonfuls of side dishes. Coleslaw. Check the next. Potato salad. Check the next. Fruit salad. Lots of prodding with tongs to select a biscuit. Really? Were these people living in a world where buffet items constituted big decisions? I gave myself a heap of everything, without looking, waiting pointedly behind her at each dish.

We ate at a white-draped table on the grass as the mountain's shadow spread over us. A candle in a mason jar sat on a miniature circle of bunting at the table's center. We talked about music, I think. The edge of the second button on my jeans dug into my belly, and I shifted in my chair and tried to pay attention to what Leo was saying. Something about a country singer I'd never heard of. The food had no flavor, and at some point the image of a grasping, malformed alien grabbing handfuls of it from the bottom of my esophagus swam into my mind and I put my fork down. Tuah's voice drowned out anything Leo said. *Whatever you decide, it'll be hard.* I was being lousy company, but Leo was still talking, so maybe I was doing a better job of functioning than I thought.

I pulled on my sweatshirt and then smelled a different quality of smoke. Dry and acrid. Not a barbecue grill. I twisted in my chair.

Flames danced and curled around a skeleton teepee of branches, easily four feet high, tickling the indigo sky. Lawn chairs made a dotted outline around the fire, and a pair of children ran past it, arms and legs silhouetted in stop motion against the flickering light. My heart started pattering against my sternum.

"When did that fire get started?" I asked.

"It just got big a minute ago. You want s'mores?"

"No, thanks. I'm full."

"Well, I do. Let's go get a seat by the fire and wait till it gets some good hot spots."

I made a show of checking my watch. I couldn't see the hands. Either my wrist was shaking or my eyes had blurred. "You know, I should go. Long drive, early morning."

"How early do you go to bed? You'd be in town by, what? Nine thirty?"

"I need a lot of sleep these days."

"You'll miss the Indian show," Leo said

with a grin.

"The *what*?"

"Indian show. Tribal dances by the fire. Then there'll be fireworks."

And that was it. I couldn't take it anymore. Indians dancing in front of the flames, explosions, cowboy costumes, the new-construction Conestoga wagon, the mini golf, the pool, the bandanas, the goddamn baked beans out of a fake kettle. And the fire. That fucking fire I could feel growing against my back. Was it smoke closing my throat, making my heart pound in my ears, now? I stood, tipping the chair over.

"Look. I gotta go."

"Is something wrong?"

I shook my head. "Thanks for asking me," I said. "It's been fun." I pushed my hands into my sweatshirt pockets and started walking toward the car, dizzy, breathing harder than I should, panic chasing me. Leo fell into step beside me. I could feel reason draining out of me as I walked, the vortex around it swirling with Florida heat and bloody birth and mountains and Tuah and goddam fucking, fucking fire.

I reached for the door handle on the Pinto.

"Look," Leo said. "Is something wrong? I mean, one minute we're talking and then —" He slid one hand against the other, the upper shooting off into the dusky sky. "Zoom."

"I just have to go," I snapped. "It's getting late."

He took a step backward, palms forward. There was a limit, it seemed, to how easy-going he was. "Okay, if that's what you want. Just thought I'd give you a chance to be honest."

"*Honest?* Like all this?" I waved a hand behind me. "Disney Cowboy Land, yipee-kiy-yiy-yoh, matching bandanas, howdy pardner? I don't think you want my kind of honest. My shit doesn't belong here."

"You do know I just work here, right? It's just a place to escape. Everybody has stuff."

"Everybody has *stuff?* Really? *Everybody?*" The tightness in my throat pushed my voice higher. "I cheated with my deadbeat apart-ment manager, and now I'm *pregnant.* I'm a college graduate with no job, living with my grandmother and babysitting *for free.* And that fun fire back there with the marsh-mallows? I started one when I was ten, just a little one, and I ended up burning twenty-seven houses and *killing* three people. *Kill-ing.* Is that the kind of *stuff* everybody has?"

Leo, predictably enough, didn't have a response. I didn't give him time for one.

"I didn't think so," I said, yanking the

door open. "Go have marshmallows. Sorry — thanks for inviting me, but it's time for me to go."

I dropped into the car, slammed the door, backed out, and drove away.

22

Paul greeted me Monday morning with his cap already on, his bag slumped by the door. He held out a cup of coffee.

"You want some?" he asked, even though it was already too late for me to do anything other than take it. He went on talking before I could say thank you.

"I got up and started the coffee like normal but I must've still been kinda asleep because I put in what I used to for two of us, you know, and then after it was already going . . ." He took a breath, then went on, "I figured it out and by then there was nothing to do but throw it away. And then I thought I'd keep it for you because I know you must get up pretty early . . . to . . . get packed, showered, dressed, you know. And do your hair and all . . . get here as early as you do, so I thought you must be pretty tired and could use a little pick-me-up."

There was nothing to say. By the time he'd

finished, my history was completely envisioned, sculpted, and kiln-dried. Never mind that no, I'd packed and bathed — not showered — in the time I had the night before, and that it didn't seem especially early because I'd been lying awake for hours and my ponytail had taken only a few seconds to pull back. Too late. But I couldn't find my old irritation, my compulsion to hammer back from inside his constructions. I knew them as something different now. As Leo had said, we all have stuff. Or at least Paul and I did.

"No, that's fine. Thanks." I took a sip. "How are the kids?"

"Well, now —" He lifted the bill of his cap to scratch his head. "Sarah's been kinda cranky. Whiny. Kevin's been off by himself a lot. Surly. I don't know." He looked down, shaking his head. "I just don't know." He looked back up at me, brows raised, forehead creased. "What do you think I should do? Be tougher? Back off?"

"I — uh — I don't know."

"What are *you* going to do?"

"I guess same as usual. They do chores first, then play or we do errands. Sarah likes her friends, and I've been trying to get Kevin out with other kids. Dinner. We read together at night. Is there something you'd like me to do?"

He'd been nodding as I spoke, in the way someone might open and close a sponge to make it absorb more liquid. In the way of a father trying to figure out how to mother his children now that their mother was gone. I could feel the ache.

"I see." Now his head turned from side to side. "No, not at all. You're doing everything just great."

"I —" I hesitated, but some part of me had already started pushing words out and the delay was only reluctance about stirring grief, not indecision about whether I should. The help I had to offer might be worth it. "Do you remember when Sarah asked you about her mom's secret place?"

Paul nodded.

"I — might know what it is. Along the Hat Creek trail? I rode up there a couple of weeks ago, and I saw a place that looked just like Sarah's picture. Really shady and green, with the creek right there."

"I think I know, if it's what I'm thinking of. We used to go there, too."

"Maybe the kids would want to go some-time."

He nodded again, lips tight. "Yes, yes. Maybe sometime."

"It sounds like they want to remember

their mom. I think realizing that you're forgetting is almost as bad as losing a person in the first place."

He looked down at his boots, then back up at me. A silent witness, the house wrapped itself around us.

"You've been there, then," he said.

I nodded.

"Who?"

"My mom, too."

He gave a single tilt of his chin in response. A code. A token establishing a partnership of loss.

"I'm sure we'll be fine," I said after a moment.

"Yes." He nodded, now as if confirming the words to himself. "That's right. I know." He took a deep breath. "I got to the market yesterday. There's cereal. And bananas. I got some apples, but they're not very good. The kids like apples if they're good, but they don't like these very much, so don't feel like you have to make them eat them, but . . . if you could think of something else to do with them that'd be good because I know you hate to waste food as much as I do. You could stew them. The kids like that. With some sugar and cinnamon. That'd taste real good . . . maybe with some pork chops. You should use Carrie's recipe. She made some good pork chops. There were some spices she used . . ."

He turned away from me as he spoke, his feet following each other toward the dim brown kitchen. He switched on the light and got a recipe box out of a cupboard, then started walking his fingers through the cards.

". . . somewhere in here. I know I saw her get it out, but there's a tab here for meat, and there's a tab here for main dishes, and I'm not sure where to look because maybe she thought it was kind of a casserole because there were onions and some sauce in there, too. I have onions. They're in the pantry . . . Oh — I think this is it."

He straightened, a single card between his thumb and forefinger, then laid it on the counter and smoothed it, pressing it into place. He finally met my eyes. "You can make pork chops with sauce and have them with apples."

"I will," I said. "Tonight."

He nodded, lips rolled in against each other.

"Well, I'd better go," he said, looking down. He gave a tug to the bill of his cap, then turned toward the door as I picked up the recipe card. *Saucy chops.* The card was yellowed, with a brown spot to the right of "soften the onions." It was less a recipe than a set of steps, too simple to need to be written down. Cook four slices of bacon, then cook sliced onions in the bacon fat, then add the chops, then cream of mushroom soup, then put the crumbled bacon back in the pan. Salt was the closest thing to a spice. Had this been written by Carrie's mother, part of a scaffolding built around a young, troubled woman about to attempt managing a household on her own?

"You'll be back Friday?" I asked as he pulled open the door.

"That's right." He paused, then turned back toward me. "You want me to call during the week?"

An ache of compassion pulled against the base of my throat. "That'd be nice," I said.

"Where's Kevin?" Poppy asked as I tucked my heels under myself on the porch step. The sun lay across my lap, warming my thighs.

"With friends," I said. Sarah sat on the ground, squealing with laughter, puppies clambering over each other to lick her face. It was their first day out in the yard. Their mother sat by Poppy's knee, heavy-bellied and sober, supervising.

"Really? Who?"

"Some kid named Scott stopped by. I think he lives over there." I twisted and made a vague gesture behind myself, toward the street that ran parallel to this one. "But I got the sense they were going to meet up with some other kids."

"Huh. You might want to watch out for that."

Sarah tipped backward under a ground-swell of puppies, and her hysterical laughter turned to wailing the instant her head touched the grass. "Ow, they're *biting me!*"

Poppy hoisted herself off the step more quickly than I did and pulled Sarah upright by one arm. "That's what they do, honey. If you want to play you should probably keep moving. Run around a little."

She looked up to Poppy with a stuttered sniffle. She tightened her shoulders under her too-small yellow T-shirt and swallowed hard, then launched herself toward the corner of the yard, puppies tumbling after her.

"Did you see that?" Poppy said as she lowered herself back onto the step beside me with a grunt, indicating Sarah with a tilt of her head. "Tough kid. She's gonna do just fine."

But I'd seen something different — a little girl swallowing pain into herself because she

319

believed she had no one to turn to for sympathy. A child I was failing. And maybe not the only one.

"What did you mean about Kevin's friends?" I asked.

Bella stood and made a low sound in her throat. The puppies must have gone farther than she liked. As Sarah paused to check over her shoulder for them, they turned as a group and started stumbling back to their mother. Sarah looked at us, the question clear in her eyes.

"Little ones need their moms," Poppy said, without waiting for her to say anything.

I winced and looked sideways, but Poppy didn't give any visible cues that she regretted what had escaped her lips.

"I know," Sarah said with resignation. She trudged back toward us and flopped on the grass as the puppies crawled over their mother. She plucked a blade of grass. This clearly wasn't the time to discuss Kevin.

"Do you think Brownies or Blue Birds are better?" Sarah asked.

It took me a moment to respond, even inarticulately. "What?"

"If you join Brownies you get a sash with the badges." She gestured with one hand across her taut little belly, shoulder to hip. "And you sell cookies. In Blue Birds you get a purse. It's red. They sell candy."

I blinked. Girls' clubs. Which meant I knew only slightly less than I did when I thought she was comparing baked goods to wildlife.

"I don't know," I finally said. "When do you have to decide?"

"Second grade."

Another year. More than. The strength with which she hurled herself toward the future caught me off guard again and again. The past, short as it was, lay undisturbed behind her.

"Well, I guess you have more time to think about it," I said. "Maybe when the time comes you can just do whatever your friends are doing."

God, what terrible advice. But maybe she hadn't heard me. She'd started pulling more blades of grass and then examining them, testing their worth as kazoo membranes between her thumbs.

"Like I said," Poppy muttered to me.

I sighed. "Maybe."

The children hung in my mind like weighted bags. I could see what Paul had been talking about. They'd been testy yesterday and last night, seesawing opposite each other in either needling or being obstinate. In my own uneven emotional state, my arsenal of responses amounted to telling them to stop it. The invitation that had drawn Kevin out of the house this morning had been a relief.

"You seen that fella that bought you the drink lately?" Poppy asked, stretching her legs out in front of her and swiveling her feet to tap the sides of her sandal soles against each other.

"A barbecue Sunday night up at the Flying J — that guest ranch? He works there."

"Know it well. Everybody does."

"I guess so. Anyway, it was a bad night. I'm pretty sure I've seen the last of him."

"Too bad. Looked like a nice kid."

I shrugged. "For somebody."

The door opened behind us with a click. "What time is it?"

Poppy answered without turning around. "Just after eleven, Mama."

"I can't find *The Price Is Right.*"

"Channel four, Mama."

"It's not there."

"Change it and try again."

"It's not there," the old woman repeated.

Poppy turned around. "You want me to send Miss Elena in there to fix it for you?"

The old woman scowled at me for a moment. "Hi," she said. Then she pulled her head inside and slammed the door.

"I'd be happy to —"

But Poppy shook her head and waved her hand. "No, no. Don't even think about it. She doesn't need any help. She just wants attention."

I looked at Sarah, who seemed completely absorbed by the kazoo making. Bella had flopped on her side and the puppies were nursing.

I lowered my voice. "What was it you wanted to tell me about Kevin's friends?"

Poppy made a sound in her nose. "Scott's not usually his friend. Plus you said it was a group."

"What do you mean?"

She lifted her chest in a deep sigh. "Kevin gets bullied a lot."

"So isn't it a good thing somebody wants him to play?"

Poppy looked at me. "You know how bullies work, right?"

"Oh," I said. But did I? I'd grown up behind a fence built of other kids' unsureness about me, not bullied but not befriended. I thought of all my urgings to Kevin to get outside, find somebody, anybody, and just play. I'd seen other kids do it. I thought that was how it worked. I always thought that if I'd been pushed to do the same maybe I would've learned to be more like the children I assumed were happier. "What are they going to do? Should I not let him play when they ask?"

"No. You can't prevent it. You can't keep him in hiding. Just — keep your eyes open. Help him figure out how to act. How to find real friends. Coach him."

I couldn't help it. I laughed.

"What's funny?"

"It's just — there can't be a worse person for *that* job."

"Oh, don't be melodramatic. You know the difference between a good kid and a little shit. Scott's a little shit. Help Kevin figure it out for himself."

She pivoted forward from her seat to her knees, scooped up a puppy that had fallen asleep, and deposited it in Sarah's lap.

"There you go, honey."

"Oh!" Grass fluttered down from her hands. She curved over the puppy in her lap like a scallop closing its shell and stroked the puppy's fur. "Thank you," she whispered.

"Can I say something?" Poppy asked as she dropped onto her backside.

"Sure."

"Look. I can see you got troubles. You're wrapped around 'em as tight as a rope. You gotta let go. We're all your friends here.

Everybody thinks you're the kindest thing in the world, looking after these children like this. You got more credit in the goodwill bank in this town than you could spend in a lifetime. So start spending. Let folks help you with those troubles."

I looked down at the sling of my arms wrapped around my thighs, the wedge of grass visible between them. Today I wore shorts with a zipper, which was cutting into my belly more sharply than the button on my jeans had done. I looked back up at Poppy — the gentle eyes, the flyaway gray tendrils, the soft little rolls along her neck. Turquoise stones the size of gumballs hung from wires in her ears, stretching the lobes long and flat.

"I didn't come here to be kind," I said.

"Well, of course not. Nobody would. Are you ashamed of that?"

I straightened my back, trying to pull away from the zipper teeth. I glanced at Sarah, still mesmerized by the sleeping puppy. I lowered my voice until I wasn't sure even Poppy could hear it.

"I'm pregnant," I said.

Poppy nodded slowly, thoughtfully. "Yes, yes," she said, as if considering whether she had enough toilet paper to lend me a couple of rolls. "That's a worry for certain." She nodded some more, gazing off across the yard, thinking. "But I believe we got everything you need around here to help out with that."

23

Kevin arrived home a little after noon, filthy and hungry, as I bent over the washing machine scraping wet socks from the wall of the tub.

"Good grief," I said. "What have you been doing?"

"Diggin' in the dirt," he said, slamming the back porch door behind himself. He had a lightness, an energy I hadn't seen before. A wash of relief passed over me. Perhaps I'd pushed him in the right direction after all.

"Wow. Did you leave any dirt outside?"

"Nope. It's all in my pockets," he said, then barked a big laugh, clearly delighted to share a joke.

"Well, shake it out tonight before you get ready for bed. Outside. Are you ready for lunch?"

"Uh-huh."

"Ham sandwiches?"

"Uh-huh."

I sent Kevin to wash up and called Sarah, who'd been asking about lunch for some time. As they ate, he tore big bites out of his sandwich and made a play out of filling his cheeks, making Sarah laugh. The cloud of bad temper had lifted.

"You wanna come over?" he asked Sarah as he finished his Fritos.

"Come over where?" I said.

"Back to the Brames' with me."

Something struck me wrong. This seemed like an odd request for an eleven-year-old boy to make of his much younger sister.

"Scott has a sister," Kevin explained before I could ask. "She wants Sarah to come play."

Sarah took an overlarge bite of her sandwich. "I don't like Cindy," she said around it.

"Yeah, I don't like sending her to a place I don't know," I added.

"She really wants you to come."

Sarah frowned, brows furrowing as her cheeks widened and slackened with chewing.

"I don't think that's a good —"

But she cut me off. "Okay," she said. She put down her sandwich and took a swallow of milk. She looked up at me as she set down the glass. "Can I go?"

"But you just said you didn't like this girl."

"Sometimes she's mean. But sometimes she's nice."

"That doesn't sound like a good friend." Was this the way I was supposed to teach them?

Kevin translated for me. "Cindy was in her kindergarten class. They play a lot. They get in fights sometime, but then they're okay again."

I couldn't automatically blame the un-known child for disagreements between them. Sarah certainly tended to be bossy herself. Perhaps this was one of the families that had had its fill of Kofford children in the months before I came. Perhaps connec-tions were repairing themselves and I should be supportive.

"Okay," I finally said. "But I'm going to walk over with you both and make sure it's okay."

Kevin gave a whine of protest, which actu-ally made me smile.

"I'm embarrassing?" I asked.

An eye roll was his only response. Perhaps I was better integrated into this family than I thought.

At six thirty I admitted to myself that I was

worried. I'd left the children at the Brames' house over five hours earlier, after the mother met me at the door, put her hand over the phone mouthpiece long enough to confirm the invitation, and said she'd send them home before dinner. But in even my limited experience, Sarah tended to tire of playmates quickly and I'd expected her sooner. And Kevin should have been pain-fully hungry long ago.

I consumed another half hour telling myself I was overreacting, waiting for worry to be proven wrong. Any minute. In just one more minute. But at seven, as the sun spread wide rays across the roofs, and the house's shadow covered the neighbor's fence, I couldn't wonder what to do any longer. Leaving a note on the table, I walked down to the corner, turned, and headed up the next road. The abandoned house on the corner. The next one with the spotted dog in the front yard. The yellow house. And then the Brames', with its faded wreath of wooden hearts on the door.

Seeing no one in the yard, I climbed the slat steps to the door and knocked. I heard toenails, then snuffles along the baseboard, but no barking. Eventually I knocked again. The dog walked away.

I left the porch and circled the house. A

tire was strapped to a tree trunk in the backyard, and the tall grass bent here and there to cup balls in assorted sizes and varieties. But no children. I came back around to the front, then went into the center of the road and stretched to see as far as I could around each of the other houses. Took a few steps one way, and then another. It felt like action. I didn't know what else to do.

I stood still enough to feel claws of anxiety scrabble at the insides of my ribs. *Where could they be?* I looked around at the homes of strangers, which stood stiff and silent, closed against me. Other than the scattering of pickup trucks and cars, the street was empty. I went to the house next door, the yellow one, and knocked on the door. A creak, voices, footsteps, and then a man answered the door, steel-haired and pot-bellied.

"Hi — I'm — looking for the Brames. Some children who were playing there?"

The man listened to me, then frowned and shook his head. "Sorry," he said. "I just got home. No idea where they are. Sheila?" he called over his shoulder. "You know where the Brames are?"

The response had the inflection of another question but no discernable words. He turned back to me. "Sorry. She doesn't know either."

I found another man home in the house on the other side and got the same response. Also across the street. On either side of that one, no one answered the door. I'd started to run from house to house, but gave up at the house with the dog, which lunged at its chain within easy reach of the porch.

I stood in the center of the road, short of breath, heart thudding, while the chained dog barked at me. What options did I have? I didn't know any of the children's other friends. Should I start walking through town and just look for them? No — driving. I would be better equipped to find them in the car. I needed to go back and get the car.

I ran down the road, along the street at the bottom, and back uphill to the Koffords', arriving at the house out of breath. I jumped over the front steps and grabbed my purse and keys, then ran back outside. Poppy hailed me from across the street, where she stood with her thumb over the end of the hose, spraying something weedy.

"What's wrong?"

I stopped by the car door. "The children. They're gone."

"What?" She dropped the hose and started lumbering toward me. "What?"

"They're gone. They went to the Brames'. They were supposed to be home by now, but I was just there — everybody's gone. I don't know where they are."

She slowed down. "Oh, honey. It's fine. They just got busy playing somewhere. You know how children are."

"No, I *don't* know how children are!" I snapped. "I know *these* children, and they should be home right now, and Mrs. Brame said she'd send them before dinner, and now nobody's home! *Nobody!* They should've been home *hours* ago!"

"Maybe so. Maybe so." Poppy had reached me by now. "You drive, honey. I'll go with you. Everything's fine."

I got in and started the car while Poppy went around and sank into the passenger seat. To my surprise, some degree of my own tension eased as the seat springs relaxed to receive her. What power did the mere presence of someone equally ignorant have to soothe? I took a steadying breath, then did a U-turn and started downhill, across the street, and rolled downhill for another couple of blocks. Nothing. I turned at another cross street and started back up toward the Brames'. I stopped in front of a house with a woman sitting on the front porch steps pulling weeds around her feet.

"Have you seen some kids go by?" I called out the window.

"Lots. Which ones are you looking for?"

"The Kofford kids. They were with the Brames. Two little girls and two boys about eleven. There could've been other kids with them."

"Oh." She frowned, then shook her head. "No, no I haven't."

I didn't bother to thank her but rolled forward again.

"How 'bout we go back up to the Brames' and try again," Poppy said.

"Okay." It was as good a suggestion as any other. And I was glad for someone to tell me something — anything — to do. I pulled up in front of the still-empty house and parked. Poppy craned her neck forward and pointed.

"Now that right there is the Clydes'. They're catty-corner from my neighbor. Did you ask them?"

I nodded.

"And the Janeks, in the next house?"

"No."

"Well, probably no point. They kinda keep to themselves. Now right there —" She pointed toward the end of the road, where the pavement ended against a weedy bank that looked more as if it had been bulldozed into place than as if the road had stopped because of it. "That's a good place to play. Kids build forts and roads and whatnot up there all the time. Did you look there? Call for them?"

"No." Calling. What had kept me silent?

"Well, now, let's give that a try, then." Poppy opened her door and hoisted herself up while I stepped out into the road. Someone walking uphill toward me caught my eye. A boy, head down, kicking a rock. I turned and started toward him

"Scott? Are you Scott?"

The boy looked up and stopped. Definitely the one I'd met earlier. Poppy folded her arms on the roof of the car as I hurried to meet him.

"You remember me? I'm Elena. Where are Kevin and Sarah?"

He put his weight back onto his heels. "I dunno," he said.

"You don't know? They were with you. Your mom said she'd send them home for dinner. Where are they?"

"I — I dunno." He angled himself so that one shoulder was turned away from me, head slightly lowered. A defensive posture. I didn't like it and took a step closer.

"Scott? What's going on?"

"I dunno."

"Stop saying that! Where are Kevin and Sarah?"

"I already told you! I don't know! I'm not a liar!"

What did I see? Something in the boy's eyes, or the tilt of his head, or the two of them together combined with the tenor of his voice, and all at once I knew. The denial was false. Something had happened. My breath caught in my throat. There wasn't enough oxygen.

"Everything okay there, honey?" Poppy's voice came from somewhere behind me, soothing, warning, but it had no power over my rising panic. I took another step closer, and my hand, of its own accord, grabbed the boy's arm. "Then why won't you tell me what's going on? Where are Kevin and Sarah?"

A car turned at the corner and rolled up the street toward us.

"Let go of me!" He twisted against me, but I wouldn't be so easily shaken off. All the strength I had left was concentrated in my hand. I clenched tighter.

"*Where are Kevin and Sarah?* What were you doing together? When did you see them last?"

The car stopped.

"We were digging! Then they went home!"

A man got out. T-shirt. Denim jacket. Bald on top. The shadowy form of a woman in the passenger seat. "You got some problem with my boy?"

"We're fine here, Frank," Poppy said. She was right behind me now. "Elena —"

I ignored them both and yelled at Scott. "That's not true! Or you would've said so from the beginning!"

"*Ma'am!* You better let go of my boy."

I pivoted toward the speaker without breaking hold. "Where are Kevin and Sarah? They were at your house! They were supposed to come home! *Where are they?*"

"Scott, you told us they went home."

"They did!" He twisted again against me.

"Really? *Really?*" I yelled as my fingers dug into his arm. My head jerked around toward the father, blurring the background of houses, rusted things, mountains, sky. "Because all I've been hearing is *I don't know, I don't know.* Now suddenly he says they went home. They didn't! He's lying!"

"Elena —" Poppy again, pointedly calm.

"Ma'am, settle down. If he said they went home, they went home. I'll help you look but I suggest we start over."

I spun back to the boy. "Tell me what you were doing! *Tell. Me. Now.* Where were you playing?"

He glared at me, surly, defiant, emboldened by the presence of a protector. He tilted his chin toward the top of the road.

"Over the hill."

I tugged at his arm. "Show me where you were when they went home."

"Hey — I understand you're upset, but you need to let him go."

"No!" My anger had radiated outward, washing over both father and son equally. "I sent two children here to play, and she" — I pointed to the car's windshield and the silent passenger just visible through it — *"she* said she'd send them home for dinner. She *didn't.* Something's happened! They're gone. Now all I've got is *this"* — I shook the boy's arm — "to help me find them. And he's gonna help, whether he wants to or not!"

I yanked at the boy's arm and started walking up the street.

"You let go of my boy!"

I swung back toward the car. "He said they were digging. *All day?"* The man stiffened, straightening behind the car door. "You ask her! What time did they leave?" No answer. *"What time?"*

He bent down to say something into the car. The engine rumbled. A moment later he stood again. His voice was lower.

"She says our kids came home about four thirty. They told her Kevin and Sarah had already gone home."

A sob lurched up from the center of my chest. "They've been gone for nearly four hours! Please! *Help me!*"

The man fixed his gaze on his son. "Scott, what did you find up there?"

Like an umbrella starting to fold in on itself, the boy shrank. If I'd first seen him as he looked now, I would've said he was far younger. "I dunno. Just a hole."

"*Shit!*" the man snapped. Something had changed, and I didn't know what it was. "*Go!* I'm right behind you."

He got back into the car and pulled around us and into his driveway while I started walking up the street again, still holding Scott. The man reached across his wife to fumble for something in the glove box as she got out of the car with a little girl.

"Give me the keys," Poppy said, catching up to me. "I'll go back to the house in case they come home."

I fished the keys out of my pocket as Mrs. Brame's voice called from the driveway, unbearably bright. "Don't worry! You'll find them!"

I didn't acknowledge it. I couldn't look at

her. Poppy squeezed my free hand as she took the keys. "It's okay, honey. Everything's gonna be just fine."

I nodded automatically. But I didn't believe her.

"And I think you can let go of that boy now," she added.

"Oh." I released his arm, which he emphasized with a twist as if to prove he'd escaped rather than been freed.

"I'll be waiting for you back home," she said.

Scott's father rejoined us. He had a flashlight in his hand, though it wasn't dark enough to need one.

"Come on," he said. "Scott, take us where you were playing."

"Thank you," I said. The fight had drained out of me, leaving me with nothing but a mouthful of dread.

He nodded. "I'm Frank."

"Elena."

"Yeah, I figgered."

We trudged the rest of the way up the street in a wary, long-armed triangle. The pavement ended against grit and rubble, and a faint path appeared, wending up the hillside. Scott led us along it, behind the hill, into a sprawl of ragged land, tufted with sagebrush clumps and dry grasses and edged by sharp-needled pines. Sun still touched the trees, but the ground was in shadow.

"Where'd you dig, son?" Frank said. It struck me as an odd question. I would've asked Scott to detail the afternoon, where they played, what they'd done, and where the children were when he parted ways with them.

The boy shrugged. "I dunno. Around."

"Show me where you dug."

Something inscrutable passed between them, and the boy slumped off across the sage, bearing slightly to the left. He stopped at a hollowed spot behind some rocks, circled by crushed and rusted beer cans.

"We dug here, some."

"There's no fresh marks. Now show me where you dug *today.*"

The boy set off along the same line. But not before he shot me another look, and this time I saw something different in him — *fear.* As invisible as radio waves, it carried into the air on a frequency I was already tuned to. I tried to pull back the breath that escaped me, then followed these strangers across the darkening field, staggering over the rocks and sagebrush roots.

At the line of trees, Scott kept going. The pitch grew steeper, and my breath started to shorten. Then he stopped and pointed to a jumble of rocks that sprouted pine saplings and buckthorn a short distance ahead.

"Over there," he said.

His father pushed past him. I'd fallen behind and stumbled to catch up as Frank dropped to his knees, doubling onto his hands near the rocks as if he was about to throw up. Then the flashlight turned on.

"Kevin!" he called to the ground. "Sarah! Answer me! Kids! Are you okay?"

I caught up in time to see him turn his head over his shoulder toward his son, his hands braced apart at the edge of a hole, an aurora of flashlight marking its opposite edge, and even in the shadows I could see a terrifying hybrid of fury and fear in his face.

"What did you do?"

"I — we — were just messing around."

In one motion the father came to his feet and grabbed the boy by the arm. "Did they go down there? Both of them?"

"Kevin did. He wanted to! We didn't make him!"

"What are you talking about? What's happened?" My voice wasn't my own, and they didn't seem to hear me.

"Did Sarah go down, too?"

"I dunno."

"Was she here when Kevin went down?"

A pause. Then slowly, a nod.

"And you left." It wasn't a question.

"What happened?" Still no one paid any attention to me.

"He prob'ly just climbed out!"

"Were you using a rope? And you took it?"

A nod.

"Then he couldn't climb out!"

This time I screamed. I couldn't help it. *"What are you saying?"*

Frank steadied himself and turned toward me. "It's a stope from an old mine — a spot where the mine got close to the surface. They cave in and open up from time to time. It doesn't sound like it's too deep, but they're not answering. We don't know if Sarah went down there, too, but I'm guessing she did. You stay here and keep calling. I'm going to get help."

Iced fingers closed around my throat. "Why aren't they answering?"

"I don't know. They probably wandered off. We'll find them."

But he didn't meet my eyes as he said it. Instead, he shoved the flashlight into my hand. "Keep the light shining down. And keep calling."

He twisted his son around and together

the two of them crunched away into the twilight.

24

"Kevin? Sarah? I'm right here. Are you okay?"

I feared the silence, so only a few moments would pass before I'd call again.

"Kevin? Sarah? Can you hear me? We're coming after you. We're getting you out."

And again. And again. The sky faded. Grit dug into my forearms and my knees cramped. My light shone on the loose rock down the hole, but the angle was such that I couldn't see the bottom. A faint draft rising out of the hole carried the musky scent of earth and dust.

"Sarah, honey? Can you hear me? Kevin? Say something back to me. We need to know where you are."

As the sky deepened to indigo, I heard steps crunching toward me. I turned on my hip to see overlapping circles of light stuttering across the ground.

"Elena?"

"What is it? Have you found them?"

"Not yet. It's Frank. I brought help. These are the first guys from mine rescue teams. The others are getting ready right now. Have you heard anything?"

"No."

They'd reached my side, but I didn't get up. Instead I called down the hole again.

"Kevin? Sarah? We're right here!" I turned to the boots beside me, more than I could count in a glance. I craned my neck to look up.

Frank offered a hand to help me stand. "Here," he said. "Let's let these guys take a look."

I staggered to my feet and four other men closed around the opening. A few murmured words and then a column of light aimed at the hole blinded me. I'd never seen anything that bright. I squinted and turned my face away. A radio crackled.

"Dan? We're here. It's on."

I turned to Frank. "What's happening?"

"It looks like this is an old silver mine, probably stopped operating seventy or eighty years ago. Somebody's at the main entrance right now, trying to see the light. There's an old guy with 'em. His dad used to work here, and he was in it some before it got closed up. Says he's pretty sure it connects but it's not a straight shot and the light won't show. If it does, they'll know for sure they can walk in that way. If not, they'll have to take his word for it. But it'd probably still be better than digging out this hole, since we know the kids aren't here anyway."

My voice swung up an octave. "So no one's even gone in yet?"

"Elena, we don't know what's down there. The maps for it look like a pile of string, and they probably don't show everything anyway. The kids could go ten yards in the dark, turn around, and be completely lost. Anybody could. We need to let professionals do this right."

Another crackle. *Ten-four. Nope, nothing. Emmett says told you so."*

My knees loosened. I was afraid I'd fall. Kevin and Sarah could be anywhere. Underground. Trapped. Lost in the dark. Cave-ins. Drop-offs. Dark water. Poison gas. Flashes from every movie or TV show I'd ever seen involving people trapped in a mine swirled around each other, forming a widening, enveloping, terrifying mass.

"It was *your kid* that did this!" I cried.

He spoke far more calmly than I deserved. "Scott said him and the other boys dared Kevin and ditched him. He explained every-

347

thing to the police. It was wrong, but it's what boys do. Kids around here get taught about not going in mines the same way kids in Kansas get tornado drills. Kevin heard it just as much as Scott did and he knew he shouldn't go down there. Kids'll be stupid. Now we're gonna find them and fix it."

Fix it. I looked at the men around the hole, silhouettes squatting over a rectangle of paper bleached like bone in the light. How many more men were gathered now at the entrance? There had been phone calls, men pulling on boots and leaving their homes, trucks bouncing through town, now lights and radios and maps, all to save Kevin and Sarah from my poor decisions. Could this be fixed, even with the whole town trying? The fault was mine, and like a coward, I'd tried to throw blame over a boy. Yet his father had just taken it gently and set it aside.

"I'm sorry," I said. "Thank you."

Three of the men stood.

"Miss Alvarez?" The man who spoke to me wore an unadorned ball cap and a dark T-shirt stretched tight over a barrel chest. He had a small mouth with a prominent lower lip that made him look like a younger, fitter Alfred Hitchcock. He stuck out a hand for me to shake, which I took automatically.

"Alan House," he said.

His hand was wide and dry, whereas mine felt vaguely tingly and somehow outside my control.

"I'm the captain. More guys are on the way. As soon as I have enough, we'll go in. We're getting our communications post set up by the portal. Frank will take you there. Chris" — he gestured over his shoulder with his thumb to the remaining man, now unfolding a lawn chair by the light — "is going to stay right here with a radio, so if the kids turn up here we'll know about it right away. Sound good?"

"Yes, sir," I lied. I could tell I was dealing with an honest-to-God grown-up who was used to being in charge, but there was no way I was going to sit on a rock, waiting, while other people looked for Kevin and Sarah.

"Good." He tucked the rolled map under his arm, and I followed their bobbing flashlights back out to the street, picking my way over the uneven ground in the dark. I got into Frank's car without saying anything else. There was no small talk to be made. Besides, I felt painfully out of place, more like one of the children in this drama than one of the adults — losing my charges in the first place, having petulant outbursts, doing what I was told while adults solved the problems, and finally following somebody else's dad to his car so he could drive me where I needed to go.

We drove downhill toward the center of town for a few blocks, then uphill and onto a dirt road that crested and then dove into a winding ravine. A few hundred more yards and I saw a pool of light in a wide spot in the road — pickup trucks shoved hard against the uphill slope, lamps, canopies strung from trees and posts, and a dizzying array of people and equipment. Bending, carrying, tinkering, talking. My fingers clenched the edge of the seat as Frank edged his car against the tailgate of one of the trucks. Gratitude twined with terror. So many to help. So many needed. And me, responsible for it all, about to step into the midst of it.

Alan slammed the door of his own truck as I stood. He put a hand on my shoulder and steered me toward one of the canopies.

"The mine entrance is just past the trucks here, straight into the mountain. The place they went in is on the other side of the hill. Not close, but we'll find them. You'll wait right here, and somebody will be with you the whole time."

"No — I'm going in."

He nodded, nonplussed. I might as well have said, "I want a sweater."

"I understand," he said. "But this isn't like a highway tunnel. If we're going to help those kids, we can't be taking care of you."

A hand on my other shoulder interrupted me before I could argue.

"Hey, how are you doing?"

I turned and stared, my bruised brain unable for a moment to place him in this setting. "Leo?"

He turned to point at one of the clusters of men. "My uncle is on one of the teams. He called me to stay with you."

"How'd he know —"

"Elena, everybody knows. The rescue guys have a calling tree, and when it's kids —" He nodded. "Well, people want to help."

"I want to help. I want to go with them."

"There's nothing you can do. You'd slow them down. Let them just do their job."

"Would they let *you* go?"

He tilted his head a little. "Probably. Maybe. But I've done some mining and safety training. It's all about whether the captain thinks a person can handle themselves and not get in the way —" He shrugged. "Maybe."

Alan had disappeared while we'd been talking. I scanned the clusters of men. *There.*

I grabbed Leo's hand and pulled him with me.

"Mr. — Alan." He looked up. Other men in hard hats continued twisting valves, and little jets of air seemed to be telling me to *shhh.* "You know who those kids are, right? Their mom just died a few months ago, and their dad is gone. They've got nobody. They've gotta be so scared. There's just me — I have to go with you."

I sounded so calm to myself, so reasonable. I felt frantic. If he'd asked to touch my hand he would have found it cold and shaking. But he didn't. And he also didn't say no fast enough to stop me from continuing.

"Leo will come with me. He says he knows what to do. He'll keep me out of trouble, and I won't slow you down at all. I promise — if you say to stop or turn around, I will."

His eyes narrowed. He looked at me for a moment longer, then looked at Leo.

"What's her story?"

I looked at Leo, panicked. What did he mean?

"She's Tuah's granddaughter. Eduardo Alvarez was her granddad."

"She got a good head?"

Did I? What did that mean? Why, *why* did Leo's last vision of me have to include me going to pieces over a campfire?

He studied me for a moment, then looked at Alan again. "She's pretty tough."

"We're following the air. You know what that means?"

"Yes, sir."

Alan finally spoke to me. "I'm only doing this because the air looks good. We'll be checking as we go, and advance a fresh air base every time we're sure we can. You can go as far as that, as long as you stay in line. The minute anything looks funny, or you make anybody pay attention to you, instead of those kids and our own safety, he's taking you out. Understand?"

"Yes, sir. Absolutely."

Alan held up a single finger, frowning so that his lower lip stood out even more. "One chance," he said. "You get one chance."

"One!"

"Check."

"Two!"

"Check."

"Three!"

Six men counted off. Little bursts of compressed air, tugs of belts, nods of heads. After Alan was a man who had been introduced to me as Dom, responsible for reading and revising the map. Bob, with a massive spool of wire, was the radio man. Stan was a medic. A man named Ramon was referred to as the "gas man," whose job, Leo said, was to test the air. Another two men, Ted and Rick, had a stretcher that carried tools, a first aid kit, more communications wire, and inexplicably, a roll of burlap and another of clear plastic. I tried to focus on the items on the stretcher and not think about any other uses for it.

Like the men, I wore a hard hat with a lamp, connected by wire to a battery pack that pulled the waistband of my jeans. A gas mask hung around my neck, and a backpack with steel bottles of air dragged down against my shoulders.

"Leo? Elena?" I felt a tug against the straps, a twist, a release.

"Check," Leo said.

Another team was going through parallel checks a few yards away. They would wait outside until called to widen the search, or to replace or rescue us. More men sat on truck bumpers or milled around a folding table, and a few more clumped around the radio unit where the wire connected to ours began. Low voices. An occasional car door slam. Carafes of coffee. Jugs of water. Uneven mounds of more backpacks, more tools, more straps and bags and tarps and coiled rope. We lived in a place where people were ready for things like this. I'd never stopped to look at the faces around town and wonder who had lost someone in the mines.

"Let's go."

I fell into line, behind the stretcher, the medic in front of me and Leo behind, the radio operator unspooling wire at the back. We walked in a stream of light created by our headlamps, which ran rough-edged over the ground.

"What's it going to be like in there?" I whispered over my shoulder as we stepped off the edge of the roadbed onto a steep downhill scree of river rocks and pebbles.

"Dark."

Any other question would be equally idiotic, but the next one asked itself without me deciding to speak. "Are we going to find them?"

"They're in there somewhere."

The ground slid away under me, and I stumbled, thrown off balance under all the extra weight. Leo hauled me upright by the straps as a cascade of small rocks bounced toward the other men, heel-stepping their way downhill ahead of me. Soon the ground leveled, the crunch of dry stones underfoot dulled, and then I felt water seep into my shoes.

"Good thing we had a dry winter," Leo said.

Within a few steps we were back on dry ground. The hillside rose in front of us and in the stuttering light of crossing headlamps I could make out a crumbling pagoda of timbers set into the soil and rocks. A pine sapling sprouted from an upper corner. Hinges clung to the frame, but what must have been the door was now a scattering of broken boards to one side, nails protruding. Ep out was spray-painted on one.

Alan stopped, and the men carrying the stretcher set it down. "Ready?" he said. He was looking at me.

I didn't want to go in. I couldn't stay out. I knew nothing about what we were doing, but I knew Kevin and Sarah, and for lack of anyone better, I knew they needed me. And I knew if I gave any hint of panic I'd be escorted straight back to the canopies we'd just left.

"Yes sir."

He nodded, then he and the other men pulled on their masks. I'd been told that we would wear them as only a safety precaution, that air movement at the mine portal said good things about the quality of air inside, that this was an unusual case of a mine believed to be dry in an area where water was the norm, that it was labyrinthine but believed to be relatively safe, but it still took conscious effort for me to act calm when the seals closed against my face and I pulled air from the tank into my lungs.

Alan turned and stepped into the opening. The gas man followed, carrying something that looked like a tall lantern with a flame in it. Behind him walked the mapper, then the stretcher bearers, the medic, me and Leo, and finally the radio man. Narrow-gauge tracks appeared as rocks gave way to bare dirt. An arbor of timbers braced the rock overhead, holding the mountain above us.

"Feel that?" Leo said. His voice was surprisingly clear through the mask. "That breeze on your neck. Fresh air coming in means fresh air ahead."

The walls narrowed quickly, and the ceiling barely cleared my head. I could see the taller of the two men carrying the stretcher start to stoop. I glanced over my shoulder at the diminishing opening behind me. Then the tunnel bent, and the opening disappeared.

The medic, in front of me, stopped. The tromp of our feet and the clatter of equipment stilled. Until now, I'd never noticed how much noise normally surrounded me. The rustle of leaves, idle calls of birds, a car in the distance. In here — nothing.

"Kevin? Sarah? My name's Alan. We're here to get you out." The voice carried but was easy and kind. Calming. "Can you hear me? Just yell or bang on the wall."

We listened. I strained to hear the way I would stretch to reach a can on a top shelf, as if by force of will I could make myself hear something. I looked at the chiseled wall beside me, the jagged timbers holding a beam in the soil above me, the woven belt of the man in front of me and the way his metal clip winked back at my headlamp. But there was nothing.

The line moved forward again. Alan rapped the walls as we walked with the butt of a wrench. The gas man raised and lowered the flame lantern. The mapper wrote on a rectangle of paper under his headlamp and called out coordinates and directions. Behind us, the wire unspooled and the radio operator reported whatever the mapper had just said. The backpack weighed on my shoulders.

Something brushed my face, and I staggered backward. Leo put a hand to my back. "It's okay," he said. "Just a cloth. See?"

I looked where he pointed over my shoulder. Yes, a cloth. A tattered rag, one end stuffed into a bracing timber and the other dangling down. Why had it been put there? Who'd left it and when? How long had it been hanging, limp and forgotten, in the dark?

Another stop. The bearers put the stretcher down. The gas man left the line and stood at a widening darkness, an intersection, waving his lamp. "All clear," he said after a few moments.

Alan nodded to the radio man as he pulled off his mask. "Okay, this is our fresh air base," he said. "Call 'em."

I removed my mask as I saw everyone else doing the same. The air was dry and smelled of dust.

"What's going on?" I said. "Why are we stopping?"

"The map says this is where things start branching off," Alan said. "It takes a lot of people to cover the ground. Teams don't split up, and nobody goes out of the line of sight of somebody else, so another team is coming in to explore that way." He nodded toward the black. "Air is fresh to here, so the next group can just walk in. We've got three more teams to work out from here. Leo will stay here with you."

My lips touched to start arguing, but no, he was right. I could see already how everyone else knew what to do without speaking, and how ridiculous it was to imagine I could be any kind of help.

And so I waited. Alan and the rest of his group walked away from us, following the rail lines, and long before their lamps were out of sight I could hear the next group coming. If Kevin and Sarah were anywhere nearby, and conscious, they would have heard us, as well. And yet, nothing. I sank down on my haunches, air tanks scraping against the wall, face in my hands.

The second group arrived, greeted us with passing nods, then started down the side passage, their own radio wire unspooling behind them. Their lights leapfrogged around each other, then disappeared around a corner. A radio operator named Ted joined us, bringing with him the hiss and crackle of reports about air and coordinates and degrees. Another group appeared only a few minutes later, trudged down the side passage the second group had taken, and disappeared in a third direction. All around me, darkness filled with banging, rapping, echoed voices, radio static.

Leo bent and said into my ear, "This is good news, you know."

"What?"

"The air — they're all finding moving air. Bad air is the big danger in mines, but when it's moving, you know it's fresh, that there's enough oxygen."

I twisted my neck to look up at him. I hadn't consciously listened to anything on the radio, letting everything wash past me as long as I didn't hear *boy* or *girl* or *found.*

"Everywhere? The air is good everywhere?"

"Well, no, never everywhere. But the main —"

"Oh, God." I wrapped my arms around my head.

A few minutes later I felt a hand on my shoulder. "Time to move," Leo said. "There's a new fresh air base ahead."

"What?"

"Follow the wire. No need for the mask. The other teams are ahead of us. They connected back up with the drift — the main tunnel. They should be pretty close to where the kids came in now."

"They're not even *there* yet?" I couldn't pull the thread of panic out of my voice. My knees were locked and aching, the weight pulling me back down, and I staggered drunkenly trying to get to my feet.

"Come on," Leo said. He steadied me

with a hand against my arm. "You're doing great."

What did it matter anymore how I was doing? How long had we been in this catacomb? How could living children have not heard us, or we them? I fell into step behind him, our lights jittering against the chiseled walls. The radio man followed. With my knees so stiff, my first steps were awkward and I caught my toe on a railway tie, my foot making a *whump* in the dirt as I righted myself, but Leo kept walking. My mouth tasted like metal.

Around one corner, over a mound of loose dirt. Walls narrowing, timbers closer to the top of my head. How long had they been in place, supporting the mountain over us? Another turn, and another. Gaping maws of darkness that interrupted the walls. Finally, another turn and light. A cluster of lamps turned toward us, blinding me. Just outside the glare I could see more lamps trained on a square of white encircled by men's silhouettes, arms extended, pointing. Islands of light in the dark.

"What is it?" I called. "Do you know anything?"

"Hey, there." I recognized Alan's voice. Calming, at ease. "Just figuring out where to go next. We're near the opening. Just waiting for you to get here so we can be quiet for a minute and listen."

"Oh — oh, sure." I could do that. I could be quiet. I could listen harder than I'd ever listened.

We stopped walking. The men at the map straightened. No one spoke. Alan rapped on the wall with a wrench. "Kevin! Sarah! Make a noise if you can hear me."

I closed my eyes. Reached, strained. Felt nausea pressing my stomach against my lungs. Did I hear something, something faint as a faraway cat, or was I only willing an apparition into existence?

"Kevin! Sarah!" My cry was a sob, pulled up from the center of my chest, my heart, my ribs, my veins. "Kevin! Sarah! *Please!*"

And then I heard it. I knew I did. A sound no louder than the breathing around me, yet not the breathing around me.

"Lena."

25

"Kevin? Sarah?" I twisted in the dark, as if I could find the source of the voice somewhere in the rock.

Alan held up his hand. "Shh, shh."

I caught my breath and held it.

"I'm here."

It was Kevin. It had to be. Sarah wouldn't have answered that way.

"Lena?"

Alan smiled and nodded at me.

"Yes! I'm here!" My voice rang against the rock. "We're coming!"

One of the men at the map raised his hand above the heads of the others, signaled ahead, then to the right. Alan nodded.

"Red team," he said. Another smile and nod to me. "You, too."

Leo and I followed Alan now, with the rest of the team in order behind us, walking along the line the map man had shown.

"Kevin? Sarah?" Alan called. "We're

headed toward you. Keep talking to me."

But all I could hear was the fall of feet, the rustle of pant legs, the creak and clatter of equipment. Were we moving the right way?

"Kevin? Sarah? We're coming. Keep talking."

We were walking uphill. A curve. Then our lights widened to reveal a three-way intersection. Alan held up his hand. We all stilled.

"Kevin? Sarah? Say something so we can find you."

"I'm here."

Quiet, but clear, from the passage to the right.

"That's Kevin!" I cried. Alan put out an arm to block me, and an extra pull on the backpack said Leo was holding me back as well. "Kevin!"

"Lena."

Like a whisper. Ovals of light swung toward the sound.

"Kevin?" Alan spoke as he walked toward the voice, with me close behind. "We'll get you right out. Don't move. We're coming to you. I've got Elena here with me. You okay?"

I heard something back. It might've been *"Uh-huh."*

"That's good. My name's Alan. I've got rope and shovels and anything you need. I got water. You thirsty?"

Another sound back. Again, maybe *"Uh-huh."*

"How do you feel? Are you dizzy, or do you feel tingly or sick?"

"No."

I understood. We were getting closer.

"Are you stuck at all?"

"No."

He was crying. I could hear it now. Choked and terrified, his throat knotted like a rope.

"That's good. Don't move, though. We're coming to you. Just stay right where you are."

"Ask about Sarah!" I whispered to Alan's shoulder. He shook his head. The relief that had run through me turned, doubled back on itself, and rose as a fresh column of fear.

"I'm Alan," he repeated. "You're Kevin, right?"

"Uh-huh."

"Well, then we found the right kid. If you were Steve or Tim or John or Rex or something I'd probably have to just say never mind, sorry to bother you. Some folks like it just fine down here, especially in the summertime. But you're Kevin. That's the kid we're looking for."

"O-o-o-kay."

I saw his foot first. A white sneaker, smudged and streaked but brighter than the ground beneath it. I shoved past Alan and ran. The rest of the form emerged in the light from my headlamp: a very small boy, seated on the ground, knees hugged to his chest, eyes wide, face grimy and streaked with tears. A boy who'd thought he was buried alive. I fell to my knees against the rocks and pulled his shoulders to my chest. My nostrils filled with the acrid tang of vomit and urine.

"It's okay, it's okay, it's okay," I repeated as I rocked back and forth. "You're safe. You're safe."

I felt his arms close around my back. His knees tipped against my hips. His shoulders heaved with gasping sobs.

"I'm s-sorry!" I started to hear as he'd catch a breath. His voice was gone, a raw whisper over gravel. "I'm sorry! I'm sorry!"

"Shhh. It's okay. It's okay. You're safe."

I put my hands on his shoulders to pull back and look at his face. I wiped the heel of my hand against his cheek. He clenched his fists to his chest, but not before I saw how scraped and bloody they were. His knees, pulled up against them, were bloody as well, the torn edges of his jeans framing the wounds.

"Are you okay?" I said.

He shook his head.

"Where's Sarah?"

His face crumpled and his head dropped over his knees. "I-I-I don't *know!*"

I felt a hand on my shoulder, steadying me, just as my own center collapsed.

"What happened?" said Alan. Soothing. Calm.

"I-I tried to find a way out, and th-then I couldn't *find* her! I *called,* and she *answered,* and then she didn't *answer* anymore!"

She didn't answer anymore.

She didn't answer anymore.

My ears rang and I felt faint. I fell over my knees.

"We'll find her, just like we found you." Alan's voice cradled us both. "I promise. I promise. Now you need to tell me what happened so we can get going."

I felt an arm around my shoulders, heard Leo's voice in my ear: "It's going to be all right."

I couldn't answer. I didn't believe it.

The story unfolded clearly enough, broken into segments as Stan, the medic, checked Kevin's wounds and examined his eyes, looked in his throat, checked his oxygen level and blood pressure. Kevin had come down on a dare, like Scott had said. Older boys had been down here the day before, helping each other in and out with a rope. Kevin had a flashlight the other boys had given him. He'd looked around and called back up what he'd seen to boys he thought were listening at the top. But no one answered. And the rope was gone. He tried to climb up, but the loose rocks kept sliding back underneath him.

A short time later he heard Sarah calling to him. She'd seen the boys gathered, but they'd told her she was too little, and a girl, and what they were doing was none of her business. When the boys left, she told Cindy she was going home and made a detour to the hole to see what all the fuss had been about. She heard Kevin calling, but when he told her to go get help she said no, that she was big, too, and came sliding down on the rubble to meet him.

The medic straightened, folding his blood pressure cuff, then nodded to Alan. Alan gave a quick nod back.

"Stan here says you're in great shape. We'll get those scrapes fixed up outside."

But Kevin went on as if no one had spoken. "My — my dad always said if you get lost to just — just *stay* in one place. You're — you're supposed to just *st-stay*."

369

His voice was papery and raw. It was easy to tell why we hadn't been able to hear him.

"That's right," Alan said. "That's exactly right. Your dad's real smart."

"But we waited a long time, and it got dark, and then I thought — I thought maybe we could walk out. So I told Sarah to *stay*. I told her. I made her *p-promise*. And — and the flashlight was going out, so I thought I better hurry. She didn't want me to go. She didn't *want* me to. She was *sc-scared* of the dark!"

The sobs took over. He sank into the blanket that had been wrapped around his shoulders and heaved great staggered breaths and couldn't talk. I wanted to hold him, but my arms were numb. Alan, squatting in front of him, cupped his hands around the boy's knees.

"It's okay," he said. "You were trying to do a real brave thing. Real brave. I'm proud of you. We're gonna find her. Just like we found you. Did your light go out? Did you get lost?"

Kevin nodded. He held up the lifeless flashlight, which might have been in his hand the whole time. Alan took it.

"Did you keep trying to find her, even though it was dark?" he said.

More nodding.

"And you probably got even more lost, didn't you?"

Nodding.

"You could hear her at first when you called, right?"

"Uh-uh-huh. A-and she was calling *me.* She tried to follow me and I told her to go back."

"But then you couldn't hear her anymore."

He shook his head. "She — she didn't — she didn't — *answer* — anymore."

"Okay." Alan squeezed Kevin's knees. "I'm proud of you. Now I want to ask you one more thing. I know you've been more scared than most people will ever be in their whole lives and you want to get out. But if you can handle it, I could use your help. Do you think you could do that? I'd like you to come with us while we look. Can you keep going? I think with light and all these people you can help us find your sister. Can you do that?"

Kevin lifted his head. His round eyes fixed on the fireman's face, and under the grime, I could see his father's shadow in the set of his jaw.

"Yes, s-sir," he said, nodding.

According to the map, the passage continued to branch and rebranch within the surrounding web of tunnels, all connected by various routes to one another and to the one where we'd found Kevin. But the map was old. We couldn't be sure. Alan radioed the nearest team to join us at the spot where we thought the children had come in so we could search outward from there. *Here,* he said, pointing at the map, and *here,* without waiting for confirmation or discussion. I sensed haste. Anxiety. Urgency.

Alan walked in front, now with Kevin and me behind. The rest of the team trudged at my back. Though Ramon continued to raise and lower the gas lantern behind me, no one seemed concerned about wearing masks as we attempted to retrace the steps Kevin had already taken. Cracked timbers supported the roof over our heads, and the walls were pocked by small caverns and cutouts that led only a few feet. The passage quickly narrowed, then took a sharp bend. Around the corner I could faintly hear voices and a jangle of equipment that wasn't ours, which meant we were getting closer to the other team. With a thud from inside my chest, I realized it also meant they had been through more passages without finding Sarah. I couldn't separate the different threads of fear winding around each other.

372

"That handle!" Kevin suddenly shouted. He pointed at what looked at first like a wooden stake leaning on a heap of dirt, but then I saw its curved shape. "That handle! It was sticking out of the dirt! I thought it was a shovel, maybe, but when I picked it up it didn't have anything on the end. So I left it there."

"That's *good*! And that was after you'd left Sarah?"

He nodded. "Uh-huh."

Alan turned his face away from us. "Sarah? Answer us! Are you there? Kevin's here! We're trying to find you!"

I only realized how large my hopes had swollen when the silence flattened them.

"Okay. Keep going."

We made it only a few yards farther before Alan stopped again. A separate tunnel angled upward to the right. Another forked off to the left and was partially blocked with a pile of loose rock and dirt that looked as if it had been spat out by a sagging timber directly above it. What I guessed to be the main passage continued ahead of us.

Alan looked back at me and narrowed his eyes, pulling on his mask. "How old is she again?" Alan asked.

"Five," I whispered.

"Does she always do as she's told?"

"Almost never."

"Uh-huh." He tugged the straps and gestured to Ramon, who stepped onto the rubble to reach the flame lantern to the ceiling and then slowly lowered it to the floor. The flame shrank, then went out. Extinguished. Dead.

"Why did the candle go out?" Kevin asked.

"Just stay back," Alan said, stepping atop the pile and then over it into the dark.

"Why?" Kevin said, looking up at me.

I couldn't make my mouth open, and only shook my head. I put my arm across Kevin's chest and pulled us both back against the wall opposite the opening. Dom, also now with his mask on, stepped onto the rubble and watched as the light from Alan's lamp faded.

Ramon knelt and relit the lantern. "It needs more air," he said. Then he stood, raised it to the ceiling above us, lowered it to the floor, and swept it from side to side. "See? Good out here. Feel the air moving? Bad air is heavier. Looks like there's some caught back in that passage and behind the pile."

He sounded so casual. He might as well have been doing a demonstration in an elementary school classroom on a sunny spring afternoon. But the only thing in my mind was that Sarah didn't have a lantern to tell her where she could breathe. Sarah, lost in the dark, could've gone anywhere. Sarah, who loved dresses that spin and bows on her stuffed animals. Sarah, lost in the dark.

I squeezed my eyes tight, pressing back against the part of me that wanted to scream, to cry, to run, to do anything but wait for a limp little body to appear in the opening.

Perhaps it was only a minute before the passage started to brighten again. Maybe more. Maybe less. Then Alan was there. Empty-handed, exactly as he had gone in.

"Okay," he said as he pulled off his mask. "Dead end. Let's assume she didn't stay wherever Kevin left her. Have an eye out for anything else she might mistake for the slide she took coming in."

He took a knee in front of Kevin. "Son, do you remember anything about what you were doing before you found the handle? Did you keep your hand on the wall? Do you remember different tunnels or turning one way or another?"

He twisted to look up at me and I could see tears start to pool against the rims of his eyes. With the blanket wrapped around his shoulders he looked like a little boy pretending to be Superman, struggling now under the weight of the importance of his answer. He turned back to Alan.

"I'm sorry —" he said, gulping back the end of the word. "I'm sorry." He ran the backs of his hands under his eyes. "I'm sorry. I don't know."

"You're doing great. Finding that handle was great. Now do you remember going across a dip like that?" He turned and pointed, his headlamp illuminating the mouth of another passage, a shallow trench across the opening.

"I — I don't think so."

"Okay, that's good. We'll go ahead, then."

"But I don't know!"

"You'd remember. You would've stumbled. I'll check for tracks, but I think you're right, and we need to meet the others. We'll send a team back if we need to."

"Okay."

A quick check seemed to satisfy Alan that there were indeed no tracks down the other passage, so with a notation on the map we started forward again. We bent around a corner, then found a rubble-filled shaft that Kevin thought he might remember. One more curve, and then I caught my breath. Another team with headlamps was already there, but there was also light falling from above. Blessed light. A faint, foggy waterfall of light rippling down a delta of rocks and loose dirt, widening and merging with the lights from the headlamps at the bottom.

Alan gave a nod to the others, who nodded and grunted greetings in return as we came to the bottom of the slide. I looked up. The hole looked so small at the top, twenty or twenty-five feet away, the slope so steep. A scatter of rocks around my feet. Had they come cascading down when Sarah slid in? Where, *where* was she now?

Alan squatted in front of Kevin. "Okay, Kevin. This is where you came in. You went down that way when you headed out, right?" He tipped his head in the direction from which we'd just come.

But Kevin looked anxious and torn. He stood with his back to the slide and glanced to the left and then the right. Left again. Right again.

"I — I think I went *that* way." He pointed away from us.

He couldn't be right. How would we have found him if he'd gone that way?

"Okay," Alan said.

"What?" I blurted.

"We haven't found her yet this way, have we? I think he's right." He stood and turned to the other men. They consulted for a moment over the maps, and then the other team left the way we'd come, directed to the intersection we'd passed, which according to the map led to another entire web of passages. We went the opposite direction, Kevin and then me again right behind Alan.

We rounded a curve, then hit a split. Radio wire showed where the last group had been, and we turned away from it. Kevin walked with his hand along the left wall, blanket around his shoulders, head down, as if intent on finding his way by feel.

"I think this is right," he announced suddenly.

"Good. Keep your eyes open."

More walking. A dip. A widening. A dead-end cutout. More walking.

"Stop!" Kevin shouted. A delta of loose rocks and soil spread onto the tunnel floor, similar to the one at the place where they'd entered, with a dome of darkness above it. He twisted away from me and stumbled toward the incline.

"I told her to go back! I told her to go back!"

Alan lurched after him. "Stop!"

But Kevin had already started to scrabble up. This pile wasn't as steep as the one that had brought him into the mine, and on this one he made progress.

"Sarah!"

I dove to follow him. "Don't go in there!"

Alan pressed his gas mask to his face as he reached to grab Kevin with his other hand.

"Sarah!"

Alan got hold of the blanket, which came away in his hand, then snatched again at anything else he could grab. I was just behind him, a finger's length away from Kevin's heels as he kicked loose stones back at my face.

"No, Kevin!"

"Both of you! Get back!"

Alan caught hold of Kevin's pants just as Leo's arm caught me around the waist. It was before I reached the top of the pile and the opening, but not before my light caught a flash of yellow T-shirt and a pool of unruly blonde hair.

26

The trucking company dispatcher was able to reach Paul, who left his load at an obliging depot for someone else to deliver and drove through the night and day to get back, arriving early the next evening. Kevin and I had been dozing in Sarah's hospital room, Kevin on the second bed, me pushed back in a recliner. Somehow we both sensed Paul's presence, coming fully awake to find him standing backlit at the door, jaw darkened, eyes lost in shadow. He didn't look at us — just stared at the heap of blankets in the other bed, the snarl of blonde hair, the twined plastic tubes. A steady beeping marked Sarah's pulse.

"How is she?" he whispered, taking a few steps forward.

"She's going to be fine," I said. I got to my feet. Yes, she would be fine, but she was in the hospital. On my watch.

Kevin sat up and swung his legs over the

side of the bed, but looked down at his shoes rather than at his father.

"They're going to take her off the oxygen in the morning, and if everything stays okay through the day, she can go home," I said.

Paul took another step. "I didn't really hear anything after — after they said she was in the hospital. What — is it, exactly?"

"The place where the kids went in — it was steep. We think after she got lost that she felt something like it and tried to go up. But it was just a dead end and there wasn't enough oxygen. Or, too much carbon monoxide. I don't know. She passed out."

"She could've died, then."

"Uh —" The answer stuck in my throat. "Yeah. Eventually." *Soon,* was what the medic had said in the mine. *Brain damage,* he'd also said. But I would leave those words where they belonged, deep underground.

"Has she been awake at all?"

"Some."

"Is she —" He took another step, then took his eyes away from his daughter to look at me. "Really . . . okay?"

So he'd already known what to fear. Had that fear been sitting beside him in the truck cab, hour after hour, driving back? "Yeah." I nodded, then swallowed. "She's herself.

She's scared to be alone and she wants to go home, but she's the same. Everything's going to be fine."

A gust of breath escaped him, and his shoulders sagged, as if that air alone had kept him inflated and upright, and now he was in danger of collapsing.

"Sit with her. I should go get something to eat."

"I — I don't want to wake her up."

"It's okay. She's been sleeping a lot. She'll want to see you."

I reached for my purse. The sooner I left the better. His child had almost died under my care. Maybe I could put off the moment when I'd have to accept his blame by slipping away right now. But between me and the bag stood Kevin, eyes on me, mutely pleading. I glanced at Paul, whose eyes were caught in a tunnel that shut out everything but Sarah. I was in no position to judge but that didn't prevent a painful stab that had nothing to do with my own dread. Kevin had suffered unimaginably, probably more than Sarah, though he lacked the hospital bracelet to prove it.

"You want to get a milk shake?" I asked.

He nodded. Paul said nothing. I left, Kevin trailing, and eased the door shut behind us. A pair of nurses murmured outside the next door. Faint beeping came from behind another. We pushed separately against the blue double doors that marked the edge of the pediatric wing. The silence between us ached.

"Your dad loves you," I finally said as the doors swung shut behind us. Kevin, eyes on his shoes, shrugged. They were the same shoes I'd seen in the mine, still blackened and scraped. "But I'm sure as soon as he heard Sarah was in the hospital, that's all he's been thinking about."

"It's okay," he said as we turned a corner and started down a different hallway toward the cafeteria.

I'd offered a platitude and gotten another in return. I wanted — I needed him to understand me. "No, it's not okay," I said, "but he's tired and worried and he's been scared about you guys for a long time. He could see you were all right, but Sarah still looks pretty bad with the tubes and all."

"It's okay." Another shrug. His shoes squeaked against the tile. "He oughta be mad."

"Of course, but that's my problem, not yours."

"You can't stop him being mad at me."

"What?" I turned on my heel and caught Kevin by the shoulders. "Mad at *you*?"

The sleep-twisted cowlick on top of his head faced me as he spoke to his shoes. "I broke the rules. It's my fault. He's supposed to be mad."

"What's your fault? *I* was in charge. And those boys *left* you! I will never forgive them!"

"Everybody knows you're not supposed to go in mines! I'm in a lot of trouble!"

My breath caught in my chest and my throat and against the backs of my eyes. I dropped to my knees and shook his shoulders, surprising myself as much as him. "Kevin! Look at me! Your dad is *not* mad at you! You were unbelievably brave. You were trying to save your sister, and you *did*. You're the one who found her! You went in that mine because you're eleven years old. Kids everywhere do things like that. But the ones who left — they're the ones who are in trouble. This was not your fault! Do you hear me? It was *not your fault*. You saved her!"

He faced me but looked into space somewhere beyond my shoulder. The responsible child. His guilt would not be banished so easily.

"Come on," I said, not waiting for him to tell me something he didn't believe but thought I wanted to hear. I stood and turned him back down the hallway. "We're getting chocolate this time."

Paul gave no hint of any anger toward me, and in fact was anxious for me to stay nearby, but he still hadn't said anything of consequence to Kevin before Sarah left the hospital the next afternoon. He'd put an arm around his son's shoulders as they stood over Sarah's sleeping form that night and squeezed him hard against his side. Whether that was the firmness of unshaken love or inexpressible anger I couldn't tell. And neither could Kevin, apparently, who continued to lurk around the margins of the room, keeping as much distance as possible between himself and his father, like a dog afraid of being kicked. Fear of punishment more terrible than punishment itself.

I hoped Sarah would settle back down when she got home. Even with her father there, I'd been unable to leave the hospital the night before. She would get panicky if she woke and I didn't appear quickly enough, so around ten a nurse surreptitiously waved me into the unoccupied room next door. Sarah was equally desperate for Kevin to be there every time she opened her eyes, but he could get along dozing in the chair while his father took the other bed.

I wanted to go home, wherever that was. Away from need and terror and grief and feeling responsible for carrying all of it. But I couldn't do it. I couldn't look Sarah in the eyes and tell her that she was fine, that her dad was here now, that I would see her in the morning, and then watch her face crumple into tears.

So we left the hospital together, and I followed Paul's truck through town and up their street, Kevin staring woodenly out the windshield beside me. It wasn't until the truck had turned into the drive that I noticed the balloons and banner hung over the door — sheets of paper taped together and lettered in red marker. Poppy, surely. WELCOME HOME SARAH AND KEVIN, it said. *And* Kevin. Bless her. I stopped in front of the house and turned off the ignition.

"You see that, Kevin?" I said, pointing. "You two are famous."

He glanced at the door, and then I saw him look over his shoulder to his dad's truck, where Paul was just going around the tailgate to get to Sarah's side.

"Uh-huh," he said.

"People are glad you're okay. Both of you. Everyone is."

He didn't answer. Just opened the door,

got out, and slammed it. I reached across to get my purse from the floor and saw the paper bag he'd used for his dirty clothes from the mine. He'd folded and crushed and crumpled it into a dense brown mass and wedged it as far under the seat as it would go.

I left it there and got out of the car, then opened the back door to get out some of the flowers and stuffed animals I'd brought from the hospital. We hadn't talked about any plans for the night, or even acknowledged Sarah's need to have me close. I had no idea what Paul might be assuming. My one idea was to get Sarah to introduce her new stuffed animals to the old ones, using them to reconnect her to Buffers, then escape to Tuah's without any dramatics. I'd already pictured a long bath, the guest room bed, and solitude.

"Lena? You coming?" Sarah stood at the door, holding it open for me.

"I'll be right there, honey."

By the time I got into the house, Paul was flipping through mail at the kitchen counter, and Kevin had already disappeared. I saw the closed bathroom door as I followed Sarah into her room.

"Well, here you go," I said, setting a bouquet of daisies on top of her bookshelf.

"Your same room exactly the way you left it. Bet you wished you'd picked up your clothes."

I might as well have not said anything.

"Buffers!" she cried, leaping onto the bed and landing on her knees. Lethargy, gone. Confusion, gone. Dizziness, apparently gone. Clearly, she was feeling better.

"Where do you want the new ones? I have the puppy and the bear and the pink kitten."

"Right here," she said, holding out her arms. She pulled the stuffed animals to her chest and buried her nose in the tops of their heads. "They smell like hospital," she said.

"I guess so. That'll go away. Why don't you help them make some new friends?"

I spent the next few minutes fetching and rearranging as she directed. Eventually I heard the toilet flush, the water run, then the bathroom door open and bang against the tub. Steps down the hall to the next bedroom. A door closed. My heart twisted.

I wished Paul wasn't here. That was it — more than I wanted to be alone, I wanted to be alone with the children. If Paul weren't here, there wouldn't be anyone holding the other end of that taut, vibrating cord that ran between Kevin and his father.

I wanted to make pizza and let the children put anything on it they could find. Have ice cream and use chocolate syrup to make drawings on it and then laugh at them. I wanted to hear the bath running, and then the shower, comb out Sarah's hair, pull the curtains and gather close together under the lamp and read *The Black Stallion,* experiencing Alec's terrifying shipwreck and discovering how overcoming fear and suffering helped him grow up. Then maybe we could cry, and talk about how scared we each were, and say how glad we were to have one another.

I straightened and blinked the warmth away from my eyes. "Look," I said. "You've got plenty to do here. I'm just going to run over to Poppy's and thank her for making that nice sign."

"I wanna come see the puppies!"

"No, you should stay here and get ready for dinner." I was only saying whatever came to mind. I had no idea what Paul had thought about for dinner. "You can see them tomorrow. It's been a long day."

"*No!* I wanna go with you! I wanna see the *puppies!*"

"Shh, now. Don't yell."

"What's going on?" Paul's head and

shoulders appeared around the edge of the door.

"I just thought I'd go say thank you to Poppy while Sarah finished getting settled here."

"But I wanna see the puppies!" Sarah shouted. Then she actually stamped her foot. My head swiveled around to stare at her.

"Behave yourself," I said without thinking, then instantly felt my face flush. I'd never disciplined the children in front of their father and wanted to reel the words back in before I'd even finished saying them.

"Don't act like a baby!" Paul snapped. My head swung back in time to see him stiffen and straighten. "I mean — calm down. You can see the puppies but not if you act like that."

Why did he have to be here? My need to get away from Paul now outweighed my duty to start easing away from Sarah.

"Okay, come on, then," I said, holding my hand out to Sarah. "Let's just go now."

At Poppy's, I could hear TV through Mama Ruth's open window, a yammering of puppies, and Sugar snarling at the baseboard, but no one answered the door. Of course Poppy would be at work — I knew that. But I'd read the banner as if it was her actual voice, calling from across the road. I tried twice. I didn't want to go back.

"Do you want to go up the road and look for some flowers for the table?" I asked.

"I'm hungry," Sarah said.

"Okay."

She slid her hand into mine and pulled. Dinner. I couldn't remember what was in the fridge but I could busy myself pulling something together for them to eat and then excuse myself. Somehow.

Sarah reached the front door first. A river of shouting poured out as she pushed it open.

"Could you even think of anything else to do wrong? Don't go in mines! Don't move if you get lost! Don't *ever* leave your sister! You're supposed to take care of her! *Always!* Can you tell me *anything* that was going on in your head? Tell me! *Tell me!*"

The voice came from down the hallway, muffled sounds of crying threading themselves into the pauses. Not a river — a flash flood, with fury and terror and blame tumbling over each other and splattering the walls. Sarah stood frozen beside me, her hand thin and limp like a piece of cloth in my own. I should have taken her and fled. Found high ground.

"I'm sorry, Dad!"

Kevin. I hauled Sarah onto my hip, no matter how far too big she was to be carried. Her arms twined around my neck like vines. I ran the length of the hallway toward him.

"Stop it! *Stop it!*" I yelled. The door was open. I saw Paul, just releasing Kevin's shoulders to swivel toward me. "Let go of him!"

Kevin darted toward me and threw himself against my hip and Sarah's legs.

"What are you *doing*?" A sob had pushed my voice up into my face, high against my cheekbones. Sarah slid from my hip as I dropped to my knees and pulled the two living, healthy children into my arms. And started rocking and crying. Crying and rocking.

I extracted the arm I had around Sarah, who pressed against my belly, and pushed against the center of Kevin's chest so I could look up into his face.

"This was not your fault! This was *not your fault*! Do you hear me? Don't *ever* let anyone tell you different! This was not your fault! You're eleven years old! You were playing! Sarah's fine! And you *saved* her!"

Kevin didn't answer. I pulled him close again.

Only then did I lift my eyes to see Paul.

He sat on the edge of Kevin's bed, hands lying limp on each side as if his knees had given out and he'd collapsed there.

"How could you say something like that?" I sobbed to him. "This was *my* fault! Not his. I pushed him too hard to spend time with those kids. He knew they were bad. He *knew* it!"

Paul bit his lip and looked down, shaking his head. I could see the trembling in the mattresses before I saw it in Paul. After a moment he looked up at Kevin, wiping at his eyes with the back of his hand. The birthmark covered his throat like a bruise.

"I'm sorry," he whispered. "I'm so sorry. I was just so scared I'd lose you. I'm sorry. I'm sorry. I was just so scared. I need you two. I can't lose anybody else."

He doubled over, catching his forehead in his hands, and curled himself around his great gash of grief.

We cried together, the four of us.

Tuah brought goulash and a bowl of mixed lettuces.

"How did you know?" I whispered. She wore a Coors T-shirt and baggy jeans and a gray cardigan. She smiled.

"I told you. It's how it is here."

I fought back a pressing urge to cry. She

handed me a paper bag with string handles, which I hooked on my wrist as I took the soup tureen in both hands.

"Do you want to come in?" I said.

She looked at the window, then up somewhere over the top of the door, then back at me. That's when I saw it, too — the membrane of grief that sealed us in the house together. She shook her head.

"No, I don't think so. You just take care of those children." She rolled her lips together. "And that poor man. Your bed's ready, and I've got more goulash on the stove if you want it. But I won't wait up for you." And she turned on her heel and strode back to her truck with her head down.

So I reheated the stew and the four of us ate together, leaning toward one another over the table like branches over a pond. I sent them all to shower and bathe while I washed the dishes. Sarah finished first and came to me with a comb and a stack of books — *The Very Big Word Book, The Way the World Works, The Book of Greek Myths* — which seemed to have nothing in common except that they were all large and long. Kevin was next, who nestled into the other end of the sofa and started to flip through the available books. As soon as his father reappeared — freshly shaved, in a clean T-shirt and jeans and socks — I dished out ice cream with no regard for the ice crystals on top. The children drizzled chocolate syrup over it, and I heard the first giggles as Kevin said his looked like a butt.

Finally we found our way to Sarah's room, where Paul sat on the foot of the bed while the rest of us huddled together on the floor to read. I told Sarah I was going to wait until she went to sleep, but then I'd be going back to Tuah's house because I missed my bed just the same way she'd missed hers. Just as her eyes widened and she started to blink faster, Paul spoke up.

"I think this is a good night for a campout," he said. "Right here in Sarah's room. What do you say, Kevin? I'll get the sleeping bags."

"Really?" Sarah squealed.

"Really. Can you let Elena go home if we do that?"

She hesitated only a beat, then nodded rapidly, chin bobbing against Buffers's ears.

"Kevin?"

They looked at each other for a moment, just a moment in which I saw something pass between them and connect them. Not a challenge. An alliance.

"Sure."

Kevin and Paul spread sleeping bags on

the floor, and we read far into the night, the stick-figure families on the walls linking arms around us. When Sarah started breathing deeply and I kissed her cheek, Kevin was already asleep. I slipped out of the room, turning on the night-light before I turned off the lamp.

I made my way to the living room, where my purse waited by the door, switching off lights as I went. Paul appeared, silent on stocking feet, as I hooked my purse over my shoulder. His voice was low.

"I — I'm real sorry about what happened earlier but I'm glad you were here," he said.

I nodded. I couldn't think of anything to say.

"I just think of him as being so grown up and I was so mad and so afraid, and I just blew up. I wish I hadn't. I wish I could take it back —"

"It's okay now."

"— but I have to tell you something else. You said you were sorry. You said it was your fault. It's not. You have to know that."

I bit my lip. "Look — I'm not a mom. I don't know what I'm doing. I pushed him out there. He just didn't want to be a coward in front of those other boys. When he went in that mine, he was making the best decision he could. And every decision after that, too. He's just a kid. If the kids had stayed to help him out, none of this would've happened. We'd scold him and tell him not to do it again, but then it'd be over." I shook my head. "It just isn't fair."

There was a long pause. I hitched my purse higher on my shoulder. "I better go," I said.

"Wait —" Paul started to put a hand out, then stopped himself. Whatever he was about to say was a struggle. "You're not — the mom. But you need to know something *about* their mom. She wouldn't have known they were lost. She would've lost track of what time it was or forgotten where they went or thought it was part of a game." He plunged his hands into his pockets. "I don't understand anything. I miss my wife. I wish I had her back, no matter what. What happened was awful. But I'd be lying if I told you my kids weren't better off the way things are now."

The inflammable, unsayable words, once said, turned to smoke that hung in the air around us. And like smoke, they permeated the carpet, the paint, my hair, and my clothes. They clogged my throat and stopped my mouth. I stood with my thumb hitched under my shoulder strap, unsure whether it was all right to move or breathe.

"I — I don't know," I finally said. Which was true.

"I do." Paul reached around me for the door and pulled it open. In the wash of fresh air, the smoke dissipated. "Thanks for everything, anyway," he said. "Good night."

I stepped over the threshold. I noticed each breath as I walked to the car, my chest widening, my shoulders lifting. I stopped with my hand on the door and looked back. Paul's silhouette raised a hand before stepping back. A haze of light I hadn't noticed was there disappeared and the front door clicked shut.

27

I was always aware that my father seemed older than other people's parents, but a week later, when he stood from Tuah's kitchen table in Leadville to greet me, I was struck by how very old he looked. What had happened this summer? He was far too old to be her son. Her second child, even. Tuah had told me yesterday that he was on his way, but I still stopped in the service porch doorway, taken aback.

"Hey," Tuah said, only barely glancing up from the beans she was snapping into the kitchen sink.

"Hi, Elena," my father said, opening his arms.

"Hi, Dad."

He put his hands on my shoulders and pulled me forward so we could meet, ear to ear, clavicle to clavicle, bent forward at the waist to just barely make contact. Had I ever embraced him the way Sarah embraced me?

"How are you?" he asked, lowering himself back into his chair, one hand on the table, the other on the edge of the seat. He wore twill pants that might as well have been draped over a stick. I stayed standing.

I glanced at Tuah. "I'm fine."

"You look good. You look really good. Mountain living suits you. Sit down — you must be tired."

Must be? Just before I left the Koffords', the children and I had been lying on our backs in the backyard, squinting up through the leaves, having contests over who could hold a breath the longest, who could show the most teeth at once, who could wiggle ears or make a tongue taco or whistle the highest or lowest. Shade was different here — brighter, more open — than in California, where live oaks closed like hands around the deep portico at my father's front door. I hadn't felt tired at all. But now suddenly I did. And I didn't want to.

"Tuah, can I help with anything?"

"You could probably wash the greens."

"Thanks," I said automatically. She glanced at me, eyes narrowed.

"Anytime," she said.

"You don't want to sit down?" my father said.

"No, I'm fine. We can still catch up." I

opened the refrigerator and doubled over to reach the bottom drawer. I found more of the garden greens Tuah had brought down from the cabin, heaped like loose pillow stuffing in produce bags. I fished a colander out of a cupboard, and Tuah edged over to give me access to the faucet. What on earth was there for us to talk about? If only the kitchen was bigger, and I could be farther away.

"So what's new?" I asked, starting the water and dumping the leaves into the sink as I plugged the drain. "Let's see — did the Howards move out?"

"Yes, and just like I expected, they left the place like a junkyard. I look out the front window and all I see are weeds, weeds, weeds. I don't know how anybody is going to buy it. Paint peeling, roof needs work. It's terrible."

"That's too bad."

"It's a simple thing to take care of a place. A little maintenance. A little self-respect. A little care for other people."

I thought of Poppy's front yard — the haphazard flowers and grasses, the sprawling potentilla, the spruce wrapping itself around the corner of the house, the wind chimes and ornaments and figurines. I doubted she owned a working lawn mower.

"For sure," I said. I shut off the faucet and swirled my hand through the water, watching the lettuces part like leaves on a pond, then close together again, trying to think of something, anything to ask that would keep him from running a cheese grater over my nerves. "And how did school wrap up? I guess I left before you were done."

"Fine. Fine enough. A lot of low grades in geometry. Those sophomores are going to be a tough bunch the whole way through. It happens every few years — one class that just has a bad personality. I don't expect to see many of them next year. They'll quit math, you can take that to the bank."

"Probably so," I said. So perhaps there was no subject he couldn't turn into a judgment. I scooped the colander through the water, pulling up all the leaves I could, then caught the fugitives with my hand and tossed them in with the others. I yanked out the plug.

"How about you?" he said. "What's new here?"

I looked over at him. He sat with one elbow on the table, leg crossed, sock piled around his ankle so that an inch or two of bony shin peeked out from under the hem of his pants. I looked back down at the sink.

Rivulets of sand had started to form as the water drained away. *How about you?* Where could I even start?

"Well, the kids take up most of my time."

"How old are they, again?"

"Kevin is eleven and Sarah's five. Almost six. She'll start first grade in the fall."

"Phoo," he breathed out, shaking his head. "Tough ages. That's tough."

Tough ages? What did that mean? I felt an irrational desire to shield them, or the idea of them, from his judgments.

"How long do you have them at a time?" he went on. "A day or two?"

"More like a week, usually."

"Oh my. That's a lot. You're doing a lot. I really don't think most people could do that."

I turned the water back on and started swishing sand down the drain. He was wrong. Had I never really listened to him before — or just never understood? My father's voice, the narration of my life to this point, now sounded so brittle and harsh and out of place. Most people couldn't do what I was doing? Tuah would do it. She had, in fact, for the children and for me. Poppy. Joan. Mindy. An entire community of people had done what I was doing now for months before I came. Then add Paul, who had dug himself in for a lifetime of supporting a wife who couldn't care for him, or his children, or sometimes even herself. A string of men had gone into a dangerous mine to look for children they didn't even know. And Leo, bless him, didn't hold my bad behavior against me, volunteered to join them, hauled me back from danger, and after we found Sarah, held on to a vomit-stained boy when I was too distraught to think of him.

I don't think most people could do that.

My father was wrong. People cared for other people all the time. And I had become one of them.

The realization stunned me. But I managed to keep my discovery to myself.

"Oh, come on, Dad," was all I said as I shut off the water. "Sure they could."

I'd always noticed that my father was different here. Ordinarily he saw the world quite clearly and settled himself onto his worn heels to make pronouncements, hands captured in the side pockets of his jackets. People were good or bad. Actions were right or wrong. Good people took right actions and good consequences followed. Simple. Only here did he defer to anyone else's opinion, and it was clearly a superhuman effort. But the dynamic was such a baseline condition of the visit that I'd never been conscious enough to bother identifying the source of the change. Tuah, I could see, was different as well now that my father was here. This was the woman I'd been slightly unsure of when I was little. Sharp. Curt. Displeased.

I'd forgotten.

Within an hour, my father had already gotten into one argument with his mother over whether a man he saw earlier was and always would be a liar because of a disagreement over a spyglass when they were children in Hat Creek. Another had almost erupted when he told me to be careful about getting "stuck" here because this was "one of those situations where people start having things done for them and start to expect it." I think Tuah bit her tongue only because she believed I had more right to be offended than she did. Shortly after that, I decided we needed some different salad dressing and that I probably had a few other unnamed errands that had to be done right then.

I left the house like a refugee from a natural disaster. The torrent of judgments and absolutes had washed the ground out from underneath me. Fragile ground, apparently, because I'd never had a problem like this before. Had he always been like this? Always? All I knew now was that he was wrong, and while living alone with him, I'd never noticed. Now, I didn't know what to stand on anymore.

I rolled through town slowly, without stopping, and found myself following the course of the river. I meandered alongside it, well below the speed limit, and eventually pulled onto the dirt shoulder at the spot where I'd taken Sarah and Kevin to make their boats, allowing the cloud of dust to clear before I opened the door. I got out and glanced up at the sky. A storm was building, later than usual. I wouldn't have an excuse to stay out much longer but I couldn't bear to go back.

My canvas shoes were ill-suited to trudging over the uneven grass clumps and boggy hollows. By the time I got to the bank I'd turned my ankle twice and my feet were soaked. And I still couldn't say exactly why I was here.

I folded my arms and watched the water rush and ripple. I walked closer, then squatted on my heels at the edge and touched the water. Unzipped my pants all the way, which felt so much better. The water ran through my fingers, clear and cold, distorting their shapes so that they appeared like the fat fingers of a baby or the gnarled ones of an old woman, depending on how you looked.

I looked upstream, toward the mountains, then back down at my fingers. Old woman. Baby. Back again. I heard a grumble of thunder and looked over my shoulder. Clouds mounded on top of each other in their haste to get to me.

I didn't want to leave this spot. Or maybe this town.

My father was wrong.

The water rippled on, leaping and sparkling. The sun bore down on my shoulders. I dropped back onto my seat, hugged my knees to myself, and rested my cheek against them. We had sat right over there, Kevin and I, talking about making mistakes. I had chastised us both for being so paralyzed by the fear of doing something wrong that we did nothing at all. But what did "right" even mean? My father had made me believe that there really was such a thing. Now it seemed such judgments must be only illusions, that what seemed bad could become good somewhere downstream, or if it was seen from another angle. Or the other way around. An effect of light, nothing more.

I felt a drop against my arm. A splash from the river? I brushed it away, then waved a fly from my face. Another drop. And another. I looked up, then twisted my neck around to check behind me. The sky above and before me was still blue, but rain reached forward from the darkening cloud over my shoulder. A peal of thunder smacked against the rocks around me and thudded in my chest.

I didn't move.

What if, perhaps, the fire wasn't an unrelieved disaster? In nature it wasn't. New growth required it, even. Did the father widowed by my actions and bereft of two daughters perhaps remarry? Was there now another child who would grow up and have more children, children who might otherwise never have been born? Was the new family a source of unexpected joy?

The drops multiplied until rain ran over my face and hair. It soaked through my shirt, and I turned my face up toward the sun that still buttered the far shore of the river, letting the water run across my cheeks and down my neck.

I would never know. But I had never considered before that it was possible.

I didn't deserve forgiveness. No good I might do could ever atone for the grief I'd caused. And I'd come to a point where it was no longer possible to avoid the risk that my actions might cause more. Should I stay or go? Go where, and do what? Give my baby to someone else? To whom, then? The consequences of my choices would stretch forward for generations. I could ruin more lives. But if Paul and the children were to be believed, I also had the capacity to render good.

In the absence of surety, maybe I could be forgiven for allotting a sliver of space in my mind to hope.

Beauty from ashes.

28

We drove up to Hat Creek the next morning, Tuah and my father and I, each of us preserving our exit options by taking separate cars. My plan was certainly the simplest: I would spend the first day being a helpful and dutiful family member, prove how well socialized I was the next day by going on a ride with Leo, then prove how indispensable I was — to somebody, at least — by leaving the following day to return to the Koffords'. Tuah and my father would have to negotiate their own interactions after that.

By that measure, day one exceeded expectations. The garden plants had grown large enough that Tuah now trusted me to weed, a pleasantly solitary task. A seepage around the neck of the water pump called for my father to take the pipes apart and reassemble them, so he was constructively occupied as well. By the time I'd finished weeding and moved on to adding a coat of paint to the porch posts, Tuah had put my father to work tightening and securing the fence around the garden.

While my father and I worked outside, Tuah shuttled between the pump and the cabin, hauling out a tub against one hip, or a stack of pots balanced against her chest, washing them, then taking them back inside. Other times she'd carry a fresh pot of water in to heat on the stove, then bring the hot one out and add it to the washtub. Smoke drifted out of the stovepipe. Pots clashed and clanged. At some point, I thought I heard her whistling.

Through the course of the afternoon, dry white clouds wandered across the sun, drawing us into light or shadow the way waves pull across the sand. The wind that carried them sighed through the pines, then drifted on. The rhythm of work served as an undercurrent that steadied and calmed us, and eventually brought us together on the porch, the scattered wreckage of the Alvarez family at last washing onto a common shore.

"That yellow is a nice color," my father said at one point as we painted the porch posts.

"Warm," Tuah said.

"Exactly," my father said.

411

We lapsed back into silence. Mac, stretched out on the dirt and dreaming, huffed little barks to himself and twitched his paws. A mourning dove cooed from the trees somewhere behind the house.

"Did the mice get into much this winter?" my father said.

"Just toilet paper. I've got all the food in cans."

"That's good."

I took my cup to the paint can, poured some more in, then went back to the post I'd been painting, squatting down to work paint into the joint surrounding the base. The sun's low angle made it hard to see into the shadowed side of the post.

"Something sure smells good," my father said.

"Goulash," Tuah said.

"That's good," my father said.

The wind stilled as the sun lowered, but it was warm and we ate outside, sitting in a row on the edge of the porch, bowls in our laps. It seemed we sat at the bottom of a golden pool, looking up at the blue surface overhead. We watched the light fade and the blue gradually deepen. Still no one spoke or got up to go inside. I reached under my shirt and ran a thumb along the waist of my pants, tugging it down a little farther.

When I could barely make out her outline, Tuah turned toward us.

"Thank you for your help," she said. "It's been a good day."

"It has," my father said.

I think she nodded.

"And thank you for coming," she said, more quietly still.

"Of course," my father said.

I looked at their silhouettes, just discernible against the darker pines beyond them, the chin and cheekbones I shared. My people, such as they were. All that I had.

Well, not quite. Plus one.

"Where are we going?" I asked Leo the next morning as the trees closed around us and the house disappeared. I looked forward to getting out into the sun soon. It was still early, and I held the reins inside my fleeced pocket. The sweatshirt covered a tank top I expected I'd want later, but right now my cheeks and ears tingled in the chill.

He turned around in the saddle and grinned at me. "Exploring," he said. "New frontiers."

" 'To boldly go where no man has gone before?' Or just go at all after I bit your head off?"

He laughed. I'd tried to apologize at the

413

hospital, after Sarah was safe, but he'd brushed it off. "Don't worry about it," he'd said. "No bonfires. Got it." Then he gave my shoulder a brotherly squeeze and put a kiss on my forehead before he left.

"Well, it's a place I've never gone before."

"Great." I leaned forward and scratched Spot's neck. It was warm against my hand.

"How are you doing?" Leo asked.

I cast around for an answer. A lot had changed since that night at the hospital. I gave the horse's neck a final pat.

"It's been — a lot," I said. "Got things on my mind."

"I bet," he said. He reined his horse around a granite outcrop, then nudged him forward again.

Bless Leo. Any answer was taken at face value. No prying, no follow-up questions demanding answers that were sure to be misunderstood. If I wanted to tell him more, I could. My choice.

"I know this path," I said. "It leads to a big meadow."

"Yeah, another guy chasing cows up this way last week told me that if you go along the base of Washington Rock you'll start following a really thin little creek that leads up to another meadow where he said the wildflowers are amazing right now."

"Washington Rock?"

He turned in his saddle and looked back at me. "The ridgeline — to the west. Are we thinking of a different meadow?"

"I have no idea."

"Huh." He turned forward again. "I guess we'll just see."

We rode in companionable silence the rest of the way to the meadow, breaking it only occasionally with little scraps of conversation about whether I'd had enough breakfast or what the name of an unfamiliar blooming shrub might be. But shortly before we got there I noticed something.

"Can we stop? I think my horse is limping a little."

"You think?" He turned around in his saddle and watched the pinto walk. "Which foot? I don't see anything."

"I'm not sure."

He studied my horse's steps for a few more moments. "Well, we'll stop at the meadow, and I'll check."

A few minutes later the trees thinned, then parted to reveal a wide bowl where the grass thrived but the trees pulled their feet back. Leo reined in and let his horse drop its head into the grass.

"There," Leo said, pointing at the rock

ridgeline that rose over the trees at one edge of the meadow. "Washington Rock."

"Well, yeah. I've seen it before. Why Washington?"

He grinned. "We'll take another look at the other end of the meadow. But hop down first. Let's see what's going on with those feet."

My horse's head was down before I was, and he let Leo pick up a front hoof as he snatched at the grass. I stood to the side, holding the reins. Leo prodded around in the hard tissue with his finger, flicking away packed dirt and small rocks.

"So how are the kids doing, anyway?" he asked.

"They're shaken up, for sure. Kevin's beating himself up something awful."

"I bet." He let the hoof drop. "A couple little rocks, but nothing he'd limp for." The horse swished his tail and shook his head, then snatched another mouthful of grass. Leo patted his shoulder, then ran a hand along his side to go around the back to the other foot in question.

"I try to keep telling Kevin he's the one who saved her. That he did everything he could, more than you could ever ask of a kid his age. But all he can think about is that he did something wrong and nearly killed his sister."

"I get that." Leo had to duck his shoulder into the horse's rear quarter to get him to shift his weight and give up his foot. How could he be so nonchalant about this? I came around the horse's head to join him on the other side.

"But he's just a kid! He's eleven years old! Kids break rules all the time, and everything turned out okay."

"That was luck. Coulda gone either way. If I were him, I'd be thinking about that all the time." More dirt flicked away. "Besides, what does okay even mean? Nightmares, don't want to be alone, afraid of the dark. I'd take a broken leg over that anytime."

"Remind me not to send him to you for comfort." I started running my fingers through the horse's mane. "So what makes *you* such an expert, anyway?"

"Are you kidding?" He glanced up, supporting the hoof between his knees with one hand while fishing in his back pocket with the other. "With my crazy brother? Childhood sticks with you. You blame yourself for stuff that's not your fault all the time. I sure have." He opened the pocket knife and turned his attention back to the hoof, digging intently at something. "He ran away one time after I took the last waffle. A stupid freezer waffle. I wasn't even hungry, but I just wanted to win. He was gone for four days. We never knew where he was, but he came back filthy and with these big bruises on his ribs. I thought it was all my fault."

"Wow."

"There!" He wedged his thumb against the knife blade and pulled a rock from the hoof, holding it up for me to see. It was irregular and about the size of a grape. "You're his guardian angel. Likely he's been walking around with this for a while."

He dropped the hoof and patted the horse's rump, then flicked the rock away into the grass. "Tell me you're not combing his mane," he said.

"I am. He could do with a little spruce-up. I'm going to put little bows in it when I'm finished."

"He's already been gelded, you know. You could let him keep a little dignity."

"I'm surprised the ten-year-old girl didn't already do it," I said. I flipped a section of white hair to the other side of the horse's neck, away from the black. "Okay, so how'd *you* figure out it wasn't your fault?" I said.

"The gelding?"

I smirked at him. "With your brother, smartass."

"Oh, right. Time, I guess. And talking —

my folks had to explain the same thing to me over and over. Kids get weird stuff stuck in their heads if somebody doesn't set them straight."

"So that's what I should do with Kevin?"

I heard a few more pats against the horse's hide. "Well, you oughta know."

"What?"

"The fire."

My mouth actually started to move, to ask what he was talking about, before his meaning struck me like a fist in the chest.

"Are you — do you mean — you think that's the same *thing*?"

"Isn't it? I mean, I don't know the details but that doesn't matter. You're hardly the first person to blame yourself for more than your share."

"It's not even close! People *died* from what I did!"

"Sarah could've died, just as easily, no matter what Kevin did. They got lucky. And you had bad luck. You didn't walk up and shoot those people, right? They were in the wrong place, wrong time. Nobody can ever know all the reasons."

I fumbled for words. Or even identifiable feelings or thoughts. Shock, perhaps, was the only one. I had never talked about the fire with anyone. Never. To my mother and father, it was taboo. As much as possible, I avoided mentioning it with everyone else. I had certainly never heard anything like this.

"How can you *say* it like that?"

"Because it's true." He pushed his hat back on his head. "Look — I'm not saying you didn't start the fire. But you were a kid, messing around, right? Just bad luck it turned into anything, that's all. If it had just scorched some grass or a building, you'd have gotten yelled at. But somehow it got away, and that's not something you did. *You* didn't make the weather. How fast did it go? And why? Did firemen respond fast enough? Did somebody not call when they should've? Did people not evacuate when they should've? Did they try, but" — he waved a hand — "I dunno, the car didn't start. Because a mechanic screwed up. Anything. A hundred things. I don't know what happened, but I do know it's crazy to think that one little kid is responsible for all of it, alone. You're not God."

My hands hung limp at my sides. I'd never, never, never, never, never thought of any of those things.

I couldn't think of them now. There was no mental structure in place for them to connect to. The idea that I could be allowed to imagine anything good growing in the scorched path behind me was still too new. And now to shift blame as well? Who had the authority to do that? Not me. And not him.

"Are you okay?" He took a step closer. "I'm sorry — did I say something wrong?"

I shook my head. He put a hand on my arm.

"There's nothing wrong," I said, twisting away. "I just — I don't know. I — can we just get going again?"

He looked at me for a moment, then pulled his hat down over his brow and nodded. He put a hand on my back to steer me around the horse's head to the saddle.

"All aboard," he said, holding the stirrup for me to step into.

I swung up into the saddle and took the reins. "Thanks," I said, looking down.

He squinted up at me. "If you don't want me to talk about it, just let me know."

I shook my head. "No — I don't know. That's not it. I guess I don't know what to think." And I didn't. I just — didn't.

He gave another nod, patted my knee the same way he had just patted the horse's rump, then went back to his own horse and swung up.

"Here we go, then."

We pulled the horses' heads up and

nudged them forward, and I followed Leo across the meadow. Wildflowers had started to open at this altitude — harebell with its cornflower-blue bells stacked on an impossibly slender stem, the bristling orange-red spikes of Indian paintbrush, blue asters winking from underfoot.

"You say the other meadow is better than this?"

"So I hear."

Leo stopped at the uphill end of the meadow and pointed. "See there? George Washington's profile, as if he's lying on his back. Top of his head to the left, chin to the right."

He was right. And it took no stretch of imagination to see it. The profile might as well have been carved, it was so accurate. Above the crown of his head and below his chin everything jumbled, but between those points, the shapes, the proportions — exact, like the head on a quarter. There was even a depression in the right spot for the eye, and a hollow behind the corner of the jaw.

"Wow," I said. "How had I never noticed that?"

"Well, sounds like nobody ever told you there was something to look for." He nudged his horse forward.

I wasn't as easy on myself. I kept looking

up at the stern profile. Smug George. *Things look different,* he lectured me from the mountaintop, *from different perspectives.* The fault had all been mine, obviously, for failing to see him the right way.

I looked away from the ridge. The sun was too bright. Had I ever seen anything the right way, ever?

"Can you tell me about how the fire happened?" Leo asked as we neared the far edge of the meadow.

I didn't answer. I meant to, eventually, but before I did he spoke again.

"Have you ever talked about it?"

"I —" The truth took over. "Not really."

"That's too bad," he said.

The words trailed along behind us. Leo angled toward the base of the ridge, dipping us back into the trees. We rode in silence, the horses' footfalls muffled by the spongy pine bed.

"Well, there's the creek," he said after a few minutes. "I think." He stopped beside a rivulet that had worn a crevice for itself between the trees. "He wasn't kidding about small."

"We go upstream?"

"Yup."

He swung his horse's head to the side and started forward. My horse followed. I looked at the line of his back, the curve of his hat brim hiding his neck, the easy droop of his shoulders, the swaying fan of his horse's dark tail.

"It started behind the garage," I said.

29

We followed the rivulet as it snaked through the trees and pulled us uphill. The story came out as I remembered it, which turned out to be fairly disjointed. It had been a hot, windy afternoon in the Los Angeles foothills, and I'd been playing with a neighbor boy. I was ten; he was nine. Trying to start a fire had been my idea, and it had skittered away from us into the weeds between the garage and the tinder-dry hillside. We sprayed it with water, thought we'd put it out. Then we heard the sirens as we ate dinner later. We evacuated to the junior high gymnasium, where the wind thundered around the building as I slept against the wall with a scratchy blanket.

Leo had a lot of questions, and it surprised me how many I couldn't answer. My memory was pierced and tattered, like a blanket that had been handled too much.

"Wait — so the whole time you've been

owning this you weren't even alone? What happened to that other kid?"

"I don't know. We moved. And he was little when it happened."

Leo twisted around in his saddle. "Elena, you were the same age."

"He was —"

"Shh." Leo held both hands up to me, palms forward, ten fingers extended, then moved his thumb back and forth. Ten, nine. Ten, nine. "You were both kids," he said. He turned forward again and picked up his reins. "How long after you set it do you think it was before you heard about the fire?"

"I don't know."

"Well, what time of day was it when you started it?"

"I don't know."

"Who were the people who died?"

"A mother and two little girls — a baby and a three-year-old. She'd been the school secretary. Everybody knew her."

"Oh, man." A pause. "What about the dad? Where was he? What happened?"

"I don't know."

I'd never known. I'd never wanted to know. The story I'd imagined might be horrible, but I feared a truth that might be worse.

With the questions, it took a long time to tell. More than once, we stopped talking for long stretches, and Leo would ride ahead without saying anything while I wrestled to pull what had really happened out of memory that had congealed years ago into one great black mass. We meandered in and out of the trees, seeing small clearings and wondering whether Leo's friend had overstated his claim, then picked the story back up wherever I'd left it.

We came to the story's end at the rivulet's source, a lip of rocks that diverted the little brook from a larger creek, wide enough for us to allow the horses to dip their heads and drink.

"So that's it, then," Leo said, pushing his hat back from his face.

I nodded.

"And you've never done this. Told the whole story like this."

A single shake.

"How's it feel?"

"I don't know. Different. Strange. I don't know if I've ever really put it in order like that before."

"Better?"

I looked at his kind face, his boyish cheeks and wide blue eyes, the sunny dimple just about to appear. A nice face. I gave a thin smile. The logic on which I'd based my identity had just turned out to be really, really illogical, so I didn't have a good answer.

"I don't know," I said.

He nodded thoughtfully. "I get that," he said. Then he pulled his horse's head up and started forward again.

"You know those trees on a cliff that get all blown one direction, so they grow on just one side?" I blurted to his back.

The brim of his hat tilted up and down. "Sure."

"That's what I feel like. Like I've grown one way my whole life and now we're cutting off the only branch I've got."

He twisted around, bracing himself with one hand against the back of the saddle to squint at me. "You know those trees are like a hundred years old."

"It's the same idea."

He turned forward again. Steered around a clump of rocks. Then, as he was tilting a little to the side to watch his horse step over the uneven ground, he said, "Maybe it's more like being one of those bean seedlings in a cup in first grade. If it's growing toward the window, just turn the damn cup around."

The creek found a path deep between

boulders, and we climbed a little rise around them to see a meadow open in front of us. "Well, well," Leo said. "Just like he said."

I stopped beside him. I didn't want to move. White flowers speckled the grassy slope leading back down toward the creek. Yellow, red, and blue dotted the green carpet laid out in front of us. A hedge of blue mountain irises outlined what must have been the bank farther upstream. Pines marked the far end of the meadow, while aspens danced and sparkled along its edges. Probably a thousand feet above us, bare slopes, tawny and pale, reached high above timberline.

A cow and calf, belly-deep in grass at the far end of the meadow, lifted their heads and turned their white faces toward us. After a few moments' assessment, they dropped their heads back down and became part of the landscape again.

"Wow," I said. There really was nothing else. The world, in this instant, was more perfect than it had ever been.

"Lunch for everybody," Leo said, looking at me with a grin.

He swung down from his saddle and held the pinto's head while I did the same. In short order the horses were hobbled and released to graze, and the picnic food and blanket were produced from the saddlebags.

"Food first or exploring?" he asked.

"Be nice to stretch my legs."

He held out his hand. "Come on, then."

He took my hand and kept it as we walked. We found a nest of lady's slipper, studied the fine lavender tracings in a white gentian, nearly missed some tiny pink flowers that neither of us knew and were almost too small to see. I allowed myself to become absorbed in studying flowers, and with a world of tiny complexity in front of me and the sun on my back, I felt my mind slowly, slowly start to settle.

"I seem to keep stopping for blue things," I said as I squatted by a mound of alpine forget-me-not. "Especially the bells." A small butterfly touched the flowers below me, then fluttered on. Leo's hand brushed a lock of hair off my shoulder. Something a nice person would do. For another nice person. I didn't flinch away.

"Let's head into the shade and look for columbine," I said.

Leo took both my hands as I stood so that we faced each other.

"I'm glad we talked," he said. "Are you?"

I saw genuine concern. He didn't seem to be fishing or trying to tell me to feel glad. But in truth, I was. I actually was. Perhaps what had come upon me, so unfamiliar and at first uncomfortable, was possibility.

"Feel better?" he said.

Different, yes. Better? It was possible. I nodded.

I felt pressure against my hands, pulling me toward him. Why not go along? A person who needs rescue is in no position to be suspicious of rescuers. Especially kind, non-intrusive rescuers with an easygoing sense of humor. So when he tilted his head to kiss me, I didn't make him come all the way on his own. Which turned out to be a good thing. He was tentative and shy, but when he pulled back from the kiss, it was with a smile.

"Come on," he said, releasing just one of my hands. "Let's look for columbine."

We meandered at the edge of the trees, closer together now. We found pink columbine first, and he reached around my waist to pull me close as we bent to peer under a spruce sapling for it. Deeper in the shade, he put his hand on the back of my head to point out the blue, with its creamy center reaching toward us and its delicate spurs drooping away beneath, then turned my face back toward his to kiss again.

We worked through a margin of trees that crowded between the open meadow and the

431

point where the mountainside lifted up at an angle too steep to climb. Found tiny mushrooms behind a rock. Peered under an overhang for signs that it might be an empty bear den.

"Hey, look," I said, pointing to another shadowed opening in the rocky face. "Maybe that one's big enough."

We walked closer and bent at the opening, peering into the darkness and waiting for our eyes to adjust, which must have happened for us both at the same time. Just as I jolted upright and opened my mouth to scream, Leo's hand against my shoulder shoved me away. But not before I saw three things:

A human skeleton.

A broken rope, with one end dangling from an anchor sunk into the rock and the other tied around the wrists.

A spill of fabric, dulled by time and weather, but still plainly calico — with flowers.

30

I threw up. At no point in my pregnancy had I thrown up yet, but for the first time now, I felt the pain of mothers and children everywhere, of lost children, of suffering children, of children hoped for and adored, of children unwanted and unloved and abandoned, of what it meant to have another life drawn out of the center of your own, and I spilled it all onto the cradle of pine.

"Oh God, oh God, oh God, oh God," I sobbed. It was a prayer and an accusation. Leo's hand was on my back.

"It's okay," he said. "It's okay."

I shook my head, still hanging it over my feet. "No, no, no, no, *no.*"

Tuah. My father. My child. My ruined family. At the spinning center of it, somehow, were these bones and scraps of fiber.

"We'll go down and tell the sheriff. They'll take care of everything. I'm sorry. It's over. It's okay."

"No!" I shrieked, twisting away and pulling myself upright.

"Elena! It's okay! Calm down!"

"That's *Benencia*! That's Tuah's *daughter*! My father's *sister*!"

"*What?* What are you talking about?"

I doubled over, feeling another wave of nausea. The gaping skull. The rope. Tuah had been wrong. How could anyone dare tell her so? Or let her imagine what I had just seen? The small comfort she'd held on to for forty years was gone. Only horror instead. And now, as I replayed the scene, I wasn't sure the bottom half of the skeleton had been there at all.

I staggered a couple of steps sideways and threw up again.

"Elena! Are you okay? What are you talking about?"

I tugged at the sleeve of the sweatshirt tied around my waist and wiped my mouth, backing away from the spot and gasping for breath. Leo grabbed my arm and dragged me out into the sunlight, then took my shoulders, hard, and shoved me down into the clean grass.

"Sit here. I'm gonna get you some water."

I nodded, then dropped my head, trapping it between my knees and crossing my arms over it. I took deep breaths through my mouth to keep the nausea down, and by the time Leo returned the breaths had turned to sobs. He sat beside me and handed me the water bottle, then wrapped his arms around my shoulders and pulled me against him.

"What's going on?" he said to the top of my head.

I had only one clear thought: we had to hide it. No one else would ever find anything, and Tuah would never know the real end of her decision to let Benencia go, on a fall day, in her calico dress with tiny flowers. That, at least, was something I could do. I straightened and pulled away to look him full in the face. "You can't tell anyone." I struggled to catch the breath to speak. "You have to — *promise.* You can't t-tell anyone. No one can *ever* know!"

"You know I can't promise that. We can't just leave that — there."

"We'll b-bury her our*selves!*"

"Elena." He was firm, paternal. "You have got to tell me what's going on."

My fingers and face tingled. I had to slow down and breathe. Look at something besides the insides of my eyelids and the picture etched there. I blinked at a clump of blue harebell that leaned away from my feet. Across the meadow were the horses, heads down exactly as they had been before any of this happened. White flower clusters of wild onion bobbed their heads above the grass. The cow and calf were gone. I think. I couldn't be sure at this distance, as watery as my eyes were. I rubbed them with the heels of my hands. Behind me, woods and —

I got up and walked away, rinsed my mouth, then stayed doubled over my knees until my head stopped spinning. In time, my breathing slowed. I took a couple of sips of water and went back to Leo, turning to face him as I sat.

"Look," I said. "Your brother. How did you feel — how did your parents feel when he disappeared — after the waffle?"

He shook his head. "Awful, of course. Frantic. Helpless."

I nodded. Breathed. "Tuah had a daughter. Older than my father. She was — slow. When she was a just a girl — twelve or thirteen — she wandered off one day and disappeared. Up here —" I lifted my chin to take in the expanse of mountains and sky. "Forty years ago. She was never found. That's why Tuah still lives up here."

I saw Leo's Adam's apple bob. A breeze caught a piece of hair that tickled my cheek. I brushed it away, then locked my hands together again under my thighs.

"She still thinks she might come back?" he asked quietly.

I shook my head. "No. But remembering living here together is all she has. She thinks Benencia got lost and hid somewhere because she was scared. It was fall. Tuah thinks she fell asleep somewhere in the cold, died, that animals got the body, and that's why she was never found. That she died peacefully."

"That doesn't seem very likely, does it?" he said quietly.

In the face of the unbearable unknown, how do we decide what to cling to? Tuah had chosen the most comforting possibility and kept on living. I had chosen the least and withdrawn.

I felt a returning tingle of nausea and took a deep breath to push it down. I shook my head. "No. I guess it doesn't." I looked across the grass. The brown horse, agreeing with me, shook its head as well, took a step, and kept grazing. "But it's what she's made herself believe. It's what she needs to believe."

He looked down and nodded. I put a hand on his arm.

"Do you see now why she can never know about this? It would kill her. I asked her a while back whether somebody might've done something, but she wouldn't hear it. She said she knew everybody too well and she knew they never would. But I think . . ." I looked uphill to where the cow and calf had been. "Now I think it was because she couldn't bear to think about anything so awful."

"Sure." Leo put his hands to the sides of his face and rubbed. He glanced over his shoulder into the trees, then looked back toward me. "What makes you think it's her?"

"Tuah said she was wearing blue calico with pink flowers on the day she left."

"Oh." He looked down. "Oh," he repeated. Then he looked up at me, brows dug together. "The story — that's why you asked me about the ghost story."

I nodded.

"It's your family." He looked away. I imagined him running the story props through his memory. The lost girl. The ghost dog. The old miner who killed them. He rolled his lips together. "And it turns out a lot of it's true," he added. He looked back up at me. "Elena, we have to tell. This was a crime. They have to find out who did it."

"Are you insane? It was half a century ago. Everybody's dead and gone. Whatever happened" — frayed edges of rope dragged between my thoughts — "it's over now. It's been over for a long time."

He shook his head. "I don't think so. This isn't our decision. This is the sheriff's business."

"Why? Why does he ever have to know? We could bury her here."

"What if you're wrong? What if it *isn't* her? What if there's another family somewhere that wants to know?"

"That wants to know *this*?" I waved one arm behind myself toward the woods, toward the — "No one wants to know this! It's better to never know!"

"Why do you have the right to make that decision? For anybody? Or even for Tuah?"

"Are you out of your *mind*?"

"Look —" He put both hands up, palms toward me. "We're both pretty shook up. Let's just let it be for now. Go home. Take some time. We'll talk about it later."

His proposal was eminently reasonable. I knew it. But I didn't like it.

We made the entire ride back down in silence. Leo glanced back at me often, but we had nothing left to say. We approached the cabin from its blind side, and after our feet were on the ground he put his hands on my shoulders and kissed me on the forehead, then said he'd find me at the Koffords' when he was back in town in a few days. Promised he wouldn't tell anyone, *anyone* before we talked again. Then he took the pinto's reins in his hand, swung up onto the brown, and rode away.

"You're back early," Tuah said brightly as I came into the cabin. She knelt in front of the stove, scooping ash out of its belly into a bucket. Her tone suggested she was perfectly happy at the chore.

"One of the horses might be going lame," I said. I tried to avoid her eyes, but I could tell my voice sounded strange. "And I'm thinking I should go down tonight, instead of in the morning. Make sure I get to the Koffords' on time. Paul has to get going early after taking all this time off."

"Really." She peered at me. "But you're staying for dinner."

"You know I don't like to drive on this road in the dark."

"It doesn't get dark until nine."

I hadn't thought this through. "Oh, I dunno. There's a few things I thought I'd do before the week. Errands. Y'know. Just some odds and ends."

She sat back on her heels. "Your father will be sorry."

I met her gaze now, finally with some confidence. "No he won't."

She looked at me for a moment more, then gave a single nod and turned her attention back to the stove. "He's taking a walk around town. If he doesn't get back before you leave, make sure you find him."

"Okay."

I escaped to the bedroom to take care of my scanty packing. I brushed my hair, poured water into the basin to wash my face, and only then dared look in the dim and wavy mirror. Had Benencia looked at herself here, too? Was my skull, under the flesh, the same as hers? I covered my face with my hands and breathed against them.

"I'm all set," I said when I came out.

"Drive safe," Tuah said without looking up.

"Like you do?"

"Only after you've lived here as long as I have."

"Deal."

She paused and turned her face toward me. I met her eyes then and saw — love. In an instant I felt the sting of oncoming tears and I blinked and looked down.

"Well, I hope that's so," she said and clanged her trowel against the edge of the bucket. I started for the door.

"I'll see you in a few days?" I heard her ask as I crossed onto the porch.

"Yes, I'll be back."

"Good."

I threw my bag in the car and eased away from the cabin. I looked back at it in my rearview mirror — bright and yellow and brave between the pines, white porch posts clean and crisp, white curtains puffing in the windows. *Where my family was together,* she'd described it. I supposed I was part of that equation now, too.

I found my father only with some effort and Mac's help. I saw the dog first, curled in the middle of the upper road, licking his flank. I figured my father couldn't be far. I parked the car and got out.

"Dad?"

"Over here."

The direction of his voice wasn't quite clear. I guessed and walked toward a pair of houses that leaned at parallel angles, like dancers.

"Am I getting warmer?"

"Over here."

He sat on the front step of one of the houses, jeans cuffed over his work boots, turning something in his hands. I sat beside him.

"What's that?" I asked.

He held it out to me. It was a horse. A tiny resin horse, prancing, with its uplifted leg broken off a little above the knee. He gestured with his head toward the house behind us.

"The Diazes' house. They had twin boys a little older than me."

"Oh — yeah."

He looked surprised. "You know them?"

"No — I mean, Tuah's told me stories."

"Of course." He held up the horse. "They had a whole set of army toys — soldiers, wagons, cannons. This is one of the horses. I just found it here by the porch."

"Do you know where they are now? Have you stayed in touch?"

He shook his head. "They moved away." He tilted his head back, then looked from side to side. "Like everybody."

I had grown up in Los Angeles. All else aside, at least the place that held my childhood would never be a ghost town. It would change, but the changes would say that yes, I'd changed, too. I wondered whether coming here, for him, meant combating a sense that you didn't really exist. That your own childhood had died. As Benencia's had.

"Um, I decided it would be better for me to go back down tonight instead of in the morning."

He nodded. "That makes sense."

"I think Paul's trip this time is five days. I'll be back as soon as I can."

"That'll be fine."

"So long, then."

"Have a good week."

And with that and a nod, I left him on the splitting pine boards of the Diaz family front step, turning the broken horse over and over in his hands.

31

"Welcome back," Paul said as he opened the door the next morning. "I was hoping you'd come early. Coffee?"

"Sure."

I followed him into the kitchen, got a mug from the cupboard, and held it while he poured. I got sugar from the bowl by the sink while he sat at the kitchen table. I joined him, sitting in Sarah's spot.

"How's everything been?" I asked as I stirred. Good or bad, the answer would give me something new to focus on.

He made a face. "Mixed bag. We missed you."

I looked down at the wake following my spoon around the coffee's surface. I hadn't asked just to fill the silence, had I? Life had passed in these brown rooms without me the last couple of days, and I genuinely wanted to capture some piece of what I'd missed. I'd pay almost anything to trade the day I'd had yesterday for one spent here.

"Sarah?" I asked, looking up.

He nodded. "I went ahead and moved the rollaway into her room. I hope that's okay. If you don't sleep in there she'll come sleep with you anyway, and I thought you probably didn't want to have her in the living room with you all night, or getting in bed with you. At least in her own room she'll stay in her bed. And she'll need a light on. You probably don't like that, but I shut it off one night and she woke up hollering."

"Oh," I breathed. "I'm sorry." God, none of this would have happened if I'd just listened to the part of me that hesitated about letting them go to the Brames' in the first place. I swallowed hard against nothing. "I'm so sorry."

He put his hand on my wrist. "Don't start with that." He hesitated a moment, then gave me a pat and pulled his hand back. "It's okay," he said.

I took the spoon out of my coffee, tapped it on the rim, and set it on the plate at the center of the table where another spoon already rested.

"And Kevin?"

"He's pretty — sober."

I nodded.

Then he leaned back and rubbed the back

of his neck. "I mighta done something stupid yesterday. I had some time on my hands and thought it might be good to start putting away some of Carrie's things. You understand."

"Of course."

"Sarah kinda went to pieces. You know what a packrat she is. She keeps everything — string, broken toys, pieces of paper. Is that just girls? Or is she . . ." A long blink. "Like her mom? I don't know."

"I'm sure it's okay."

"That's right. That's right. I'm sure it is. You must know all about it. But she wants all her mom's stuff to stay right where it is. And I can't do that. I just can't go on doing that forever. I've got to start moving on."

"Of course."

He nodded to himself. "It's true. It's true. But I should've talked with her about it, that's for sure. It was the wrong time. I know that. You must know that."

"I have no idea."

We sat in silence.

"I left some extra money in the jar. It's Boom Days this week. You can take the kids to the parade, maybe. Play some carnival games. Get some food. They'll like that."

"Oh — that sounds great." I took a sip of coffee.

"Uh." Paul rubbed the back of his neck. "One more thing, just a heads-up, I'm going to ask about work in the mine. I have to get off the road. We need to be a family. God knows we need the money. And you need to get on with your life. I know that."

"But I'm sure —" I cut myself off as I realized that perhaps his reasons for not going to work there long ago were none of my business. At some point, without a doubt, my capacity to sort the threads of what I was and wasn't supposed to know, of past and present, would fail spectacularly. But he didn't seem to notice.

"I should have done it a long time ago," he said, looking down into his cup. "A long time. Maybe, then — everything could have been different. For Carrie. For us. Maybe."

I heard a door creak.

"Lena!" Sarah thundered into the room and threw herself against my side, arms around my neck. I felt silky fabric under my hands. I tipped my head back enough to see what she was wearing. An emerald women's blouse. I looked at Paul, who nodded, lips pressed together.

Figuring out what to do with old bones, it seemed, was a thorny issue for everyone.

"I wonder," I said to Poppy later that morning, "if you lost someone, would you rather know or not know if something bad happened to them?"

We sat on aluminum lawn chairs in her backyard, backs to a broken bed frame, and watched the children try to get the puppies to chase bits of string they dragged around. The sun sparkled off wind chimes and baubles that hung in the trees, and it was easy to imagine the laughing children as untroubled.

"That's an odd question."

"It's just — with the kids in the mine . . ." I shrugged my shoulders, trying to indicate discomfort in a way that would ward off further questions. "It's just been on my mind. A lot of what-ifs. Like, what if we'd never found them? Would you want to know what happened or just always wonder?"

She tilted her chin over her shoulder, toward the house. "Ask Mama Ruth."

"What?"

"Her no-good drunk shit of a son, who ran off and left her stuck with me. I think she'd like to know."

"Her son? Your — brother?"

"My husband. Ex-husband."

"She's *his* mother? Not yours?"

"Yep."

I stared. "You are a saint," I finally said.

"She's not as bad as you think."

"I bet she's worse."

Poppy tilted her head. "Have you ever figured out my collection?"

"I — haven't thought about it, I guess. It's just" — I shrugged my shoulders — "part of your house."

"Think about how they're arranged."

I tried to picture the living room walls, the chaos of found items that covered it. I'd never been able to spot a connecting thread. The materials? Paper, wood, plastic, metal, twine. Purpose? Things that illustrate, things that inform, things you play with, things that decorate. The shapes? Squares, circles, pieces of clothing, leaves, cutouts. No, it was a purely unsorted jumble of colors and shapes and subjects and textures, crowded together in a way that suggested the articles were either shoving their way to the center or that the collection had started in the center and expanded outward —

"Everything touches?" Hardly a deep thought, but it was the only one I could muster.

Poppy threw her hands up in triumph, muumuu rising with them. "Ha! That's it!" She leaned toward me against the arm of her chair, torqueing its aluminum frame. "Every kind of thing in the world, everything touches something, that touches something, that touches something else. Everything connects. Everything comes back. If you're two hops away from one thing, you're next to another, and by touching one you touch them all. A postcard is a postcard and a fork's a fork, but they all touch each other. I try to do good. Even Mama Ruth, no matter what's happened, has touched other things and left good behind. I know it."

She put a hand on my knee and peered intently into my face. "You came here to help those children and you are. Oh, you are. But honey, you're touching other things, too." She gave my knee a pat and leaned back into her chair, which relaxed into balance. "You're a good girl. That's just the shape you are. Good will come of whatever you do, sooner or later. That's just how it works."

I sat on the Koffords' sofa, angled slightly so I could see a patch of light coming from Sarah's room. I'd sat here earlier to convince Sarah that she could see me from her room and it would be all right to fall asleep alone. Baby steps. But now it was nearly midnight, and Leo was here, after driving down from the ranch this late so we could avoid having this conversation around the children. He hadn't changed his mind. He was determined to tell the sheriff what we'd found, and didn't want to have to explain a longer delay than it already was. He faced me while I sat cross-legged, hands in my lap. I hadn't seen him in light this low before. In the shadows he looked . . . older.

"Look," he said. "There's no point trying to guess what Tuah *would* want to know because she doesn't. Your question only matters if she actually knows she has a choice. She's accepted one idea, but that doesn't mean she wants it to stay that way no matter what."

I shook my head as I had over and over again. "If we'd found the body just lying there I would agree with you. Absolutely. But whatever happened, it was more horrible than anything she's ever let herself think about. It would break her heart. It would completely break her heart."

"It's not something she *wants* to know — but she has a *right* to know. Would you want somebody to hide something from you because they thought you couldn't take it? Something that was maybe the most important thing in your life?"

I looked down at my hands. "I would. I already wish I didn't know. And if that's true for me, it's a thousand times that for her."

He leaned forward and took my face in his hands. I looked up, startled.

"You're lying," he whispered. He held my gaze for a moment, then dropped his hands and leaned back. "You're lying to yourself," he said, now in a normal voice. "And you don't even know it. You like to hang back, and I get that. You've had some gut shots. You'd *like* life to be safer, but I really don't think you'd want somebody else picking and choosing for you."

Truth, like water, finds its own path. The beaver dam of sureties I'd pieced together over all these years was already leaking badly, and it didn't take much to tear a new hole. He was right — there was no such thing as safety. I'd known it for years, even while I continued to look for places to hide. But just because I could acknowledge the truth for myself didn't mean I thought imposing suffering on my grandmother, at this particular point of her life, was the right thing to do.

"Look — this is tough," he went on. "I'm not saying it won't be awful. But your grandma has you."

Did she? To what extent? What would her reaction be, and how long would it last?

What kind of support would she need and for how long? Especially after I ripped away faith in her community. The implied commitment was terrifying. But I was sick of being governed by fear. I put my face in my hands.

"Hey," he said. He picked at my fingers until I gave up and lowered my hands. "Look, you're probably right and it's your aunt, but there's still a chance you're wrong. There could be another family somewhere.

"Have Poppy watch the kids in the morning and then you and I are going to tell the sheriff what we found. We have to. But that's all we'll tell them. Let them figure out if it's Benencia, decide how to handle it themselves. It's their job. This isn't all on you. You're not responsible for everything that happens in the world, you know."

I sat without responding for a time. Eventually, against my own will, I nodded.

32

Leo escorted the sheriff's officers to the cave by himself. I wanted to be there, felt I owed it to Benencia to stand as a witness, as family, when she was finally rescued. But I couldn't figure out what to do with the children, and in truth I wasn't sure how I would react to watching the actual process of gathering up what remained of my aunt and loading it onto a packhorse for the trip down the mountain. Still, I spent all that day looking up toward Hat Creek and back at my watch. Fix breakfast. They must be driving to the ranch for horses. Dry dishes. They must be riding to the meadow. Fix lunch. They must be at the cave. How long would they stay? Sort laundry. Surely they were on their way back down by now.

Finally I fished the extra cash out of the jar, shoved it in my pocket, and announced that we would be going downtown to see what was going on at the festival. We found a parking place behind the Powder Keg, which seemed like unusually good luck until we came around the corner and I realized that a lot of setup was still going on. Men on ladders stood at opposite ends of the bandstand tent across the street, hanging a banner above the stage. BOOM DAYS! it said, with bombs for the Os and at each end a prospector with a pack burro laden with dynamite. At the curb, more men unloaded speakers from the back of a pickup truck. Vendors' booths lined the street, and though much of the activity involved tables being moved, I could smell food and did see a few other visitors roaming around. We starting drifting from one booth to another as vendors arranged wood carvings or turquoise jewelry, taking food samples where they were offered.

"Try this," I said to Kevin as I saw bored annoyance start to rise, handing him a sample piece of a lemon cookie. Or, "It's like a doughnut," as we sat at a plastic table and Sarah made a face at the twisted brown lumps of a funnel cake.

"Why aren't you eating anything?" Sarah asked.

"My stomach hurts," I said.

"You should drink some Seven-Up," she

offered, taking a mouthful of whipped cream.

"I will."

When the funnel cake was finished, we wandered over to the pen where burros waited for tomorrow's race. A foal, its eyes furrowed under a thick tuft of fur, glared at us from beneath its mother's neck.

"Lookit the baby!" Sarah squealed, pointing between the fence rails.

"Yeah," I said. But my eyes were more focused on the traffic behind us. At some point, one of the vehicles would be a coroner's van carrying Benencia's remains. Would they be able to figure out who it was? How would I talk to Tuah? How long could I put it off? The questions chased each other in my own hopeless, endless effort to find a way to contain and control what would happen.

Someone turned on the speakers at the bandstand across the street, which gave off a quick, sharp whine and startled a couple of the burros. I glanced over my shoulder. The courthouse glowered at me over the banner, now swagged jauntily above the stage. Of course the sheriff would figure it out. Of course the body was Benencia's. And I owed it to Tuah to tell her myself and not leave that job, like a coward, to someone else. But how?

"This is boring," Kevin said. "They won't have games till night."

"Let's try the gold panning."

"That's so *stupid*. I've done it like a hundred times."

"Sarah hasn't. Come on."

I led the way across the street, past the front of the bandstand, stepping over cables being dragged across the ground, to a dirt lot behind the barbershop that had been cordoned off as the children's area. They could dig for prizes in a sandbox, ride a four-car train of mine carts through a corrugated metal tunnel, and pan for flecks of gold in a sluice box with flowing water fed from a hose and sand lining the bottom. From the gold-panning area, I had a decent view of the street.

"I'm not riding that train," Kevin said.

"Nobody's asking you to. Let's try the gold panning."

A bearded man with canvas pants and a floppy hat was already helping another pair of boys, so Kevin and Sarah picked up unattended pans in the sluice, scooped some sand and water, and started swirling the pans. Sarah spilled most of hers immediately, then as I started to show her how to scoop just a little sand rather than fill the pan, I saw it: a sheriff's car, headlights flashing, another behind, and then the van, just making the turn at the top of the street. An honorary procession. I let go of the pan and stood, arms hanging by my sides, watching them pass the burro pen and the pickup truck with the speakers, drive slowly past me, then disappear beyond the brick wall of the barbershop.

"Are you going to cry?" Sarah said, voice small.

I looked down at her. "Maybe," I said.

"Does your stomach hurt bad?"

"No, it's okay."

She paused to consider that, then her own face started to fold. "Are you going to go away?"

"What? No! Of course not!" But even as the automatic response came from my lips, her question, her tears, and her history all twisted and fused together. I glanced at Kevin, standing with his hands in the water, also watching me warily. I dropped onto my knees on the ground and took hold of her arms.

"Sarah, did your mom cry sometimes?"

She nodded.

"And did that scare you?"

Another nod. I glanced at Kevin.

"When she said good-bye to you the last

time, when she took you to your friends' house before she went to go see your grandma and had her accident, was she crying?"

"Uh-huh."

"Oh, honey." At that, I really did start to cry. I pulled Sarah into my arms.

"Ma'am, is she okay? Do you need some help here?" The prospector's shadow lay on the ground. I shook my head without looking up.

"We're fine," I said. The shadow withdrew.

I pulled away, still holding Sarah's arms. I looked at Kevin to include him.

"Sarah, Kevin, I need you both to listen to me. I'm crying right now because I'm sad about somebody else who died and I'm sad about your mom, too. People die, and when you love them you cry, no matter how old you are. I think your mom cried sometimes about other things, too, and grownups do that. We all do. But I want to make sure you know it was *never* about you. Never. I know that. Do you understand?"

I made sure they both nodded.

"And it doesn't mean someone is going to leave, either. You might see your dad cry sometimes, because he's sad, too, but you're not *making* him cry and he's not going to leave you. You're probably going to see me

460

cry some more times. And that's okay."

I paused. Secured both of their gazes. Discovered I could say what all three of us needed to hear.

"You didn't make your mom leave," I said.

It felt nice, I realized, to hear how those words sounded.

We heard a knock at the door Friday afternoon, as I held Sarah to the task of cleaning up the doll kingdom she'd spread all over the living room before her father came home. At the sound, Sarah jumped to her feet and opened it to find a sheriff's deputy standing on the stoop, turning his hat in a circle in his hands.

"You're Sarah, aren't you?" he said with a smile. She looked at him for a moment without answering, then looked back at me over her shoulder. "I'm Sheriff Bales," he added.

Not a deputy, then.

"Sarah," I said. "You can go out back and see what Kevin's doing. The sheriff is here to talk to me."

"Why?"

"I think he's looking for Tuah." I glanced at the sheriff. His eyebrows lifted very slightly.

"That's right," he said.

"Why?" Sarah asked again.

His response was mercifully smooth. "I think we found something that might be hers."

"Oh." Sarah's interest dwindled visibly. She looked back up at me. "Can I go outside now?"

"You bet."

She sprinted away, disappearing down the hallway before I might have a chance to change my mind about her cleanup chore, then confirming she'd left with a bang of the door.

"So you knew," he said when she was gone.

I hesitated, then nodded. "I thought so," I said. "You want to come in?"

"Thank you."

I swept a handful of Lincoln Logs onto the floor and sat in the beige chair while he took the matching sofa, leaning forward onto his knees, still turning the hat in his hands.

"I was just at your grandmother's house. Do you know where she is?" he asked.

"Hat Creek."

"Have you said anything to her?"

I looked down and shook my head. "I was waiting for you to be sure," I said. Then I looked back up. "Are you?"

"Enough. The medical examiner says the remains are the right age, female. Did the best we could with old records." Another circuit of the hat. "You saw everything, then," he said. He rolled his lips together. "In the cave, I mean. So you know what — was there."

It was sure, then. Bone of my bone, the girl in the cave as much as the baby in my belly. I tried to swallow, but the muscles of my throat stuck. I nodded.

"We need to talk to her. Then talk to anybody we can find who was around back then. No matter how old, it's still a murder."

Spoken aloud, the word took on form and substance. It was real and would change Tuah forever. What words would I use to tell her? How does one confirm the worst fear in a woman's life? Yes, your lost child has long been dead. Not only that, but she died terrified and suffering. And I can't sit beside you as you hear the news, absorbing the blow with you, but instead I'll sit across from you, delivering it. Hadn't she suffered enough?

"I know this must be real hard," he said. "I'm very sorry for your loss."

Stock words. How often must he have said them over the years? The same acknowledgment of small losses and great ones, made exactly the same way to the young, the old, the fearful, the happy, the virtuous, the evil. Sorrow was no respecter of persons. Tuah would suffer. Everyone suffers. It wasn't a question of who deserved it.

I looked down. It was my duty to tell her. And yet, as I asked the sheriff to give me time to get to Hat Creek before him in the morning, I realized something else. I wouldn't have wanted to do anything else. This was my family. This was my home.

As I shut the door behind the sheriff I looked at the clock on the mantel. Two hours until I could expect Paul. Hours beyond that I would spend in the empty Leadville house, wishing I could be in Hat Creek instead. For the first time in my life, I didn't want to be alone. I looked at the kitchen, where I had left off cutting carrots and cucumbers when the sheriff came. I straightened the hem of my shirt and walked down the hall to the back door.

"Kevin! Sarah!"

Sarah, squatted over something in the grass, looked up at me, and a moment later Kevin appeared from behind the barn with a ball in his hand.

"Come inside. I want help with dinner."

"Isn't Daddy coming home today?" Sarah said.

"Yup."

She popped to her feet. "You're *staying*?"

Her innocent question, wrapped in so much hope and joy, struck me in a far larger way than she intended. My answer was a revelation, and I hesitated for a moment before I said it, confirming to myself that it was real.

"Yup."

I lowered my standards for Sarah's cleanup chore. With Kevin deputized at the stove browning chunks of beef, and Sarah soon at the sink tearing lettuce for salad, I made stroganoff for four. Paul seemed more pleased than surprised when he came home to the smell of onions and butter and I asked whether it would be all right if I just stayed.

We chatted and laughed around the table, the children slurping noodles and trying to outdo each other in making our mundane activities of the week into exaggerated stories. Poppy's puppies could run — no, drive — no, *fly* now. Elena's car almost ran out of gas — no, it *did* run out and had to be towed — no, it burst into flames! Paul in turn told them about the fantastical places he'd been and things he'd seen during the week. The idea that Waco was wacko would stick for a while, I could tell.

Afterward we took the children out for ice cream, where we ran into the high school principal. He introduced himself with a slightly sticky handshake and said a little bird had told him a certain Miss Alvarez might be the solution to his science teacher problem. I glanced at Sarah and Kevin, solemnly licking their ice cream at a picnic table, at the mountains that stepped up toward Hat Creek, and said it was something I was actually thinking about. At the medical clinic we passed on the way home, I noted the phone number on the sign and quickly memorized the last four digits, all anyone needed up here.

Back at the house it was time for the children to get ready for bed, then stories, and then for Sarah to show her father how she could go to sleep by herself now. We said we'd sit in the living room and wait until she was asleep.

"Kevin," I heard Paul say at his son's door, while I switched on the night-light for Sarah. "It sounds like you were a big help this week. I appreciate that."

I couldn't hear Kevin's answer, but I pictured him lifting his chin, even as his head lay on the pillow, and felt a squeeze in my throat. I blew a kiss to Sarah.

Paul and I sat across from each other, chair and sofa, lights low, while evening settled around us like a cat around its tail. I looked down at my shirt, bloused over my midriff, hoping that Paul just thought I'd been making too many cookies, but also realizing it would be fine whenever he knew it wasn't. Birds in the bush outside the living room window rustled and groused as it got dark, and voices from a neighbor's porch faded away with the slap of a screen door. From time to time Sarah would call out, "I'm still in my bed!" but eventually that stopped as well.

"So you're going up in the morning?" Paul asked as conversation about daily life at the cabin wound down. A distant chime of laughter from a neighbor's TV drifted through the window. His arms rested on the chair arms, and a bottle of beer hung by its lip between his fingers.

"Yeah." I glanced at the clock on the mantel I had succeeded in forgetting since the afternoon. "I should get going."

"Well," he said as he pushed himself to his feet. "Thanks again for dinner."

Had I really felt uncomfortable here before? In the instant it took to wonder I realized I felt more connected here than to any home I'd lived in growing up. The home of a stranger and children I still didn't believe I fully understood. What made the difference?

"No — thanks for letting me stay. I probably would've had crackers or something if I'd just gone back to Tuah's house." I picked up my bag and hitched it onto my shoulder. He took the two steps necessary to open the door.

"I, ah, should let you know," he said. "Alan House stopped by last weekend. He brought by a check."

"What?"

"The men on the rescue team. If it's not just a problem in the mine, if it's a person, it turns out they" — he looked down, cleared his throat a little — "they never take their pay. So they put it all together and handed it over to me. For the kids, you know. It's a big help. I've got a few more hauling contracts, but I stopped by the mine on my way into town. I'll be able to start working there in another month or so. Mechanic's shop. So we're gonna be okay."

"That's great. That's fantastic."

"I just —" He pressed his lips into a thin line. "Here's the thing. You've been like family. Better. I don't know how we would've made it without you. I can't ever thank you enough. And now . . ." He looked through the open door into the dark, then back again at me. "Look, I want you here as long as you can be. Hell, I hope you take that teacher job, stay in Leadville, get married, raise a nice family, be my kids' aunt for the rest of their lives. But only if that's what you want. I don't want you thinking you're stuck here. That's all. Whatever you do, I need you to know we're gonna be okay."

We faced each other across the void created by the open door.

"Thanks," I whispered. "It's been —" I didn't have a word. And I couldn't have spoken it if I had. So I ducked my head and stepped out into the dark.

The door closed behind me. I tipped my head back and looked up at the ceiling of stars, visible to me here as they never had been in Los Angeles. The Milky Way washed overhead like grains poured from Zeus's jar, blessings or curses streaming from heaven to earth. Or I could see instead something true and much less frightening: countless stars and galaxies, suns with their own planets and moons, bodies and systems incomprehensibly large, bits of matter invisibly small, stars expanding and stars collapsing, dense and interconnected, all of them pushing and pulling against each other with their specific masses and gravities in infinite complexity, across a vastness of time beyond my comprehension. A universe in perfect balance.

And me in my place within it.

I drove up to Hat Creek as the morning sun lay across the road, counting the landmarks off as I went — the gnarled ponderosa growing alone out of a rubble heap, the taut wire fences of the Bar Triple C Ranch, the knob near the intersection with the dirt road that had always made me think of an ambush spot from an old Western. The trip rolled along as a series of images now so deeply imprinted that I knew them before I saw them. The final one was of Tuah, standing in the center of the garden, one hand holding a hoe and the other shading her face, watching my car roll toward her.

"Well, this is a surprise. We weren't expecting you so early," she said as I opened the door and stood. My father appeared on the porch with a dishtowel over his shoulder. Mac, lying on the porch with his forepaws drooped over the edge, raised his head to look at me and thumped his tail a couple of times against the boards.

"Hey, Dad," I said.

"Is everything okay with the Koffords?" she asked.

"Yeah." They continued to stand looking at me, waiting for the explanation. Mac rolled onto his side with a long sigh. "I need to talk to you. Both. Can we sit down for a minute?"

Tuah cocked her head a little to one side, then smiled and pushed off against her hoe. "Roberto, grab another chair."

We formed a little arc on the porch, my grandmother upright in a kitchen chair, I in an uncomfortable rocking chair we rarely used, my father in the deep porch chair his father had made. He looked uneasy. He didn't like situations in which he didn't already know what was going to happen. Tuah, on the other hand, sat relaxed and pleased, and all of a sudden I realized what she must be thinking — that I had come to the side of reason and decided to tell my father about the baby.

There was no way to ease into this.

"Tuah," I said. "On my ride last time with Leo, we went someplace I'd never been before. Neither of us had. You know the meadow at the end of the elk trail?"

Tuah nodded. "Yes, of course."

"By Washington Rock?" my father asked.

I really had been blind. I shifted in my

chair. "That's right."

"That's a pretty spot," my father said.

"Yes, very," my grandmother said.

I steadied myself with a deep breath. "We went past there," I said. "We followed a little creek a few miles past it to another meadow. We were going to have a picnic and do some exploring —"

"My," Tuah said. "You went a long way."

My father squirmed in his chair. It looked as if it didn't fit him.

"We found — a cave and . . . there was — a body."

The sentence hung like an egg thrown against a wall, where it clung for a moment before it started to slip and fall.

"A — *body*? A human body?" my father said. Tuah sat frozen in her chair.

"Yes." I looked at Tuah. "I thought it might be Benencia."

She stared back at me, still motionless. Blinked. Blinked again. I tried to read in her face what she was feeling. When she spoke, her voice was papery and pinched.

"That's — that's not possible. That's too far. And it's been too long. There couldn't be a body."

"It was —" I couldn't bring myself to say *skeleton*. "Bones."

Tuah gripped the edge of her chair, and

her gaze now focused somewhere in the space between us. "That's too far. That can't be her. It's too far; she couldn't have gone that far." She turned to my father. "Did you go that way? To the meadow?"

I looked at my father for the first time. He looked stricken, pale. I didn't understand what was going on between them. "I don't know," he said. "You know I don't know."

Tuah turned back to me. "What makes you think it was her? It could've been anyone. Miners, hikers, so many people . . ."

I forced myself to breathe. "It was — there was fabric. Like you said she was wearing — calico with flowers."

She sat still for a moment, then shoved the chair back, hard against the porch boards, and went into the cabin. My father stared woodenly ahead and wouldn't look at me. I heard Tuah's steps in the cabin, walking away, then getting stronger again as she came back. She stood in the door opening, now holding the quilt from the guest bed, the one I'd been using and had been here for as long as I could remember. She shoved it into my lap, pointing to a square caged by surrounding triangle teeth. Blue calico with pink flowers.

"That," she demanded, pointing at it with one finger. "Did it look like that?"

The fabric swam in front of my eyes. I pulled folds of the quilt into my hands. There was another square. And another. And another. Blue calico with pink flowers. Benencia's dress, tucked around my shoulders at night. Holding my dolls. Crushed against my cheek when I was sulky or sad. Wrapped around my back on a chilly morning as I twisted my feet into it at the kitchen table.

"Did it?"

I looked up at her, eyes wide and aching. I nodded.

She dropped against the edge of her chair, almost missing it, and fumbled to right herself. It was only then that little sobs started to work in her throat.

"How would she get so far? How? It's too far. Roberto, did you ever go to the meadow together? *Ever?*"

"I — I don't know."

My father had hardened into my grandfather's chair as if he'd been carved there as well — chest hollow, following the shape of the chair back, hands locked onto the arms, face gaunt and frozen. Not once had I thought of his reaction to this news. He'd been a child when his sister disappeared. But in his own way, he seemed as undone as his mother.

474

"Maybe she kept wandering because she was lost." Tuah was talking to herself. "I suppose she didn't have to do it all at once, did she? Maybe she stopped, and then she walked some more." A sob caught her breath. "For how *long*?" She breathed the question into a breeze that picked it up and carried it away across the meadows and slopes and hills. She buried her face in her hands. "How *long*?" she wailed in a voice I had never heard, and I could see the shape of her pain by the way she wrapped herself around it.

"I'm sorry," my father whispered. "I'm sorry. I'm sorry."

I don't think she heard him. She had sunk too far into grief for anything to reach her. And it was still only half as far as she would need to go.

33

I never found a way to finish the story. Tuah kept crying, rocking over her knees, while my father clenched in his chair and apologized again and again and again. Sitting between them, I didn't know who to comfort and I didn't know how. Putting my arms around either of their shoulders felt too foreign to even try. I finally put my hand on Tuah's arm.

"Tuah," I said. "Tuah, the sheriff is coming. Soon."

"The sheriff?" She lifted her face from her hands, bewildered, adrift. Her eyes had swollen, but the skin underneath them had collapsed over her cheeks.

"The sheriff. They got the body a few days ago. They think it's her, too. They want to talk to you."

She started to nod. "Of course. That's right. Of course. Yes." She started to catch her sobs and pull them down into herself.

She wiped her cheeks with the heels of her hands.

"No!" My father's voice surprised me. "No, no, *no!*"

"Dad?"

"Not *again!* I can't do that all over again!"

"Dad!"

But it was as if he didn't even know I was there.

"Roberto, stop it," Tuah said. Her voice sounded familiar to me again.

"I don't remember! I couldn't remember! I can't have somebody asking me all over again!"

"No one is asking you to. No one ever expected you to. You don't even have to be here. Go, if you have to."

"Dad! No!" I reached for his arm. "How could you leave her alone right now?"

"Elena. It's all right. Roberto — go. I'll come get you after they're gone."

I sat between my father and grandmother as they looked at each other.

"I'm sorry," my father whispered again.

"This has nothing to do with you," she said. "It never did."

He shook his head. "I have to go," he said.

"Go on, then."

He pushed himself out of the chair, stepped off the porch, and disappeared around the side of the house.

"Tuah?"

But she put up a hand and shook her head, then got up and went into the house. I was afraid to follow her. I don't know how much time passed, but I was still sitting on the porch, rocking under Benencia's quilt, when Mac gave a single sharp bark and I heard the moan of an approaching vehicle.

I sat close beside Tuah through the interview. The sheriff, now, sank low into my grandfather's chair on the porch, while Tuah sat straight and proud above him. Mac lay by her side, panting. The afternoon had grown warm, and the air smelled dusty. She told Benencia's story to him as she had to me, hands folded in her lap, voice level and calm. In answer to his follow-up questions, yes, Benencia was simple, incapable of guile, trusting and open. Yes, perhaps three hundred people lived in town at the time, and she knew them all. Yes, a few others had lived and worked alone on their own claims scattered across the surrounding hills.

"Why are you asking about all these other people?" she asked after he began to explore how the search had been conducted and who had helped to look for Benencia.

The sheriff glanced at me. I was within

Tuah's line of sight and couldn't shake my head. I only stared back at him.

"I need to conduct every investigation as a homicide," he said evenly. I think the hesitation and the check with me were too slight to draw attention.

"Homicide? You mean murder?" I could hear a frantic note dangle off the edge of her voice.

The door behind me swung open. I twisted in my chair.

"Dad?"

He pulled a kitchen chair with him and set it on Tuah's other side. She frowned at him. "Robert Alvarez," he said, ignoring her and extending a hand to the sheriff. "I'm sorry to be late."

The sheriff stood halfway and reached to shake my father's hand, accepting the appearance of a new person without any visible reaction. "Pleased to meet you." He sank back into the chair. "Your mother had just finished explaining to me how Benencia got lost, and I've been asking some questions about who lived nearby."

"It was my fault," my father said. "My fault she got lost."

The three of us spoke at once.

"Roberto, stop it."

"Dad — what?"

"Excuse me, sir?"

My father ignored Tuah and me and responded to the sheriff. "We were playing hide-and-seek. I decided to play a trick on her. I told her to hide and then I went to my friends' house. The Diaz boys. When my parents found me and saw that she wasn't with me, they asked me to show them where we'd been playing and I couldn't find it. I didn't know. I still don't. I can't help you any more than that."

Tuah had never told me this part. Clearly, she didn't blame him. He wasn't part of the story at all. God, he was just a child, doing what children did.

But she might as well have blamed him. I recognized the face he wore. I'd seen it when he tried to explain to me that my mother was gone, the final injustice in a world that had always been against him. It was anger — the rims of his eyes thickened, the skin across his nose tight, the lips thin and pale. But I saw it differently now. It wasn't directed at me. It never had been.

And then I understood. I understood everything. Past, present, future. The way a laboratory experiment that doesn't turn out as you expect is the one that suddenly shows you the way things really are. All the anger I'd felt at a self I judged through my own eyes only, at a world that was imbalanced and merciless and unfair, at what I did and didn't deserve as a consequence of what turned out to be just a childish thing done by a child — it was *his* anger. At himself. It had been his all along, polished and perfected and passed on to me, ready to use. But I didn't have to keep it.

In a wash, I had as much pity for my father's pain as for Tuah's, different as they were.

"It wasn't his fault," I blurted. "There was a dog. He always went with her. The dog always watched out for her, and if he'd been there she wouldn't have gotten lost. But he'd been shot just a couple of days before."

My father swung his attention to me. "What?"

The sheriff turned back to Tuah. "Shot?"

She shook her head, dismissing an unrelated, unimportant detail. "It was hunting season. We found him out away from home. But yes, ordinarily Gus would've been with them."

"That was only two days before?" my father asked.

Tuah nodded. The sheriff looked at me, then down, then put his elbows on his knees and leaned forward.

"Mrs. Alvarez, I'm sorry if I've been at all

unclear. I need you to understand that this is a homicide investigation. We believe your daughter was murdered."

"Because of a hunting accident? That had nothing to do with —"

"Mrs. Alvarez, the body was found nearly eight miles from here. It's very unlikely that a child would have wandered that far on her own. Also, the circumstances in which we found the body —" He stopped. Fought to clear something in his throat.

No amount of delivering terrible news can make doing so any easier, I realized. Though stock words might be part of the apology, the message and the suffering is fresh every time. *Mr. and Mrs. Jones, your son has drowned. Mrs. Smith, your husband had a heart attack. Mr. Kofford, your wife — there was an accident. We found the car.*

"Mrs. Alvarez, the evidence indicates that your daughter was held captive. If your dog was shot two days before, that's an important piece of information. We will do everything we can to find out what happened. I'm sorry."

It was as if I could see something fall out of Tuah's center and her shell collapse around the empty place. She grabbed the edge of her chair and turned hollow eyes to me.

"What did you *see*?" I didn't hesitate this time but reached to draw her toward me. She fought back. "What happened? What *happened*?"

My father put his hand on her arm. "Mama, I'm sorry," he said, pleading, but she jerked her arm away and slapped at his hand. She jumped up and staggered backward, knocking the chair over with a clatter and a puff of gray from the floorboards.

"No!" she shrieked. "Get away! All of you!" She thrust herself toward the sheriff. "Tell me what happened!"

The sheriff alone remained calm and matter-of-fact. "We found evidence she was held in a cave," he said. "I know this is a shock. I'm very sorry. But you knew everybody who lived here better than anyone, and only you know the sequence of events. I'll need your help to understand who might have been involved."

Her body looked like clothing caught on a hanger — shoulders loose, sleeves dangling at her sides. She lifted her eyes over the sheriff's head and turned her face toward the trees that separated us from the ruins of her town, the houses that had sheltered people she knew. People who had borne her suffering with her. Houses that were now nothing but bones.

"I don't know," she said without looking back at us. And then, as if she had just opened a drawer where she was accustomed to seeing familiar objects and found it empty, added "I don't believe I know anything."

I awoke to the gray light of morning, the chilled quiet, the blanket of night being prodded and tugged by the drowsy mutter of the first birds. Then crunching footsteps and a car door slamming. The car started. It drove away. I should have run after it, but the process of understanding what I heard and analyzing the distance between my bed and the place where I could make a difference convinced me I would be too late. Perhaps I should have acted rather than taking the time to think.

I got up shortly afterward, pulling Benencia's blanket with me. As I expected, I found my father's bedroll on the floor by the stove rolled up and pushed into the corner. I eased the door open to look into Tuah's room. Only the top of her head was visible, gray waves hazed over the pillow, face buried under the blanket. Mac, lying on the floor at the foot of her bed, lifted his head to look at me, then put it back down. He wouldn't leave the room until she did. I closed the door. Every minute she spent asleep was a gift, but long habit would probably wake her soon.

I opened the stove door and started stirring the coals to life, feeding them pine needles and wisps of bark from the kindling bucket. In time it started to crackle and I was able to put on water for coffee.

"Where's your father?"

I turned to see Tuah in the doorway, barefoot, hair pinned back in an untidy knot, a canvas barn coat over her nightgown. Mac detoured around her ankles and went to the door. I let him out.

"Gone. I heard the car leave a while ago."

She came the rest of the way into the room, pulled out a chair, and dropped heavily into it. She sat for a moment with her hands loose in her lap, then crossed her arms over her belly and doubled over.

"He won't be back," she said.

"What do you mean? He didn't —" But as I spoke I looked to the corner where the bedroll was tucked and realized his satchel was gone as well.

"How did you know?" I said. "Why?"

She sat up slowly. Her head hung slightly to one side as if its weight was more than her neck could carry. Her gaze fixed on the wall somewhere to the right of the stove.

She looked so, so old.

"You saw how he blames himself. He's never gotten over it, never listened to reason, no matter what I've said. Sometimes I've been just so angry that he won't stop thinking about himself. But bad as it's been for him, now to think she suffered something worse —" She stopped herself. Caught a breath. Looked at me. "He's hardly been able to look at me for forty years. Even while he keeps trying to make it up to me somehow. Now . . . it can only be worse."

I didn't have an answer. I cooked oatmeal while Tuah sat motionless in the chair, served her a small bowl, and sat with her as she pushed it from one side of the bowl to the other. Eventually she put the spoon down, then took my hand and pulled it into her lap. We sat that way for a minute or more, with no sound but the muffled crackling from the stove.

"You started the fire," she finally said.

"Yeah. It's okay, now."

She nodded, slowly. "That's good."

Another minute passed. Mac scratched on the door. I got up, let him in, and came back to my seat. Took Tuah's hand again.

"It seems a person is never finished learning about sorrow," she said.

"No," I agreed.

There was a pop and a faint hiss from the stove, probably a wet knot in the wood. She squeezed my hand.

"I'm glad you came," she said.

"Me too."

Another pause.

"You've been a blessing." She stopped. Squeezed my hand again. Then she shook her head, correcting herself. "You *are*. You *are* a blessing."

There is a balm for every wound. An atonement, however inadequate, for every wrong. Or perhaps proportion and balance are measures we don't understand at all. I felt the oil of healing break over my head, pour through my hair, down my neck, and over my shoulders. In the cabin kitchen we found rest on each other's shoulders and wept together, the two of us.

I packed up the food, pulled in the porch furniture, and waited until I was sure the stove was cool, then told Tuah I thought we were ready to leave. I closed and locked the windows, then locked the door as soon as Tuah was through it. I had to be back at the Koffords' in the morning and I didn't want to leave her alone.

"Come on," I said, putting a hand on her elbow. "Let's get you home." The wrongness of the final word coated my lips as it passed.

She'd been about to step off the porch but pulled up. She straightened and stood still for a moment. Put a hand on the porch post. Took a deep breath. Then without looking back she stepped off the porch and walked to the truck.

The story, as we pieced it together later, was that my father had appeared at a ranch a couple of miles up the road beyond the Hat Creek turnoff while the family was eating breakfast. The ranch was owned by a man he'd grown up with, who was about my father's age and had come into Hat Creek for school when he could. My father asked for a horse, was gone all day, then at the end of the afternoon handed his weary mount over to one of his friend's sons, along with a twenty dollar bill, and left. We found a note when we checked Tuah's mailbox by the road on our way out of Hat Creek.

I have to go home, it said. *I'm sorry.*

For the rest, I have only my imagination. The way to Washington meadow he already knew well. The creek along the base of the hillside wouldn't have been difficult to find, and by this point, the path to the cave was surely well worn by the many horses that had traveled it recently. The anchor in the rock would have still been there. I don't know whether any rope remained. I don't know how long he stayed there. Whether he sat in silence. Whether he cried. Whether he threw his head back and screamed to the wind and the empty mountaintops.

Out of pity, I never spoke of it to him again.

34

Tuah was up early the next morning, moving ghostlike through the Leadville house long before I needed to get up and go to the Koffords'. I heard the scuff of her slippers against the long boards of the hallway, the softened clack of a door closing, the shuffle of things being sorted and moved. I opened my bedroom door to find her standing on a stool in front of the coat closet, nightgown loose around her ankles, pushing something onto the top shelf.

"You didn't sleep much," I said.

"No."

She reached slightly to the side, then pulled a small box against her chest and stepped backward off the stool. Glanced at me. "Things of Benencia's."

"Oh."

She turned and disappeared into the parlor.

"Should I start coffee?" I called after her.

"That'd be nice."

I went to the kitchen. Yesterday afternoon's paper lay on the table with the headline, *Body Found May Be Long-Missing Girl,* staring up at the ceiling from its front page. I folded it over, started the coffee, and sliced bread for toast. When everything was ready I carried the mug and plate to her in the parlor and set it on the lamp table. She sat on the stiff sofa under the window, with articles from the box arrayed on the cushion beside her. A bonnet. A pair of baby shoes. A tiny silver bracelet. A baptismal certificate with gold leaf around the edges.

"I've never eaten in here," she said, looking up.

"Seems like a good time to start." I sat on the matching settee across from her and set down my own mug. "I hate that I'm leaving. I don't want to leave you alone."

"I'll be fine."

"Maybe I could come over with the kids later. Sarah would love to see you."

"That'd be nice." She didn't sound convincing or even as if she'd really heard me. Her eyes were in the box, her fingers rifling through objects inside.

"I think Paul said he'd only be gone four days this time. We could go back up to Hat

Creek after that."

She removed a tiny piece of crochet work from the box. I wasn't sure what it was — a cap of some sort, perhaps, or a little lace collar. She held it up against the pale light from the window for a moment, then laid it on the sofa beside the shoes.

"I don't think I'll be going back," she said.

"What?"

"To Hat Creek. I don't expect I'll want to go back."

"Why not?"

She looked back into the box. She removed a pair of crocheted booties that had perhaps once been pale pink, holding one in each hand. She ran her thumbs over the undulating stitches that had once touched the tops of her baby's feet.

"I think I told you once that the whole reason I went there is because it's the place where my family was together." She caressed the booties for a moment more, then set them on the sofa. She still hadn't looked at me. "That's changed, now. Now it's the place where my family came apart."

"Tuah —"

"Could you get some sugar? I think I want sugar in my coffee this morning."

The faint light from outside shone through her hair, the cloud-gray wisps that had escaped the loosely wound braid at the base of her skull.

"Okay," I said.

Sarah sat at the kitchen table, hunched over her cereal bowl, kicking her feet, and flipping pages of the mythology book.

"That's the chair that pulls the sun across the sky," she said, pointing to the picture of Apollo.

"Chariot," I said.

"It doesn't work that way," Kevin said. "The earth goes around the sun. The sun doesn't move. The earth does."

"Nah-ah," said Sarah.

"Does, too."

"It's in the book."

She was clearly arguing for the sake of needling him. A day started that way was not headed in a direction I wanted to go. I needed to intervene. "Remember how I said these were stories people made up? Just stories. Like if you said the reason you have clean clothes is because an elf washes them."

She squinted a grin at me, cheeks puffed around a mouthful of cereal. She wiped a dribble of milk from the corner of her mouth. "*You* wash them."

"That's right. And I think it's time I showed you how to wash them yourself."

"That's silly."

"We'll see."

I spread a spoonful of jam across my toast, then carried it and my coffee cup to the table. She flipped a page.

"That's the man who got stuck looking at himself," she said.

"Now *that* might really happen," I said.

"Nah-ah."

"Okay, maybe not. But there are a lot of people who spend too much time looking at themselves."

"Miss Melanie," Kevin offered.

"Who's that?" I took a bite of toast.

"She was my mom's friend. She worked at the hair place."

The offhand way he brought up his mother's life was something I hadn't seen before. "Did you used to see her a lot?" I said.

He nodded.

"Do you miss her? We could go see her."

He shrugged his shoulders. "Nah. It's okay. She wore red lipstick and tried to kiss me." He made a face.

"You need to tell me or your dad if you ever think of people you want to see."

"Okay," he said, scooping a mound of cereal against the side of his bowl.

"Smaller bites," I said automatically.

He spread his mouth open as far as he

could, added the cereal, then mugged at me with his cheeks and lower lip swollen from the contents. I had to laugh.

"Okay," I said. "Funny once."

I sensed an ease about him I didn't think I'd seen before. Then I remembered something Paul had told me.

"You tried to find your mom's secret place yesterday, didn't you?"

He nodded.

"Yup!" Sarah crowed, kicking harder.

"Did you find it?"

"Nope," said Kevin, with no trace of disappointment.

"I caught a fish!" Sarah said.

"Wow! You went fishing? Did you catch any?" I said, looking at Kevin.

He held up two fingers. Gave a sly smile.

"And *Kevin* stepped in the *water*!" said Sarah.

"So you had a good day with your dad?"

Kevin nodded while Sarah bounced in her chair. "It was the *best* day in the *whole world*!" she said.

I looked at Kevin. He met my eyes with a faint smile, then looked back down into his cereal bowl. I had to catch my breath. At Tuah's house, only sorrow. Here, a ray of light. Until yesterday, it had been the other way around. And would be again, certainly.

The threads of joy and sorrow, light and darkness, blessing and grief were woven together too tightly to tell one from another.

Sarah went back to flipping pages, two or three forward, one or two back. "That's the girl getting borned out of her daddy's head. That doesn't really happen."

"Nope. Not at all."

Another page.

"Those are the girls that sing and make the sailors crash. Why do they do that?"

"Just causing trouble. You don't ever want to be like that."

"But it doesn't really happen."

"No, but you want to stay away from girls who just want attention."

She didn't seem interested in a morality lesson but continued flipping pages.

"And that's the one with the jars of good and bad things," Sarah said, pointing to the picture of Zeus overlooking humanity in all its insignificance. "It doesn't happen like that."

I looked at the picture, sideways to me and shimmying slightly as Sarah kicked and jiggled the table. The white jar of blessings, the black of curses. My father's way of viewing things. We needed a different picture, a different story: joy and sorrow, light and darkness, blessing and grief, all coming from the same place. We needed Tuah's magpie jar, a way to explain that nobody really knew what anything was.

"Well, it kind of does," I said. "But there's more. Right after they made this picture, a kid was running around and knocked over the jars."

"Really?"

"I'm making up a story. Right now. We'll say it was a girl named Sarah."

"Did she get in trouble?"

"No, nobody saw it. Not even her brother. Because he would've told on her."

"Nah-ah," Kevin said. "I would've helped her."

"You're right. Let's change the story. Sarah and Kevin came running through the picture because . . ." I cast around for a moment. "They were chasing puppies. Lots of puppies. And the *puppies* were wrestling and they knocked over the jars."

"That could happen," Sarah said.

"Exactly. The puppies knocked over the jars, and the blessings and curses spilled out and made a big mess. Like sand, everywhere. And the puppies were running and rolling in it, and Sarah and Kevin were yelling at them and trying to get them out, but by the time they were done you couldn't tell what was what. All the blessings and curses mixed up, and some of them had spilled over the edge." I pointed at the picture, where the gods' patio hung over the edge of the mountain. "So they fell on the people way down in the valley."

"I bet that dad would be mad," Sarah said, looking at Zeus in the picture.

"Oh, you bet. So mad. He wanted to control everything, and now people had stuff happening to them that he didn't plan. So Kevin thought he'd make things better by cleaning up. He got a broom and swept up all the mess because he's really great at sweeping. Especially in kitchens."

"I don't want to sweep today." Not a fool, that boy.

"No, you're great at it. Nobody does it as great as you."

He wrinkled his nose. "Yuck," he said. But his objection was automatic and not delivered with much effort, and he returned to chasing the ribbons of sugar at the bottom of his bowl.

"And Sarah's amazing at mopping."

"I love to mop!"

"I know. So those are our chores after breakfast. Anyway, Kevin gathered everything together, swept it into the dustpan, and Sarah got another jar to put it in. One jar for everything, good and bad. But here's where things got really weird. Zeus, the dad" — I pointed to the picture — "kept watching the people so he could figure out who had bad things fall on them and who had good things, so he could fix it if he needed to. But it turned out that he couldn't tell which was which. Some people had stuff happen to them that he *thought* was a curse, but it turned out to be a blessing. Other people had good stuff happen, but then bad things came out of it, and then the bad things became good. Then bad again. Turns out that the whole reason the stuff that spilled got mixed up was because it really was the same. Or at least by the time people touched it and messed around with it, you couldn't tell which was which anymore."

I must have gotten unintentionally emphatic as I went on because Sarah's expression became worried and concentrated. She looked at me scowling, chewing slowly. When it was clear I wouldn't say any more, she looked back at the picture. "It doesn't really happen like that," she said.

"Not exactly," I said. "But it kind of does."

She stretched her chin to look at the picture again.

"I like this story better," she said after a moment.

"Suit yourself," I said.

■ ■ ■ ■

At the last minute, I called Mindy and Joan to join us for lunch at Tuah's. Joan wasn't home, and Mindy said that Alex had woken up early this morning and needed his nap. She wouldn't be able to stay long but she'd try to be there.

I made enough peanut butter sandwiches for everyone, got some grapes and a bag of chips, and called the children home from Poppy's to go on a picnic.

"Again?" Kevin said.

"You'll thank me in January," I said. "Get in the car."

As we passed the park, Kevin said, "Where are we going?"

"Tuah's house."

"*Really?*" Sarah squealed, kicking and bouncing her seat.

"Yup. Just a picnic in the yard. She's been feeling kinda lonesome, so I thought it would be good to visit."

Kevin didn't say anything. I doubted lunch at an old lady's house sounded very compelling to him.

"There's a great tree to climb," I said.

"Uh-huh."

I hadn't been completely sure how we'd

find Tuah and I was relieved to see her come to the door, dressed and with her hair re-pinned, while I was getting the food out of the back hatch.

"Tuah!" Sarah yelled. As she had on the day we met, she ran to my grandmother and threw her arms around the old lady's hips.

"Hello, Kevin," Tuah said. "I think you've grown since the last time I saw you."

He nodded solemnly. "Yes, ma'am."

I pointed to the cottonwood that leaned over the shed. "Climb that," I said. "I'll get us something to drink."

"I'm okay, you know," Tuah said as I passed her at the door.

"Just had to see for myself," I said. I got an ice tray from the freezer and whacked it against the counter.

"Losing her was worse."

I turned.

"The hardest part of grief is getting over trying to go back and change things. I already did that. This is terrible, but you need to know there's relief, too. We can have a funeral now. She can be buried there by Eduardo."

"Sure we can," I said. "Everyone will come."

She nodded but said nothing further. After

a moment I opened a cupboard for a pitcher.

"She was perfect. Do you understand that? She was perfect in every way. *Every* way."

I looked down into the pitcher, the countertop tiles wavering through the glass bottom. A human free of judgment, error, malice, grudges, spite, self-destruction, fear, blame. Perfect. I looked up at Tuah.

"I know."

She put a hand on my shoulder, a little rub and a pat, then took the pitcher from my hand. "Go on now. I'll bring out the water."

Mindy pulled up just as I shook out a blanket on the grass. Tuah, unfolding a lawn chair, looked up, surprised. Then she looked at me. Back at Mindy.

"Good Lord," she muttered to me. "How much watching over do you think I need?"

"I just thought it'd be more fun for the girls," I lied.

Katy bolted out of the car without waiting for her mother. Sarah, in a low crotch of the tree on its back side, darted out and the two little girls hugged, staggering in a circle together as if they hadn't seen each other in weeks.

"Katy, honey, we can't stay long," Mindy

called after her. Her daughter showed no signs of having heard, and the two girls disappeared together to the far side of the tree. Kevin was already up along the angled limb.

"Hi, Tuah," Mindy called as she hoisted the baby out of the backseat and onto her hip, where he kicked and fussed. She slammed the door and came over to greet her, putting her free hand around Tuah's shoulders and leaning forward to kiss her cheek. "I'm so sorry," she said as she straightened. "I read about it in the paper."

"You're very kind," Tuah said. She put her hands on the arms of the lawn chair and eased herself down into it. There was a certain stiffness about her, and I started to think I might've done the wrong thing by inviting Mindy.

"I've got sandwiches," I said, sitting as well. "They're just in the bag. Kids can grab whatever they want."

Mindy eyed the tree. "It might be a while before they think about eating," she said. "Not too long, I hope. Alex is gonna pop a vein any minute now."

Mac shambled around the corner of the house, tail waving. The girls squealed and pulled their feet up.

"Sarah!" I called. "What are you doing?"

"Sorry," Mindy said. "That one's Katy's

503

fault. She's allergic. Gets hives on her hands if she touches a dog."

"Oh! Should I put him in the house?"

Mindy put a hand out to stop me from standing. "No, she's fine as long as she doesn't pet him or get licked. I was the same way when I was a kid. Now it's not so bad, so maybe she'll grow out of it." She dropped cross-legged onto the blanket. Alex shrieked and grabbed hold of her neck. "I don't know where it comes from," she went on, ignoring him. "Nobody in my family has any allergies."

"Your grandma sure did," Tuah said. "And maybe your dad, when he was young."

I shot a look at Tuah. How distracted was she?

"Really? Grandma Rodel?"

"Yes, of course," Tuah said.

But she was looking at the tree as she said it, the shuddering of leaves and the laughter of the little girls. She looked back at Mindy, whose whining baby now reached for the blanket. She put him down, and he swung his fists out and wailed angrily, then buried his face in her lap.

"Yes," Tuah repeated. "Your grandma had allergies. I had another dog when we were younger, and she could scarcely come into my house."

"Wow. I never knew that."

"I imagine not," Tuah said.

"I didn't know her real well," Mindy said. "I'd love to hear more sometime."

"I suppose. Sometime."

Alex gave another wail, so I don't think Mindy saw the way Tuah watched her, then had to look away. But not with sorrow. With tenderness.

"Okay, that's it," Mindy said, standing. Alex shrieked again, and she reached down to pick him up. "I tried. Katy's gonna have a fit, but this guy needs his nap before he explodes."

"Let her stay. I'll just drop her off when we're done here," I said.

"Would you? That'd be great."

She called good-bye to Katy, then took the baby to the car and left. The other three children remained in the tree.

"Are you going to tell her?" I asked Tuah after Mindy had gone.

"About her family? No, of course not. But I'll tell her what her grandmother was like. It doesn't matter who she thinks it was."

I leaned back on my hands and felt the grass, cool under my fingers. Kevin, who had climbed higher than the girls, shook a branch above them and they shrieked in overacted fear.

"I made a doctor appointment," I said.

Tuah looked at me sharply. "You did?"

I nodded. "Thursday. At the clinic. When they found out my dates they wanted to see me soon."

Tuah studied me for a moment. "You're staying, then," she said.

I looked down. "A couple people think I could teach high school, but" — I waved one hand over my stomach — "I don't know how they'd feel about this."

"I couldn't say," Tuah said.

"But it can't hurt to look into it."

"No, that's right." She shook her head, then looked toward the tree. Laughter cascaded down the trunk and scattered across the grass. She cleared her throat. "You know, I don't want you thinking you have to be here for me. I've been fine before. I'll be fine. I just have to get used to a different way of thinking."

I looked down at my lap, then back up at her. "So do I. Maybe we can help each other."

She nodded but didn't speak. Kevin had worked himself down the tree until he was beside the girls, then jumped to the ground from there. They shrieked, and he promptly went back to the trunk and started climbing again.

"I need to start making some plans," I said. "No matter what I do, it'll be a while before I can afford my own place."

"That's true."

"I don't want you to feel like I'm taking advantage and wonder whether I'm ever going to get out on my own. I'm asking if I can stay here for now, but I want you to know that I intend to support myself."

"Elena, you don't ever need to go."

I looked back at her, not speaking.

"I've been alone a long time. And not because I prefer it that way. You staying with me — well, now, that'd be a gift."

I swallowed hard. Looked at the tree. Mac, bored with the inaccessible children, had flopped in the shade and lay with his head up and his eyes half closed, smiling and panting.

"Well, it'd sure be helpful to have you there, with the baby, if that's what I decide to . . ." The sentence had come out of me before I knew where it would end. I bit my lip. "But that's asking a lot."

She shook her head. "No. No, it isn't."

"I could help with stuff around the house and I could start paying rent. Soon."

"I don't care about that."

"And maybe it'd be good to have me at the house whenever you're ready to go back

507

to Hat Creek."

Tuah laid her hands in her lap. "I meant what I said earlier. I don't think I'll be going back," she said. "For the funeral. That's all."

"I just can't imagine that."

"I was thinking all night. That town I thought I knew, where we all took care of each other . . ." She shook her head. "There was evil. Why wouldn't there be? It's everywhere. I was a fool."

"No — Tuah —"

"There was no hunting accident. Somebody was watching Benencia, planning it. The police will work on it for a while, but no one will ever solve it, no one will ever get what they deserve." She stopped, straightening slightly as if correcting herself. "Well, no one ever does, really. You know that. And if I go back up there, I'll just walk around looking at those houses, suspecting everyone I ever knew. It would poison everything — the life I had, the life I have now. I won't do it. I just can't. I have to believe better than that."

I looked up at her. "But you told me about the way it holds your memories. Your family. Olive. It's your home. And it looks so beautiful now."

Tuah smiled at me. "Olive is here, now.

508

Not there. And so is my family."

I looked down at my lap. Tuah leaned forward over her folded hands. I looked up into her face, shadowed in the strong sunlight. She wore a denim work shirt, and the points of the collar were frayed.

"Elena, this is my home. The past is past. This is where my family starts over."

Epilogue

The position of physical science teacher at Lake County High School was cursed, it seemed, which served to my benefit. My competition to replace the poaching, marijuana-growing teacher from last year developed his own problems with the law when his wife was discovered to have embezzled somewhere in the neighborhood of thirty thousand dollars from her employer and he was the one who had bought a truck, a motorcycle, and a snowmobile with some of the proceeds.

By comparison, an illegitimate pregnancy was a minor inconvenience, and the job was mine. Of course, I would need a substitute after Christmas break, but the principal identified that as a small problem, considering. An actual teaching certificate, as well, could follow later, and he had every expectation of offering me a permanent position when the various loose ends were tied off.

I was with Leo on a Saturday afternoon at the end of the summer, sitting on a bench outside the malt shop with a strawberry shake in one hand, the first time I knew I felt the baby move. I froze in place, staring at my abdomen, my empty hand suspended over my lap, astonished at what had just happened, afraid to miss it if it happened again.

"Elena?" he said. "The cookout. Were you listening?"

I shook my head, afraid to speak.

"Are you okay?"

Another touch. Tiny, like a nerve twitching, but unmistakable. Another human, inside of me, alive and doing something I couldn't see. I looked up at Leo.

"The baby moved," I whispered.

"Really?" His eyes widened. "Wow!"

An understatement of mythic proportions. I looked back down at my belly, waiting.

He tapped the side of my cup with one knuckle. "Staring isn't going to feed anybody," he said. "Finish your shake. Baby wants some berries."

The Koffords adopted one of Poppy's puppies, which helped mitigate some of the tears as the others left for their own homes. Paul had gone to work at the mine by then, and I made a habit of stopping by the house on my way home after school, purportedly to check on the puppy, but mostly to spend an hour or so with Kevin and Sarah.

Late in October, as snow brought the last of the aspen leaves to the ground, Poppy threw a baby shower for me, her already overcrowded front room becoming chaotic as it filled with people and pattern and movement and noise. Mindy and Joan came, along with Kim and Lizzie and Leslie, as well as other friends of theirs who had become mine as well over the past few months. Fellow teachers and a few parents came, too, plus a couple of neighbors I'd never seen before. Mama Ruth had combed her hair and dressed in polyester slacks and a blouse, and sat by herself in the corner eating potato chips from a soup bowl.

Tuah was there, of course, pointing at items on Poppy's walls and discussing something with one of Poppy's neighbors with great animation. One of the other women came up to her and gave her a hug. Two others laughed near the kitchen. Sarah slipped in and out between their hips, offering carrot sticks and crackers from a plate. Gifts, garish in yellow and white and green and in frilled ribbons — plus one from the Koffords in Christmas paper — leaned against the wall by the door.

I sat in the corner, hardly knowing where to look in this room so full of people and warmth and life. Finally Tuah seated herself beside me and put her hand on my knee, patted it, and gave a squeeze. I looked back at her and she nodded, then looked away and squeezed again, blinking. My own eyes filled, as they did too easily these days, and I put the heels of my hands against them before anyone would be able to ask why I was crying.

The fullness in my chest was almost more than I could bear. I had been given so much. These people, this child, and most of all, a future, however criss-crossed with joy or trouble it might be. I was the recipient of gifts I had almost failed to recognize, and had done nothing to deserve. But which I now knew I should keep anyway.

I had been blessed, indeed.

ACKNOWLEDGMENTS

No story idea makes it to the printed and published page without being touched by many hands along the way. One name appears on the cover; the others get squeezed onto a page or two at the back. So I want to make sure those names get their due here.

Overwhelming gratitude goes to my agent, Sandra Bond, who first believed in this book when it was just a few chapters old and rode with it through family upheavals and tragedies on both sides, waited for it to go with me to Saudi Arabia and back, and knew the importance of finding just the right home for it. She's been my guide and my cheerleader and an unerringly clear-eyed business counselor. Really, everybody should have one of her.

Sandra's top target, early on, was my editor, Chelsey Emmelhainz. At the time she first saw this book, she was with another publisher, and made it her first order of business to ask for it as soon as she arrived at Skyhorse Publishing. I am beyond grateful for Chelsey's vision of what this book could and should be, her enthusiasm and advocacy for it, and her extraordinary talent as an editor.

I've been around the publishing business long enough to know that Chelsey serves as the captain of a boat that has a large crew. As I write, I am only peripherally acquainted with the rest of the team at Skyhorse Publishing who will put their skills to work in copyediting, proofreading, graphics, design, marketing, publicity, and more, who think what they do is totally normal. It is beyond me. And I'm deeply grateful.

The original set pieces for this book included a lost child and a girl who started a fire. They did not include molybdenum, mine rescue, Colorado mining history, gold mining practices, or the specific town of Leadville and its history. While the ghost town of Hat Creek and its setting are fictional, Leadville is not, and I am indebted to experts and historians there that I hope will say I got things right enough. At the Lake County Public Library, resident local historian Janice Fox took me to 1970s Leadville. Bill Nelson and Vince Matthews at the National Mining Hall of Fame and Museum, also in Leadville, answered my questions about mining practices. Eventually, all roads led to Joe Nachtrieb at Colorado Mountain College, an extraordinary teacher with a long career in mining and mine rescue, whose expertise in chemistry, physics, geology, history, and humanity left me in awe. Plus he was irrationally generous with his time. You should check out America's highest incorporated city yourself. As Joe told me, "For nine months of the year, the skiing is great. For the other three, it's pretty good."

For the writing itself, I am indebted to all those who read and gave input along the way. Michelle Crystal, my critique partner, brainstormed with me and kept me on schedule. Marcy Gardner, Bonnie Wetherbee, Terry Young, Cheryl Glasset, and Ann Stanz, my longtime friends in books and ideas, were able to step in at the final stages and comb through the manuscript for inconsistencies, discrepancies, and unanswered questions. My goal all along has been to write a book folks like you would want to read.

My gratitude in writing and in life goes above all to my family. I have one of those moms who thinks I can do absolutely anything, and that whatever I do is brilliant.

Any screwups built on a foundation like that are purely my own. My children, Cheryl, Jill, and Danny, with their respective spouses Benjamin, Kory, and Michelle, have read and reread, kept tabs on everything going on, and supported me with laughter, encouragement, and the best company I know.

Finally, my husband, Stephen, is the one who made it all possible. When the ideas and characters that had been circling each other in my head for years finally decided they were ready to step onto the page, we were grinding through a phase of unemployment and could ill afford for me to write. But he insisted that I must. Without his determination, faith, support, and refusal to let me off the hook, there wouldn't be any pages, least of all the one that gets his name on it. Of all the intertwined threads of my life, the ones that run through his hands have turned out the best, no matter what they looked like when they started.

ABOUT THE AUTHOR

Margo Catts grew up in Los Angeles and has since lived in Utah, Indiana, and Colorado. After raising three children in the U.S., she and her husband moved to Saudi Arabia, where her *Foreign Girl* blog was well known in the expat community. Originally a freelance editor for textbooks and magazines, she has also done freelance writing for business, technical, and advertising clients, all the while working on her fiction. She is a contributing author to *Once Upon an Expat. Among the Lesser Gods* is her first novel. She now lives in Denver, Colorado.